CONQUEST OF CANAAN

BRITTANY SHANNON

BookWise
publishing

OG

BookWise Publishing
Riverton, Utah
www.bookwisepublishing.com

Library of Congress Control Number: 2016953157

Author Portrait by Elise Orozco: http://mospicsandvids.com

Cover and interior book design:
Francine Eden Platt • Eden Graphics, Inc.: www.edengraphics.net

ePub Design and Formatting:
Dayna Linton • Day Agency

ISBN: 978-1-60645-168-7 (eBook)

ISBN: 978-1-60645-167-0 (Paperback)

10 9 8 7 6 5 4 3 2 1

First Printing

To my family. Have faith in deliverance.

Whosoever he be that doth rebel
against thy commandment,
and will not hearken unto thy words
in all that thou commandest him,
he shall be put to death:
only be strong and of good courage.

— JOSHUA 1:18

1406 BC

KAYA

A Day in the Life

I HATE PEOPLE.

I lump myself into that group for those who immediately jump to the conclusion that I'm an egotistical misanthrope.

I am just a misanthrope.

So these people I hate. They are dying. All around me.

And that's how my day's going.

KAYA

Now That I've Got You Cheered Up

APPARENTLY BEING LOCATED WEST of forsaken and just north of bored to death makes you a target. Being a pompously nonviolent territory along the spine of Canaan makes you a history lesson. Avoca is under attack. The rebels are everywhere, doing what they do best. Pillaging. I realize, with horror, their objective is to kill every male first.

I force myself to stumble down the road, weaving through an alleyway. A rebel is dragging a woman through the gravel by her hair. Her turbulent eyes meet mine, and she cries out for help. Before the rebel notices me, I turn and dash down the next passageway. Pressing my back against the wall of a building, I close my eyes tightly only to see her desperate face again on the back of my eyelids.

For a fleeting moment, I wonder if I should intervene.

I crack an eye open. The wall opposite me has an ax stuck in it, remnants of flesh pinned behind the blade. I stare at it, holding my breath. Avoca's slogan of amity flits through my mind. I don't believe in happy endings, but the fate of the woman in the alley is more than tragic. Her screams are silenced before I peel myself from the wall to begin running again.

Unfortunately, I'm not out of the kill zone.

Avoca is not just a neutral province. It is a sore, a lesion, resting upon the skin of the Canaan. War is the sickness. Violent crusaders pick, and pick, and pick at the sore until the earth bleeds. And now we're all going to die.

KAYA

How My Morning Really Began

In Ignorance.

War has caused a great destruction among the people. Barbarism replaces culture—*defines* it. And not in some sexy, man-wears-loin-cloth, kind of way. It reduces human nature to desperation. And desperation reduces humans to the lowest of evils. That is why my tribe fled to Avoca before I was born. Here, I've lived twenty-two years too many. I am part of the sore.

For years this contention has continued, with kingdoms and kings gaining strength, each determined to besiege the other. A repulsive disease has further diminished the population. It kills what the sword does not. Avoca residents think they've outsmarted the bloodbath by living in this passive province, but peaceful politics have a way of welcoming disaster.

It is sometime before sunrise. I'm staring at a deteriorating cave, the one hollowed out in the sandbanks of the Salt Sea, listening to the moonlit waves crash in repetition.

I hate that cave.

Contrary to most nights, I allow myself to step back to a moment many years ago. The memory plays before my bleary eyelids. Skin and silly laughter. That was before the threat of incursion loomed on our horizon. Before the mass death of entire kingdoms turned a normal person into a desensitized mechanism.

I'm not going to think about it anymore. Instead, I'll take a drink. What is it they say—take everything in moderation? Including moderation.

I am out of wine?

I hate being out of wine.

I twiddle the drained bottle in my fingers, eying *that cave* but erasing any memory of it. Midnight swims are a particular favorite of mine, both because I have trouble sleeping and because I'm drawn to the sea. There's something wholesome about being underwater. No conflict, just serenity and isolation. No fear, no risk, no war. It's something in the salty smell, the lull of the waves gurgling onto the shoreline, and the unique color of the water that's sage green or teal blue depending on the angle of the sun. Oh, and I do love the way the sea salt creates a wedding-night look to my hair. *Something* should.

Tonight the moon is high, exposing the beach with a silver glow. Sighing to the stars, I abandon my empty bottle and stagger to my feet.

"My name's Kaya Lucan," I announce to no one. "I'll be here all week."

Without my wine bubble, I typically get that crawling feeling that someone is lurking behind me in the shadows of the night. Watching, waiting, stalking. Right now the excessive numbness keeps me from feeling *anything*. This is my happy place. I sidle away from the banks of the Salt Sea without looking over my shoulder, not noticing the figure that steps into the moonlight to watch me leave.

The night is quiet and lonely, as always. Avoca people rarely venture out here. Not these days. I trudge back across the hill to our desolate, *neutral* conurbation of tents and huts, and approach my home. Hustling inside, I rest my forehead on the wooden door and lock out the world.

There's nothing out there. No one is after me. I have nothing of interest or value to thieves and soul-catchers.

Not anymore.

KAYA

Several Unenthusiastic Thoughts Later

IT'S A NEW DAY, despite rumors of wars, the constant fear of invasion, the need to stay far away from the sick lying in the streets, and . . . it's just another morning.

At least dawn is a nightmare-free zone.

Not wanting to accept that I have to get up, I lie motionless, half off the bed. My brain sensors twitch, recovering. My wine bubble is gone. The sun is casting annoying shafts of light through my curtained window. It must be late morning. I pinch the bridge of my nose to ward off the hostile migraine, knocking another empty bottle to the floor. It rolls against the wall with a *clank*.

That's when I hear them.

I swing my legs over the side of the bed and tuck back a corner of my curtain. Then I *see* them.

"If it isn't the happy couple," I mumble, shaking my head.

They're standing at Avoca's single intersection, adjacent to my home. I stand and watch *him* a moment. *With her.* He is dressed for manual labor, a belt of miscellaneous gear around his waist. Finding work is hard, but even harder for a Shelomo.

After thorough hydration, I prep for being seen and head out into the daylight. The weather is in rich spirits today. That makes one of us. Squinting, I pace toward the disputing pair, equipped to make an entrance into another one of *her* amusing rants. With a closer glance at my friend, however, my thoughts scatter.

Travin.

He is the only person on my list of people I do not hate. His full name is Travin Samuli Shelomo, but he would kill me for saying so. The mousy hair atop his head is askew, a common and favorite attribute. But his enormous eyes, usually bright and smoky, are dull. He has a perturbed glare on his face, aiming the subdued irritation at his romantic interest. He's never dealt well with contention. Poor fellow.

His companion, on the other hand, takes on the form of The Fanged Serpent quite impressively. She has eyes the color of cistern water that has been bathed in time and time again. Her fawn-colored tunic hugs her middle, hanging down to her duck feet. She lives on one end of Avoca, and I live on the other. Travin lives between us, both figuratively and literally.

Trav glances at me, the typical look of defeat etched on his features. A shadow of whiskers dusts his cheeks and chin. His simlah is as worn as his patience. I can see the mental groan. Bon-won turns up her nose. Just kidding. Her name is actually Bronwynn. It is her way to go about life acting like I don't exist. Impervious, I wait, intruding on their squabble. I must have interrupted something important, because neither of them knows what to say.

That's when Bronwynn lets out an obnoxious snort, indicating her disapproval of my presence.

I roll my eyes and smile cheerfully at her. "I'm doing fine, thanks."

More silence.

Travin gives a nearly imperceptible shake of his head. He drags his gaze over to Bronwynn's condemning frown. Noticing her thin brownish hair, I twirl a coil of my own around my finger. Hers is fine and cropped sleekly below her jawline. Nonetheless, she makes an effort to toss it at least once every ten seconds. I go out of my way to shuffle my long, thick waves over one of my shoulders.

Travin clears his throat and fingers a tool on his belt, obviously anxious to get on with the day's work. He has enough on his shoulders without Bronwynn's heckling. If he can't earn enough to provide for his family, they might leave Avoca. The thought scares me into ending the silence.

I tap Travin's bicep with my knuckles and quip, "Want to go get some wine?"

"Stop," he mouths back.

"What is she talking about?" Bronwynn whines. Her voice is shrill and congested. It's clear she's been "crying".

"Nothing," Travin replies, failing to sound soothing.

"I'll take that as a hard no," I grumble, having personally found it a wonderful excuse to replenish my empty stash.

To each their own misery. I turn on my heel and leave unannounced, the hello-goodbye with Travin dissatisfying.

There isn't much work at Lucan Care today. I'll get to it, later. Instead, I head toward the fields to collect olives. I am out of manna, and I loaned my rekheb to Travin several months ago after creditors took off with his upper millstone. He grinds grain to make bread for his family every morning, which is fine, as I prefer a diet of mostly fruit. The fields are near the Rox's dwelling. I may stop by there after breakfast.

It's not too far of a walk, but an intriguing one to say the least. You pass by all the different classes of society—the rich, the poor, the poorest. Most of our quaint homes are built of scrap wood from the wilderness, clay, and tarps. The underprivileged live in tents, the least of them in the dirt behind said tents. Despite demographical differences, most tribes own at least two oxen or one mule. They plow the fields and harvest their own crops. We are self-sustaining and self-preserving.

Avoca is on the northeast corner of the Salt Sea, not that I've been anywhere else to know that. My knowledge of the land of Canaan is minimal, substantiated by late night conversations in the taverns. I prefer to keep it this way. The land is rich with cultivated plants. Figs and vines are abundant. The wine is richly spiced. There are vast quantities of oil and honey, with many fruit trees, wheat, and barley. To the east, the brush develops more densely, forming the wilderness that separates our village from the mountains. I've never been more than two feet into the forest. Never much cared for trees.

A few children scuttle off to the schoolyard ahead of me, an imitation of a promising future. Most Avoca residents have only one child, and that's if one even makes it to wedlock before dying to achieve such a goal. Expansion transpires, but at a controlled rate. It's safer, easier, and cost-efficient. This is one of the strange rules of Avoca. It is not spoken of what happens to unwelcome conceptions. Only elect few have multiple children, like the Roxes. The rest are inexplicably shunned.

I cut through the venue, stroll by the market, the blacksmith, and the animal clinic my father used to own. I helped tend to the animals, heal the sick ones, and provide the immunity remedies and branding. I never intended to take it over, but he was stricken with the disease when I was seventeen. He passed away after only nine days.

I turn down the road behind the distillery. Cutting through the slums makes the trip to the fields quicker. If a giant broom swept the scum of our city into a dustpan, this would be the dustpan. The slums overflow with every manner of abomination. Disreputable taverns line the streets. The weakest morals make the strongest wine. I wave to Cam, the owner of the most profitable of these establishments, The Cellar.

"Good day, Kaya," Cam calls.

Miki Rox's strident laughter carries out the window of The Cellar as I walk by. He's "networking." If you want to stay in office, keeping the slums on your side is vital.

Exiting the undesirable precinct, I head toward the north end of Avoca. These larger homes, built out of smoothed wood and the twinkling stone from the mountains, overlook the Salt Sea. Rich people live in a luxury I couldn't dream of, purchasing linen, thick wool, and carpets from traveling merchants. They dine on the finest of foods, order in the finest Egyptian products. This is where the Rox tribe lives.

The Roxes are the leaders of Avoca. They are good people. Well, most of them. Maeve and Max Rox are fair governors. They oppose warfare and conflict. In fact, they use a manipulative form of coercion to forbid it. Aggression in any form is discouraged. They worship Asherah and plant asherim in the Temple court each spring.

Our neutral territory will stay neutral as long as they can manage it.

Of course, aggression doesn't need encouragement. There are men who offer underground programs in the slums—or so I've heard from Cam. These secret combinations keep tabs on the destruction of nearby villages, pinpointing patterns of armies or sneaking out to ruins of evacuated cities to collect maps and weapons left behind. But the Roxes do not know it happens.

A few weeks ago, rebels assaulted Avoca. The Roxes tried to calm the village. Those men I spoke of, the ones secretly "training" soldiers, captured several of the enemies and killed them. In a true act of insurgence, the mock soldiers staked their victims' heads on pikes and placed them at our furthermost borders. They wanted to ward off inquisitive rebels and armies, Cam told me, at the taverns.

The Roxes were horrified, cleaning up the mess the way a young woman who did not have children would replace a baby's soiled loincloth. Mikyla Rox threw a town carnival. Daughter to Maeve and Max, she helps her parents organize volunteer support groups who raise funds for Avoca, with which they construct sanatoriums, collect food storage and medical supplies, and accept clothing donations for the poor. But no weapons. The Roxes don't want to encourage violent behavior.

No violence! More *peace!*

Mikyla initiates these merry diversions to distract the people from distress. Rumors of wars and the frequency of death cause unwanted pressure for our city. Overall, the Roxes do well for the people of Avoca. If only they knew about Miki.

Miki Rox is Mikyla's older brother. By four minutes. Being her twin has provided him with equally good looks. Raven-colored, curly hair. Tall, built stature. Eyes the color of pure obsidian. The Roxes are esteemed for such a miracle—two children in one pregnancy. Not disgraced the way most second births are. They are *elect*.

As a result of the double birth, Mikyla and Miki grew up . . . distinctive. Miki uses his over-the-top ego to slither around the popular taverns and do that which is most abominable. No parental guidance. No prospective marital objective in sight. Charm does little to sway a virtuous daughter. And when virtue runs thin, Miki

Rox is a man of force. What are politicians good for?

Miki is a quandary, considering Mikyla is probably as close to a sister as I'll ever have. She is a natural beauty and as ignorant as her parents. In our teens, she picked up the art of styling hair, forcing me to reinvent my looks. I don't have her fancy perfumes, but I can set my hair into loose pin curls after late night swims. Letting the sea salt set the waves, I twist segments up onto my crown, fastening it with a cloth and some twine, and by morning my hair is comparable to hers. Our similarities end there.

We grew close during our schooling. Let me rephrase that—as close as I'd let myself get to her. It sounds foolish but, like I said before, I try not to form any attachments. Attachment means vulnerability. Vulnerability means weakness. Weakness is not something you can afford if you want to survive.

Mikyla might tell me her secrets, chat about boys, and cry on my shoulder about both. It helps develop a kind of bond universally associated with friendship. But I keep my secrets safe inside. I try not to worry about when she'll decide to get married and forget about me. Or get infected from the disease. Or die from a rebel assault. It is what it is. She balances my cynicism with optimism and tells me to smile when I'm in one of my moods.

Today is going to be one of those days.

TRAVIN

When We Were Young

SHE WALKS BRISKLY AS though she does not want to be followed. The Lucan girl. Her braids bounce against her back, where dirt is smeared on her makeshift dress. Her skin is much deeper in color today than the last time I saw her. Maybe that is why she's missed school lessons the last couple of days. She's been on an *adventure*.

I follow her out of the schoolyard, thrusting my imaginary sword forward. Some of the other boys have fashioned knives out of sharpened rock or fragments of iron scalped from the blacksmith shop, but others are quick to tattle if you are discovered with one. Rebby's own father gave him a knife—a *real* one—two summers back. I don't even have a slingshot. Thus the sword of my imagination must suffice, as it does regularly. In my imagination it can exist larger than any of the boys' knives.

Weapons are not allowed in the schoolyard, and children are most certainly *not* allowed to possess them. The Roxes would have them confiscated. *My sword will forever remain in my possession*, I think gladly. I find it impossible not to dream of adventure. My adventures must always include a sword. Maybe the Lucan girl has a weapon, the one she took on *her* adventure. Maybe she rode on one of her horses, out into the enemy's lair. I wonder if she encountered soldiers on an ill-fated quest.

The Lucan girl is a couple years younger than me, but she is often in her own mind, the way I am. She does not play and laugh the way the others do. She avoids them, kind of how I do. But at least *I* have Rebby.

Pacing through the venue like an adult, the Lucan girl is treated like nothing less as people move out of her way. Weaving in and out of mingling grownups, I follow her to the animal clinic where, instead of going through the front entrance, she walks around to the back door. Grabbing the handle, she tugs it open and disappears inside.

I can't follow her there.

Skipping back to the front entrance, I look up at the faded words. Lucan Care, they read. Then, in smaller print: FOR ANI-MAL CARE INQUIRE WITHIN. The signs are painted with a chipping varnish, so antiquated you can hardly decipher them, but they are scrubbed clean by careful hands. On my tiptoes, I gaze through a window, a square opening in the clay building. With the cloth curtain rolled up, I can see into the shop. An exceedingly tall man stands beside a crate containing a colorful bird. That's her fa-ther. I can tell because she smiles the same way he does. They both have green eyes that tell the world they have stories.

Just then, I see the Lucan girl walk up to her father. He pats her head and she looks up at him with that smile. It originates in her eyes. Greener than grass, they light up brighter than the star show-ers, when the sky is full of rhinestones. *Even prettier.* She trusts her father. Perhaps he is a kind father.

Afterward, she moves to the back of the shop and starts to feed the horses. She carries barrels of hay as big as my bed. Her father, unbeknown to me, moves closer to the window, where I notice him watching me. Contritely, I shrivel away.

I am spying like no well-behaved boy does. *Worse on a girl. In front of her father.* Father Lucan is much bigger than most, and I gulp, envisioning his hands, each the size of a hen, striking me.

But he gives me *that* smile. The story it tells isn't an angry one. Tilting his head to one side, he scratches his chin with his thumb before moving to the door.

I nervously try to straighten my untrimmed hair. My palms are clammy and dirty. Embarrassed, I tuck them into my torn robes. I scan the street sideways, marking various escape routes through the venue. I'm a fast runner—nearly as fast as Rebby.

As Father Lucan comes outside and stares down at me from his towering height, I give up on a reckless getaway, utterly and totally petrified.

I wasn't lying. I wasn't stealing. I wasn't . . .

"Hello, there." He squats, and his green eyes are at the same level as mine.

His beard is a mixture of silver and black, same as the hair atop his ears. Everything about his demeanor is much more overbearing up close. Having a stable job, one that requires physical effort, has provided him with a large build and the essence of grand adventure. A head as big as an ox. Muscled arms. Chunky hands. I'll bet he gets to eat dinner *every* night.

"Hi," I manage. Very doormat-like. "Sir."

Father Lucan rubs a large, unclean palm across his knee. "What do you call yourself?"

I don't answer. I'm not supposed to tell anyone my name.

He jerks his chin toward the door to his shop, asking, "Would you like to see inside?"

If he knew my name, he would not invite me in. But he does *not* know who I am. If I follow, I can see all the creatures within.

Timidly, I nod.

"Well, then," he says, standing tall again, "follow me, my boy."

The interior of the shop smells funny, but not bad. It is larger than it appears on the outside. The walls are lined with lofty shelves, cluttered by unidentified tools and implements. There are various crates with smaller animals like cats and dogs in them. Down the hallway, the clinic stretches into stalls for bigger animals, like horses and cows. Huddling by a shelf, I glance down the hall hoping to catch a glimpse of the girl I'd followed or any storybook creatures perhaps in hiding.

"What interests you, boy?" Father Lucan calls from the entrance.

I try to find my voice. I can't lie to a grownup.

Just then, his daughter exits one of the horse stalls. Locking the gate behind her, she starts walking in my direction. Her cheeks are the color of flowers. A few pieces of straw stick to her hair. I can't think of anything to say, my mind emptied by the possibility of *her* speaking to *me*. Father Lucan reappears, jingling a coin purse in his hands. Between the two of them, I hurriedly decide to stare at my feet.

Father Lucan eyes me, and then his daughter, who walks toward the shelves on the wall. She almost bumps right into me, so impartial to my presence, I barely refrain from checking to see if I am, in fact, as imaginary as my sword. When she tries to reach a metal object on a high shelf, her father strides past me to get it for her.

"Here," he says, handing the item to his daughter.

She takes it from him and marches by again, without a glance, without a word, down the hallway and into a different stall. I did not realize I am stretching my neck to watch her leave, until I hear the gruff clearing of a throat. My face heats, and I lower my chin.

After a minute, Father Lucan asks, "Do you know how to shoe a horse?"

"Nay." I dare to peek up. "Sir."

"Would you like to learn how?"

I try to look straight at him. He puts down his coin purse and drops onto his heels by my side, itching the stubble on his chin.

"It is fun," he says more brightly.

Finally, I force my gaze to his eyes. He has a bigger smile on his face now. The expression looks unnatural. He must not do that often.

"Come," he states, rising and beckoning me. "I'll have my daughter show you."

I follow Father Lucan hesitantly through the hallway of stalls. The animals are talking to one another, and the smell intensifies. It's a very curious shop. So many things you could climb up or hide behind. The rafters up above would give me and Rebby good makings for a fort. My feet shuffle along twice the speed of Father Lucan's, while I attempt to keep up with his long stride. Eventually, we reach the open stall. He rests one hand on the top of the gate. With his other, he motions for me to go ahead inside.

I peer around the wall. His daughter is sitting on a large, wooden stool dangerously close to the stern of a horse. The beast's rear left leg is bent backward, the foot resting in her lap. A table of strange tools and big nails is set up next to her. At the sound of my fidgeting, she cranes her neck to look at her father, and then her eyes fall on me. A crease forms in the center of her brow as her gaze narrows. Much like her father's.

"This fellow is interested in learning how to shoe a horse," her father says matter-of-factly. His daughter flicks her eyes up to his. "Would you like to show him how?"

At first, she doesn't move. I start to worry that the horse might kick her in the head. She looks me up and down, takes her time, and deliberates. Decisions are important to her. I turn to leave, ashamed I have even presented her with such a decision, when thick fingers press between my shoulders. Father Lucan's palm gently pushes me forward into the stall, and then he is gone.

"You're quiet," his daughter states abruptly.

She's inspecting me, like Mother does when I'm suspected of doing wrong.

"Come here," the girl demands, waving me over.

My feet move of their own accord. I stay more to the side of the girl, away from the horse's legs. *I* don't want to get kicked in the head. She begins to pick up different tools, explaining to me their use. Her fingernails are filthy, her hands chapped. She holds up a big metal object.

"This is the shoe," she clarifies, holding it out to me.

Something flares in her eyes, bringing a new luster to the green. They're smiling at me, even if her lips are not. She likes animals. They make her happy.

I take the shoe from her and hold the heavy thing in both my hands. It's rough and rusty.

"I'm Kaya."

I glance up. Not taking her eyes from mine, she reclaims the horseshoe.

"I'm Travin," I hear myself say.

Her gaze lingers a moment on me, and then slides back to her task. "I know."

KAYA

My Day Getting Better

POPPING AN OLIVE IN my mouth, I gaze across a cornfield to the familiar front door of Mikyla Rox's home. The Roxes have the best view of the Salt Sea. The sand is pure white and soft as cotton beneath your feet. Huge boulders lie cracked and covered in a pale, powdery deposit lining the edge of the shoreline. Palms provide plenty of shade. It's wondrous.

Some people just have beach in their souls. Which is why I spend many of my evenings there. Sometimes with Travin.

I met Trav as a gentle, floppy-haired boy. Being a Shelomo has made him a target his whole life. Town jackals often antagonized a juvenile Travin into a group-on-one altercation. It was bad enough to be bullied, but worse to go home to an emotionally absent mother who neglected him for any aggressive behavior. I've watched boys, several years his senior, bring him down in the schoolyard. He did not even raise a fist to block them, nor has he made any grand effort to defend what folks say about him. Epitomizing nobility, he goes about his business using actions, instead of claims, to verify what kind of person he is.

One of these actions I'm quite fond of is befriending the cynical girl who owns Lucan Care. I've never done yard work a day in my life.

The yard surrounding the Rox's home is immaculate. One of Travin's many trades is landscaping. I referred him to the Roxes, since they would not have batted an eye in the Shelomo direction had I not been friends with Mikyla. He decorated their yard with several pottery vases, the latest modeled loom for spinning linen, and a hot vat for dying cloth. Maeve is very particular about her yard. As far as mothers go, she is a good one.

I have no recollection of my own mother. She left when I was two years old. I found an epistle from her in Father's chest shortly after he died. It was dated a year after she'd left us, and most of it was just a bunch of excuses as to why she never returned. Father never showed me the letter. I'm told I get my looks from her. I'm five feet tall and svelte.

My father was six foot six. His long arms could reach into a pigpen and haul out a barrow like it was a down-stuffed pillowcase. I look nothing like him, but Trav says we have the same eyes. My father loved my thick hair. I know it reminded him of my mother's. As a child, it used to drive me crazy, but he would patiently brush and braid it down my back, cursing words that he thought I couldn't hear with each knot.

Mikyla will have something to say about my disheveled locks today. Styling would've been useless in this heat wave. Besides, the animals at Lucan Care don't give two oats what my hair looks like.

I love my profession for that reason. Nothing smells more nostalgic than a chicken coop. Nothing sounds friendlier than the swish of a horsetail against the stall door. Animals possess an uncommon innocence. An unfathomable loyalty, too. Sometimes I can sense my father's presence there. It feels like home.

Since the disease is lethal to animals, Lucan Care has become a part-time trade. I should probably feel guilty about that, after how many hours I watched my father put into the clinic. But, frankly, I'm kind of relieved. The job provides me with sufficient revenue for my needs, yet time to do whatever I want. Having a profitable business is something I take for granted, since I'm not seeking yield for two more mouths to feed. Travin has always been a fair reminder of that. A respectable, *honorable*, example of selfless love.

Maleah was quite a surprise for their family. Avoca residents eschewed the Shelomo tribe for her birth, among other things. This dishonor was *heartily* resented by their father. Luckily, he passed away only months after Maleah was born. He was a drunk with a hard hand. Upon learning this, I understood why Trav has always had father issues, and I admired him for what he did to provide for their family.

Honor is important to Travin. Probably because it's never been associated with the Shelomo name. He's done everything he can to prove himself to the people of Avoca, putting forth his best effort to undo what his dead father created. Sometimes, Travin can find honest labor. He'd prefer it that way. Other times, he'll take what work he can. Whatever keeps his family off the streets. He doesn't know I know.

The town has persecuted him, his mother, and his little sister Maleah, even after the death of Trav's father. Apparently, the Shelomo tribe was in great debt. Creditors swore in every manner of maliciousness that Trav's family would live in ruin.

They live in absolute poverty.

Travin's last name has never bothered me. They're just letters. What does bother me is how little I see him these days. We used to spend a lot of time together, led by none other than our personal ringleader, Ranvir Daan.

I have no idea why we call him Rebby, but everyone does. He happens to be Avoca's most *un*married bachelor. And he knows it. I try to hate him, but every day Rebby manages to convince me otherwise. He is Travin's less decent, better looking, comrade. The two go back farther than Travin and I do, with some kind of unseen connection between them I covet. Growing up, we were the best of friends, sometimes rivals. We were a three-man circus. That is, until Trav started romancing *Bon—won*.

The last time Travin and I spoke it was concerning war. He had worrisome views on Avoca's neutrality. He wondered at the life of a soldier and battle like it was an adventure. He mentioned an Israelite army with promising numbers that is awaiting the opportune moment to take down opposing kings. It is his belief we must join the fight or be lost to destruction. I think Rebby feeds his fantasy.

Rebby's father has always been a known supporter of the secret combinations in Avoca. The Daan tribe migrated from

Kadesh-Barnea, an Israelite territory, before Rebby was born. Rebby's father believes children should be baptized by the blazing flame of combat, discussing this openly around town. The Daan tribe does not believe in Aton, or Asherah, and poke fun at idolatries. A God that does not see, hear, eat, or smell is nothing more than an inanimate object. The Roxes have sent Father Daan before the judges a number of times for this scandalous belief. Rebby was raised with many scandalous beliefs.

He was an infamous kid, the kind the elderly still drone about. He invented miniature knives from home goods and brought them to school, handing them out to children, before facing a week of expulsion. Tipping scales, or creating false weights, were his areas of expertise. A grumpy tradesman chasing Rebby out of the Commerce Centre would often be chasing a scrawny Travin, too. Of course, a couple of bouncing braids might have been somewhere in the mix as well.

Even facing slight prejudices, both men seem moderately happy with their positions in life—Rebby delighting in the women vying for his attention, Travin absorbed in pleasing everybody but himself. Me? I'm happily moderate. I tend to the animals at Lucan Care and avoid the people I hate.

During our last conversation, Travin asked if I would want to become a soldier if presented with the prospect. He may as well have asked me if I wanted to eat the cow manure I was shoveling. My answer must have been funny, because he laughed. I remember because I haven't heard him laugh in months. Our paths barely cross, even when he does help out at Lucan Care.

I went home that night thinking about Canaanites, Israelites, and rogue rebels. The latter of these are non-affiliates, wayfaring throughout the land, wreaking havoc. They've caused mayhem a few times here in Avoca, the last of these occurrences a few weeks ago. The Roxes threw a town carnival the next day with anti-war propaganda. The Daans held a bonfire and celebrated the death of the rebels with burnt offerings.

Rebels are known to be a main source of the rampant disease. This plague has only affected a few victims in Avoca. It either claims their lives quickly, or the infected individual develops tolerance but loses all sense of humanism. A contaminated survivor demonstrates . . . how do you say it? Cannibalistic behavior. Just imagine how the Roxes react. When these diseased persons become too problematic, they are taken far into the wilderness. I don't know what happens after that, but I doubt it involves anti-war propaganda.

My pockets stuffed with olives, I descend toward the Rox's. I start up the walkway, smirking at the boastfulness, when something slams into my chest. I stumble. Catching a conglomeration of feathers in my arms, I quickly discover that it's a bird. One of my favorite species. The peafowl to be exact. Her sleek down is sticky with her blood. The velvet tail feathers I love to watch stream against the blue sky lay frazzled in my hands.

Instinctively, I cradle the wounded fowl, medical impulses flashing. I know what I could do to save it, but all my tools are back at the clinic. Wanting to retrieve them, I turn away from the Rox's. A small paper is clenched in the bird's claws. I gently open the scaly feet and uncurl the scroll attached the bird's foot. There are a few illegible words and a picture of two triangles pointing toward each other, just touching at the tip.

The message appears ominous, written hastily on parchment that is stained with pomegranate juice. It has weathered a journey. Stuffing the paper in my pocket, I resolve to get the peafowl to Lucan Care for treatment before delivering the scroll to one of the Roxes. Just as I think this, an explosion occurs behind me. Startled, I whip around to see smoke rising into the air. The vapor thickens and swirls like coal dust above the distillery. Hordes of shouting people run from their homes into the streets. A horrible, ear-splitting cry pierces the air.

The eminence of evil creeps up my skin. Even the sun hides behind the abrupt appearance of clouds.

Conflicted, I abandon the dying bird and prioritize my next actions. I catalogue the animals at Lucan Care and belongings at home that I need to assemble. I slip through the crowded streets of the venue when another burst ruptures. Crouching, I shield my eyes from spewing dust, wondering if the star showers have commenced.

The bakery door is busted. More people flood the streets. Dogs wander out the gaping doors, barking at the ruckus. A young child is crying. The smell of smoke reaches my nostrils.

A twinge of unease triggers my quicker pace, when a hand catches my arm, jerking me to a halt.

"Kaya!"

I spin frantically to find my aggressor is only Rebby. His auburn hair is pulled back and fastened at his neck, displaying his square jawbone. He smells like sawdust. There are flakes on the tops of his shoulders. Remnants of his employment. His dark eyes are uncharacteristically puzzled. There's an arrow sticking out of his bicep.

"What is happening?" I shout above the commotion.

Before Rebby can respond, mutineers galloping bareback on horses burst through the trees, unashamed of their nakedness. These are rebels. Murderous, merciless, unpredictable. They wield ordinary farm tools for weapons and use mechanical slings to propel giant rocks through the air.

To my right, a rebel dismounts his mare and charges Rebby and I, his tongue swinging maniacally out of his mouth. Old blood stains his flesh. Scars corrode his face and arms. His eyes look in two different directions. It's clear he is infected with the disease. Lifting an ox goad, the rebel utters a gargled cry.

Frozen, I stand motionless. The iron-tipped point of the ox goad nears my face, the shaft raised above the rebel's head. Rebby releases my arm and swings a hand in a large arc. The rebel falls, Rebby's knife protruding from his jugular. The ox goad hits the ground, sliding towards my toes as the blunt end scrapes up a puff of dirt.

Rebby grabs the arrow protruding from his arm and breaks it off at the tip.

"Come on," he yells, retrieving his knife.

I've been reduced to paralysis. Rebby gives my arm a yank.

"Look," he continues, leaning close to my face. I tear my gaze off the nonliving rebel. "Do you know the escape route into the wilderness?"

"Yay, but . . ."

"There's a parish in the trees. Can you make it?"

I trip, unable to match Rebby's ardent stride as he pulls me east. He shoots me an impatient stare, demanding a response.

"Can you make it there?" he asks urgently.

"I've seen the drawings," I stutter. "But . . ."

"Follow the others," he commands. His grip on my elbow tightens, and he tilts his forehead against mine. The concern on his face, the face of a protector—*ready to kill*—rebirths him. "Don't pause for anything. *Don't* look back, Kaya."

And like that, Rebby is gone.

I *do* look back.

A banner promoting peace has caught fire, floating like a paradigm of carnage above a burning city. Powdered soil fills my lungs. I can hardly make out my surroundings as horses stir up dirt in furor. Heart racing, I search for a course between incoming rebels. A pair of competitors spars close to my right, the armed Avoca local carrying a comprehensive weapon. I sprint by them, olives tumbling from my robes.

I tell myself to keep moving. Crawling a few feet in front of me is a little girl. I help the child to her feet and clutch her arm tightly. Right then, an enemy stallion gallops over us. I fly with the little girl in my arms, shielding her body with mine as we topple to the ground. When the rebel is gone, I pick the girl up and scan her for injuries.

"Here, come with—"

But her mouth opens in a scream. She scurries away into the dust, gone. Trying to call out to her is useless. She will never hear me.

The outline of trees is just ahead. Behind me, the foray is centralized near Avoca's city gates. Large boulders catapult through the air, knocking down village buildings. A javelin strikes a running man, Cam. He continues staggering into the wilderness, clutching the staff of the weapon penetrating his belly.

A procession of Avoca soldiers-in-training has assembled at the top of the hill, armed with slingshots, handcrafted bows, and tools. A dozen of them, ready to retaliate against the rebels. One of the men raises a hand and shouts, "We don't go home, they don't go home!" It is Rebby's father. His son stands at his side. I watch Rebby and the ersatz soldiers plunge into battle.

Ascending the hills, I push my legs to move faster and harder. Cam made it. I can make it.

As soon as my feet reach the shadows of the overhanging branches, I forget everything but my instructions from Rebby.

Run.

TRAVIN

She Knew My Name

MOTHER ISN'T MAD THAT I get home late from Lucan Care. She doesn't often get mad anymore. She doesn't talk anymore. She doesn't care anymore.

I climb into bed, telling her about Kaya and the animals. There is so much to recount about horseshoes, and green eyes, and a kind father.

"I'm strong, right, Mother?"

She gives me one of her sad smiles and nods.

I know I can't lie to adults, but sometimes adults lie to children. If I were strong, her eyes wouldn't be so sorry.

"I'll be strong someday," I murmur, curling onto my side with a yawn.

Someday.

Mother yawns, too, despite sleeping the majority of the day, responding with, "You're only eleven years old."

She kisses me goodnight, and I listen to the sounds of her footsteps tread across the main room to her bedroom. It's always the same routine. As soon as the curtain closes, Maleah appears at my bedside, dragging her blanket behind her. I let her crawl under the covers with me, where we'll share the space for dreams until sunrise. At dawn, Mother will wake, aged years older than the day before.

For hours that night, I lie awake next to Maleah's tiny slumbering body. A slit of light entering through the window illuminates her thin infant hair, stuck to her cheek. Her fingers clutch her scrappy blanket. One day she will be old enough to understand all of this, why they treat her differently, why they treat *us* differently, and why Mother is the way she is. I wish there was a third Shelomo, and a fourth, and a fifth. That way, our *second* wouldn't have to face all the disgrace of our tribe.

Sometime in the night, a bottle clashes through our open window, shattering on the floor. Maleah startles, but I hush her back to sleep. I creep off the bed, staying low to the floor, and pick up a sharp piece of the broken bottle. Huddling below the window, I listen to the men laughing and mocking until they have wandered down the street. Certain we are safe, I gather each broken fragment. Then I clean up the broken bottle.

KAYA

Into the Wild

I know there are two pathways that lead into the wilderness. It is one of the few things the Roxes allow in the schoolroom regarding any aspect of attack. And that aspect is *fleeing*. I don't exactly have the map memorized. Judging by the chaotic flow of people entering the woods next to me, not many do. We scramble to locate these paths. When violence erupts in a non-violent community, apparently the result is disaster.

I'm following a man who is slamming his way through the brush with a sense of direction. As we run deeper and deeper into the wilderness, the people fleeing town become more and more scattered. Many of them are caught by rebels. Arrows zing through the trees, the only noise other than footsteps and eerie nature sounds. Leaves swishing, twigs cracking, rocks crumbling.

The man in front of me is distancing himself. I tell myself to keep up. There is no clearing in the brambles. My arms and face acquire generous cuts, scratches, scrapes. Over my shoulder, a woman cries out. I try to swallow, but my mouth has become too dry. My lungs begin to ache, sending a pain through my chest. My simlah is clinging to my breast.

The man breaks right, diving through a cluster of bushes. Asthmatically, I slow my pace to more cautiously part the shrubs. The plant, as it turns out, is covered in thorns. I groan as they tear at my hands, drawing blood. But I break through them, landing on my hands and knees. I find, to my despair, the man is nowhere to be seen.

Now immobile, the urge to continue running is gone. I sit, stationary, allowing the unbearable throb in my sternum to hit me. My lungs labor for air. I crouch, gasping, finally noticing the path underneath my knees. A path that stretches in either direction. Wiping my forearm across my face, I listen. The wilderness is quiet beyond my wheezing.

It may sound so temporal, but I can't help worry about my little shack, how I have worked so hard to preserve the modest place just for me. The little jewelry case my father gave to my mother as a gift, and I inherited after she left. Its contents. The washroom I keep stocked with half a dozen fragrant soaps I buy at the venue, because just one never totally removes animal scent from my skin. I picture Lucan Care, my father's hands keeping the clinic tidy. Frightened horses whinnying. Chickens flapping in a frenzy.

I think of the Salt Sea.

The cave.

With a quick assessment of my surroundings, I realize I am lost in the wilderness, fleeing from anarchists. I have no idea what kind of creatures—both animal and human—live in these wilds. And I am unarmed. Perhaps my guardian angel drinks wine, too.

Feeling hopeless, I sit back on my hind and stretch my legs out in front of me. At least I have a trail to follow. With any luck, it leads to the parish. I've met some people from *the wilderness*. Native woodland folks with odd facial structures, bizarre dialects, humorous fashion choices. They come into Avoca to mingle and trade, but off they go back into the trees. I'd be lying if I said I've never thought of going with them.

I transition onto one knee, when a branch cracks down the path. My pulse does that thing when you're sure it's completely stopped, once and for all. I try to make out any moving shapes down the trail, to no avail. In a greater act of stupidity, I call out.

"Hello?"

No response.

A couple of minutes pass. I'm almost certain the sound came from my left, so I start slowly placing one foot in front of the other. This is the genius in me. Follow the sounds of cracking branches, especially when you're alone. And female. Practically a virtuous one.

The path bends slightly. I follow it, continuing to tiptoe along the rim of the foliage until the jostle of plants brings me to a halt. I steal a suspicious glance behind me, my smartest move yet. But when I turn forward, I see a man emerging from the rustling bushes. His face is stone cold, his clothes torn, every inch of his visible flesh covered in dirt. He's the man I have been following, camouflaged. A soldier tactic. In that instant, I appreciate Avoca's secret combinations.

"Please," I say, "help me."

"Cease following me," the man orders, raising a sword.

Against my better instincts, I persist. "But I don't know my way—"

"Be warned!" he growls. "Do not follow me."

He takes a few steps back, lifting the pointed blade to eye level. Then he vanishes into the forest, feet thumping as he effectively flees. I really hate people.

Feeling the size of a lone ant, I am swallowed by the wilderness. I take one step forward, but my foot does not meet earth. I fall. Down, down, into a pit. I hit the bottom, as a net crumbles down onto me.

"Oof!" I wince, tossing the net aside.

A centipede slithers over my palm, and I scuttle backward until my spine collides into the cold, dirt wall. Looking up, I estimate I'm around ten feet below the forest floor. Perfect. Flexing my arms and legs, I surmise nothing is broken. Nothing physical, at least. My appreciation for Avoca soldiers *is*.

I convince myself it could be worse. I also convince myself I can escape. Problem: the walls of the hole are perfectly chiseled, leaving no easy way to climb out. I try clinging to divots in the dirt but make no progress. I have tended mountain goats, but it doesn't mean I can become one. It's useless. *I* am useless. Pounding my fists into the hardened earth, I yell until I can't think of any more bad words.

As the time drags by, the confined space begins to make me uneasy. Minutes accumulate into a full hour. I try again and again to climb the walls, the way one living in a delusory state of optimism might, only to fail miserably. My fingers, my back, my head, *ache*.

Keep calm, I tell myself. *I need my wine bubble.*

I wipe the cuts on my arms against my tunic, unsure of how I feel about seeing my own blood. I notice my fingers are trembling. I also feel the pangs of hunger. *When did I eat last?* Reaching into my robes, I search for olives. None remain. It's only a matter of time before I die of dehydration. What's the average lifespan without water? Three days?

Another hour later, my growing discomfort has increased to alarming levels. My head is dizzy, my stomach churning unpleasantly. The walls of the hole seem to be closing in on me from all sides. No matter which way I spin, there they are. A third hour passes. Either I imagine it, or I at long last hear a voice from up above. I hold my breath and strain my ears. Learning from errors one through three, I choose not to call out.

"Mercy," I whisper, gnawing a fingernail.

Then, I hear it.

"*Stay put.*"

The voice is close, definitely within calling range.

My fingernail begins to sting so I switch to another. What if it's a rebel?

I jump, getting a great view of the dirt eight inches above my forehead.

"I told you, just stay put," the voice says, much closer now.

And it's a voice I could recognize anywhere.

My heart pounds against my ribs.

"Travin!" My voice cracks in desperation. "Travin! Travin, over here!"

Silence answers.

Perhaps it was a delusion, brought on by trauma. A thorn bush above me crackles in two loud, short bursts. I cringe my eyes shut. My mind fills with imaginations of the Canaanite army and all manner of wickedness. It would be better for me to die in this pit than be caught by rebels. I am, in fact, the best worst-case scenarist.

Footsteps scuffle onto the dirt path, drawing nearer to the pit.

I open one eye and watch a silhouette materialize above me. The figure tucks something shiny into his belt and drops to his stomach, stretching his arms toward me.

"Kaya!"

He's here.

Travin curses. A very rare occurrence. It is followed by, "What happened?"

"Help me!" I gasp, my optimism of escape renewed. "Help me get out of here!"

I claw at the dirt repeatedly and jump. Acrobatics are not my specialty. Nonetheless, Travin encourages my embarrassingly ineffectual efforts.

"There you go. Keep at it. You've almost got it."

He slides forward until his torso hangs over the edge. Pointing, he rattles off a few suggestions. With his calm, stoic instructions, I maneuver my legs and arms.

"On the count of three," he says. "One, two . . ."

I bend and lunge as hard as I can. Travin's hands clasp onto my wrists. As he wriggles backward, I kick against the dirt walls until I'm miraculously freed from the all-consuming pit. I roll to my back, kissing the dirt path.

"Are you alright?" Travin questions, face directly above mine.

He drags me to my feet, fingers awkward, pushing strands of hair from my face, lifting my hands, jarring me forward and examining the cuts on my arms.

"Where are you hurt?" he demands. "You're covered in blood. You look like you've been in a fight." His eyes are two enormous spheres, black pupils swallowing up the tepid gray of his irises. "You're hurt. Are you hurt? How did you get in that pit? How long were you down there?"

When his gaze focuses back on my face, he grimaces. He lifts his fingertips toward my cheek, and then his palm falls to my shoulder.

"Thank you," he sighs, closing his eyes.

It must be dusk. There are no signs of a massacre, other than the tattered clothing we wear. Travin appears unharmed, although the sleeve of his outer robe is torn and blood is spattered on one of his sandals. Leaves and dirt are jammed into my own. I look around, too full of questions to think clearly, but willing to add my sincere gratitude to Travin's prayer.

"I saw Rebby," I gasp.

Travin nods. "I saw him too—" But he's interrupted by the untimely entrance of Bon-won.

She approaches from the wood disdainfully. I'd forgotten Travin had been with someone before discovering me in the pit. It was Bronwynn whom he told to "stay put," and I can tell by her expression she wasn't in congruity with the idea. They both escaped the rebels unscathed. It is a miracle.

Bronwynn does not appear grateful for this achievement. She gets even more excited when she sees *me*.

I realize Travin's hand is still on my shoulder. In a not-so-subtle wiggle, I let it slide off. His eyes open, turning immediately to Bronwynn. The look on his face translates his forgetting she was here, too.

"Don't be afraid," he states. "You can come out. The area is secure. Kaya fell into this pit. I just pulled her free. Now we can head to the parish together."

His words are quick and apologetic. Bronwynn joins him but resists his embrace. I shut my eyes a moment, wondering if it wouldn't be better to leave *her* in the pit, but the woman in Avoca being dragged through the alleyway by a rebel suddenly flashes into my mind.

"We should depart," I mumble, opening my eyes.

Travin's expression is complex. He glances over at Bronwynn, worry outlining his features.

Bronwynn wraps her hand inside his arm. She leans her head against his shoulder, while his arms embrace her.

"I'm so scared," she squeaks. Her eyes skate over to mine, sliding up and down my body like the tongue of a lizard.

"Come," Travin mutters, tugging her along.

I walk feebly behind them, making an effort not to limp, but making a larger effort to avoid staring at their affections. Travin holds Bronwynn's hand, helping her through the woods while I trip and get the swishing branches in my face. I observe the looming trees, rodent burrows, the scent of wilderness. Had this not been part of a dangerous escape, I would call it a kind of adventure.

"Travin?"

"Hm?"

My thoughts quickly turn to Maleah and his mother. "Your family . . ." My throat croaks, both from dehydration and the inability to express what I fear.

The look on Travin's face *does* express it, and perfectly. A grief grips my chest, like a ravenous snake coiling around a squirrel. Like nothing I've ever felt, except when . . .

"I haven't seen them," he replies forlornly. "I ran home, but . . ."

Bronwynn and he exchange glances. He tightens his grip on her hand.

If Avoca is destroyed, our families, our livestock, our businesses, everything will be gone. To me, that means my home and my beloved animals. For Travin, it means Maleah. His single most cherished entity in the universe.

It takes me exactly two minutes to then ask, "Did your parents fare alright, Bronwynn?"

"I don't know," she retorts. "It was all such a blur." Her eyes slide sideways to meet mine. "Travin and I did the best we could to find *our* families, but our homes were already destroyed. There was just too much danger. The rebels were devouring Avoca. Travin was kind enough to help me escape."

In honesty, I'm not listening to her. I am overcome with this strange and very real heartache. Like . . . like I'm losing someone all over again. And it is consuming, inasmuch as that pit. I feel a tightness in my bosom and a shortness of breath.

I clear my throat. "The man I was following . . ." *Breathe.* "How did he dig a pit so quickly?"

"It was already there," Travin answers. His voice is devoid of emotion, and I suddenly long for his teasing smile, the one that reveals a barely-there dimple in his left cheek. He adds, "They're used for detouring unwanted followers. The parish is neutral, but wise in its diversions. These woodlands are full of them. We must be cautious."

Travin pushes aside a fallen tree limb. Bugs squirm out from beneath it as he steps over first, then Bronwynn. I follow, not realizing it is odd for Travin to know that information.

"The diversions work well," Bronwynn says, stomping directly on a bug that squishes under her foot.

"Right," I mutter. "Diversions."

Travin leads us to another trail, the map of the wilderness learned by rote. His stride is wide and purposeful, requiring me to wield excruciating energy. My right knee buckles, and my left ankle smarts with every step. We don't commune during the rest of our travels. Mourning presides as my thoughts are distracted by flashbacks. Watching Rebby at the top of the hill, beside his father . . . what happened to Cam . . .

It is evening by the time we clear the forest. A valley opens up before us, the landscape drier than Avoca but still fertile. The parish is constructed in a half circle, facing the vast wilderness where a range of purple-fringed mountains rises in the distance. Villagers dwell in small homes or tents. Goats and sheep and horses roam through the lodgings, bells jingling. Down the center street, a group of Avoca survivors are huddled around a well. Natives assist them, dunking the bucket and pulling it back up, water sloshing over the bricks.

I cross to the well and lick the stones, the water pure rapture on my tongue. Hours of hiking through the thicket have wearied us. Travin urges Bronwynn to take a drink before approaching one of the nearest homes. He knocks on the door, glancing over at me. His head splits into two and begins swirling in my vision. Blackness encloses. Overcome with sickness, I faint.

TRAVIN

Didn't We Meet

SITTING CROSS-LEGGED ON the floor, hair braided, Kaya waits for the teacher to begin our lessons. Maybe Kaya won't pretend I'm a ghost today. Not after yesterday with the horses. I locate my assigned seat on the floor, gazing around the schoolroom. Kaya does not usually express outward signs of agitation, which is why I find the stiff set of her jaw and frequent movement of her hands uncommon. When she peers over at me, I wave. She doesn't react.

Her eyes don't smile.

When lessons are over, Kaya hurries out of the room and into the schoolyard. I gather my supplies and follow, squeezing through the bustling children who scrap over toy sticks. Rebby comes out victorious. I sprint past them to catch up to Kaya, reaching for her hand. She startles and comes to a halt, eyes snapping to my face.

"Hi," I murmur, retracting my hand. "Are you . . . going to the animal clinic again today?"

"I go every day."

"Are . . . you sick?" I inquire.

Her eyes darken to the color of a wet forest. She folds her arms glancing sideways.

I stammer on, "I – I – I didn't mean . . . I wasn't talking about the disease, Kaya—"

"What do you want, Travin?" she demands. "I can't let you watch me anymore. It will distract me. I didn't have time to finish all my chores yesterday because I spent time teaching you about horseshoes. And I could tell you didn't want to listen. Look, I have work to do. Why don't you get back to playing with the *children*?"

She twirls, her braids whipping across my cheek as she stalks away.

"Wait!" I holler.

Pausing, Kaya pivots slightly toward me. Her eyes perform one methodical blink.

"When do you get done working?" I ask.

"I'm always working."

"I want to show you something. Like you showed me something."

She rolls her eyes, but it only partially conceals a hint of interest. "Maybe I'll meet you after lessons." Then, she rushes off into the venue before I can stop her.

BUT KAYA DOESN'T SHOW up to lessons the next day. I stare at her empty seat on the floor in disappointment. When the teacher releases us for the day, I make my way out to the street. Rebby thinks my sullen mood could be fixed by playing with his knife. He reveals it with pride, lifting the hem of his tunic to expose the hidden blade while bragging of his father's latest smuggled weaponry. Several boys nearby gawk. One of them runs off to tell the instructor.

"There you are!"

I twist around.

"Travin!" Kaya calls.

She stands just beyond the schoolyard, her clothing clean, her long, brown waves loose on her shoulders. The sun glistens through them, varying the pigments from dark copper to red clay. Like a doll. With a shy gesture, she beckons and then knots her fingers together. An uncommon action.

I skip up to her, Rebby's knife forgotten. "You weren't in lessons today."

"My father let me stay home," she replies with her 'Kaya' smile. *What story is she trying to tell me today?*

"You don't have to go to Lucan Care right now?" I question.

"Nay," she sighs, an expression close to relief spreading across her face.

"Why not?"

"My father told me to do whatever I want. *Today* . . . is my birthday."

"Birthday?" I exclaim. "Happy Birthday, Kaya!"

She giggles accidentally, quick to repress it. It is a sweet sound, like Maleah makes. And the first real smile she's shown me. Her eyes twinkle a brighter shade of jade. She's not sad, like yesterday.

"Thanks," she murmurs, smashing her lips together and peeking up at the sun. "I am nine years old. Father said I should go with *you*, when I told him you wanted to show me something, that is. So," she hesitates, "what was it you were going to show me?"

"Come on!" I spin around and dart out of the schoolyard.

Kaya follows, and we run through the town, toward the hills. Hopping through sage, I pause at the top of a slope as Kaya tags along a few feet behind. We take a minute to catch our breath. I can already smell the salt. My favorite place.

Enthusiastically, I point down on the other side of the hill.

"The Salt Sea?" Kaya asks, shielding her eyes from the sun.

"Ever been?"

"Nay, but—"

I grab her hand and pull her with me. Together we run down the incline, over the relics of an ancient fence post, evading several animal burrows. I shoot an impish grin toward her and take the lead. This is *my* adventure.

Soon, the hill dissolves into sand. Kaya follows me across the shoreline where I break into a full sprint, reeling toward the water with a whoop of delight. The waves pound the beach and creep up toward my toes. Bubbling water fizzles and then retreats back into the sea.

"Hurry, take your sandals off!" I shout.

Kaya copies me with a skeptical indent in her brow.

The next wave hits the sand and inches closer. I jump up before it can reach my feet and splash back down. The water sprays up my ankles, cooling my skin in the gentle breeze. Kaya smiles, a genuine face splitting grin. It tenderizes all her edges. The wind whips her hair, and she coyly tucks it behind her ears. She looks happy. Enchanted.

"Try it," I say.

The wave comes again, worming up the sand. Kaya bounces up next to me, her nose crinkling just the slightest as she looks at me out of the corner of her eye. At the same time, we both jump to avoid the initial hit of the water on our feet. As we land back in the sand, the water splashes up to our knees.

"Let's go!" I laugh, charging into the tide.

Kaya does not follow.

I return to grab her hand a second time. "Kaya, let's swim."

A look of alarm crosses her face, and she shakes her head.

I give her hand a futile tug. "It's fun," I state adamantly.

She resists my efforts. "I can't swim, Travin."

For the tiniest of moments, the breeze ceases. Kaya's eyes lock on mine. She looks frightened.

I step forward. "I'll teach you."

KAYA

Homeless and Harangued

"*Hold still.*"

His words slur together as one, the latter coming across as the sound a drunken snake might make. That's exactly what he is—and, always and forever will be. Drunk. And by far the slimiest snake of a man I've ever come across.

At this point, I want more to wipe away the specks of saliva he's just sprayed onto my cheek than fight against his heavy body restricting me against the ground.

The piercing shriek of a kettle springs my mind into consciousness. The nightmare is over.

I'm lying on a small bed, heart slamming against my ribs. An oil lamp rests on a windowsill, swaying light over my surroundings. I sit up and wipe the cold sweat from my forehead. My hands shake profusely. And there is an *awful* pounding in my skull. *Thirst. I need to quench it.*

Throwing my legs off the side of the bed, I head toward the curtain separating this room from whatever else there is. My fingers barely reach the cloth when a woman pushes it aside.

She stands before me with a tray of teacups. "You must be Kaya."

Drink. The thought pounds into my head with each physical thrum. *Drink, drink, drink.* The woman slips into the room and places the tray on the bed.

"I'm Yespin," she continues, turning and taking my hand in hers. "Yespin Roteruth of the Roteruth tribe. Welcome to Taavetti."

Her grip is warm and steady, and if she notices the quiver in my hands, her face gives nothing away. She is dressed ordinarily, her hair hanging silvery down her shoulders.

"Taavetti isn't much of a resort, but it's a nice enough town," she says talking to herself. "Anyone from Avoca is welcome here. Why, we just had an attack in Taavetti . . . what was it? One month ago? Or was it two—"

She looks at me and stops.

"You must be hungry," she declares affirmatively. "I'll bring you a change of clothes. Drink the tea. It will settle your stomach."

She disappears out the doorway. I inhale the liquid, letting it burn down my throat. Mint tea. I wouldn't mind something stronger, but I drink every cup on the tray. Yespin returns with some folded clothes in her hands. She asks if there's anything else I need, before she returns to cooking supper.

"A-actually," I stutter, feigning a glance down at my ensemble, "is . . . there a place where I might . . . clean up?"

Yespin motions out the doorway. "I'll take you."

The little washroom is whittled into the wall just beyond the curtain. Another lamp burns on a shelf, next to clean cloths and a basin of clean water. On the floor, a plank of wood covers the waste depository. Gingerly removing my clothes, I begin by tying my hair up. My fingers stick to the tangles, fixed together by dirt. I dunk a hand into the water, running it over my hair, when the curtain rustles.

"Kaya?"

I notice his silhouette behind the fabric.

"Uh—just a moment!"

Grabbing a towel, I wrap it around my body. I pull back the curtain a bit, and for a moment, I see an eleven-year-old boy. The boy who stared meekly at me across the stall in Lucan Care. All big, fearful gray eyes, recklessly abandoned wayward curls above a worried forehead, malnourished shoulders, and knees like grapefruits. I blink, and he's my twenty-four-year old friend again, fidgeting as he notices the towel around me.

His eyes snap up to my face, his expression as easily read as words in a book.

"Er . . . sorry," Travin says demurely. "Yespin told me you were awake, and I just wanted to make sure you were well."

I exhale, brushing an invisible hair off my face. "I am well. Just trying to clean up, you know?"

"Right."

Disgruntled by my response, Travin runs a hand through his hair. The color has changed from buttery blonde to dishwater brown over the years, and it's a little longer than he used to wear it. Damp from a recent wash, the length reveals tiny ringlets that appear only around his nape. He smells pleasingly of soap.

I tighten the towel around me.

"Are you hurt at all?" Travin continues lowly, "From the fall or . . . or anything?"

"I'm fine, really," I reply. I keep my trembling hands behind the curtain and tilt my head backward. "I'm going to clean up."

He smiles genuinely but with concern. "That will be well."

The creases at the corner of his eyes and the small dimple on the side of his left cheek make him look fourteen again, when his facial features all grew at different rates. As his twenty-four-year-old self, they've finally sorted themselves into a pleasant collaboration. His nose is perfectly proportionate. As for the rest of his physique, manhood helped him fill out his over-sized, hand-me-down clothes.

As he fusses with the back of his hair, his gaze drops to his hands. I know he's displeased by this emblematic tick. When I cease to engage in conversation, he glances up and steps closer.

"You don't have to block me out, Kaya."

I push the curtain open. "Did you want to join me then?"

Travin's smile vanishes. He glances sideways, using his left hand to scratch his right ear. "Hurry or you'll miss supper," he mutters before retreating.

The curtain falls.

I almost call out to him, but I don't know what to say. A sickening twist of my gut sends me dashing to the depository. I clutch my stomach, hunching over it, letting the smell of waste distract my mind from the terrible thoughts in my head. My burning throat and watering eyes remind me I'm only human. Weak. Wiping the back of my hand across my mouth, I stand and begin bathing myself.

My movements are automatic, my brain still dizzy, my bowels upset. I make a tight face, mentally slapping myself. Frustration and embarrassment collide with my nausea. I am unable to stop the replay of the day in my mind, the way the rebels raided Avoca, the image of that woman being dragged through the alleyway.

"Ugh," I moan, scrubbing my face.

That alley. *Was it the same one from my nightmares?* Every time I see her face in my head, I'm struck with guilt. Should I have helped her? But what could I have done? The rebel would have easily killed us both.

Flee.

The command I've been trained to obey repeats in my head.

Flee.

I did. And I feel cowardly.

When I finish bathing, I dress in the clean clothes, somewhat missing my old, animal-smelling ensemble, but glad the new robes cover my bruises and swelling joints. For a moment, I pause outside of the washroom, trying to think of something to say to Trav. As awful as I feel, he must feel worse. I know firsthand what happens to a girl at the hands of a wicked man. Nothing comes to mind, and I give up, gulping my pain in an effort to keep others from tasting it.

I follow the sounds of clanking dish ware to a kitchen where the smell of food makes me salivate. The room, not quite large enough, is crammed with people, seven occupants hovering around a square table. It has been set and prepared for a meal. Travin and Bronwynn sit next to each other, having refreshed themselves in the washroom. Bronwynn's cheeks are red from crying. The look on Travin's face as he holds her head against his shoulder makes my stomach roil. He is in pain. The other three faces belong to an older man and two identical twin boys. The older man has feathery brown hair and a smile that matches Yespin's. The twins are tall and sinewy, with dark curly hair and sculpted cheekbones. They are young, attractive boys approaching the end of their teen age.

Yespin places a basket of bread onto the table. "Kaya, sit here."

She points to the twins, who speak simultaneously.

"I'm Gring."

"I'm Grond."

Perhaps they are Maleah's age. I distinguish between them by their only different features: Gring has a pit in his chin, and Grond is missing the lower half of his right earlobe. They are of the Bottker tribe, a relative of the Roteruth's. Sons of a traveling merchant, they moved to Taavetti to pursue a trade-craft of their own and find wives. I gather they have not found wives by the way they're staring at me.

I acknowledge their greeting and back-story with grim interest.

"And I," the older man proclaims, "am Hartle Roteruth. You may call me Hart."

I nod, spared his life's endeavor.

"Let's eat," Yespin states, placing more dishes of food on the table. She sits next to her husband.

I suddenly feel like the black sheep in the room. Two people sit at every side of the table except mine. On my own, like always. Hart gives a blessing on the meal, while I watch Bronwynn and Travin. The twins watch me. Then I feast on supper like unto a wild beast.

In spite of Yespin's discouragement, the males discuss Avoca's unfortunate events. Travin speaks intelligently of Avoca's secret combinations, but I am too lost in my own thoughts to wonder how he attained such knowledge. The Roteruth's tell us that in the morning we can congregate with the other survivors at the tabernacle, but until then they ask us to stay indoors.

Taavetti has very different laws than Avoca. I fear they are an aggressive people. They are a neutral territory, but not quite as pro-peace as our home. The pits they dig in the trails leading to their parish stand as evidence.

After supper, I offer a quiet thank you and retreat to my room. Travin retreats to his, meaning Bronwynn retreats to hers—*mine*. I guess we are sharing, being fair, unwed maidens. She doesn't talk to me, and I realize I do not wish to congregate with people tomorrow, but with the living, breathing, beings of Lucan Care. I'll never be able to confirm the survival of my animals. Travin's troubled eyes and incessant fussing with the back of his hair during dinner remind me of what *he* has to lose.

Unable to find rest, I pace the Roteruth's home, searching the kitchen for wine, before tetchily succumbing to the nightmares awaiting me in bed.

TRAVIN

I Thought We Were Friends

KAYA DID NOT LET me teach her to swim the first time I took her to the Salt Sea, nor the second. It happened yesterday, on our third visit, and we both returned home soaking wet, too angry to speak to one another.

All throughout lessons today, Kaya has remained in poor spirits. I decide to make it up to her by playfully chasing her with a piece of animal dung on a stick. The other girls scream with glee and run around the schoolyard. Rebby races after them, trying to steal a kiss. But Kaya does not flee. She simply stands there staring at me until we are face to face.

"Aren't you going to run?" I pant, soiled stick in my left hand.

"Why would I run from you?" Kaya asks.

"Because," I laugh.

She transfers her weight, contemptuously watching Rebby kiss the girls.

"Won't your mother be upset if you come home with animal dung on your clothing?" I ask, waving the stick at her. "Or would she be *more* upset if you were kissed?"

Kaya's eyes dart back to my face. Her expression is molten as she circles away.

"Kaya?" I call after her.

She says nothing, running out of the schoolyard. Dropping the stick, I tear after her until we reach the venue. At Lucan Care, Kaya goes straight to the rear entrance. Her fingers close around the handle, but I stop her before she can go inside. She shoots a glare at me. I can see something in the depths of her eyes. It's goodbye. Not just for the day either.

I leap in front of her, my back against the heavy door. Kaya's thick eyelashes cast star-like shadows across her cheeks. Her eyes contain a multitude of emotions like unto a hailstorm. A small lock of hair has sprung out of one braid, fluttering over her brow. She brushes it back derisively, masking her pain. It has taken me until now to realize what we have in common.

"I'm sorry," I say softly.

We are silent several minutes. Kaya's breath calms, and the storm in her eyes diminishes.

"You're not going to leave me alone?" she sighs. "Are you?"

"I will if you want me to," I answer.

"You don't *want* to leave me alone?"

"Nay."

"But you're going to someday."

"What does that mean?"

She doesn't reply.

"Do you *want* me to leave you alone?" I ask her.

After a moment, she responds with a nonverbal, "Nay."

"Do you want to be my friend?"

She thinks about this for a few seconds and nods once.

Just then, Father Lucan yanks the back door open. I nearly fall into him. Kaya catches me by the front of my tunic. Her father glances between the two of us.

"Ah," he exhales, "you're never late."

He addresses Kaya, but his eyes remain upon me.

Kaya groans, "Sorry, Father. I was just—"

"It's my fault," I cut in.

Father Lucan's eyes smile.

Kaya gives me one more glance, her green eyes sharp, and then she stalks into the clinic, chin lowered. Father Lucan stares down at me from his gigantic height, a serene and strong presence. He reaches a hand out. Terrified, I remain still.

He touches my shoulder. "We could use some extra help around here," he states.

My eyes scrape up to his. Behind him, Kaya stops walking.

"I don't know how to do anything," I say quietly.

Before Father Lucan can reply, Kaya returns. She reaches through the door and grabs my hand.

"I'll teach you."

KAYA

It Dawned on Me

By DAWN, MY EYES and fingernails sting. My headache is worse. I mope into the kitchen with a limp, obviously the first one awake. Locating the kettle, I make a pot of mint tea over a fire. It is unexpectedly satisfying. I drink another two cups before the Roteruths and the others rise. Yespin carefully arranges breakfast, but I can't find it in me to eat. My stomach feels worse than the bruises.

"Have trouble sleeping?" Gring asks me.

"Something like that."

Hart tells us the villagers will host Avoca's survivors at the tabernacle, and that we may search for our loved ones there. Travin is the first to leave, Bronwynn only a half second behind him. I exit the Roteruth's home because I have no reason to remain within it, following Travin toward the tabernacle. The twins, Yespin, and Hart join us. The streets are crowded by the time we arrive. There are guards, *armed* guards, and patrons organizing family searches. Their organization reminds me of Mikyla Rox, working diligently for the people of Avoca.

I avert my eyes toward the northeast horizon. Billows of dust grab my attention. Gring and Grond Bottker, who have made a habit of staring at me, follow my gaze. Grond tugs on Hart's sleeve and points. It is not dust, but smoke. Something is on fire.

"The city is burning," Yespin mutters in fright.

By now, the greater part of the Taavetti populous sees it. Travin and I exchange glances. Accompanying the smoke, the ground starts to rumble.

"Look!" Gring states.

Across the desert hills, below the thick black smoke swallowing the blue sky, fresh dust from the earth swirls as the infantry of an army comes into view. They are marching toward us. Chariots follow, with more men on horseback. Their numbers are beyond measurable. They cover the entire landscape, like shadows from the clouds. Behind them, the smoky haze of the burning city increases. It is a sight I cannot describe in the words of man.

"They march from Heshbon," Grond says mutedly.

"They've destroyed it," Hart agrees.

All I can think is that the Canaanites have come to butcher us all. And yet, frozen in awe, I gape at their majesty.

Smoke covers the sun until it appears to be dusk, though it is only daybreak. A dust storm ensues from their footpaths, causing some of the Taavetti women to return to their homes, ushering little children indoors. The soldiers advance faster than imaginable, by the thousands, until they are upon the parish. Chariots and horses ride into the streets. More men than I knew inhabited the earth take up positions around the perimeter, establishing a blockade so no person from Taavetti may go forth unto the wilderness. Soldiers, in an *exceedingly* sexy man-wears-loin-cloth kind of way, march unto the steps of the tabernacle. Their armaments offset the sepia of their skin, long hair glistening under the ocher sky.

One man emerges, atop a beautiful stallion. He gallops in front of the infantry, coming to a halt before us. A man on foot steps beside the horseman, carrying a shield. The villagers and visitors fall so quiet I can hear Heshbon burning from miles away. I gape at the man astride his purebred horse and marvel. He is the largest man I've ever seen and not just by physical appearance. His horse is equally as spectacular. Dried blood covers the man's body, sticky in his hair beneath a metal helmet. His upper half is layered in armor like unto the scales of an armadillo. The other soldiers are armed and bloodied from battle, waiting perfectly still, as they regard him with absolute reverence.

Everyone around me begins to murmur. Many of the Taavetti inhabitants drop to their knees.

I don't understand.

The man on the horse starts to speak. "Arise, faithful servants." His voice echoes like thunder, commanding the attention of all who are in his presence. I have never seen an army, and I have never seen an army's High Commander, but the image before me surpasses anything I could have envisioned. Each soldier stands erect, immobile, and alert. Breastplates and swords gleam under the saffron clouds. All of the equestrians cease their whinnying, their only movement the flick of their hair in the wind. The canvas behind them is like a scene from the underworld.

The High Commander continues, "I am Joshua, servant of the Most High God, High Commander of the Israelite army. We come from Heshbon, where we have destroyed the high walls that defended every city. Nophah, Medeba, Dibon, and all their lofty citizens have we put to death. And we did burn the cities to ruins. Sihon, King of Heshbon, is dead. And his spoils, and all the cattle, have we taken for ourselves."

At this, several of the villagers cower. The Bottker twins, standing in front of Travin and Bronwynn, whisper in one another's ear. Hart leads Yespin to the back of the tabernacle.

"The Lord has given us this land to possess it," Joshua declares. "Our wives and little ones and our cattle shall abide here in these our cities. The country situated between Arnon of the south and Jabbok to the north, and the Jordan to the west, are under our possession. We will soon march on Bashan. Og, king of Bashan, has the height of a cedar and the strength of an oak. His cities are threescore, all with high walls and mighty fortifications. Nevertheless, I say unto you, Og shall fall because of his wickedness. The land on this side of Jordan, from the Arnon River unto the mount of Hermon, and every coast and all of the dirt our feet will step upon will be ours. All of the cities of the plain, even Gilead and those on the west of the Jordan, shall be ours, saith our God."

Beside me, Travin is captivated. You would think he was staring at God Himself. He absorbs the words of this Joshua with the hunger of a suckling child. *How is this man, this High Commander, more righteous than the bloodthirsty Canaanites?*

I think of poor Maleah, possibly *not* making it safety, or out of Avoca, being scooped up by the hands of a nasty rebel. Being dragged behind an alley.

"Our army has gathered," Joshua preaches, "over the goodly mountain. We have a stronghold in the valley of Shittim, led by righteous leaders. Our numbers exceed forty and a thousand. All worthy men of Taavetti aid us, and you shall receive land and provisions. Do not fear our enemies, for God will fight for us."

All this talk of God makes me nervous. I've never seen Him, or met Him, or spoken with Him, which is why I don't comprehend people who act like they have. Joshua seems rather convinced that he is acting for, and in behalf, of said God, and that the burning of Heshbon was a commandment. A smitten city, every living thing, young and old, sheep and ass, put to an end.

My chest burns at the thought of dying women and children and animals, Canaanites or not. A God who could command such a thing is frightening. And then I remember Joshua saying the Israelite army exceeds forty thousand soldiers. This frightens me more than God.

The Taavetti people don't feel the same way, apparently. They run toward Joshua, begging to be received into the Israelite army. Gring and Grond enlist. Many young, able females also join them. To my dismay, some of the peaceful residents of Avoca desire to join the battalion of fighters. Unless perhaps, they are not so peaceful at heart. The kindest of souls, Trav, is one of them, Bronwynn in tow.

Our friendship has been at an awkward standstill, mostly due to the barrier Bronwynn has created between us since they began courting. I didn't help matters with my comment last night, but I would like to share a farewell with him, at least.

I glance around at the strangers surrounding me, watching those interested in following Joshua evacuate the tabernacle. Even those who don't join the army emerge from homes, congregate in the street, and praise the soldiers. Several holy men raise their graven images, chanting toward the darkened heavens. Joshua removes his helmet, trotting over to them.

"Oh, be wise," he states. "Worshiping false idols is a sin in the eyes of God. Behold, there is to be a new law. We will teach you all the ways of the Israelites."

I can smell the smoke. War. Destruction.

The Israelite army commences the process of enlistment. Several officers organize a conscripting site as the majority of the infantry retreat beyond the homes to tend to cattle and water their horses. Men, and some women, both Taavetti locals and my neighbors from Avoca, diligently join ranks with the soldiers. Glimpsing the rolling plumes of inferno over their shoulders, I don't blame them. *Would Joshua just as soon burn all of us if we resisted?*

I've heard tales of Israelites ruining generations and eliminating bloodlines, or conquering evil and providing for their posterity, depending on who speaks of them. Rebby claims the Israelites *protect* the freedoms of the land and fight for a righteous cause. But Avoca was a free people. We sought no one else's gain. A neutral territory has been destroyed, and the Israelites were not there protecting it.

All around me the faces of family members grieve and pray and smile proudly. I spy Travin near the recruits. He's holding Bronwynn against him. She is sobbing hysterically, fingers clasping his tunic. His face is a fusion of anger and pain and something else. I feel no small amount of antipathy toward this God that Travin has lost so much. We both have.

Nobody stands next to me. No one will ever stand next to me, to worry over whether I shall return or not, unless you consider a lactating dairy cow that person.

I turn to the nearest tabernacle pillar.

"Good talk," I quip and descend the stairs.

I think of my drawer of keepsakes back in my home. My jewelry box. The animals at Lucan Care. My beloved, beloved animals. The flaming banner floating above the street in Avoca, eviscerating my link to a home and neutrality.

On the street, I pace straight toward an Israelite officer and state vehemently, "I am going with you."

The fierce warrior stares blankly at me. A glare of sunshine reflects off of his breastplate. I squint at it, my eyes darting between his stoic face and the girdle around his waist. His weapon is almost as big as me. Over his shoulder, a Taavetti female is signing up. My agnostic attitude is overruled by my vengeful one. I take the chance to persist, falsified in confidence.

"I'm only five feet tall, but I'm ten pounds of wheat in a five-pound bushel. I have no remaining kin, and my occupancy and occupation have been destroyed. I need a place to live and food to eat. For reimbursement, I can care for your beasts."

In response, the Israelite officer takes my name and sends me toward the recruits who are being prearranged into four traveling companies. It takes the remainder of the day. Taavetti men and women donate belongings of use. Those, combined with the supplies of the Israelites, are divided and dispersed into each company. These companies are under the direction of an officer, each officer reports to their High Commander. Joshua. I regard him in the distance, presiding over the people in a calm, benevolent, yet executive demeanor. Notwithstanding our differences, I owe this High Commander a bit of respect.

Amongst my company, I let the possibilities of my near future flash through my head. I am joining an army, where I will live alongside soldiers. I'm leaving home for the first time. I will see the world. *What a vision will it be to behold?* I will see the River Jordan. I will see . . . Bashan in conflagration, like Heshbon. *What is war like?*

Night falls upon us. I ignore any looks of judgment from the older, wiser, and stronger people and move into the congregation of my traveling company. Yay, the most difficult part of this enlistment will be tolerating *so* many people.

Around midnight, the four companies merge into the ranks of the Israelite army, depart the village of Taavetti. Our destination is Shittim, further east. Above us, the charcoal smoke of Heshbon hovers sinisterly. Avoca is left to memory. The people I worry may be left to memory also rise in my mind. If Mikyla survived the attack, she would probably stay behind as a successor and rebuild her community of peace. And Rebby, if he's alive, I know I will see him again. He will be among Joshua's men.

I wonder what will become of our neutral territory if it is overthrown by Canaanites. Somehow, I am glad I won't be there to find out.

TRAVIN

Rebby to the Rescue

I TAKE A THIRD punch to the face, swinging a fist blindly and connecting with someone's ribcage. Two boys grab my elbows behind my back. The third takes my face and smashes it into the dirt until my teeth feel like they may break.

"Your mother is a harlot!" they shout. "Say it!"

I wriggle against them, swallowing gravel.

"Say it!"

"Your mother is a harlot!"

"Your sister is a harlot, too!"

"Hey!" Rebby's enormous voice yells as he breaks into the brawl.

The boys scramble immediately, Rebby's mere reputation scaring them away. Freed, I tuck my knees beneath me.

"But this is the good part!" Rebby shouts to my aggressors' retreat. "Now the odds are more even."

I gaze upward to Rebby. My vision is impaired, my eyes swollen and black. I lick my lips, cracked and bleeding. Rebby came just in time to spare me from saying what those boys wanted me to say. I would have said it.

Hiding a few feet away, concealed by the shrubbery outside the schoolyard, Maleah is hiding. I glance in her direction so she knows to wait for me there.

"How many times do I have to ask you?" Rebby says, hauling me to my feet. "Don't start a good fight without me. Now I've missed all the fun."

"All of it," I spit, words and blood and saliva alike.

Maleah reveals herself, but I hold up a hand to keep her from approaching. Rebby composes his attitude, his eyes sliding over to where she stands by the bush.

"We have a witness," he says, although I'm not sure if he means it as a good thing or a bad thing.

"My mother will find out anyway," I retort dryly, pointing a thumb in the direction of my face.

"It was her, or you. Wasn't it?" he demands.

"It doesn't matter."

My mother does find out. Violence is not tolerated in the Shelomo home.

"Oh, Travin," she says in that perfected, hurt-bunny voice. "You bring me so much shame. Why do you have to be just like your father?"

She does not speak to me for a week.

Despite her disapproval, Rebby invites me to his work after lessons one day. I soon find out it is not to assist him in carpentry. He pulls me to the back of the shop, addressing me in a low voice.

"I have a proposition for you." He glances at an employee who walks by us, waiting until the man is gone to speak again. "What would you say if I told you that you'd never have to face the persecution of another bully, ever again?"

I know he means well, but my humiliation responds for me. "I don't need you to defend me, Rebby. It only makes them ridicule me more."

Rebby's eyes gleam. "You're going to learn to defend yourself."

KAYA

To Burning Cities We Go

THE FIRST DAY OF travel passes painlessly, but my mind is full and concentrated. I monitor everything. Israelite vernacular, how they walk and eat. Their bodies amaze me, mostly because I didn't know that much muscle could be contained under one human's skin. There are weapons I've never seen, and strengths I've never seen to wield them. Most of the soldiers wear breastplates and greaves on their shins. The officers also have coats of mail and scale armor. All of them wear tse'adah, a battle bracelet than jingles when they march. The Roxes would be mortified.

Joshua, discernible throughout the mass of men by his red cape, drives us north. If we make haste, we can reach Shittim in two or three days. We trek past dead carcasses, some human, others indistinguishable, over vast plains, down streams, and through heavily wooded hills. The men forage for useful remnants in vacated cities, the women put the remnants to use. Emotion is diminutive. Personal conversation is minimal, but the soldiers who have seen the battlefield brag of their victories in songs of praise. It is fascinating.

"I'll never forget Jahaz," one man boasts to the new recruits. "As soon as the Amorites gave ground, we pursued them briskly."

"We are skilled in slinging and very dexterous in throwing darts of any kind," the soldier's friend adds, much to the admiration of the draftees. "Our armor is light, and we were quicker then they. We overtook them, and all those who managed to escape were later slaughtered when we found them crowded around a stream, quenching their thirst."

Come evening, the men set up camp. A camp worthy of city walls. Women, and there are more of them than I expected, tend to the cooking. All the recruits fall into the Israelite's system as if they'd been there all along. The horses are tied up around the outer perimeter. I wander over to them. A beautiful, black stallion glances at my approach with large eyes. I run my hand across the coarse mane. The cattle graze just beyond, a flock of sheep and chickens among them. It reminds me of Lucan Care. Home. Leaning into the beast, I murmur comforting sounds. The mare nods and snorts in response.

"Kaya!"

I look up. Wave. Mikyla jogs over to me and gives me a hug. She pulls back and smiles. Her face is worn, grimy cheeks strewn with dried tears.

"Miki and I, we're okay," she declares, "but Mother and Father . . ."

She cuts off by cupping her hand over her mouth. I know her grief.

"I'm glad you're alright," I say.

She continues, "Since they are—can't be found right now, and Avoca is uninhabitable, Miki decided to it would be best for us to make league with the Israelite army. Many people have fled their homes in fear of Joshua. I swear, under Aton, I didn't want to leave Avoca. We didn't know what they would do, if they would slay us. Isn't it awful?"

She gazes over at the soldiers. Apprehension lines her pretty face. Wrapping her arms around her waist, she looks at me and shudders.

"Miki is all I have left—so, until they find Mother and Father—well, I couldn't stay in Taavetti alone."

"I'm sorry."

"Aren't they fearsome?" she gasps, gesturing to our new venture.

I nod. "Let's see what they have for supper."

Mikyla sniffles and nods.

We gather around one of the several small campfires. A basket of manna is passed among us. The fruits of the land are divvied and shared on trays. A few minutes later, a handsome soldier joins us.

I leap up and hurl myself into his arms before realizing it. He's as surprised as I am by the affection, squeezing me tightly for several seconds. His copper-brown eyes meet mine and, without a word, relay the message I've dreaded hearing. His family is gone.

"Thanks for saving my life, Rebby," I tell him.

No charming smile replies. He relaxes his hold on my hips, looking down. I touch his cheek.

"You'll always have us."

He pats my hand, squeezes it once. When he gazes back up, he gives me a warm smile, sharing it with Mikyla. "Alright, I didn't want to say this but . . . I can only marry one of you."

I punch him. Mikyla giggles. Our mood is somber as we finish our meal, but I find relief having the two of them beside me. It softens me for a moment, recognizing I don't hate all people.

Night approaches with the sun turning the desert pink in its descent. Soldiers have a curfew or a station, in some cases both. Joshua sees to the new recruits who are housed in the same general location, a flat mesa at the base of the mountainside. The veteran soldiers post guards around the perimeter, and the officers pour over maps and schematics. Mikyla and Rebby return to their traveling companies, and I to mine, where I'm sharing a tent with a few burly women. They are extremely built, one of them with facial hair. I stand beyond the tarps a moment, admiring the vast span of the Israelite army, the detailed structure of it all.

Upon the hill to my left, setting up a tent with a handful of draftees, I see Travin. He is glaring at me. Our eyes have only met a couple times since leaving Taavetti, but those scowls are all I've received from him since our excursion began. Perhaps he is still aggravated by my insensitivity at the Roteruth home. His heart must be broken by his loss. The officers have stated that, once we reach their stronghold at Shittim, a unit of soldiers will return whence we came and scour cities that have been destroyed by our enemies. But that prolongs Travin's ability to search for his sister and mother.

I glance away, wishing I'd comforted him better.

Evidently, Bronwynn has chosen to do something more than weeping and wailing. She joins the other female members in matronly duties during the day, but right now she is by Travin. The two of them comfort one another.

As usual, I lie awake for quite some time. The camp grows silent until only sounds of the wilderness are audible. It's all very foreign. Dust whispers in the gentle breeze. Animals scurry over sandstone. Every so often, the night guards march past my tent. Curfews are not the only laws upheld by these soldiers. The men are not ordinary in discipline.

Without realizing I've dozed off, I awake from another nightmare to scuffling outside my tent. I wipe a tangle of hair from my face and sit up. Quietly, I open the tarps and peer out into the torchlit campsite. A young man is seated at the fire's edge, some four cubits away. He is alone, digging through his satchel. The blaze illuminates his angular features, though I can only see part of his face. A face that resembles an age similar to mine.

Intrigued, I climb out of my blankets, careful not to wake the other women. Unsure whether or not I will be scolded for being out of my tent, I exit warily. I have never spent a night in the wilderness. The drop in temperature is surprising. Bitter winds hit my flesh. I quicken my pace to near the flames. The boy at the fire senses my approach. He stops his search for only a second, without looking up at me, and then continues.

Taking a seat on the log opposite from him, I extend my hands toward the hot embers.

"Kaya?"

I squint against the darkness.

"Do I know you?" I inquire.

"Nay."

He's still digging through his satchel.

I shiver and say absentmindedly, "It's cold."

He looks up to meet my gaze for the first time. I've never experienced such an immediate self-consciousness. His charcoal hair looks like he cut it himself and then styled it perfectly to seem like he just rolled out of bed. Even across the fire, I can see that his eyes are a strikingly light blue, almost white. The reflection of the red embers flickers in them. Like hot and cold. The sun and the moon. Heaven and hell . . .

The corner of his mouth twists up into a half smile. Also striking. "Colder out here than in your tent," he replies, and commences his search again.

I shudder and take a quick glance around me. The sky is obscured, either by low clouds or the expansive smoke of Heshbon. I'm not sure. Little moonlight shines down, therefore the lamps and torches are all that provide the minimal vision at this hour. Glittering specks out in the hills identify the living things staring back at me. The same intrigue that drew me from my tent draws my eyes once again to the boy across from me.

He has discovered what he was looking for. He withdraws a small bottle and tosses his satchel aside. Pulling out the cork, he leans back onto his elbows and takes a long swig. His eyes slowly make their way up to my face. I've been unable to tear my own eyes away, so remarkable is he to gaze upon. High cheekbones connect to the distinguished slant of his jaw. The tip of his chin forms the shape of a heart. His ketonet is dark blue, extolling his complexion.

He releases a heavy sigh and extends the bottle toward me.

I shake my head and mumble a worthless, "I don't think so."

I love wine, but I don't love a strange man's wine.

The strange man gives a passive lift of his shoulder.

"I'm Westin," he offers. "Westin Fahim."

"Westin," I repeat, dumbfounded that my voice sounds so abnormal. "Where are you from, uh, Westin?"

I fantasize about battlefields, and victories, and watching him twirl swords and shields.

"Doesn't matter now." Westin lets out a soft chuckle, an attractive sound I want to hear more of. There's something perceptive in his diamond-like gaze. And I become avidly aware of my neglected appearance.

That face. I'd remember if we had met . . .

"You don't like sleeping?" Westin asks.

"I don't like nightmares," I reply.

Crossing his ankles, Westin transfers his weight to one elbow and takes a drink. "What's your story, Kaya?"

I shift on the bench, warming my other side. *Where is my quick wit when I need it?*

"Story?" I cough.

So much for witticism.

"Your father used to look after my mother's peafowl at Lucan Care." The way he says it tells me he knows details I haven't made known. I examine him carefully through the flickering flames, unable to procure my hate for people momentarily. "Your best friend is Mikyla Rox," he says, "though you despise her twin Miki. You're cynical, reserved, and I believe you have something against Travin's girlfriend, 'what's-her-name.'"

"*Bon-won*," I reply, glad he, too, finds Travin's romantic interest a bore. It cancels out my previous concern over his knowledge of odd facts about my life. Westin is henceforth added to my short list of less-hated individuals, but I have my reservations.

"Right." Westin grins again, charmingly. "Bronwynn. Tell me something I don't know."

Maybe I shouldn't have joined him by the fire. For all I know, he's just like Miki Rox. Just what I need. I take another glance around, part of me wanting more company as an extra precaution, and part of me wanting all of Westin's attention to myself. The latter part wins, and I'm distracted by his commendable genetics. Maybe it's the way his glacier eyes stare into mine, like he isn't afraid to blink or make me blush.

Except I don't blush.

Squinting into the orange coals, I try to think of a clever response, something to disguise my unrest, but also something that might prove I'm an estimable contender. I will not be fooled by a pretty face. And I will not have him thinking he knows everything about me. Not even the bed I sleep in knows my innermost thoughts.

But Westin continues before I can answer.

"I hope you don't find me uncouth," he commentates. "Your animal clinic, I spent quite a bit of time there over the years." Again, I sense him delving into my unspoken past. "You see, my mother's favorite pet was her peafowl, Gem. She treated that animal like her firstborn child. Whenever the bird got sick, or so she claimed, she'd take it down to your father and get her treated." And then comes the big bomb. "It didn't take me long to realize that wasn't the only reason she went to the animal clinic."

My face is suddenly too warm for the fire. I stand.

"Maybe she just belonged with the other she asses," I remark hatefully.

"Relax," Westin calmly replies, setting his bottle down. His words float atop a stream of smoke. "Your father's affairs are none of my business. *You*, however, were the reason I chose to go."

For the record, I missed that last part.

How would *he* know my father's affairs? Simply being a client of Lucan Care gives Westin zero credibility.

My thoughts must have been delivered by my expression.

"I know what you're thinking," Westin says. "And no, we've never really met. But I know you."

"You don't know me."

Westin rubs his eyes. I can tell he feels the same yearning need for sleep that I do. Yet, somehow, I know neither of us will be able to.

"Never mind," he sighs. Leaning forward, he drapes his arms across his knees and glances up. "We've gotten off to a bad start. I just *want* to know you."

Sure. Know this: "I euthanize sick animals."

And I fold my arms across my chest.

Westin's brow rises teasingly. He drags his satchel between his knees, reaches in, and withdraws a second bottle. He crosses the space between us, setting the bottle at my feet. I examine him from his extended height. The way his tunic pulls tight across his sternum and reveals a triangle of exposed chest. A knife is sheathed in his belt. A big one.

"You want this?" Westin asks.

Maybe.

He continues, "It is wine, from Avoca."

My heart pounds. Oh, wine. *Do I want the wine.*

I'm not ready to accept any sort of gift, even a gift from home. Accepting would automatically mean I'm indebted to Westin, and

I don't owe him anything just for being overly observant. Whirling away from the fire, I warm my backside. Also, because the access to a whole bottle of wine has my hands itching. And my face feels aflame. And I don't even know what I'm doing.

Westin rises and wishes me goodnight. I glimpse over my shoulder at him. He gives me another torturous half-smile, sending my insides in a nosedive. Then he spins and retreats from the blaze. No "I'll see you tomorrow." No offer for courtship.

He's arrogant. And he has broad shoulders.

My neck begins to prickle. *What just happened?*

My eyes travel downward.

I hastily retreat to my tent, jamming the bottle I've obtained, with the concession that I've welcomed much more, under my blanket. I'll save it for a night I really need my wine bubble. If Westin only knew how many headaches he's saved me from . . .

And then it hits me. *He knew.* He knew all kinds of things.

I think of his eyes, and that smile, one last time. And then I sleep.

TRAVIN

A Whole New Battlefield

REBBY IS WAITING FOR me at my front door at the end of the week, when I am permitted to see him again. He has no qualms about taking the blame for my misbehavior. My mother always says he instigates my poor manners. She says we engage in violence together, and it is shameful. Rebby finds it quite enjoyable and proudly flaunts his conduct at lessons. He *earned* his reputation.

"I've found you another girl who needs courting," my instigator declares.

I roll my eyes, approaching my porch tentatively.

"Cease to be wary," Rebby adds, grinning. "She's of good virtue."

"Like the last one?"

Rebby regards me cunningly, "Her name is Channa. Channa is in desperate need of courtship, and Kymme and I have volunteered to chaperone. You remember Kymme, right? We go to lessons with her."

"I remember Kymme," I reply.

"Channa is her cousin. A beauty. Long hair. Her bosom has grown since her youth."

"Great. Why don't *you* court them both?"

He laughs. "Actually they're courting each other. I was hoping to court *you*."

"I'm high maintenance."

"You know I like a challenge."

"I'm a Shelomo."

"Come on!" he groans. "Don't give me that, okay? Not tonight."

"I don't know," I exhale, trying to find some excuse to get out of this. I think I've already used them all. Twice.

"I know what you're thinking," Rebby chuckles. "And there is nary time to waste. I told them to meet us here."

I moan, my eyes shifting to the contemptuous words painted on the side of my house, my efforts to obscure them fruitless. "My home? Really?"

Rebby's eyes follow mine. "You just get ready, and I'll take care of everything else."

I escape into my house, dubious. A half hour later, a knock sounds on the front door.

"Just remember, he's kind of meek," I hear Rebby say.

The girls must know whose home this is. They must know I am a Shelomo. Tonight will go one of two ways. Either I will be hounded with questions about my father and Maleah, or I will end up chaperoning a three-way courtship.

A second knock.

Begrudgingly, I reach for the handle and pull it open.

"Hi," I say to Rebby.

He's flanked on either side by his, so-named, virtuous female friends. Kymme looks the same as she always has, with medium length, chestnut hair, narrow eyes, and full cheeks. Her simlah is dandelion yellow, in contrast to the beige one her friend is wearing. Channa, as Rebby already described, has very long, hair, and a large bosom indeed, contained by a sash around her waist. The story in her eyes doesn't intrigue me.

"Channa, this is Travin," Rebby declares, beckoning to me. I close the door behind me and wave. "Travin, this is Channa."

"Oh, he is cute," Channa giggles into Kymme's ear.

I force a smile. Wonderful. The *cute* title again.

"Come," Rebby ushers us into the street. "Let's do this."

Inconspicuously, I glance over my shoulder at the wall of my home. As I'd suspected, Rebby covered the vile words with wet clay. The two girls walk ahead of Rebby and I, holding onto each other's arms and snickering while they peek back at us.

"So," Rebby asks under his breath. "What do you think?"

"I think I'm bored already," I answer, giving the cap atop his head a one-sided smirk.

"Really? You've got to *try*." He notices my gaze and tosses the first and last debuted cap behind him. "There's more to life than just Kaya."

I blanch, trying not to take offense. Rebby means well, and he's right. But what does he expect?

"Kaya isn't hard to be around," I respond, trying not to sound defensive. "*These* girls, they're all just . . ."

"They are interested in courting you," Rebby interjects. "That's the difference."

"Nay."

"Look," he states, motioning to Kymme and Channa, "I know it's not your favorite activity, but idleness is the devil's handiwork."

I send him a sardonic glare. "And courting all of the town's fair maidens at once isn't?"

"How will I find my wife?" he shoots back. "Which gets me back on track. If you're ever going to take up a wife—"

Two pink dots rise to my cheeks. "Cease—"

"Channa isn't any less virtuous than Kaya. It will be well. Just relax and act like you're talking to your longtime friend. If all else fails, pull out your knife. They like soldiers."

I glance at the females. "You didn't tell them—"

"Not yet," Rebby replies with a wile grin. He pats his ezowr, the fancy belt his father gave him. Hidden in a pouch is his knife. Mine is tucked beneath my tunic. "The girls won't mind. Channa already likes you, and her father approves of the secret combinations."

"At least we'll have something to talk about," I mutter dryly, my thoughts turning to Kaya and our lack of conversation as of late. I have not shared with her my involvement with the secret combinations. She would think I've become a violent man, and I know she fears violence. I didn't join the association of secret soldiers to learn to beat people up. I wanted to learn how to fight so that it wouldn't happen to me, *ever again*. Kaya would understand that, but she won't understand my support for bearing arms and protecting freedoms.

"Channa's father is in total support of the new way of life," Rebby encourages. "And he is in total support of *you*."

"In other words, he doesn't mind that I'm a Shelomo," I retort.

Rebby grasps my hand and swings it. "Neither do I."

KAYA

I Still Don't Know What Happened

I'M DREADFULLY DISAPPOINTED THE next day when Miki Rox joins Mikyla and I for breakfast. He gives me a wide grin with food sticking out of his mouth.

The nerve.

"You're disgusting," I groan, and I mean it in more than one way.

Miki is a one-man-pestilence. I never could understand how someone could be as handsome on the outside as they are ugly on the inside. Five more minutes is all I last, sitting next to the two of them before I start to crawl out of my skin. I tell Mikyla I'll find her later and wander off through the camp. Rebby, Travin, and Bronwynn are eating around a nearby fire pit. Rebby gives me his typical smile of grandeur, the one that was missing yesterday. This pleases me, and I let it show. Bronwynn scoots closer to Travin who, perpetually, glares at me. Behold, it is grievous.

I shake my head, not in the mood for anyone's companionship. Except for the light-eyed man leaning against a tree by himself, hacking away at a piece of wood with a small knife. I cross in front of the sanatorium and head his way. Like last night, he doesn't look up at my advance. He only grins lazily and states, "I've got another present for you."

It lures me in more than I'd like.

He holds up the wood he's carving. It's a tiny cup. He chisels the letter K into the front of it and then tosses it to me. I trace the K with my finger. A stupid hotness rushes to my cheeks. I try to deflect the absurd reaction by clearing my throat. I must be getting a fever.

"Get any sleep last night?" I ask, smoothing the front of my simlah. I have only two very plain robes to last me until we reach Shittim.

Westin shrugs and responds, "You?"

Those eyes. I can't stop staring at them, and I sort of wish he just wouldn't make eye contact with me. Maybe it's the contrast between their pastel hue and the dark, tan of his skin. Exotic. He's wearing the same cerulean ketonet as last night, but has donned an ezowr this morning. At the belt on his left hip is a dagger.

"I made one for me, too," he states, pulling an identical cup out of his pocket. Pushing himself to his feet, he takes a step toward me. "I thought we could celebrate our induction into the army. Just the two of us."

"Celebrating *with* people isn't really my thing," I reply sarcastically.

Westin leans down. "I can walk on all fours if it makes you feel better."

It works. I crack. I smile.

Today's journey won't be nearly as lonesome.

The army marches from dawn to dusk, Westin and I talking through most of it. It is a nice break from soldier jargon. He is a couple of years older than I am, which is why we never went to lessons together. His mother didn't make it out of Avoca, and he's never met his biological father who was an Egyptian. It explains where Westin got his exotic looks. I apologize about the comment comparing his mother to a donkey, but he only grins, telling me he wished he'd come up with it himself. She favored possessions to posterity.

Apparently, Westin was a regular at the taverns of Avoca, which makes me wonder how we've never met. In a way, his charisma reminds me of Rebby. But Rebby has a fun-loving air about him that no one can take too seriously. I take Westin seriously, and I think about him a lot during the day. More than my sore feet and torn sandals.

Although the majority of our time has been spent marching, setting up camp, taking down camp, and marching again, the new recruits have been appointed minor assignments until we reach Shittim and can be segregated into appropriate ranks. My assignment is to tend to the horses. This duty comforts me while traveling with the strange Israelites. It reminds me of my chores from home and the animals I wish I could've saved.

On the third day of our expedition, the army encounters a great valley. Before us, the land stretches into a flat pampas encircled by mountains. It is the outer limits of Shittim. Joshua leads the soldiers through this fertile dale, where we approach an abandoned barricade. As we advance, the stench of something foul hits me swift and sharp. A buzzing sound accompanies the odor. Several recruits begin retching off to the side.

The barricade is not made of rock, but of human corpses. The buzzing is thousands of flies. Transfixed, I gasp and cover my nose. Without pause, the veteran soldiers remove a section of the barricade to allow the army to march beyond.

As we descend into the valley, a massive colony of soldiers comes into view. I'd thought Joshua's Israelite army was innumerable before, but now I see that there are more Israelites than there are stars. Rows and rows of tents form a large square. Soldiers wander up and down the torch-lit aisles. In the center, a large bonfire releases smoke into the evening air.

My stomach begins to flutter.

Shittim.

It is much warmer here in the valley than last night in the open desert. I never did like the cold. It's also a lot noisier. The lodging is substantial with more tents than there were homes in Avoca and Taavetti combined. There are even gainful venues, armories, bakeries, infirmaries. A stable has been constructed on the outskirts of the camp where I can smell the familiarity of animals.

Two guards take the horses to the stables. A team of men drives the cattle to a grassy knoll, guiding the other animals to pastures behind the barnyard. The care provided for the beasts turns my heart to the hearts of the Israelites, just a little. Meanwhile, Joshua and his officers lead our promenade of recruits to the center of camp. Hundreds of soldiers are assembled around the main fire pit. Their eyes welcome our arrival in inquisitive, convivial, and competitive surveillance.

At the sight of Joshua, they jump to their feet and honor him. I find it fascinating how quickly the High Commander switches from general of their army to friend. With his helmet tucked under one arm and his shield-bearer carrying his shield, Joshua looks younger and more casual. He exchanges a few greetings, even laughing with some of the men. His smile is radiant.

Part of me feels so out of place, but the larger part of me is delirious with exhilaration. This is all really happening.

When all of the new recruits are present, Joshua prepares for another one of his speeches. Large in stature with an opulent countenance, it is obvious he is well respected. Every soldier stands erect, regarding him. Almost worshiping. He is not just honored, but well liked.

Joshua calls his commanding officers to his right hand. Two of them, Jair and Nobah, are the highest-ranking lieutenants. Lachlan, Gorrow, Orren, Carac, Azsh, Mert, Dank, Tabor, and Charkish are below them. These officers are allocated the new draftees. The males are delegated to an officer first, based on their knowledge and experience in combat. The females go next. I wind up under the order of Officer Mert, with pretty much every other female from Avoca.

Officer Lachlan gains those individuals who have seen a battlefield, which are few, and only residents of Taavetti. Gorrow obtains those who have experience in combat training. Orren receives those with the greatest potential to become educated soldiers. Charkish and Carac are given men and women with communication and literacy skill. Tabor and Dank accept who is left. That is the most information I gather on army ranks this evening.

When the divisions are complete, the High Commander concludes his sermon. Joshua's breastplates and girdle compliment the strength in his arms, chest, and voice. A cape of vermilion drapes down his back with brass embellishments on his shoulders. Sandals are tied up his muscled legs. Strands of mahogany hair cascade below his nape. Eyes of ebony pore over the multitude, sharing the depth and illustriousness of the galaxies above.

"My people," he declares, "are masters of a wide region of splendid pastures. The streams are abounding, The highway—all connecting Edom and Moab to Bashan, and from the westward road into the Jordan Valley—is open to us." I didn't know a violent man could be so convincing. As his speech continues, I understand where and how he gains his loyalty. "You are of the chosen people. God has called you to come forth and inherit the land of Canaan. Do not be afraid. We will come off conqueror."

Ovation erupts from the audience.

Looking around, I examine the variety of people here. Men with jungles for beards. Clean-shaven men in jeweled tunics. Gnarly women dressed in rugged clothing. A handful of young, decent females like me. People of all shapes and sizes. Scores of tribes. All united here with one purpose. *Their* purpose. *God's* purpose. I can sense the power of . . . belonging.

I don't know if God exists, but I *want* Him to in times like this.

With surprising organization, Joshua arranges our housing. Men are on one side of camp, women on the other. Mikyla and I register together, offered the dwelling of a tent the size of my home in Avoca. The night then turns into a commemoration of Joshua's recent victories. Music, dancing, singing, feasting. It reminds me of the carnivals Mikyla used to assemble back home. Many wild boars are hoisted above fires and roasted. Manna, corn, fruits, and communal wine bottles are dispersed. Mikyla and I immerse ourselves in the festivities.

After the brief separation of getting our housing established, Westin seeks me out amidst the congregation. We sit together, hand-carved cups in hand, wine bottle between us.

"*This* is from home," he states, uncorking the bottle. "It is good to have something from home."

I sit beside him. "How did you manage to save it from Avoca?"

"It's what I thought of first," he answers. "When the rebels attacked, I ran home to get my satchel. What did you save?"

He pours the wine into both of our cups, and I drink it. It is strong wine. The scent burns my nostrils, the effect almost immediate as it rests in my belly. Numbing.

"Nothing."

Together Westin and I watch the people dancing, sharing songs, and war talk. Mikyla is being twirled around by a tall, dark-haired soldier. I'm glad she's smiling, despite the hurt I can see in her eyes. It's not particularly easy to lose one's parents. Grond Bottker is holding a woman much older, and hairier, than he, while they move to the rhythm of the music. Gring is not far off, dancing by himself and looking hangdog. Predictably, Rebby is smack in the middle of several long-legged promiscuities, no doubt willing to test their virtue.

Bronwynn even has Travin dancing. Well, not really. He's mostly just standing on the periphery, looking unpleasant, as she moves around in front of him. I know he hates to dance and, from the look on his face, I'm sure everyone else knows, too.

Westin shrewdly gauges my observations. Finishing his drink, he stands, offering me his hands. "Here's *my* story," he says. "I'm a remarkable dancer."

Reluctantly, I place my fingers in his palm and allow him to pull me to my feet. My head responds a little more slowly. I take a second to find my balance, relying upon the support of his grip. He leads me into a twirl, wrapping one of his arms behind me. It brings me in close. He smells . . . spicy.

I've not been held so close for so long in quite awhile. Men don't easily breach my walls, if ever. Not to mention such close proximity between opposite gender individuals is discouraged. I don't trust Westin, but a part of me doesn't care. What I do care about is making him aware that I'm going to make him earn my trust.

"The stars," I say with a sweeping motion of my hand. It allows me to subtly break contact. "Aren't they abundant?"

Westin's returning smile suggests he is aware of my motives. He does not acknowledge it, however, and we sit once more, gazing upward. Brilliant white dots dazzle against the black night. I've never seen stars like this. It is glorious. I'm so glad the sky is not clouded with smoke, and that I can no longer smell Heshbon.

The crowd begins to thin. Soldiers retreat to their barracks. The music softens, those playing the drums, jingling bells, blowing horns, plucking zithers, and strumming harps concluding their orchestral entertainment for the night. I no longer see Mikyla, Gring and Grond, or Rebby. Travin is holding Bronwynn in an embrace, one I distinctly believe a chaperone should split apart. My only hope for Travin and that girl is that he finds a temporary comfort during this grim time.

"Where's your tent?" I ask Westin abruptly.

"Huh?"

"Where. Is. Your. Tent?"

Westin's eyes are closed, and he peels them open, offering that irresistible grin at only one corner of his mouth. "Such is the precipitate request of my modest lady?"

I roll my eyes at him. "It is just a question."

"Then the answer is over there," he replies, pointing. "Come. I'll walk you to yours."

I don't know if I feel rejected or relieved when Westin leaves me at the entrance of my tent with no more recognition of my "precipitate request." He doesn't ask to see me again. He also doesn't look back. I stare as his figure retreats down the torch-lit aisle and out of my sight.

I blame the bubble.

Inside my dwelling, Mikyla is already asleep. Her steady breathing is a reminder that for once, in a very long time, I am not all by myself.

WESTIN

There Comes a Time When Your Time Comes

TODAY BEGINS WITH WEAPONS training for the new soldiers. The Israelite commanders give us a lecture on how and why we fight. There will be strategy sermons, disciplinary requirements, and hand-to-hand combat simulations between soldiers for personal evaluation. Joshua truly believes his soldiers are capable of anything, even defying death, when following God's commands in congruency with proficient practice and dedication. He also employs extreme control. It is so beyond the neutrality of Avoca, most of my fellow neighbors are stunned with disbelief.

Yesterday, the recruits were each placed in a unit of the army, under the order of an officer. Each unit consists of between one and five thousand men, depending on their proficiency. Some of these soldiers are delegated as lieutenant officers if they build a good rapport. The lieutenants report to their superior officers, who report to their High Commander in instructive and detailed epistles. The system is very complex and tactical. Every man is always accounted for.

While there are close to twenty thousand men camped here at Shittim, another twenty thousand are dispersed in nearby regions, including the logistics base in Gilgal. Joshua travels frequently between these base camps, and there are always Israelite spies traversing the mountains, documenting maps, gathering intelligence on the enemy.

Shittim is a bustling beehive, every bee busy and buzzing. I long to taste of the honey.

Orren is the officer over my unit. He is of average height with shaggy hair and a slim face. He is taller than I, but is of a sinewy build. His clothing is finer than the typical soldier, proudly representing his wealth. He speaks often of dominions and the wrath of God. He is not friendly. I notice the soldiers regard him with a kind of fearful approbation. No one dares contravene his command.

Out in the designated weapons training sector of Shittim, our unit surrounds Orren while he displays a plethora of sharp knives and spears, pointing to different parts and explaining their uses. Avoca has never seen such finely crafted weapons. *I* have never touched a weapon. When Orren picks up a sword and thrusts it into my arms, I nearly drop it. The weight is so heavy, like unto a crucifix. Gasping slightly, I try to recover before anyone notices.

"Now," Orren instructs, "partner up! You," he says pointing to me, "you will be my partner." He maneuvers my fingers around the shaft of the sword, teaching me how to hold the hilt. My biceps are already tired. He then moves in front of me. "I'm going to instruct you on how to attack. Everyone spread out. Those with a weapon, do as I do."

I check the sword in my hands, holding it directly out in front of me with the tip pointing at Orren. After some basic tutorials, we engage in light swordplay. I follow his thrusts perfunctorily and awkwardly. Nearby, the other soldiers practice similarly. Some of them appear to have knowledge in the art of weaponry. It points out the awful truth that there were, in fact, secret combinations in Avoca.

After an hour of basic instruction, Orren calls us to a halt. He demonstrates a difficult decapitating maneuver. He offers to practice on me, just for show, of course. Naturally, I hesitate.

The officer smiles acridly. "If you're afraid of simulated battle, you will never last on the battlefield."

He says it loud enough for the others to hear. My ears heat with humiliation. Avoca education was extensive, but it did not involve taking the life of another. I could dance circles around this man in finance and agriculture. An Israelite knows only bloodshed.

Nevertheless, my instinct turns to defiance. I will not allow some proud soldier to prove me an unworthy opponent.

I resume my stance. "Go forth."

Orren grins and then aims his sword at me. Adrenaline causes my pulse to accelerate. The blade swings toward my torso. My initial reaction is to buckle my knees and arch my back, extending my arms out to the side for balance, but I'm not fast enough. The swish of the blade nicks my forehead, catching a lock of my hair and slicing it free. I land on my back in the dirt.

Orren appears above me, clapping a hand against the hilt of his weapon.

"This is a perfect example of why we do *not* believe in *neutral territory*," he says, emphasizing the fact that Avoca does not raise men worthy of war.

I push myself up onto an elbow, touching the raw skin on my forehead.

The officer smirks, striding past me, and shouts, "Next!"

KAYA

The Morning After

I STARTLE AWAKE TO Mikyla kicking my bed. "Arise, Kaya Lucan!"

I groan, feeling the light throb at my temples. It progresses to an independent drumbeat in my skull. The aftereffects of strong wine.

Mikyla continues kicking. "Up, up!"

"Alright, I'm up."

I flop out of bed, my simlah rumpled. The cataclysm in my head is increasing by the minute, and my mouth is dry.

"You were up pretty late," Mikyla muses.

She's doing that thing where she doesn't know she's being condescending and judgmental. I try to ignore her pressing comments, blinking rapidly until my vision settles. Managing the ache of an empty stomach, and the unremitting thrum in my brain, I dig through the provisions we've been afforded as members of the Israelite army and find a brush for my hair. Last night resurfaces in my memory. Remembering Westin, I also remember my stupidity. He must think me no better than a harlot.

"Well, if you're not going to tell me who you were talking to last night—" Mikyla follows me out the door and into the bright morning sun. *Too bright*— "I have something to share with you."

"Is it tall, dark, and handsome?" I protest.

"*It* has a name," she rebukes, taking my hand. It's a good thing, too, because I refuse to torture my eyes with the sunlight. "His name is Jac."

The whole way to the center of camp, she goes on and on about

Jac. How he was such a gentleman, and how he taught her to dance. He's from a prosperous family, like her. An employed engineer, Jac will see less battle than the other soldiers. His duties include trenching, architecture, and commerce. This pleases Mikyla. If her father were around, Jac would ask him if he could court her.

She has this little glitter in her eye that I haven't seen in a long time and, at first, I think this Jac could be just the thing she needs during her loss. But two days pass, and she's still talking about him, spending every second she can with him. It's like Travin and *Bon-won* all over again.

My third day at camp is horrible. The veteran soldiers have begun training with all the new recruits. Well, all the new *male* recruits. Joshua has a strict policy for his army, one of the rules being males are superior warriors. So far, all the females have been assigned to stations that require minimal combat training. I selected the barnyard, where I will work as a stable maid under the supervision of Tildeh. The other females have accepted positions in cooking, cleaning, basket-weaving, agriculture, and garment mending.

If I wanted to do that I would've stayed home and gotten married.

On top of this, I've been stranded as an unwanted third wheel no matter whom I'm with.

Mikyla, Jac, me.

Travin, Bronwynn, me.

Gring, Grond, me.

And Rebby who always has a lady on his arm.

Today I take the long way to the stables, exploring parts of the camp I've yet to see. I stroll by the twins, who are out in the grass practicing their aim. They each take turns throwing metal spikes into the trunk of a tree. A red circle has been painted on the bark, and when Grond's spike pierces it perfectly in the center, he hoots and punches his twin, roaring, "Beat that!"

I round a corner of tents dreamily, wondering how Westin is progressing in his training. I would fancy the sight of him in breastplates and armor. Kicking a rock ahead of me, I glance around in vague assessment. I have to admit, the Israelites are impressive, if weirdly God-fearing.

My eye catches a lone figure exiting a tent down the row to my right and I halt.

Miki Rox.

He runs a hand through his hair, rolling his shoulders that are now dressed in Israelite costume. Conceitedly, he adjusts his leather weapon's harness and looks up. He sees me and sneers. I spin and start walking quickly away, but not resourcefully. There's nowhere even to hide. Miki drifts up to the side of me.

"What's the hurry, little lady?" he purrs.

"Leave me alone."

"You know, we could be friends," he persists. "I would ask your father's permission to court you if he were alive."

It is the lowest of lows, and he knows it. But I don't grant him response. Henceforth, I dart down the next row of dwellings made of wood and stone. At this point, I really have no idea where I am, or where I'm going. All I sense is stabbing memories. Sieving flash-backs. I can smell the smugness undulating off Miki in waves. I confess, it frightens me.

I decide to try and run. But Miki's hand shoots out. He seizes my arm, wrenching me toward him.

"Hey!" he barks.

"I should just out you, you pig!" I spit back in his face.

Miki rapidly glances around. With no one near enough to over-hear, he glares back at me. His eyes are dark and pitiless.

"Don't pretend like you didn't want it," he hisses.

"Have you lost your mind?" I can't conceal my fear. He's too close—too *here*—and I can't even look him in the face. "You're lucky I care about Mikyla and the harmony she strives for! You're nothing compared to her. You're an evil, worthless mule—"

He grasps my shoulders in such a force that I shut my mouth. Slamming my back into the structure behind me, he pinions me to it, his elbow painful against my chest. He speaks in a voice sharp as steal.

"You're the one who is nothing. And you *did* want it," he adds. "I could do it again, right now. No one is here to stop me."

I want to cry out, to do anything to defend myself. But just like a year ago, I am paralyzed.

The morning after it happened, Miki came to Lucan Care and tried telling me it was consensual. This, even if it was somehow true—*and it isn't*—doesn't excuse the degrading nature in which he acted and *still* acts when he sees me. Like I'm a piece of meat. Raw meat.

My biggest regret is that I didn't put up a fight to stop it. This was a man with a vital image that Avoca relied upon. I was compromised with wine, and I will have to live with it. At least I *lived* and was not pregnant. According to stories, other victims don't come out so fortunate.

"That's right," Miki continues in a slithery voice.

His massive torso crushes into me, his knees suggestively widening mine. He leans in a little closer until he's breathing on my face.

"You're not going to shout. You're not going to tell anybody. Like a good girl." He releases one of my arms and touches my cheek with his big hand. "Aren't you a good girl?"

I jerk away, but Miki only laughs, grasping my chin firmly this time. His thumb squashes my jawbone, holding my head in place. I can feel myself trembling, and I hate him for it. I'm helpless. Weak. And I hate myself for it.

He leans in, his mouth only an inch away.

"What do you think about trying this again?" he asks, fingers trilling down my stomach. His lips begin to touch mine.

Something snaps inside of me.

Finally, the screams that have built up in my chest explode through my throat. I thrash about, trying to kick at his legs and bite at his fingers, but a beefy hand covers my mouth. Strange, inhuman cries ricochet off his palm but go no farther as he restrains me with his other arm. Two seconds flat, and I'm incapacitated. That's it. That's all I've got. Two seconds.

Lord, please. Not again.

Suddenly, Miki's body is ripped off of me and thrown into a nearby stockpile of supplies with an ugly crunch. In a whir of black hair and fists, Westin appears. He punches Miki squarely in the nose. Blood spurts as Westin hits him on the side of his face and then again. Again. Again. Miki, unaccustomed to such aggression, is caught defenseless. Westin, unaccustomed to hitting a man, gropes his wrist after the feat. His attack was more or less slovenly in method, but full of impact. With Miki debilitated on the ground, Westin wheels toward me. His eyes are bright and wild like a snowstorm. When he tries to put his arms around me, I flinch backward.

"What did you do to her?" Westin demands, turning slowly to face Miki, who is holding a hand over his face. Several streams of blood run down Miki's chin. When he doesn't respond, Westin grabs the neck of his tunic and raises his fist again. "I said, what did you do to her?"

I clutch Westin's forearm, tugging him away from Miki. Such behavior is uncommon in Avoca. I am unaccustomed to preventing it. Westin's nature has changed since joining the army. His temperament is less constrained with the allowance of violence. Touching him, I can sense the adrenaline pumping through him, causing the veins in his neck to bulge. He resists my efforts for a moment and gives Miki one last forceful shove.

Turning his crystal eyes on me, Westin bodily lifts me a few feet away from Miki. He looks enraged and dangerous, and all the more handsome for it. I find I am attracted to the aggression, and it both frightens and confuses me. But I don't want to be hugged, or touched, or seen. I feel violated and exposed. My jaw aches. My chest feels tight. My face is ablaze. A wet drop escapes my eye, and I wipe it away frantically. Everything is spiraling out of control.

"Did he hurt you?" Westin asks throatily.

Did Miki hurt me? He ruined me.

I can't speak. I'm reliving that moment a year ago.

Things get that much more awful when a group of soldiers emerges down the row of tents, a brigade returning from a training session. Travin is among them. He's mingling with the others like they're longtime friends. Camaraderie. Acceptance. Equality. Everything he's longed for.

I try to hide behind Westin's shoulder, but I fail. Travin looks over and stops. Westin keeps a guarded stance in front of me as

Travin drops his gear to the ground and jogs over, his left hand on the hilt of his knife. He's the one person to whom I truly hate to appear weak.

With each step Travin nears, his eyebrows furrow deeper. His trenchant gaze sweeps over to Westin.

"What's going on here?" he asks, the way one solider is obliged to greet another.

It doesn't hide the suspicion I see in his eyes. He glances between Westin and I, and then to Miki who has sat back against a post. Travin does not cringe at the blood. He returns his gaze to me. I feel my cheek to make sure that what I think was on my face isn't on my face. I do not cry.

"This man has a real problem," Miki sputters, wiping his sleeve across his battered mouth.

"*I* have a problem?" Westin snaps, flexing the muscles in his arms.

He and Miki begin an oral dispute that transitions into a semi-physical spat. I grab hold of Westin's elbow with both hands as he lunges again, barely keeping him from attacking. The Israelites have introduced combat to the draftees but have not yet instilled enough discipline.

Travin's eyes dart from Miki to my grip on Westin's elbow. Westin loops that arm around the front of me and subtly pulls me behind him in a protective fashion. I tuck my chin, avoiding all six eyes gaping at me.

"Kaya?"

"Just forget about it," I manage to say.

My voice cracks, and I chastise myself.

Travin says it again. "Kaya?"

I can't meet his eyes.

Westin stands stiffly between us, but Travin shoulders past him and reaches his left hand out to me. I instantly melt into him. He holds me, unmoving, and I bury my face into his chest, wanting to disappear. There is horsehair in his tunic. It is *so* much like home. I close my eyes and breathe it in. A squeaking sound escapes my mouth, and I burrow deeper.

I do not *cry.*

Travin lowers his mouth to my ear to softly ask, "Do you want to go back to your tent?"

I nod but don't let go of him.

"Somebody tell me what's going on," he demands menacingly from the other boys.

"Actually, I'm not really sure," Westin finally answers.

"Your little queen," Miki barks, "made me an offer I couldn't refuse!"

"You'd better watch what you say—"

"She would never—"

The males fall quiet. I peek an eye out. Westin and Travin crisply eye each other, clearly unaware to whom Miki was speaking. Westin's hands clench into fists again, his pectoral muscles tightening under his tunic. He reminds me of a cockatoo, whose feathers ruffle and puff up when it gets set off. Defending me is one thing, but irrepressible rage is another.

I don't care to explain anything to either of them. I simply want to get as far away from Miki Rox as possible.

"Please, can we just go?" I mewl against Travin's collar.

Travin agrees but gives the two soldiers a final warning, "You'd both better stay away from her."

His voice is more authoritative than I've ever heard. I poke my other eye out over his shoulder. Using him as a shield, I watch Miki stand and retreat back into camp, cursing along the way. Westin watches Miki's exit with a cold glare.

"Keep moving, you prodigal waste of a man," Westin mutters contemptuously. My blue-eyed conqueror shifts that contempt to Travin.

Westin is angry. At both of us. I realize I have chosen to seek comfort from the man who did *not* rescue me.

"Westin, be at ease," I state, releasing my grip on Travin.

Travin tightens his hold on my waist.

"I'm sorry," I say ruefully. I know Westin deserves gratitude from me, but I can't face him right now. I need some space from the violent nature of soldiers and the violent nature of memories. He stands inert as Travin begins to urge me away.

Travin guides me to my tent. Fortunately, it's empty. He then sits me down on the bed and squats in front of me.

An overwhelming and despicable regret smothers me. I will not talk about Miki to Travin. He doesn't need to know. I turn my face away, pointing to the bottle at the foot of my bed. When Travin hands it to me, I throw the cork and take a long swig. It burns down my throat. I cough but take another.

"Settle down," Travin murmurs calmly, taking the bottle from my hands. "Why was Miki's nose broken, and who was that other soldier?"

"Westin," I reply, leaving out the first half of the story.

"Do you know him?"

"I met him after we joined Joshua in Taavetti. Westin—"

"What's his business with Miki?"

"It's none of his business, really," I explain, though I know it will be different from now on. "Miki and I were just . . . talking. Then, it sort of turned into a misunderstanding."

I'm a horrible liar. Travin knows this.

He asks dryly, "And Westin just happened to be there when you and Miki were *misunderstanding* each other?"

"What is your problem with Westin?" I blurt out. "Miki was the one transgressing! Worry about him."

"I don't know Westin, that's my problem." Travin lifts the bottle to his own mouth and takes a slurp, only to force it down with a face of revulsion. He prefers pure wine from the vine to fermentation. "I know Miki and his family, and I'm wondering why a fellow soldier punched him in the face."

"You do *not* know Miki," I counter, stealing back my bottle. I take another fulfilling drink, ignoring the inscrutable expression that crosses Travin's face. He has adamantly avoided wine since he was a young child. I don't blame him, but he mustn't blame me either. "And *I* know Westin. He's fine. He's a friend."

Travin eyes me carefully as I take yet another sip.

"Nay," he states, reaching for the bottle. I hold it out of his reach and his gray eyes narrow. "Be wise. That's not going to help anything. I'm sorry. If you say Westin's fine, then he's fine."

"Just forget about Westin. Keep Miki far away from me."

"I will. I promise."

Travin doesn't ask me anything more, and I don't offer any information. We sit in silence—compatible on my part—for several more minutes, while I gather my emotions and place them carefully back into their bubble.

Numbness.

No one has ever seen me cry. Maybe my father—once. He smelled like horsehair too . . .

"I'm late for work," I mumble without conviction. "Tildeh will be mad."

"I'll handle it," Travin replies with a lopsided smile.

I give him that look, and his returning one says, *"I can do that."* He places the back of his hand on my forehead and states, "You're burning up. I think it's a germ. As your male superior, I order you on strict bed rest until tomorrow."

I roll my eyes. "You order me?"

He grins. He loves being a soldier.

"You seem . . . really happy, Trav. You like it here?"

He plays down the rapture in his eyes by answering simply, "I do."

When I don't jump to congruence, his brows dip. It gives his grin a flummoxed shape.

"Joshua is the wisest man," Travin tells me. "The way he utilizes his soldiers, how he plans his siege attacks. He has special storm troops, delegated sappers who dig trenches, engineers who build weapons, mining tools, and battering rams. I—I'm sorry. You don't look like you want to hear about this."

I crook a smile at him. "You sound like Rebby."

He licks his bottom lip, his shoulder lifting towards his chin. "I suppose."

Quick to pat the top of his hand, I add, "But even more like a proud Shelomo." His clever expression perceives my ill-timed accolade. "How is the legendary Ranvir, anyway?"

"I'm telling him you called him that," Travin teases.

"I dare you."

His grin wanes as he glances around the room then back to me. I know it isn't proper to be without a chaperone, but it's just us.

"I should go," Trav states.

"Is *Bon-won* wondering where you are?" I ask.

"Probably." Travin chuckles, shaking his head. He raises just enough to slide onto the bed beside me. "Lo, I may need more wine."

"Why are you courting her, anyway?"

His eyes slant over to mine.

I regret it the moment I say it. Wine makes me more honest than I'd like to be when it is fermented.

Their courtship has long been a tense subject between us. With Bronwynn controlling Travin, and with his compliance, he and I spend minimal time together. Before we fled Avoca, it had been weeks since we held a solid conversation, gone swimming, or just hung out with each other. Swimming in the Salt Sea is something Travin and I have done since our childhood. I don't believe it's fair she has taken that away. Just saying.

It was our little place to get away to together. We could share anything, *any* part of ourselves. When Bronwynn came into the picture, I became the abandoned frame.

"I mean, you just make an odd pair, that's all," I state.

This doesn't help.

"I wouldn't expect you to understand," Travin answers.

It stings. I thought we always understood each other.

"I don't get it, Trav." I get up and pace the room. "She doesn't treat you well. You don't deserve it. I hate to see you miserable."

"Who says I'm miserable?" He stands and continues with bold hand gestures, "And you're one to talk. You're always in a fight nowadays, or drinking your problems away with *this*. It's no way to live. It's *wrong*."

"Oh, save your sermons for Joshua and those who believe in God."

"Kaya!" Travin snaps.

I poke a finger roughly into his chest, the chest I'd recently been nuzzled against. It's like poking a rock wall. *When did that happen?*

"You don't have to idolize him, you know," I retort. "It's not like

Joshua is your *father*."

Hurt and offense coalesce into a deadly combination. Travin curtails the emotions and adjusts his leather weapon's harness.

"You should remember your place," he says quietly.

I'm angrier with myself than with him. My comment about Joshua struck a nerve of his I didn't mean to strike. "Just because they say you're superior doesn't mean you have to act like it," I argue anyway.

"And *you* don't have to *act* like a stranded lamb."

He strides to the exit. Just as he pushes back the tarps, Mikyla comes running through with Jac in hand.

"Oh!" She jumps, bewildered at the sight of Travin. Travin jostles his way past her as she looks up at me. "I'm sorry. I didn't think anyone would be in here." And she pushes Jac back out of the tent.

They didn't want a chaperone either.

I'm glad Mikyla is gone. Looking at her only reminds me of her twin brother.

Murmuring, I clutch the bottle, almost empty now, and curl up on my bed. A small shard of guilt from Travin's words creeps into my head. Why must I always push him away, when I need him to be near? I know he does not approve of my conduct, but he does not know my pain.

I should want to cry more, to release the frustration and fury, but no tears come. I am numb.

WESTIN

The Art of Oppression

I AM QUICK TO discern what quality of human my officer is. Orren knows every one of his one thousand soldiers by name. He knows their strengths, their weaknesses, and he knows exactly where he wants them to rank in Joshua's army. If a soldier appears to be performing with skill that outshines the officer, that soldier is appointed a station at Shittim where his talents will not be discovered. It is the pecking order. A man will always do what he can to succeed, but what he will do with that success, and whom he will hurt with it, depends on the kind of man he is.

Men like Miki Rox and Orren seek success for the power to hurt others.

This knowledge has put me in an awkward position. I need to learn the Israelite ways, but I *cannot* be buried by an oppressive officer.

I often conceal my abilities with weapons and stay silent on my education of the maps of Canaan to fly under the eagle eye of Orren's inspection. While doing so, I study my officer and the other soldiers, gathering the use of sycophancy involved in our military unit.

"Soldiers," Orren orders, "today we will be swimming in the stream fully girded in armor."

We are commanded to swim upstream. Those not completing the task within the allotted time are required to repeat the exercise again. The skill of swimming has not come naturally to me. With the extra weight of my breastplates and weapon, staying afloat is a treacherous sport. Nonetheless, I finish swimming the distance in the appropriate time. This is both to my benefit and to my misfortune.

When one of the soldiers in my unit, Rionn, begins to sink, I am charged with helping him finish the drill. Instead of exhibiting my skills in flattery to talk my way out of it, I choose to keep them concealed. I splash back into the water and pull Rionn, his armor and gear, upstream. There is more to be learned of Orren today and more to learn of myself.

KAYA

What Rhymes with Bubble

I CLOSE MY EYES, and when I reopen them it's nighttime. The effects of the wine still linger in my body. As I sit up, the walls go slightly askance. Mikyla is not here. Lamplight flashes through the tarps, across her empty bed. I stand and wobble my way to the exit, out into the night.

Our camp is active and busy for evening, with soldiers following through on their unending duties. Guards pace the perimeter. The weapons refinery has the largest congregation with construction of armor and armaments imperative. Copper-laden rock is the most common ingredient. Iron is desirable but a costly rarity. Crushing copper ore, the soldiers attain the pure copper. In a furnace, charcoal is heated to produce fuel. The ore reduces, emitting a green flame when it is molten. Once it is smelted, tin is added to strengthen and offer fluidity. After it is all melted, the mixture is poured into molds made of clay.

Outside the manufacturing plant, a large bonfire hosts a multitude of soldiers amicably conversing. I look for familiar faces, but I don't recognize anyone. The embers are rich, the heat pleasant on my skin. I stand in solitude for a while, watching the flames dance, paying no heed to the soldiers that pay me no heed. After another hour, I spot a shape across the fire. A Westin-sized shape. The inferno illuminates his face as it did our first encounter. A very strapping face. I move around the pit until I bump into his shoulder.

"Hi," I garble.

Westin doesn't meet my gaze. "Sorry. I couldn't 'stay away' from you."

I glide in front of him until he looks up at me. His eyes are even more entrancing with the reflection of the flames glimmering in them. *Fire and ice.* I reach up and touch his brow.

"Do you know that and can I tell you I just love your eyes?"

He smiles a little. "How much of that wine have you finished off?"

"All. Of it," I hiccup.

"It appears so," he replies.

"*Hiccup.*"

"Kaya," he says, catching my hands as I tip toward the fire, "we don't have to talk about it right now if you don't want to. But if we're going to establish some trust, I do want to know about you, Miki, and Travin."

"Ugh, I don't wanna talk about them. One bit."

Westin raises his eyebrows. I mimic his expression animatedly, but he doesn't find this amusing. He has not released my hands. I have not pulled them away.

"Well, if that's the way you want it—" he starts.

"Fine, fine," I groan. "What do you want to know?"

"Why was Miki trying to violate you?" he inquires, disdain on his tongue.

"He's perverted," I mumble, hoping it was an efficient response.

"Curse be upon him," Westin agrees.

"And Travin and I *were* best friends," I babble. "Then, he started courting that bully Bon-won. You know, she's probably the meanest person I've ever met, which is ironic considering Travin is the nicest. We grew up together. We've been through everything—well, a lot of stuff. We hardly ever see each other anymore. And when we do, she's always . . . like—and I hate her. It takes a certain level of evil to sabotage someone daily when an entire village already persecutes them. Did you know she actually tells him when he can and can't talk to me?"

"They deserve each other," he replies.

"In a sick, opposites attract kind of way. I guess."

Westin represses a grin. I decide that's my favorite expression he makes. Intertwining his fingers in mine, he links our hands behind my lower back. I arch to gaze up at him.

"And that's all?" he asks.

"That's all."

"Then why did Miki refer to you as Travin's 'little queen'?"

"Huh?" I start to teeter again but Westin holds me upright.

"Miki said, 'your little queen'. I thought he was speaking to me, but he wasn't. He was talking to Travin."

"I don't know."

Westin's hand grazes my jawline where Miki grabbed me. It's alarmingly gentle, and I begin an incline toward him. "I'm really sorry about Miki. He will never lay another hand on you. I will make sure of that."

I let my eyes wander over him. His tunic reveals his taut muscles. The muscles he used to defend me. Muscles I kind of want to feel.

Maybe I do want his comfort.

"Can we go somewhere?" I ask quietly.

"Anywhere you want," he responds.

"Where's your tent?"

Westin squints at me uncertainly, deliberating. "It's occupied," he eventually answers. "Yay, I think I know where we can go."

He leads me down an empty row of tents while I ramble meaninglessly about the stars above. The nights out here are unreal. The way the mountains seclude the valley makes the sky look like a tunnel into the infinities when you peer straight up. There's never too much wind, and it's never all that cold. All it needs is a shoreline.

At last, we come to a halt at the edge of the camp. A smaller shelter made of aged wood sits a short distance out in the plains. Westin plucks one of the torches from the ground and takes my hand. When we reach the shed, he cracks the door open and shines the light of the torch inside. It's dusty and cluttered and free of people.

"Your humble abode," he whispers.

I step inside. Buckets, tools, saddles and reins, and a few abandoned weapons lie strewn around the ten cubits of space. Westin kicks them aside, places the torch in the entrance, and then retrieves a horse pad for us to sit on.

I position myself next to him, my movements lackadaisical from the excessive wine intake. It makes me giggle.

"I do not think the Israelites like wine."

"They like their wine," Westin counters. "They just preach discipline in consuming it."

Right. Another rule. Drink wine sparingly. Eat meat sparingly. Abide the law of chastity. Do not worship false idols. The Israelites are confined by rules.

"Discipline," I mutter.

"They condemn gross intoxication," he responds, pointing to me with a defiant smirk.

I toss my hair aside. "There are worse things."

"Trust me." His eyes narrow thoughtfully. "I understand. And I may as well ask. Do you approve of our courtship?"

"I approve," I answer immediately, wishing I'd thought more properly about the response. I didn't know we'd transitioned into a courtship. I don't know if I want one. Then again, wisdom and wine do not coexist.

Westin gives me a funny look. "I know it's been untraditional, but . . . I just . . . I don't want our involvement with the Israelites to complicate things."

"What things?"

"Whatever is going on between us."

There's an us?

"Besides," Westin hurries on, "if we break their rules, we may be punished. We have to be careful."

He looks at my lips and grins, a teeth-baring smile that makes my insides quiver. Persuasion. I didn't know such a thing could be so powerful. My heart beats faster and the resistance emplacements thereupon flee like unto defenseless Canaanites.

Westin kisses me. I contemplate the rules. The punishments. I think of Travin's frowning at my wine, of the way he has adapted so quickly to this new people. He has taken to the Israelites like molten ore filling a clay mold. And they are creating a weapon out of him.

KAYA

People Are Not as They Seem

DAY AFTER DAY, OUR free hours are spent in that shed. We don't have many, but during breaks in our vocations, or a meal reprieve, it is Westin and I, me and Westin. Our "courtship" is a budding surprise to this new soldier life. It is fulfilling to be a source of pleasure for someone else, to feel like you bring them joy. Westin is happy with me. We have not broken *that* rule, but . . . we have bent it.

Typically, we are apart through the day. Westin observing the strategies of tacticians, learning the language of the Israelites, and increasing his stamina for war. Most of the soldiers are fluent in many dialects. Hoping to become one of them, I busy myself in the stables, repeating words I've recently learned. Thus each chicken and goat has a name.

I prefer my time amongst the animals to my time with people, but I make an exception for Westin. He is different than other men—well, different than Miki Rox, to whom I compare almost every man. Westin brings me colorful bouquets of wild flowers and compliments me. We delight in our wine, and cynicism, together.

Today at breakfast, Mikyla tells me Orren is taking his unit out into the wilderness overnight. The specific factors are limited to those involved, including Westin and Jac, but Jac did let it slip that medical evaluations would be performed. I begin to speculate why, when Mikyla giggles and tells me Joshua plans to have all the men circumcised after they conquer Bashan.

"What?" I gasp, appalled.

"It is called of God," she replies, grinning childishly. "Joshua wants all the men of Israel to be circumcised. Jac told me so. But you can't say anything! We'd be punished if he knew I spoke outwardly about it."

"Ouch," I murmur.

"They will be gone three days," Mikyla whines. "What will I do without Jac for three days?"

"Oh, thanks," I reply sarcastically.

"I'm sorry. I didn't mean to sound rude, it's just—"

"I understand." I smile so she knows I'm not angry. It's not like we've seen much of one another anyway. She's busied herself as a seamstress, and I've busied myself with the animals and Westin.

"Aren't you going to miss Westin?" she questions.

"I guess."

"You *guess?*" she responds baffled.

"Sure, I'm going to miss him," I swiftly amend, so I don't have to explain why I don't feel the same way she does. I *like* Westin. I don't *need* him.

Westin has replenished my bottle of wine, anyhow. And no matter how lame that might seem to Mikyla or anyone else, I know perfectly well it will keep me occupied.

"Miki mentioned Officer Lachlan is going back to Avoca," Mikyla announces. "They want to seek survivors from every city."

"Oh?"

"Joshua wants to build his army as large as possible. Did you know there are over eight thousand soldiers just in this quadrant? I didn't even know there were that many men alive. Joshua seeks every living person to join the Israelites. Miki thinks he can be promoted within the ranks soon. He'd like to go with Lachlan and search for our parents."

"Let's hope," I murmur.

"What's that?"

"I said let's hope . . . they find your parents."

"I know," Mikyla replies enthusiastically. "I've talked to Jac about it. It's so sweet how he listens. Can you believe we both found soldiers to court us? I never thought I'd court a man who had a violent nature . . ."

Mikyla continues talking, but I've stopped listening.

Across camp, Bronwynn is leaning against a tent post, talking with a few soldiers I don't recognize. Male soldiers.

"Yay," I answer to Mikyla's commentary.

Bronwynn is not at her station, hemming soldier garb. She's *there*.

" . . . so, I'm going to be with him before he leaves. I'll see you later," Mikyla states, not noticing that I haven't heard a word she's been saying.

I mumble, "Alright."

Bronwynn reaches out and touches one of the man's forearms coquettishly. They laugh. It is indecent!

Travin would be hurt if he knew how she was behaving. Not only that, but the Israelites have guidelines for morality. With new recruits from all kinds of backgrounds joining the camp, the principles and values are increasingly mingled. It is often confusing. Needless to say, I assume exclusivity in courtship is a unanimous morale. Witnessing Bronwynn's indecency makes me nervous about Westin. I've seen the way women lust after him. If Bon-won finds exclusivity difficult, an eligible, *beautiful*, soldier would find it increasingly more so. A primal instinct within me to mark my territory evolves.

I picture the recipient of Bronwynn's flirtation being circumcised and turn to head to the stables.

If there is a God, I bet he surrounds himself with animals.

WESTIN

Adapt, Survive, Repeat

"Exercises are complete for the day," Gorrow announces. "Report back at the same time tomorrow. Bring your overnight gear."

Combat practice was extra rigorous on the mountainside today. Joshua has been traversing the plains, recruiting more soldiers, and making plans for our impending attack on Bashan. His top engineers travel with him, mapping out the landscape where they intend to build trenches. He has left his officers in charge of keeping the camp organized and active. Orren finds this especially welcome, relishing the opportunity to implement authority. We are pushed to our limits, punished, and both go overlooked.

Today, our unit combined with Gorrow's, the next best soldiers to Lachlan's. We were first educated on the king of Bashan. Og. A known giant, Og sleeps in a bed of iron that is nine cubits long and four cubits wide. He is exceedingly strong with great fortifications around his city. I have never seen a giant, nor did I believe in their existence. The thought of confronting one in battle causes fear in my heart.

The two units were then led in groups of ten up the mountainside, each required to carry an excessive load, to prepare our bodies for the exertion of war when we will be girded with heavy armor and supplies. Gring and Grond Bottker mount the summit in record time, slowing only on the straight vertical sections, hardly losing their breath. They are skilled climbers. Gorrow makes a note of this.

My accomplishments weren't as rewarded. When a less than

competent soldier, Gebidiah, ceased to find strength in carrying his load, Orren ordered me to carry it for him. Sore from the activities, I lope back to my tent to bathe my face and prepare for our overnight excursion. We are to receive medical evaluations prior to being circumcised. I couldn't refuse anymore than I wanted to refuse carrying Gebidiah's armaments. The Israelites penalize wayward behavior and condemn it as a sin in the eyes of God.

I remember my mother speaking of religion when I was a boy. She told me God had allowed her to suffer. Her husband—my father—had been unfaithful to her, later leaving in the night for another woman in the village. *God lets bad things happen to good people, so why be good?* she would question.

I wonder what Joshua would say to that.

After I bathe and pack, I decide to be with Kaya a moment before I must depart. I enter the women's barracks, stopping by a blossoming bush growing out of the side of the path. I pluck a flower, stooping over a pot of water to check my reflection. Mother also told me that how you present yourself to others would determine how you are treated. It was under her clever discretion I learned the tricks on flattery.

At Kaya's door, I knock on the tent post and let myself in. The smell of fermentation wafts throughout her room. Kaya is sitting on the floor, staring at an old horseshoe. Her upper body sways lightly from side to side as she holds it in both hands.

"Are you, uh, well today?" I ask from the entrance.

She mumbles unintelligibly. I walk around in front of her and grimace. Her eyes are bloodshot, empty, with a translucent layer of pain I rarely glimpse. Notwithstanding, this condition of inebriation is something I *often* glimpse. In a few seconds, she'll start rambling about horses.

I squat at her side, extending the flower to prevent it. Her eyes graze over the flower and then return to the horseshoe.

"Matthieu was a purebred, you know," she slurs.

Here we go with the horses.

"He was so beautiful. Fourteen hands tall. His eyes were the color of molten ore."

I exhale. "Do you want to go exercise him?"

"We had to put him down today."

I pause a moment, adjusting to the animal-human bond I don't quite identify with. Kaya considers the beasts of the earth precious above jewels. Above people. I wiggle the hand with the flower, desirous to see her smile.

"You don't have to buy my affection, Westin."

I glance at the flower, then at the exit, then back at her.

"What *do* I have to do, then?" I retort. "I'm not Travin, Kaya."

"Excuse me?"

"I don't *understand* you when you get like this."

And now I've just revealed what I've worked the hardest to convince myself is untrue. I *want* to understand her. I *don't* want her to be close with anyone else. And Travin still knows her better than I do. She trusted him over me.

"Sorry," I sigh tersely, moving to sit in front of her. It is likely just the wine influencing her mood. Usually it influences her mood in a way that is beneficial for me. "Tell me what grieves you. I can lessen your burden."

Suddenly, Kaya tosses the horseshoe across the room. "I wasn't ready to let him go," she mewls.

"He was just an animal," I reply.

Her frown tightens. She rubs her eyes with her thumb and index finger.

"Look at me," she murmurs.

"I am looking at you."

"Nay," she says again. "Look at *me*."

"You must speak to me concerning the desires of your heart. I do not speak in tongues."

She stands and motions around the room. "Is this what you want?"

"*You* are what I want," I respond.

I try to place the flower in her hand but she circles away.

"What about me?" she questions.

"I'd like to figure out what it means when you do this, for starters," I say. Then under my breath, "You are in some personal contest for impenetrability."

Kaya doesn't seem to hear, thankfully. "I am beginning to feel different things."

This time, I grab her wrist and pull her back down. She sits clumsily, noticing the flower. She takes it and smells the petals. Tracing a finger beneath her chin, I lift her head slowly.

"Kaya. Tell me what your heart desires."

"Do you believe in Joshua?" she asks softly.

"The other soldiers do."

"But do you?"

I scratch my forehead. "I have hope that we will receive this inheritance he speaks of. Think of all that land! Joshua has an army of more than forty and a thousand, Kaya. He has killed even more men than that. You should hear the things people say about him. The soldiers speak of him as if he is a mythical creature that cannot be beaten."

"And God?" she asks. "God is a mythical creature?"

"It does not matter as long as we prosper."

"I fear it *does* matter."

"Why?" I respond. "Why this interest in religious beliefs? You have never cared for what the Israelites think before. Your *father* was not an Israelite."

The look she gives me is so intense it deserves sound effects. "Do not speak of my father."

"What do you want from me?" I demand, partially standing. "Just tell me what you want!"

She bites into her lower lip, dropping the flower. "I want . . . to have hope. These soldiers—they have a purpose. They seem . . . happy in their purpose. You know? I want a purpose. I don't want to be a useless maiden."

"You are not useless."

"Yay, I tend animals."

"But you *love* animals."

"You don't—I don't—feel like my life has purpose."

I murmur with dissatisfaction, standing to pace the room. "Thank you. Thank you for letting me know that *this* means nothing.

Our courtship means nothing!" I stomp on the flower petals. Kaya's eyes follow my movements, widening vaguely with trepidation. "*I* am a part of your life, too, you know. If your life has no purpose, then *I* have no purpose to you."

Kaya remains staunch. "That's not what I meant."

"But it's what you said!"

"Wes—"

"Is nothing I do enough? If you want some . . . thing else, just say it."

She pauses, backing towards the corner of the tent where Matthieu's horseshoe sits. Her motions are contrived.

"I didn't mean to—look, I'm calm. I just want to know what you want. Kaya, not everyone is out to get you."

"I don't know what I want."

"Me?" I snort. "Did that thought cross your mind?"

Her eyes travel to the horseshoe near her toes. "What's my favorite breed?"

"Breed? You're acting crazy right now," I exhale.

Kaya looks up, her eyes pained. "You think I'm crazy?"

"Nay." I walk to the exit. "I said you are *acting* crazy."

"Wait," she pleads as I reach for the tarps.

"You need some time by yourself," I respond, pulling them open. Three days apart from Kaya will straighten all this out.

"I don't want to be alone," she says quietly.

But I let the tarp flap shut behind me and grunt in departure. "Women."

KAYA

An All-Time Favorite

I AWAKE FROM A nap feeling ill. The faces from my nightmares loiter on the edge of my conscious memory. Not even the wine subdued them this time. Westin is gone. He left amidst our contention, which has left me feeling spiteful. I laboriously resist the wine bottle and decide to clean my tent.

Over the next few hours, I tidy up my room. Finish some laundry. I've collected old horseshoes from the stables that I stack beneath my bed. They remind me of home. I make up my mind to head to the barn and exercise some of the stallions, to *feel* more at home, when I hear a knock on my tent post. It's followed by a, "Whoop, whoop!"

"If it isn't the Catastrophe Crew," I say dryly.

Travin and Rebby burst into my tent, glittery eyes gazing my way. Travin immediately trips, hitting the floor hard.

Rebby laughs, dropping to his knees on top of Travin's back while shouting, "Shwabaam! And take that, woman!"

He punches Travin in the side of the head.

"I can fight you!" Travin prattles back, rolling over. Rebby flops off of him. "And don't call me woman!"

"Aw, man-love," I mumble.

Rebby stands, sort of, and exclaims in my general direction, "You should've seen him! Tell her, Trav. Tell her how I got you to play Grab."

"Travin," I turn on him. "You played *Grab*?"

Obviously. The game, Grab, is an excuse, more or less. Soldiers do not moderate their intake of wine during such diversions, straddling the verge of gluttony. It was not the Israelites who created the game, but some of the newcomers. Giving it a title is like pulling the wool over the others' eyes. Many of the staunchly religious avoid the game altogether. It seems my two friends gave in to temptation this evening.

Travin has never liked wine, let alone consumed it excessively. I can count on one hand the number of times I've seen him drink the strong beverage. It might have something to do with his father's tendencies. I respect that about Travin. I also respect his diligence to these laws, God's laws, which he is trying so mightily to obey.

Still lying on the floor, Travin blinks his large eyes up at me, pointing at his face like a small boy who is about to confess to his mother that he ate the last piece of manna.

"Kaya, I played Grab."

"Well," I laugh, returning to the row of empty bottles I've been lining up at the foot of my bed, "it seems like you lost."

Travin prowls to my bed. Pushing off all fours, he slumps onto his belly while watching me arrange my collection. His eyes rake over my limbs slowly. In my defense, I was about to head to the stables. My *clean* laundry is put away.

Meanwhile, Rebby jumps onto the bed, feet first, which shifts the frame of the tent and knocks down a few of my bottles. Travin sinks toward the middle of the bed where Rebby's weighted down the cushion. I give them that look out of the corner of my eye.

"Do I need to sit between you two?" I scold the raucous scoundrels.

"Yay!" Travin cries, reaching off the side of the bed and grabbing hold of my wrists.

"I was teasing!" I screech, digging my heels into the ground.

But it's no use.

Travin yanks me toward him. His strength has profited from the rigorous training. He picks me up like a weightless doll. It's hard for me to envision, this boy from my childhood wielding swords and shields. I do not like to think he is the violent type. And yet, it seems he has never belonged so well somewhere. These men do not care that he is a Shelomo.

Rebby moves to the head of the bed so Travin can slam me into the straw pallet. It's not as soft as back home. I wheeze on impact. Nonetheless, both boys lie on their backs on either side of me.

"See, isn't this great?" Rebby asks, folding his arms behind his head.

"It is great," Travin replies. He's looking at me with a carnal gleam in his eye.

Rebby leans over my head, his armpit effectively placed above my nose. "We have to stay in here, at least until the effects of your loss at Grab wear off. I'm not going to get punished for gluttony because of your deficiency in a simple game. If we receive any visitors, I will claim to be the chaperone!"

"Tsk, tsk," I smile. "Maybe I should get you something to eat. It's about supper time, is it not?"

"I'll bring us a meal," Rebby announces, getting off the bed. "I can already smell it cooking. What do you suppose it is? Lamb? Roasted urchin?"

"In your dreams," Travin chortles.

"I thought you just said you have to stay *in* here?" I ask.

"I'll return," Rebby declares flamboyantly. Pointing an index finger at me, then Travin, he smiles at a private thought. Then he disappears out of the tent.

"Don't trip and fall into another woman's chamber!" Travin bellows to the tarps.

I cover my mouth to hide my reaction.

A few seconds pass. I wonder if Trav will mind that we are without a chaperone. Joshua preaches of high moral values, but also of agency—the freedom to choose whether or not an individual wants to abide by those values. Travin reveres Joshua. I'm still riding the fence on these rules. Besides, it is just me and Travin.

"So, " I'm unable to think.

Travin says nothing either.

I remember what Mikyla mentioned about the soldiers being circumcised. I will certainly *not* talk about that.

"Do you enjoy the army?" I ask instead.

"Yay," Travin responds, rolling limbs at random until he's on his side. "We all have schedules. It will not be long until we march into Bashan."

"I see," I pause, trying to find more words to say. I can still feel his rounded shoulders digging into my body when he picked me up. They felt like sculpted oranges on either side of his neck. *Since when is Travin so strong?* "Is training going well? I mean, what are you even learning to do?"

"Much," Travin answers nonchalantly. "My favorite is hand to hand combat."

His eyes light up as he launches into a very long, one-sided conversation about different defense mechanisms and camouflage techniques he's learned, accompanied by boyish sound effects.

"Well, as long as you don't run up behind them screaming *'whoop, whoop,'* I think you'll be fine," I joke.

"Ha!" A burst of laughter bubbles out of him. He contains it, only to let it out again. "Ha, ha!"

"Yay," I muse. "I can be funny."

He stares at me for a second, hawk-eyed. "I've always thought you were funny."

"Sure."

"What's under there?" He rolls, almost falling off the bed.

I grab the back of his tunic as he points beneath my bed. I don't want to tell him about the horseshoes, for it embarrasses me. Changing the subject, I suggest, "You ought to have some water."

"Water is good," Travin agrees. "Is wine supposed to taste so objectionable?"

"If it is fermented," I remind him. "Have some water. I don't want to have to take care of you."

A dopey smile spreads across face. "Am I out of hand?"

"Nay, just tempting the laws of propriety."

A mixture of apprehension and perplexity cover his face before washing away. I'd meant it to be funny, but I'd forgotten how seriously he takes his honor.

"I shall cease my unseemliness, but my soul mourns," he says, helping himself to a drink of water from a vase beside my bed. His eyes graze around the room. "You wouldn't take care of me?"

I almost answer with another joke when I'm abruptly reminded of Bronwynn.

"Where, uh, is Bronwynn?" I ask tentatively, unsure of meddling in their affairs uninvited.

"Oh, she's met some new friend," Travin answers. "Arabella, or something. They work together as seamstresses. Bronwynn wanted to be with her tonight and didn't seem to mind if I spent time with Rebby. Strange, right?"

"Except you're not with Rebby. Anymore."

"I know, but . . . " Travin stops to judge his words. "I need this tonight. I want to remember what it felt like at home."

I decide to leave Bronwynn's misdeeds out of this happy moment. "Me, too."

"This is nice," he adds, nudging his shoulder into mine. "We haven't done this in a while."

"I know. Don't you think Rebby should be back by now?"

Travin makes a sound of lacking interest. "Meh, I'm not that hungry anyway."

I stand and make my way to the other end of the room. "Maybe I'll go find him to make sure he's not keeping all the lamb and urchin to himself."

"Nay!" Travin whines. "Stay."

I join him on the bed again, lying opposite him so that his feet are near my head. It is acceptable in my eyes. We've known each other since childhood. A chaperone is not needed. Besides, even in his state of immoderation, Travin is still the saintliest person I know.

"This was a bad idea," he finally says with a burp.

I burst into laughter but cover my mouth when I see he's deathly solemn. His eyes swivel lethargically back and forth. He manages to haphazardly move around on the bed until he's kneeling in the fetal position, his head leaning on my shoulder. I hold a pillow across my face to muffle the laughter I can't seem to repress.

"It is certain!" he blathers. "This is awful. I have sinned. I did not mean to consume so much . . . I just . . . it happened."

He tries to yank the pillow from me, but it only makes me laugh harder. I easily pull it from his grasp.

"Relax, ye doer of evil," I snicker, patting his head. He lies back down at my side, this time draping one arm across his eyes. I see the trace of a smile on his lips. "Try to go to sleep. It will all be over in the morning."

I stare at the ceiling a few minutes before making the mistake of glancing over. Trav remains moribund, using his arm to block out the light. Another unstoppable flow of the giggles creeps its way back into my throat, but I take a deep breath and repeat, "I'm sorry, I'm sorry!" while he smacks my leg weakly. After a few deep breaths, I've gained control of myself.

He grins beneath his arm and murmurs, "You are forgiven." Then, through a yawn, "I must never drink wine again in all my days."

Lucky him.

"Remember that time," he begins, "you and I were scrubbing that horse and she started kicking back, all angered, and knocked the back wall of your clinic down?"

"I do," I smile.

It was before my father died, and he'd asked me to bathe one of his customer's mares. Travin stopped in as he did often and offered to help me. Travin's always been skittish around equine, which added to the comedy. Neither of us knows what we did to make that horse so mad, but she neighed and kicked until there was a huge hole in the back wall of my father's clinic. I don't think Travin ever recovered.

"Officer Gorrow was complaining that his stallion had a braided tail," Travin slyly confesses. "You wouldn't have any idea who would spend such loving time doting on a warhorse, now would you?"

I zip my lips shut.

He tugs a strand of his hair over his shoulder. "Remember when you tried to braid *mine*?"

I toy with his tresses. "I still could."

"And . . . and remember that time," Trav pauses to laugh so hard no sound comes out, "when we went swimming—in the—Salt

Sea? We decided our underclothes wouldn't be necessary since it was nighttime. I let you go in first and then followed after you. While we were down there, a windstorm came through and blew our clothes away. Has it already been a few years since then?"

"I believe so."

"You made me get out first and find you something to cover yourself with. I'll never forget the look on your face when I held up that rag I found. I only had my hand to shield myself with!"

"I covered my eyes!" I retort.

"So did I," Travin whispers, and then he grins much too indecently.

"You little . . ." I grab his arm off his face and shake it.

His head tilts back and laughs hard this time, the kind of laugh from deep in his gut that only a stone gargoyle could resist.

"I'm telling Joshua," I murmur.

"I dare you."

I fall onto my back, covering my face with the pillow again. It drowns out at least most of his laughing. But he pulls the pillow aside, still eying me with that smug look. Shifting his position, he lies on his side, facing me. His eyes close with another yawn. The curls around his hairline are matted—in a good way—and his bronzed cheeks showcase a week's worth of beard. The mature veneer becomes him.

"Trav?" I ask gently, in case he's fallen asleep.

"Hm?"

"What is it like to be in love?"

"I don't know," he slurs. Dragging his eyes open perhaps a quarter of an inch, he grins and says drowsily, "I mean, it's good. It's a happy thing."

"Such a Travin answer," I tease. "Very descriptive."

He only smirks, closing his gray eyes again.

"Trav?"

"Hm?"

"Are you scared to meet the Canaanites?"

"I am."

"Trav?"

"Kaya?" he replies more monotonously as his mind begins to drift away.

"Do you think I'm a crazy person?"

"A little." The corner of his mouth turns up, creating brackets around his lips. "You were hard to approach when I first met you. Sometimes, you know, you're like a porcupine. And you're a little prickly, but that's a good thing."

"Isn't that the *same* thing?"

"You've grown."

"Trav?"

"Hm?" he half snores.

"I'm really, really sorry about Maleah."

His eyes are closed, his lips slightly parted as he breathes a slow, rhythmic sound. Then, he suddenly reaches his left hand out. Grinning, I grab hold of his fingers with my own and direct them safely between us.

"God has a plan for all of us," he murmurs, fingers closing tightly around mine.

"How do you know there's a God?"

Travin is silent a moment, before replying with absolute clarity, "Because he just answered my prayer."

A chrysalis in my tummy ripens.

Several minutes pass with me hoping he will speak again.

"You know," he says softly, "I have one memory of my father, and one memory only."

Travin has spoken of his father as much as I've spoken about my mother. Never. I don't dare to move. I hold my breath, listening intently as he opens a secret chamber of memories.

"Maleah was so tiny, and so precious, and I just kept thinking, *'How could he want to hurt her?'* Father didn't want the second baby. I know he was going to kill her. If Mother hadn't stepped in his path, *I* would have. Mother did it to protect us both. But then she was lying on the floor so bruised, and Father came after me anyway. When it was over, he fell down and didn't get up. He'd had too much wine.

"I remember Maleah screaming, but she was alive. Mother was alive, too, but she would not come out of her room. When I could move, I went for Maleah. Father lay there for four days until men from the distilleries came looking for him. He owed them money. I remember his stink, wine and rot, when they took him away. Him, and everything of value we owned. Mother barely spoke after that."

I've never held Travin's hand for more than a childish tug-and-pull, but in a moment like this I want to hold more. His palm is calloused and rough. Much bigger than the hand that used to push and shove me around as a kid. His slender fingers have lost all femininity and are now the epitome of a warrior's hand. It almost saddens me. I feel like I've missed so much. Where has time gone?

The dim lights cast shadows along his face, enhancing his features the slope of his jaw, the curve of his lips. A lock of sandy hair flops down his forehead. I sneakily tuck it back. There's still youth in him, but he's developed so much, from the child that was bullied, to this warrior that is magnificent. He hasn't let his past, or pains, slow him down. It's difficult to visualize him out in the middle of a war, shedding blood and ending lives. I would never want him to get hurt.

"Trav?"

"Hm?"

"Are you afraid to be alone?"

He doesn't answer. His mouth hangs farther open. A gritty sound vibrates in the back of his throat, and he clamps his lips shut while wriggling involuntarily deeper into the pillow.

"I am," I whisper back.

I get up as carefully as possible, releasing Travin's flaccid fingers one by one, and loosely fasten the tent tarps. Silently, I remove my sandals. I grab a blanket to cover Travin, returning to the bed. For just a second longer, I stand staring down at him. *How could you not adore him?*

Inching my way onto the bed, I gently lie back down, watching him sleeping there so peacefully.

And then, catching me entirely off guard, he whispers, "Don't be."

I close my eyes and immediately drift asleep.

WESTIN

Mine Eyes See

MIKI ROX'S EYES MEET mine from across the ring. Officers Orren and Charkish are inside the combat station, instructing two soldiers on fighting hand-to-hand.

I know why Joshua runs these drills. Each regulated fight is for practice, and so the officers can observe us. They gauge where our skills are strongest and where we need to improve. The soldiers are to learn to feel no pain, to act on instinct, and to triumph no matter their afflictions. It is why the Israelites are unequaled on the battlefield.

There is no fair paring when it comes to the combat simulations. Sometimes one's contender is larger and faster, stronger and wiser. Sometimes one must fight against his friend. Sometimes they blindfold one, requiring him to learn to listen keenly. Sometimes they restrain one of a soldier's arms, or tie a weight to one of his ankles. Today, the competitors are female. I learn something more important than weaponry and tactical violence watching them engage. Women may never have the amount of physical strength a man does, but they are matchless in dauntlessness.

A woman with a goal is to be feared above the devil.

KAYA

La La La La La

THE SUN SHINING THROUGH the tiny window flutters across my face, awakening me. Blinking rapidly, I yawn away my sleepy disorientation. *Husky breathing.* Not Mikyla's. The memory of last night seeps back into my conscious as I become fully awake. I sharpen my vision with some thorough eye-rubbing and stare across the bed.

Travin Samuli Shelomo is snoozing soundly beside me, in the same position he fell asleep in. He's absolutely dormant. On the other side of the room, Mikyla's vacant bed swears us to secrecy. Without making a sound, I shift enough to look into Trav's face. The thin skin of his eyelids is tinged a pale, pale blue. The curls around his hairline lie adorably unkempt above them. His lips are agape. I almost giggle.

In the quiet light of morning, I study the changes in him. Trav has always been lean, but his adult form is hardened by diligent work. He's definitely more muscular, barely covered at all by my scanty blanket. His face has browned from being out in the sun so much. The stubble on his chin is paler, blending into the bristles at his sideburns. A subtle line carves its way across his forehead, the line that wrinkles when he's frustrated or mad. Right now, it's hardly noticeable.

His face looks so . . . soft.

Silently, I creep off the bed. Travin mumbles something incoherently and instantaneously sprawls across the mattress. Smiling to myself, I change my clothes. I place the water vase beside him and close the tarps on my way out.

It's a beautiful *day.*

Several birds dance across the brilliant blue sky, singing their morning chorus. I watch them, overcome with a decided urge to do something close to twirling. As I roam the walkways, I follow the scent of breakfast toward the center of camp. Food sounds great right now. Which reminds me—I wonder why Rebby never came back with supper last night.

When I reach the brick fire pit, I scour the surroundings for Mikyla. I'm sure the story of her whereabouts last night is juicier than the meal I'll be provided with. Over at one of the tables, I see the Bottker twins. They wave at me excitedly.

"Good morning!" I exclaim, joining them.

"Someone's in a good mood," Gring grins.

For a brief second, it seems he knows of my sleepover with Trav. Butterflies escape the chrysalis inside me, but I shoo them away. It isn't the first time we've slept side by side. Many evenings at Lucan Care, Travin would enter to find me asleep in the straw. Sometimes he would carry me home, to ease my intoxication. Other times he would spend the night on the floor with me.

"Catch!" Gring tosses me a roll of bread. "What is the meaning of your smile?"

"Can a girl smile without a meaning?" I tease.

He blushes, but replies with poise, "Each and every day."

That smile mutates the moment I see Mikyla. Bronwynn is with her. They're chatting. Real, amiable chatting. I know they both work as seamstresses, but I didn't know they'd become so . . . acquainted. I excuse myself from the twins and meet the two girls near the stove.

"Hello," I direct toward Mikyla. I try to give her a look that demands an explanation as to why she's accompanying the one person I hate almost more than her brother.

"Kaya!" Mikyla smiles and gives me a hug. "Guess who I ran into on my way down here?"

"I was just on my way back from bathing in the stream," Bronwynn declares caustically, without actually looking at me. "Mikyla invited me to eat with her."

The two of them exchange a friendly expression that makes me feel like I'm eating toenails for breakfast.

Mikyla continues, saying something that Bronwynn finds funny. Bronwynn cackles. I swallow the toenails. Bronwynn asks for a second helping of bread and then complains to the cook when she doesn't get enough. It's no wonder Bronwynn's gaining weight. Subtle weight, but I see it in her cheeks, beneath her chin, and around her waist like a spare wheel.

"By the way, have you seen Travin?" Bronwynn twists around, and I avert my judgmental assessment. "He's supposed to leave today for Joshua's medical evaluation."

"I haven't seen him," Mikyla answers. "Have you, Kaya?"

"Nay."

"That's strange," Bronwynn sighs. "I checked Travin's tent this morning, and he wasn't there."

The memory of Travin asleep on my bed flits through my mind. The stories we shared last night. His confession about his father. Then a viridian awareness that Bronwynn is welcome inside Travin's tent, which isn't even close to the stream.

"I thought you were on your way here from bathing when you ran into Mikyla," I point out.

"I was," Bronwynn replies smoothly, still not meeting my gaze.

"But you checked Travin's tent this morning, and he wasn't there? The men's lodging is clear on the other side of camp. And the stream is over there."

"And?" she counters defensively. "I walked over there to see if he was awake so we could be together before he departs. He has an ache in his shoulder, and I've been massaging it for him. I purchased some olive oil and planned to work on his tight muscles." She shares a wink with Mikyla. "He loves it when I do that. His eyes roll back in his head—"

I cough up a toenail.

"I hoped to find him in his tent," Bronwynn continues. "When he wasn't there, I went to bathe, and then met Mikyla on my way here."

"That's a lot of walking," I mutter, without adding, *for someone who is gaining weight.*

If she speaks honestly, she would've had to be awake before sunrise, and I highly suspect she does anything honest.

"Why do you care?" Mikyla glowers. It devitalizes her beauty. "Bronwynn can walk wherever she wants to walk."

"It is well." Bronwynn turns her vinegary remarks on me. "Kaya's just jealous that she has no one looking for *her*."

"News flash," I bark back, "I had parental supervision when it was needed. So did Travin. We don't need petty micro-managers as mature adults. We all have our agency."

I'm proud for reciting that last comment and *meaning* it. It's true, the Israelites allow us to use agency in discerning their laws. We're adults *and* soldiers. The effect of reminding Bon-won how exasperating her unnecessary superintending of Travin is satisfies me. Her mouth opens in shock, but it's Mikyla who comes to her aid.

"Kaya's just in a bad mood," Mikyla says dismissively. It isn't the first time she has acted like a Rox, but when she takes Bronwynn's arm in hers, it is the first time she lands on my list of hated people. With a flip of her long hair, she states, "You always get like this, Kaya."

"Me?" I sputter.

"Every time I fall in love first, you just hate it."

"*Love?*"

"We understand," Bronwynn smiles acerbically. She meets my gaze finally, and I feel a stab of evil. "Summer must be dreadful when you're not in love, and have no family, but even worse in a time like *this*. I have Travin, and Mikyla has Jac. When we inherit these lands, we're going to be married. *You* have no one."

I try to claw my way out of this stupefaction and say something back, or plant my fist in her idiotic reproductive organs. To my misfortune, I remain stupefied.

"You must know," Bronwynn continues, her eyes skewering mine. "You did this to yourself."

"Come," Mikyla says to her. They begin to walk away. "Let us find peace lest our moods be ruined like Kaya's."

I watch them leave as my face simmers hot with rage. There's so much more I could say to Bronwynn, so many things built up that I could scramble together with a bundle of bad words and stir into her breakfast, but the two of them are gone and the opportunity lost.

Mikyla's relationship with the prosperous Jac has exaggerated her haughtiness, something I could overlook, but her newfound friendship with Bronwynn insults me.

In a fury, I tramp back toward my tent, kicking through the entrance, forgetting I had an overnight visitor. But Travin has already left.

I throw the tarps shut behind me and uncover my wine bottle, carrying it to my bed where, sitting on my carefully folded blanket, rests one of my horseshoes.

WESTIN

Incentive

EVERY SOLDIER IS TO be circumcised. After the Israelites have ensured the downfall of Og, the medicus will remove the foreskin of all immigrant recruits. Joshua has ordered his men to sharpen their knives. The medicus and his employees use shards of bone to chisel flint into blades. But this will not happen until after we conquer all of Bashan. Thankfully, today, we will just be evaluated for health purposes.

The infirmary has become increasingly full from a widespread contamination of the disease. Many are afraid of even going near those afflicted. This outbreak struck an entire quadrant of Shittim last week. Some have already passed away. The medicus has been ordered by Joshua to have each soldier thoroughly inspected. Every officer will take the men of his unit to be assessed. After which, the soldiers are to visit the priests and confess of any sins, for this is why, according to Joshua, we have been smitten with the plague.

Orren orders his company of soldiers to line up and, one by one, we enter the tent where the medicus awaits. Orderly, faithfully, each man is examined. When my turn comes, I enter to find the medicus seated near a table of tools and implements. Standing over him, Orren regards me with contempt. It is the way he regards any soldier who does not idolize him like they would Joshua. A fantasy, Orren believes he can outrank the general, be placed upon a pedestal by the lower-standing soldiers, and revered. But *Joshua* does not indulge in harlots and gambling and personal gain.

My officer orders me to undress, which I do. The evaluation is painless and results in the removal of one bad tooth in the back of my mouth.

"Good news," the medicus states. "You're not infected with the disease."

When the medicus is finished, Orren asks the man to fetch a pail of clean water. I follow the medicus to the exit when Orren stops me.

"I have a task for you."

Rubbing my jaw, I turn and await some assignment customized by his direct and personal ridicule.

Instead, Orren lowers his voice and states, "I want you to collect some information for me from a few of the officers."

"What kind of information?"

"Joshua has thus far appointed Lachlan and Gorrow to second in command beneath Jair and Nobah. They have access to maps and war plans."

"And you don't?"

He smirks. "I believe I have a few more battlefronts to see before Joshua will consider me a val-ua-ble ass-et." He annunciates disdainfully. "Rather, he relies on my unit to be the clean up squad. Is that what you want to be? The clean up squad? I would think not, seeing how you display emotion when having to pick up after incapable soldiers."

He pauses, letting that sink in.

"Joshua sees our company as the clean up squad. But . . . if the odds are in my favor, I can turn things around—for both of us. If I knew where our enemies were located, if I knew what Joshua's spies know about possible Canaanite attacks on us, and how he plans to react, I could finagle the circumstances to allow me *and* my men to prove their validity."

"Look, politics aren't my thing."

It's a half-truth.

"Many of the officers and their spies congregate in the Violet Room. If you become a regular attendee, you can ascertain the information I seek."

"Why would an officer reveal private information to me?" I question.

"They wouldn't," he replies. "But they often . . . over-share with the hired company."

I balk. "You want me to do your dirty work?"

Orren's right shoulder lifts toward his chin.

"I'm not a spy."

"Joshua calls plenty of Israelite spies," he argues. "Why shouldn't I be allowed to do the same?"

"Nay," I reply. "If you're on some mission to feed your arrogant soul, you're on your own."

Danger winks at me from the mirthless smile on my officer's face. "You cannot refuse your superior's order, you know."

"Maybe I'll just turn you in to Joshua," I bite back, losing some of my nerve.

He barks a laugh. "Are you threatening me with exhortation?"

"I'll . . . expose you."

"With what?"

I swallow.

"Tell me, Westin. Would you rather dig trenches the rest of your military life?"

I don't immediately respond. He withdraws a handful of precious rubies from his robes, juggling them in one palm.

"It's your word against mine," Orren remarks, just as the medicus returns. He plasters an expression of comradeship on his face. "Think about it. There are plenty of ways for a man like you to improve his rank."

I blow past the medicus, wondering what kind of man Orren thinks I am. Improving my rank would be desirous, but I am not interested in some defamatory ploy. Rubies will hold little value in court if I am caught tampering with the Violet Room's contributors. Surely, Orren will not require this of me. *What if I say no?* Then again, *what if I say yes?* I could profit in more than one way. If exposed, I could convince someone I was acting under my officer's order, but I would need sufficient proof. Orren would be demoted, I would be a richer man, and I would know priceless information concerning the Israelites strategies.

That night, I listen to many of the soldiers talk of God and the mouth of His servants.

"Twenty-four thousand have already passed on," one soldier states with apprehension. "We have given in to sin by toying with pagan gods and Midianite women."

"No one actually worships Baal de Peor," his friend retaliates. "The Canaanite shrine inside the Violet Room is a charade."

"But the harlotry isn't," I jab, having heard plenty of details about the activities happening in that establishment. Miki Rox is often seduced by immorality. It's his favorite topic of conversation outside of political exploitation. Perhaps the two are interlinked.

Joshua has preached of commandments, laws the Israelites must abide by. We are told it is a mandate for the men of Israel to be circumcised and promised that if we are obedient to God, rich blessings will pour down upon us. No sickness will plague our armies. Every battle will be won by the hand of the Lord. The lands we inherit will be sufficient and bountiful.

Blessings, health, and inheritance are incentive to do what I'm told, but so is bringing down the diplomatically wayward of Joshua's men. Revealing Orren's motives will benefit my accommodations within the army, but destroying Miki Rox will help me gain favor with Kaya Lucan. Fortunately, using my power of speech and all manner of flattery, I know how I can achieve both.

KAYA

When I Do Not Moderate My Moderation

I WAKE UP WITH my head and right arm dangling off the side of my bed. The wine bottle now lies tipped on its side on the floor, clearly empty, and there's a single sandal that doesn't belong to either Mikyla or myself beside it. Squinting against my headache, my mind retracts to its most recent memory. Bronwynn and her beady eyes. Mikyla and her scornful frown.

Holding my head, I make my way to the exit and thrust the tarps open. It's still daylight. And noisy. Streams of smoke slither up into the air, penetrating the lake-water sky. To my right, a rather overweight group of soldiers are gathered around an even larger female brewer, who is stirring her cauldron proudly. A pair of goats jingles nearby and I groan. Tildeh is going to be angry I flaked out on my duties.

I take a few steps outside. A brigade of men carrying their gear through camp is heading in my direction. Toward the center of them, I spot Westin.

My headache increases instantly.

When Westin sees me, he breaks free from the group to run and gather me in his arms. It is slightly inappropriate, but the appreciative rumble of his throat makes me grin.

"Good morning," he states cheerfully. He fluffs my nocturnal hair. "You are as beautiful as the sunrise."

He's lying. I look like cow pie. Speaking of cow pie, I'd better get to the stables.

Wait.

"Morning?" I inquire.

I have already been up once this morning.

Westin gazes at the sky then back to me. His black hair glistens under the sun, his blue eyes lucent. He blasts me with that fabulous smile. "I have all day free."

"Did you come home early?" I ask, confused.

"Kaya, it's been three days. I told you I'd be gone for three days. Were you hoping I'd be gone longer?"

"Nay." I force a smile. *It has been three days?* "I'm happy you're back."

Westin picks up his bags and follows me back inside my tent. "I see you enjoyed my present," he comments, nodding to the empty bottle at the side of my bed.

I did not enjoy anything. I could *not* feel more miserable. I feel as if hate has consumed every part of me. Oblivious to my unrest, Westin drops his pack and approaches me from behind, wrapping his arms around my waist. It is both unusually and portentously affectionate.

"Are you alright?" he asks.

"Fine," I lie. "Just a little tired."

I sit on the edge of my bed, and all I can think about is the other warm body that had last lain here.

Westin excuses himself temporarily to bring back enough food to last us until supper. He's free *all* day. *Isn't that splendid?* If I've missed three days of work, what's another one?

You did this to yourself, Bronwynn's voice smites me.

Did what? I stubbornly argue.

When Westin returns, he smiles, beautifully, and I ask myself if summer *would* be better if we were in love. Would life be better?

"Brought you the good stuff," he declares, handing me a bowl of stew and manna. From his back pocket, he reveals a slightly smashed flower. "For you."

I crook a grin, against my best efforts.

We sit on the floor with our backs against my bed and eat in silence. It's about as romantic as two lamas mating. At least the stew tastes fresher than it has the past few weeks. The officers send out scouts to nearby villages and farms. They map out the surroundings but also return with fresh fruits and vegetables, ore, and other materials. The meal sits well in my stomach, probably soaking up the surfeit wine. When I'm finished, I rest my head back and sigh. I can't do this anymore.

Is it impossible for me to exert the same discipline as Trav?

"Are you sure you're alright?" Westin finally asks, finishing his last bite of bread.

"I don't know," I answer truthfully. A part of me wants to be by myself, but when I'm by myself I feel claustrophobic and lonely. It doesn't make sense. I reply, "I feel a little off."

"What can I do to make you feel better?"

"I don't know," I grumble.

"I do," he answers slyly.

His eyes are like snowflakes, glistening against his dark hair. He lifts one of my smaller hands into his tanned one, sandwiching my palm between his.

"My Kaya," he whispers, kissing a fingertip. "Having your hand to hold is a greater blessing than being allotted an entire kingdom."

I smile, taking pleasure in the fluttering of my stomach.

But behold, I make unwise decisions this night. I allow Westin to kiss me until I become uncomfortable. The interaction causes a vision of Miki Rox to appear before my eyes.

"Cease!" I shout, shoving Westin away from me.

Lips plump and out of breath, he retreats to the opposite side of the room. His voice has an edge of defensiveness. "*You* wanted this, too."

I press my thumb to my forehead, closing my eyes. That's exactly what Miki said. All men are the same. I hate them!

"Just go," I mumble.

"You're joking, right?"

"Go!"

He leaves, churlish, and I feel even angrier than before. My hatred for myself intensifies. It is such that I wonder if Bronwynn was right about me.

TRAVIN

What It Means to Be a Shelomo

"WHAT'S THAT LOOK FOR?"

"Huh?"

"You're giving her the death look," Rebby states, nodding toward Kaya.

She's leaving the barn, her shift having ended. A twig of straw dangles from the back of her braid, and she has animal dung smeared on her robe.

Earlier today, two of the Israelite officers and several soldiers returned to camp with prisoners they'd captured in the mountains. Identified as Canaanites, the young men were marched through our camp like a cluster of bulls heading to a slaughterhouse. The convicts were impaled and then taken out to a mountaintop, where they were left to die a slow, agonizing death. That wasn't even the worst of it.

I noticed Kaya watching from the pasture, where Officer Carac and Officer Azsh put an end to the enemies' horses. She stood there, frozen, both hands clasped over her mouth. She remained there long after, before disappearing into the barn. She has not emerged once, until now.

I would know, because I've busied myself at the refinery station across from it and waited, all day, memories of Maleah flashing through my mind. It is torturous for Kaya to witness such violence, like unto my younger sister being a bystander to the beatings I would take in her place. But it is exceedingly more painful for Kaya to watch the death of a precious mare.

Rebby clears his throat, reminding me of his presence.

"I don't know why she chose to be here," I declare, and I hide my perplexity over a saw.

Rebby runs a hand through his thick, coiffed hair. I'm not sure whether he does this out of habit, or because he finds himself particularly attractive with tousled tresses. "She's actually the best stable maid here. I heard Tildeh say it."

"You heard *Tildeh* say it?"

"Well, one of Tildeh's . . . younger . . . more svelte . . . assistants."

"That's what I thought." I suppress a roll of my eyes and murmur to myself, "Women do not belong in a war."

Rebby's lips quirk. "Don't say that around the feminists."

"Kaya is *not* a soldier. She seldom manages to stay on her own two feet, let alone live out here, in *this*. She should be safe somewhere, making a new home. Not here at camp."

"She'd miss me," he states confidently.

I drive my left fist toward his arm. He dodges it.

"Kaya will be fine, Trav. She has us to look out for her. And Westin."

My eyebrow touches the clouds.

"He's not bad, you know." Rebby fans his face as if scooping the aroma of his dinner plate towards his nose. "He has a sort of—rugged bravado."

"Thanks. I'll log that away someplace useful."

"I went to his second combat simulation. He almost won. If it makes you feel better, I think Kaya would be a very difficult hostage," Rebby chuckles. "Canaan would send her right back, and then some."

I cut a glare at him, ambling over to a stockpile of glaives. He follows.

"*And*," he continues, leaning an elbow onto a barrel, "I'm glad there are so many women here. It gives me variety."

Yay, Rebby forgets about the rules.

I wipe the sweat off my brow with my forearm. We pass the hour mending weapons, the heat of the day rising on our backs. Without a tunic, my knife is exposed in my belt. It gladdens me I no longer have to hide it. Father Lucan gave it to me. My first knife. He did not always agree with the way the Roxes governed Avoca. He was a mild man of passive nature, but he still believed in the tradition of giving a son a knife.

It happened, one day, during my formative years. A few rebellious teens followed me after working late at Lucan Care. With a dislocated shoulder and bloodied face, I returned the following day. Father Lucan was legitimately worried about me. Which gave me legitimate reason to be worried about myself. Would I *ever* grow out of the Shelomo shadow?

I take my knife from its sheath and turn it over in my fingers. I can remember every detail of Father Lucan's face when he bestowed upon me this finely crafted weapon. He held myrrh to my swollen lip with one hand and extended the knife with the other. My heart soared with gratitude. Then plummeted with mortification.

Despite how easily the veteran soldiers here have accepted me, it is hard to forget old times.

With a final twirl, I shove the knife back into my belt.

Picking up a weapon's harness, Rebby begins polishing the thick leather, whistling a tune. I smirk at him and offer a sarcastic statement about his promiscuity under my breath.

He scolds me, "That was inappropriate."

"I'll repent."

"Travin?"

I turn my head to see Bronwynn approaching. She has our afternoon meal in her hands.

Rebby and I look at each other. He subtly lifts his right hand, palm flat, with the pinky tucked in. The silent signal for *danger ahead.* I smile and give the same gesture in return, extending my left thumb skyward. *Destroy the danger ahead.*

"If you're just going to pretend I'm not here, I'll go hiking with Arabella," Bronwynn is speaking. "We don't have any more work for the rest of the day. I figured I'd be polite and spend it with you. You know, Travin, you've been really distant lately, and it grieves me."

Unconsciously, my left hand forms the silent signal. *Torture.*

Rebby snorts a laugh.

"Here," she states, handing me my share. "Don't use your hands! They're filthy. Use this."

She gives me a spoon. Rebby mimics her behind her back.

"Are you ready for the fight tonight?" she asks, mouth full.

When she finishes her portion, she sticks her spoon into my bowl.

"It's not like they're going to try to kill each other," Rebby replies. "It's just for practice."

Even though I know it is just training, I still have a troubled feeling in my stomach.

"You don't want to lose, though," Bronwynn speaks between mouthfuls. "That would be embarrassing."

"Not really," I counter, looking down at my feet. "I saw the man who lost yesterday, and he wasn't feeling too bad. He was glad Charkish gave him corrective criticism. How else are we supposed to learn, to know where we are strongest or weakest? I'm exceedingly new. I'll probably lose."

"I know," she balks. "That's what worries me."

"You'll do fine," Rebby remarks, ignoring Bronwynn. "Let's go practice together."

Bronwynn reaches out and snatches my hand. Her eyes narrow obsessively and then soften. "Oh, you really do need the practice. I'll be with Arabella today. See you tonight, at the fight?"

Without a response, I nod. Rebby has an incredulous look on his face, clearly as perturbed as I am. When Bronwynn's back is turned, he gives the silent signal, *venom*.

We make the long walk out to the training stations. A session of weapons handling has begun with Dank and Tabor's units. The Bottker twins are amongst them, speaking in unison, the way they always do. One of them is paired with Rionn, a soldier who has bounced between units as each officer has a struggle enduring him. A devout follower of Joshua, Rionn reminds me a lot of my adolescent self. The more I've been around him, however, the more I realize it isn't a name he is trying to elude, but a disability. His mind does not work the way a grown man's should. This mental infirmity is terminal.

Rebby and I move to the far end to keep out of the way.

"Are you ready to show everyone what you've been practicing since your youth?" Rebby asks. His tan pectorals are damp with sweat, his auburn hair held back with a leather strap.

"I do not feel ready," I sigh.

"Your mother would roll over in her grave," Rebby replies.

I try not to take it personally. "Yay, she would disapprove."

"She would whip me for encouraging you."

"You *did* encourage me."

"I'm gonna make you eat your teeth, you know." He smiles a gap-mouthed grin, circling and thrusting a roundhouse toward my face. He's always been the better fighter. Contending one another, we will have to adjust to each other's strong arms. He is right-handed. I am left.

Dodging his heel, I grin. "There's a first time for everything."

"Think of it this way," he hops left and positions himself for a joust, "and you won't feel so bad tonight. See? Pain of failure is only severe the first time you experience it. After that, you'll look forward to it. Nobody expects anything from a failure."

"Is that what you tell all your disappointed lady friends?" I jeer.

"Are you so sure they're disappointed?" Rebby wiggles his fingers in the air and smirks. "I can test my *failures* on Bronwynn, if you'd like."

"Ah. Please do."

He guffaws. "Are you kidding? I'd rather court you."

"That's not the first time you've offered to court me."

"It isn't?" he scratches his head with a finger. "Well, then. You see? There's some wisdom in this brain, after all."

I tap my temple with a finger. "From my good friend and his river of wisdom."

"Care for a swim?"

"Can't," I reply, lifting my hand to my chest in a reflection of apology. "I'm afraid I'd drown in your sense of self-worth."

"I know a few people who could resuscitate you," Rebby states, lifting both fists up to his jaw. He punches the air on the sides of my ears.

"You mean, you wouldn't be willing yourself?" I state, slapping one of his wrists speedily.

"Kiss a man?" Rebby shrugs. "There's a first time for everything."

"I find it absolutely expedient, if you are planning to court me."

He slaps me back, raising his eyebrows. *Are we going to fight, or what?*

"Don't go easy," I mutter wryly.

"I never do, dearest," he laughs and punches me in the face.

KAYA

The Milk Maid

I FINISH MILKING THE cows and carry the pails to Tildeh. She distributes the fresh milk into jugs. The women from the bazaar retrieve them after dropping off our noonday meal. Through the open barn door, I hear a harem walk by. I am not an expert on their language yet, but I can tell they are talking about their substantial earnings. Miki Rox strides across the threshold, first noticing the passing girls, then noticing me.

"Hey, your hands dirty," he calls, a guileful smirk on his face.

I glance down at my hands, tinged white from dairy. Dirt rings my fingernails and manure is smudged on my wrists. But I know that's not what he's referring to.

Benjamin, the sheep, bawls as Miki kicks it aside. I glare at his back until the voice of Officer Jair grabs my attention. The man is hardly ever seen. He's speaking to Nobah, an equally enigmatic lieutenant who is often with Joshua in the Tent of Meetings. They pass from one walkway to the other.

"Did you offer them terms of peace?" Jair questions.

"Accordingly," Nobah replies as they turn a corner, "they denied it."

Rinsing my hands in the water trough, I catch a glimpse of my reflection. My father's eyes stare back at me.

Avoca had peace all wrong. Peace comes from within. But just in case, I decide to join the next Israelite directive on weapon's handling.

I'd rather lift a sword than my simlah.

TRAVIN

The Tortoise Leaves the Shell

THE FIGHTING STATION IS the furthest structure behind the barnyard. Gorrow, officer of our unit, stands near one corner of the dirt square. Many of the officers are present, including Lachlan and Orren. They've lit torches around the area to give light to the spectacle. Slowly, more and more people have filtered out of their barracks to attend.

It seems larger than the simulated matches I've attended, but that might just be because I'm nervous. Staring down at my fingers, I clench them into fists and release them with a whoosh of breath. My knuckles are a little scabbed from my bout with Rebby. All my instructions in fighting an opponent hand to hand run rampant through my mind. How to block a punch, keep your hands up and stance firm but agile. Jab, straight right, right cross.

Gorrow gives the signal, blowing a whistle. It is followed by a collective round of spectator murmuring. My opponent enters the fighting square. And he is huge. His long hair is held back by a rope, the sides of his head shaved. The muscles on either side of his head have replaced his neck. The muscles of his bare chest and stomach create deep canyons of flesh. The muscles of his *muscles* are thick as oxen.

I feel myself shrinking with each step as he approaches, until I am the mouse and he the elephant. He stops before me in the middle of the fighting ring, in front of all these people, his mouth twisting into a smile.

"You. Travin?" he asks in his native dialect.

"Yay."

"Luko," he announces with a grating voice. He thumps his fist on his naked chest.

Any and all optimism for an evenly matched spar drops to the pit of my stomach. Bronwynn's hope of me not failing flutters through my head, that and a fleeting image of Rebby disinclined to "resuscitate" me.

"Be true and be well," Luko states encouragingly.

I nod. "Be well."

Gorrow blows the whistle to commence, and the audience hushes their wagering. Peering over at the crowd, I see Rebby and Bronwynn. The expression on both of their faces makes me gulp hard. They know it, too.

"Behold," Gorrow calls. "These two men will assist one another in strengthening their intelligence as soldiers. No biting and no hitting in the groin. Raise both hands in the air to forfeit. You may begin."

The torch light dances across Luko's features as he begins to circle me. I mimic his actions, holding his gaze. He doesn't seem like the type who'd wail on a man a third his size and take pleasure it. But that doesn't mean he isn't going to batter me to mulch.

Keeping my hands in front of my face, I open with a *one-two jab, cross*, jabbing toward his face. Luko's head bobs from left to right. His massive hand with hairy knuckles flies toward my face, making contact. *Jab, cross, hook, cross.* His precision causes me to stumble sideways seeing black spots.

He's right-handed. I quickly alter my plan of attack.

The multitude claps. Refusing to make eye contact with Bronwynn, I instead shoot a glance toward Rebby. He holds up a congratulatory gesture.

"Right," I mumble under my breath, rolling my eyes at him. "Focus."

Stepping vigilantly, I advance toward Luko again. I fake a jab with my left fist. He moves swiftly to block, and I cross right, hitting him in the temple. His robust body hardly flinches. We loop around for another minute or so, while I try to think of more combinations. The audience grows impatient, scuffing feet and shouting. I remind myself that this is just for practice, and I shouldn't be afraid to get hurt. This is an experience I need, or I'll never get better. Besides, I can always surrender if he's about to knock me out.

The pain of failure is only severe the first time you experience it.

Luko jabs right, followed by a left uppercut. I elude the first, but the second knocks me in the chin, harder than before. The ache jostles my vision, spreading up through my jaw. All of the punches I took as a kid surface in my memory. I have experienced failure before. This is not as severe.

I spit blood out to the side and try to react quickly. *Go for the body.* To disrupt Luko's rhythm, I throw fast punches, moving up and down, causing him to work double-time on defense. When I have a clear shot of his face, I put full power into the hit. My knuckles crack on impact.

This time, he staggers from the contact.

The viewers holler instigating remarks. But Luko comes at me with more determination, swinging a right cross. I intercept his hit with a left jab straight to his head, making sure to hold my left shoulder high to protect my face. More soldiers clap in approval. Then Luko is wrapped around my waist, hoisting me upward, slamming me into the dirt. We scuffle like this a moment, my smaller size benefiting me as I weasel away.

On my feet, I circle him, each of us acting as if we won't engage. Swiftly, Luko charges at me by stepping with his left foot to the outside of my right foot. He throws two wide right crosses, followed by a right hook to my body. The power behind the last punch cripples me to my knees. A searing pain perforates my ribs. Contrary to the golden rule not to show pain, I grimace.

The crowd cheers as Luko steps back, allowing me to find my breath. I wipe the back of my hand across my mouth, staining my skin red. Blood, but not teeth. That is good.

Gradually, I find my footing. Rebby whoops positively from the sidelines. He's smiling like an imp at me. I challenge him to do better. Turning back to my rival, I face a sudden comprehension. Luko is panting. He's tired. I'm not nearly as out of breath as he. I still have much strength in me.

Rolling my shoulders, I start to ring around him once more. He fakes a jab. I evade it. His massive arm swings out toward my face again, and I duck beneath it, rolling to the ground and coming up behind him. I am the squirrel and he the tree. I punch his left side repeatedly until he doubles over. By now his breath is coming harshly. I speed around in front of him. Without hesitating, I throw an uppercut that catches him under the chin, followed by a right cross.

Luko slumps to his knees, leaning a hand against the ground for support. Someone from the crowd shouts, "Finish him!" I back away a few steps, scanning the audience that stands illuminated in the torchlight. My adrenaline is pumping the blood through my joints, giving me a surge of energy. I can do this. I can keep this up. I can *fly*.

All of a sudden, Luko raises both hands up.

"Cease," he gasps.

His eyes sort of roll into the back of his head.

"What?" I ask bewildered.

"You've done well," Luko declares between deep breaths, stumbling to his feet with unfocused vision. "I am finished."

Gorrow blows the whistle again. "Marvelous!" he calls, and the crowd erupts into applause. "Both of you, very nicely done."

Luko takes my hand and raises it skyward. The roaring of the spectators is deafening. Even though my eyes are swelling, I can see their excited faces. Officer Lachlan claps proudly. He leans over to Charkish and says something. They both nod. My challenger pats me once on the back of my shoulder, before exiting the fighting area. I watch him go, stunned.

I'm still conscious. I'm still standing.

I won.

The congregation deserts the fighting area, some exchanging funds they've wagered. Actual *funds*, not just *chores* that they'd wagered on *me*. Which means people thought I'd win.

The whinny of a horse grasps my attention. Over the heads of the dispersing soldiers I see Joshua, mounted on his steed, a look of fulfillment on his bold features. He nods once and then tugs on his stallion's mane, directing the beast back into camp. My sense of contentment only thickens when I recognize Kaya barreling her way through the disintegrating audience.

She's been here? Watching? Squeezing through the mass of people, she sprints the remaining distance between us with a big grin on her face.

"Trav! That was astonishing!" Kaya reaches a thumb up to my cheek and makes a face. "Aye! How do you feel?"

Westin swaggers up behind her. He's chewing on a stick of grass, looking elsewhere. Casually, he hooks two fingers into Kaya's sash, a subtle, possessive claim. Rebby saunters over a few seconds later, a very self-righteous expression dominating his face. He shoves a substantial bundle of new wealth into his pocket, eyes me up and down and whistles through his teeth.

"You look pretty," he states.

Kaya grins sideways at him. "Half of that is mine."

Rebby nudges her roughly.

They planned on capitalizing off my win? They thought I'd beat Luko?

I gaze down at myself, unsure of how to feel. An ache pulsates through my whole upper body. My ribs are red and puffy. The flesh on my fingers is raw. My head feels like it might burst. I can only imagine how my face looks. And yet, I feel invincible.

"I hate to break it to you," Rebby smiles, "but you've just marked yourself. Joshua was here. He never has time for these matches. If I were you, I would have lain right down and flopped like a dead fish."

"Silence," Kaya commands, elbowing him in the ribcage. "I can't imagine what they must be thinking. What they'll expect from now on."

"That's what I'm saying," Rebby responds tauntingly. He turns to me, award-winningly grave. "Dead fish."

He and Kaya exchange yet more playful punching, which becomes awkward with Westin still attached. After a moment, Rebby gazes at me. His eyes flare with pride.

"What is it like?" he asks.

"I'm still alive, aren't I?" I mumble.

"Not just that," Kaya exclaims, backhanding my fist. "You were good! I've never seen you hurt a soul, Trav. Where did that come from?"

"I've been practicing."

More than she knows.

Rebby and I exchange glances, one that secures our mutual agreement in omission. I am not ready to tell Kaya about my involvement in Avoca's secret combinations.

"Perfection," Rebby states with a slap to my already bruising shoulder. "Simply perfection."

"Keep that up, and *you will be* the dead fish," I reply.

Kaya's eyes glimmer exceptionally green under the moonlight. She glances at my abdomen. Concern mixed with something complicated crosses her face. I'm reminded of the time she laughed uproariously when I almost lost a finger at Lucan Care. Got my stupid hand stuck in a rope trying to tame a stubborn mare. It was one of the largest horses to ever be brought in Avoca, and she insisted I aid her with the *docile* beast.

Docile? So *docile* I thought for sure I'd be scooping up phalanges like sausages. Kaya was laughing so hard, and she was also so worried about me. She'd smiled at me then like she is smiling at me now. How I have missed that smile.

I open my mouth to say something self-deprecating, hopefully funny, when another voice enters our conversation.

"There you are!"

Bronwynn sashays over, bumping into Kaya's shoulder as she throws her arms around me.

"Ouch." I cringe, trying to shift her off of me.

Bronwynn squeals, kissing my cheek. "I can't believe it! That man was enormous, inasmuch as a giant. I thought you'd last two minutes at most."

"I'm not going to lie," Westin interjects. "I thought the same thing."

He drapes his arm around Kaya's neck in that way he does. Kaya shoots him a scolding look, before turning back to me.

"You're . . . strong!" she praises. "And fast. I think you're a natural."

"Thanks," I huff, suddenly weary of the attention. "I really want to go lie down, though. I'll see you later."

Rebby chortles as if he deserves all the credit. "Just remember who taught you everything you know!"

I send him a partially amused smirk. Stiffly, I wiggle out of Bronwynn's grasp, but she rubs a hand across my bare chest to keep me close. Her fingers on my skin spurn my contentment.

"You look so hurt, dearest. Come," she purrs, eyes darting at our friends, "I'll treat you to something *extra* tonight."

It is an insinuation I've never heard from her and one I have no interest in. She pulls at my hand to lead me away, but I linger just long enough to say, "Goodnight, Kaya."

And without a second thought, I wink at her.

KAYA

Bubbles Are Transparent

Rebby lays his opponent out in nine seconds flat.

Am I really surprised he wins all of his combat simulations? Nay.

Several weeks have passed. The Israelites are in constant preparation for the march to Bashan. The men are whittled and refined and
sculpted into the finest warriors I have ever seen. They barely rest
from their drills. Commerce is on the rise, with shipments coming
in and out of Shittim. Traveling merchants sell oil to Egyptians,
which is carried partway by river and the rest of the way by camels.
With the profits, Joshua expands his army's provisions. I've been
charged with sixteen recently purchased warhorses and a sprightly
mule I named Sinai.

Tonight, however, we take a break to celebrate and honor the
Israelite God. I have attended their worship once or twice. I prefer
to attend their celebrations.

As the feast is prepared, I invite Rebby back to my tent so he can
brag about his victory longer than the nine seconds it took him to
prevail. Travin follows, hand linked with Bronwynn's. Jac, Mikyla,
and Westin enter a few minutes later. A flash of annoyance darkens
Westin's handsome face, but it disappears when his eyes meet mine.

"Smile at me and make my worries disappear," he states, tapping
beneath my chin with a knuckle. "Let's go dance."

"Dance?" I question.

"We are celebrating our march to Bashan," Jac answers. "A dance
is a formality."

"Formality?" Travin mutters under his breath, his lip curling in disgust. He is bent over some maps. Bronwynn is bent over him.

Jac leads Mikyla into the steps of a traditional dance. Westin takes my hand, and we do the same. Rebby critiques us from beside Travin.

"Kaya you spend far too much time around animals. You move like a newly born calf."

I laugh, but I do not feel happy.

My heart is overcome by my resentment toward everyone, especially Joshua, for taking me from my home, toward Travin for excelling as a new Israelite soldier, toward Rebby for succeeding at anything he ever wants, toward Mikyla for her new romance, and toward Bronwynn for existing. In an attempt to numb my unhappiness, I consume more wine, but it does not lesson my pain or distort my nightmares. I worry I am ruined.

"You're doing it all wrong, Westin," Rebby says with a roll of his eyes. "Let me."

He replaces Westin in front of me, his dancing worse than my own. Out of the corner of his eye, Travin watches us. Westin paces over to him, discussing several locations on the map. It attracts the interest of Jac. He leaves Mikyla to join the soldiers conversing of spies and warfare.

"You two should do this," I state, swinging Rebby around to dance with Mikyla. I return to sit on my bed.

Jac and Westin burst into laughter.

"What's so funny?" Rebby asks, checking his pheromones. Mikyla shakes her head at him, giving up on dancing to come sit by me. Rebby steps to the other men, gazing at the map of Bashan. "I detect scandal. If you're perpetuating a fraud, I want in."

Westin gives him a cocky grin. "Travin wouldn't partake in any kind of fraud." For the first time, he and Rebby actually jointly agree on the joke. They begin talking about the pathways to Bashan the Israelite spies have been tracking.

"Arabella mentioned that a shipment of clothing and jewelry has arrived," Bronwynn announces. Her hand sweeps across the back of Travin's neck as she strides over to Mikyla. "We can purchase whatever we'd like. Isn't it wonderful?"

She takes Mikyla's hands into hers, solidifying the union of their friendship which I've yet to approve. The females leave to purchase elaborate dress robes and tsamiyd from the shipment. The earrings and bracelets sparkle as they return to the tent. I've spent most of my earnings on the cluster of empty bottles around the room, but I wouldn't want a new robe or jewelry anyway. It is impractical and pretentious.

The men left at the same time, washing and dressing, but they return shortly after Mikyla and Bronwynn, entering with a buoyant waltz. Westin's thick hair is glistening. He's groomed to flawlessness. I admire his choice of a light blue ketonet, finding it marvelous compared to his eyes. He will doubtlessly turn heads this evening. Equally devastating, Rebby has washed his auburn waves and smoothed them back into a rope. His brown tunic matches his brown eyes which twinkle in merriment, his smile catching. Jac is the vision of maturity and affluence, a leather band around his head and tse'adah on his wrists.

They're something to behold, all of them, when not covered in a week's worth of dust and grease. And then I see Travin step into the tent, reluctant. He moves to the corner of the room where he stands, fingers knotted together. Very Travin. He's clean and modestly clothed in an eggshell tunic and patterned ketonet. The chagowr around his waist is new, a gift from the officers because of his victory against Luko. This type of battle girdle is earned, unlike the common ezowr of the recruits. Without his armaments he looks like the Travin from Avoca. His hair is damp, the trademark ringlets forming around his ears and nape. Every few seconds he reaches up and tries to flatten them. He's freshly-shaven, and his velvet cheeks offer a youthful appearance to his new soldier facade. I remember him looking this way as a thirteen-year-old boy. Before puberty. Before he could grow hair anywhere besides the top of his head. He looks good.

Westin presents the group with a full wine bottle. All but Travin partake. I established my bubble when they left to get ready, so I linger toward the back of the room as the others indulge themselves.

Travin weaves over to me, smirking at my attire.

"I noticed you didn't dress up."

I sneer back, "I noticed *you* are going to a dance."

"Are you eager to see me move my hips?" He leans down toward my ear conspiratorially. "Don't get your hopes up."

At that moment, the bottle lands in my hands. I glance up at Westin.

"Here, beautiful."

But his eyes are on Travin.

I contemplate not drinking anymore. Not just tonight, but anymore *ever*. The night Travin fell asleep in my tent is the last night I spent completely sober. I hadn't wanted to drink at all that night. And I had felt a contentment that drifted into a nightmare-free sleep. Could the wine be causing me some of this anger? Some of this misery? It used to numb me so well, but now I am unsure. The Israelites are good people with good morals. It seems their list of rules bring them great joy.

My positive musing evaporates, when I see Bronwynn and Mikyla across the room. They look exceedingly fair, next to their men. Happy. Content. In love. Jac escorts Mikyla to the front door. She smiles up at him, elation beaming from her eyes. Bronwynn takes Travin by the arm and grins teasingly at him. His eyes gaze at her, fondness illuminating them. She twirls him around.

"Alright, no dancing," he laughs and is swept out the exit with the others, like a leaf in a current.

I remember celebrating Travin's eighteenth birthday. Mikyla organized the celebration utilizing her carnival supplies. It was just us close friends, out on the beach. During the frivolity, I'd asked Travin to dance with me.

He'd complained, "People will stare."

I didn't care. I'd twirled around him, giggling, linking my arms behind his neck.

"I'm going to get you back," he'd stated out of the corner of his mouth.

I'd replied, "I dare you."

It feels like this is my punishment.

Rebby bolts past me and out of the room, his pockets overflowing with conceivably unwise not-too-distant-future purchases. This leaves me alone with Westin, who reaches for the bottle still in my hands, asking, "Ready?"

"Not even close." I take a long swig.

It is just enough to tip me over the edge into a negligent abyss.

Self-control is not my strongest suit. Neither is even-temperament. At the dance, I end up flirting with a soldier, who lets me borrow his loaded crossbow, which I proceed to shoot into the mass of dancing bodies. The arrow very nearly punctures the leg of one of the officers. Had I been an honorary, high-ranking soldier, I would have faced a much more severe punishment and demotion. As it is, Westin smooths things over with the officer in that oily way he can, and my punishment will be a lousy slap on the wrist.

Meanwhile, a flustered Travin drags me away by the elbow. He displays the depth of his provocation only by infinitesimal pulses in the veins in his neck, a skill he's exhibited since his youth.

"Will you free me?" I ask. "I am not—*hiccup*—going back there."

"Do not resist," Travin grunts.

He walks me beyond the bonfires, past the frivolous multitude, toward the gully at the edge of camp. The night quivers with sound. As the celebratory music diminishes with distance, the song of wilderness and wildlife becomes sonorous. The moon is high and large, blending land with sky. Most people say that darkness falls, but I feel as if it lifts. Without the torchlight, I feel like I have floated up into space, surrounded by colorful, twinkling stars, so close I could pick them like olives.

It's beautiful out here. Honestly, beautiful.

Travin stops near the fighting station and whirls around to face me with a quelling look. "Here," he declares, releasing my elbow with a bow. "Be free."

"Thank you." I try to curtsy, but fall sideways instead.

Travin lurches to catch me.

"*This*," he grumbles condescendingly, "is unacceptable."

Looking back up, his face is only an inch from mine. Back is the little cranky indentation between his brows. I can feel every line of muscle in his body contracted. Anger. This is anger. Welcome to the club, I think. But the soldier in him suppresses it. He's trying to be the smart, patient one.

In an effort to avoid becoming his father, Travin developed this incapability of conveying much negative emotion at all. It is fascinating and infuriating at the same time. Too bad I know his face well. His gray eyes always give away everything.

"Don't think I'm stupid, Kaya," he says steely.

"I never said—"

"You are wine blind—raving!" His attempt at an insult. "You almost injured an officer!"

His eyes blaze, his angular jaw resolute. A strand of hair cascades over his brow, but he doesn't move to brush it aside. He's staring at me.

"I know what's happening here, Kaya."

"Do you?"

He's awfully close to me. The ill-tempered wrinkle in his forehead expands out to the corners of his eyes. He pinches the bridge of his nose and closes those dove-gray eyes a moment.

"Someone could have been exceedingly hurt," he states.

"Maybe crossbows and pointy projectiles aren't the only things that hurt people."

"Are we being philosophical now?"

"You tell me. Apparently it's easy for you to leap from one denomination to the next. Now that you're an Israelite, you're an expert on all philosophies."

"Oh, grow up, Kaya!"

"Me? Redirect your allegations to your own beloved. Bronwynn called me a liar and . . . "

"I'm sorry she called you a . . ." Travin stops and swallows as if something nasty has landed on his tongue. The soldier responds stoically, "A certifiable second-born."

My face reheats hearing him say it. I'd rather be called a harlot.

He continues hurriedly, "You know how girls get when they have wine." He begins to motion toward me but decides against it. "All of this is just exaggerating her emotions. She's lugubrious, you know?"

"And that is you *not* bearing false witness?"

The ninth commandment. *See? I've learned the ways of the Israelites.*

"I'm not going to say anything horrible about her," Travin disputes. "You and I know how Bronwynn gets. That's just how it is."

"That's not how it is, Trav!" I shout, feeling the drunkenness take me to a new level of angry. "It doesn't have to be that way."

He only shakes his head grimly. "It doesn't have to be this way with you either, Kaya Lucan."

"Why are you turning this around on me?"

"It takes two to argue," he says, adding under his breath, "clearly."

"I'm not arguing."

"Just like you aren't poisoning yourself?"

I raise both hands skyward. *I forfeit.*

Travin delves into a series of indictments. "I noticed it back in Avoca, Kaya," he begins heatedly. "This has been going on for a long time. You're a fool to think I wouldn't pay attention, but even more foolish to be doing this to yourself. You're out of control. Your conduct grieves me. If you cannot exercise control, I will report you to Tildeh and Officer Mert. I'm not just saying this because of Joshua, but your intake of wine has become increasingly—"

"You'll report *me*, Travin Shelomo?" I spit his last name in a wicked retaliation. "You don't have to till ground or scrape cloven hooves or place fraudulent weights on scales anymore—you get a stupid little knife and suddenly you're as big of a deal as Shamash."

"That's not—"

"Tell me what you really think of me," I bark. "Bronwynn already has."

"I'm not excusing anyone's actions, particularly Bronwynn's. But I *had* to help you."

"Nobody has to help me."

"You always have an excuse, Kaya."

"Take me back to Westin."

"Nay."

"Then, I'm returning to the dance without you."

I spin and take a step but stagger again from dizziness.

"Good luck," Travin scorns, unmoving.

I glower back at him. A rage builds in my chest. I struggle to contain it as I grunt, "I don't need your *help.*"

He folds his arms, carving one eyebrow heavenward. Every time he finds me unreasonable this happens. Since we were children.

I turn my back to him. The night encompasses me. Many Israelites use the stars as a compass. Right now, they are bright enough to light my way back towards the congregation. But when I take another step, I trip over a stone and plummet toward the earth. Travin's hand is quickly there to stop my fall. Wrapping an arm around me, he tugs at my waist and pulls me tight against him.

"Are you eating?" he questions. "You're too skinny. You need to stop drinking and eat more."

"Really?" I grind out, trying to extricate myself from his grasp. "Will—you—remove yourself?"

Travin shifts a centimeter, leaving his hands resting on my hips. I try not to look at him. Strain hums in all the small places between us. A full moon the color of his eyes hovers just above. I look there instead, for I will not see it so whole for another twenty-nine days.

"Kaya?"

"Am I eating? Am I—." I take a moment to balance myself, ignoring the way my voice sounds because my drunk tongue has gone limp in my own mouth— "Am I a fool? Am I *foolish*? Am I *grieving you*? Am I *out of control*? *Am I a comical waste of human life?*"

"Stop that."

His temper rises in his face. It's almost a relief to have someone to fight with. Westin always walks out on me if a quarrel occurs, but Travin is good for it. Tonight, he has a predatory demeanor about him, like a wild canine that has been domesticated. All that anger, all this time. *Let it out. I dare you.*

I realize I'm talking to myself. The desire I see in his eyes is my own, a mere reflection. My anger is pouring out of me against my will. A mass of defiance forms in my throat, clogging my rehearsed excuses. After a moment, Travin reclaims himself.

"Don't go back."

Too exhausted to persist, I instead stare stubbornly into the night. Our quarrel abruptly ends.

"I don't need your help," I croak for the third time, ignoring the crack in my voice. In my peripheral vision, I see Travin's expression tighten. I hold up a finger when he begins to speak. "I already know what I am. And I *don't* need any reminders. I've been on my own long enough, and I can very well take care of myself."

Before I can push Travin's arms off of me, I notice he's already let go.

Oh.

I back away a few steps, managing to remain upright.

"Maybe *you* are the one that needs help," I allege, distancing myself from him with a look that dares him to disagree.

"Maybe," he answers rigidly.

He stares at me, cold and hard. We're both angry, but my anger isn't what it started out to be.

"Stay out of my business, and I'll stay out of yours," I force out. With that, I walk away.

I trip a few more times, but no hand is there to catch me. *Did I expect one to be?*

Rather than search for my dwelling in my current state, I fumble through the grass, without a glance back, without fulfilling the need to know what state I left Travin in, without seeing him standing there in the field, bathed in moonlight, disappointment on his face. I trudge on until I reach the dark shed on the outskirts of the barracks. It takes me a minute to open the door. The room is empty, inasmuch as my heart.

I lumber across the floor, collapsing onto the blanket. I can't focus on anything. The room is spiraling. A drumbeat throbs in my head, the sounds of the merry soldiers traveling through camp. I feel sick. An alien sensation of tightness grips my chest, accompanied by a wetness on my cheeks, a flaming in my throat. Regret shreds my heart.

Just when my head hits the pillow, I'm out cold.

TRAVIN

Being Noticed for the First Time

REBBY WAS RIGHT. My fight with Luko was perceived by the officers and Joshua himself. The approval of the High Commander accelerated my advancement. He transferred me to Lachlan's unit, and I was honored with a tse'adah—a battle bracelet—and a chagowr. The chagowr was custom-made since I am left-handed. My knife fits nicely into the sheath on the right side of the belt.

Today, when Lachlan was conscripting a squadron of men that would be returning to Avoca and nearby villages, I was one of the first recruited.

"I personally recommended you," Gorrow tells me, as we line up to receive our scale armor. Two other soldiers from my original company have also joined Lachlan's unit.

When it is my turn to be fitted, Gorrow holds up a shiny sheet of armor consisting of tiny scales fastened together.

"What do you think?" he asks.

I slide my palm over the metal surface and swallow. "It's perfect."

Gorrow grins. "We'll have them engrave Shelomo right here."

Just to be accepted into the cachet of Lachlan's unit pleases my heart, but I never imagined I would be able to own such fine artillery. My soul is glad.

"Do you want to head on over to the artillery lodge?"

"Oh, I am fine with this knife," I reply.

"Are you sure? It's on me."

"I'm sure. I know this blade well."

Gorrow's smile broadens. "And God knows *you* well. You've been blessed for your righteousness."

"Thank you, sir."

When the soldiers are prepared, Lachlan discusses our travel campaign, which will include marching through several towns, Avoca among them, in search of tools, men, and food.

The fate of my mother and Maleah has weighed heavily upon me. When I hear we will journey through Avoca, I am all too eager to depart.

The voyage will take two weeks. We visit several villages, all burned like unto Avoca. Part of Joshua's tactical brilliance is the psychological effect his domination of kingdoms has on other fortresses. Some are vacated before the Israelites even pass through. Others, after being offered a peace treaty, and refusing it, have been subjugated.

When we reach Avoca's city gates, I feel an instant wave of remorse. It is heavy and thick and unbending. The wreckage is catastrophic. Just inside the village, we find three human beings. Two are alive, feasting upon the third. They are diseased. Lachlan has them killed. He orders us to disperse and explore, search for anyone in hiding, collect supplies, and return in an hour.

"Let's make this a quick infil," he commands. "There could be others."

These veteran soldiers are awarded more liberties than the untried ones. My first officer, Gorrow, gave succinct, detailed instruction that I heeded precisely, for I knew not what to do on my own. This is my first venture out of Shittim with a new officer and new apprehension. Lachlan's unit consists of experienced soldiers. He can trust them with a broad-spectrum command and know they will perform dutifully. After a simple hand signal, the men disband. Most of them ignore me. I will have to earn my ranks among *them*.

Unsure of how to proceed, I tap a passing soldier on the elbow. "Shall I go with you?"

He scowls and glances at the old, handed-down knife at my chagowr. I've been saving my military funds. Not gambling them nor wasting them on harlots. I will soon have enough to manufacture a wonderfully crafted weapon, but even then, this knife will forever remain on my belt.

The soldier jerks his chin down the street and grunts, "Take that end."

He spits into the dirt and adjusts his shiny, posh glaive, moving north down the road.

My feet crunch into the shattered clay and splintered wood lining the street while I examine the demolished homes. Skeletal remains lie across the roads, dangling out of window frames, and hanging from trees. The whole town is leveled. Everything is charred.

At the end of the street, I turn left. Though it is hardly recognizable, I find my old home. The roof is caved in, the walls barely standing. I enter through a gap in the sidewall and slink down the hallway to where mine and Maleah's room used to be. Everything is torched. My mother's room is the same. I don't know why, but I'd been hoping to find their bodies. What if they are out there somewhere? Or lost? Or looking for *me*? Maybe they were taken prisoner by the Canaanites. Maybe they were eaten by rebels. I may never know.

I nearly collapse, squelching an irrepressible sting in my eyes.

Do not show pain.

I slam my fist into the wall, causing it to crumple around me. Powder catches in my lungs, and I submit to a fit of coughs. By the time I exit the home, the soldier who'd disliked my knife is walking toward me. I tell him there is nothing of value on this street, both grateful and hateful that it is true. He nods and moves on.

Solemnly, I make my way to the remains of the Lucan home. Scores of memories filter into my mind. A little girl with braids used to run through these halls. And a blond-haired boy used to follow her everywhere. Near the center of what used to be Kaya's room, I spy a crispy piece of parchment held down by a chunk of ceiling. The edges are singed black, fluttering in the wind. I step beyond the broken posts and pick up the scrap of paper. Some of the words are still legible. It is a letter. Signed N. Lucan.

Kaya's mother?

I remember the day after Kaya's father passed away. Up until that time, I'd always seen her as such a strong person. Stronger than I ever was. She grew up fast, learned to work and take care of herself, and never once claimed the lesser because of it. At her father's burial, Kaya was devastated. She'd sold her only milk cow to purchase a plot of land in the town cemetery. It meant Father Lucan's remains would be honored.

That day—the whole ceremony—she didn't shed a single tear. It tore me apart. Kaya's valorous personality fragmented. And I was powerless to stop it.

I admired Father Lucan. It was crushing for me, having him taken from our lives. Kaya would never admit to it, but I know she was as hurt by not having a mother, as I was about not having a father. It is one of the elements of the earth that I think drew us together. We were both . . . incomplete. After her father died, she became a different person.

I hear Gorrow's whistle blow and realize I've spent the majority of the hour in the Lucan's home. I keep the letter and return to our unit, unaware of the tear streaks cut into my dirt-covered face. The soldiers exit Avoca, marching by a dozen pikes at the edge of town, where rotting heads of citizens are displayed, at which point I notice a pair of sandals walking beside mine. It is the soldier from the street in Avoca. His face is set in the indifferent manner of our first encounter, but his eyes display an understanding. We don't say anything to one another, walking side by side the rest of the night.

KAYA

Maybe I Don't Know Anyone at All

SUMMER HAS BEEN A BLUR.

Autumn encroaches Shittim, as hot as summer, therefore the only noticeable change in season is the progression of the draftees. The march to Bashan looms near. I stare at the ceiling of the aged shed with a bitter taste on my tongue. The sun shines through the cracks, illuminating dust particles. This is where I come when I don't want to deal with people.

Yesterday I was placed on probation. After my exhibition with the crossbow, Tildeh issued a citation claiming I am always late to work. I have to dispute the claim with my superior officer in front of judges in order to return to work. While I have been late a dozen times and missed a few altogether, I'm still the most proficient employee of the barnyard. None of the stable maids have the extensive knowledge about the beasts of the field and fowls of the air that I do. Besides, Tildeh doesn't like that the animals favor me, especially the demon rooster who always attacks her. She said I'd be better off making a living as a harlot. I told her it takes one to know one.

So, I cannot report to the stables today. Favoring procrastination, I avoid disputing Tildeh's claim with Officer Mert and the judges. When I decide to venture outside the shed, I roam along the perimeter of camp. A flurry of soldiers are running through camp and grouping in dwellings. Joshua is marching to Bashan within the week. Different companies will depart at different hours. Each of Joshua's officers will follow detailed orders of their expedition up to the capitol of Ashtaroth and then to every other city under King Og's control, employing espionage and laying siege to enemy cities.

My heart begins to mourn for the impending battle seeing these soldiers, young and old, wise and wiser, rush to heed their commanders' orders. There is also a level of exhilaration involved. I ponder which I want to focus on more. I fear I am drawn to the excitement of violence, but it also brings me worry. On the other hand, the diligence of the righteous and their unyielding faith in their God is notable. The law-abiding soldiers are undeniably blessed.

They speak of this land as being sanctified. *A holy land.* Idols are not worshiped, nor the stars or sun, as majestic as they are. Even Joshua, who is considered a general over clan chieftains and tribal elders, remains assured that his covenant relationship to his deity, does not make him superior. He works alongside his army and retains a soldier's ethic, leading by example. Covenant adherence has paid off for him. Those I know who have slipped by way of the law have seen afflictions. Could it prove religion is not about control, but about a two-way, obedience-reward affiliation between man and God?

My confusion is interrupted when I'm unexpectedly greeted by Mikyla.

"Kaya, you have to come see this!" she blurts animatedly.

"Not now," I reply, rubbing my temple.

She grabs my hand regardless and pulls me down an aisle of tents. I follow unenthusiastically, wondering when we became friends again. Behind the barnyard between two tool sheds, a cluster of soldiers has formed a circle. Men and women alike. They are roaring and cheering loudly at whatever is in their midst. Most of them are the less devout sort. Gring and Grond are the first boys I recognize. They are casting lots with the soldiers around them.

An uneasy feeling grips my stomach.

Mikyla pulls me closer yet. We reach the edge of the crowd, but I can't see over their heads. The congregation collectively shouts and then winces. A man grudgingly hands the Bottker brothers a lump sum.

The group parts and a mangled man stumbles through. As he passes by me, staggering, he knocks my shoulder, leaving a stain on my shirt, and then wanders away as the spectators bark mocking jeers. Next to me, Mikyla smiles with glee and turns back to where the circle of soldiers has hollowed out.

I gasp, catching sight of Westin. He is pacing around the circle like an exultant gorilla. His hands are covered in the other soldier's blood. A few men around him offer congratulations. On the ground on the inside of the ring a second sanguinary soldier sits limply, propped up by the legs of those around him. It takes me all of ten seconds to understand what is going on.

"This is not a regulated match."

Next to me, Mikyla nods. "That's why you had to see. Westin is winning against everyone he challenges. He hasn't been beaten yet."

Her tone is laced with pride.

"How long has this been going on?" I ask.

"I don't know. Who cares? That's your man out there. Go give him a kiss!"

She nudges my shoulder.

Mikyla has relaxed her version of decency, I see.

I fall toward the inside of the circle, where Westin stands victoriously, laughing with his comrades. He doesn't see me as he raises his arms and yells, "Is there anyone else?"

The soldiers chuckle. A few female observers blush and wave scarves.

"Anyone?" Westin calls. "Anyone at all?"

I try to protest, but Westin continues his crowing.

"How many more will it take?" he declares, directing his gaze to one man in particular.

I recognize this man, across the circle. Officer Orren. He is watching the scene with bitter amusement. Westin is not fond of his officer. From what he's told me, Orren likes to bend and use Joshua's rules to his personal benefit. Both men look alarmingly unsafe at the moment.

"Him!" someone bellows.

"No, him! Fight him!" a second and third shout.

A small, scrawny soldier is thrust into the ring. Rionn. He is a delicate boy, young and slow of mind. A God-fearing lamb that often finds merriment in feeding the chickens. He's never spoken to me, but our paths have crossed when I gather eggs. I've heard Travin mention Rionn's disability, his struggle with speech and capacity for blunder. Some of the soldiers find it a hindrance, Westin included. Nonetheless, Rionn's inefficiency in combat has not diluted his allegiance. He has been named one of Joshua's priests.

Rionn has also never won a simulated fight. He didn't come here to increase his stats, he came here to encourage these men to cease their doings.

One of them came to increase their stats. Taking a glance down at Westin's fingers, I see that tiny pebbles have been laced to his knuckles with twine.

"Fight! Fight! Fight!" the group chants.

Orren sneers at Westin.

"If that's what it takes," Westin shrugs.

Rionn's doe eyes widen in fear. He turns and tries to escape the circle, but the other soldiers laugh and block his exit. One man takes him by the shoulder and twirls him around to face Westin.

Fight! Fight! Fight!

Westin shakes his head derisively. Only enough to make me glad he isn't enthusiastically anticipating hurting the innocent boy, but not enough to make me forgive him if he does.

"I don't see what this will prove," Westin comments toward Orren. "But alright."

The officer is mendaciously calm. "It proves you aren't weak. Mercy is reserved for the weak."

The look on Rionn's face—his shock at the traitors betting on his doom—saddens me. I realize that it is not the weak who are bullied, but the *strong*.

The crowd claps their hands.

Fight! Fight! Fight!

Rionn is thrust toward Westin, his pleas to stop going unheard. Westin moves, his eyes glinting with menace. I take a step forward. Just then, another man enters the ring, and I stop.

Rebby.

The crowd quiets, eyes and mouths agape. Rebby grabs hold of

Rionn's tunic and pushes him aside.

"Depart," he grunts under his breath.

The soldiers chuckle and split for Rionn, who crawls by their feet to flee. Orren spits into the dirt at Rionn's retreat. Slowly, Rebby advances, stepping into the center of the ring of men. He gives Westin a devil-may-care smile.

"I thought I was aware of all the scandals that take place in Shittim," Rebby exclaims.

It is a charming tease, but I know these men. I see the challenge in their eyes.

"Really?" Westin asks. "You mean you're not above scandal, like your righteous friend?"

"I haven't thought to look between the tool sheds." Rebby motions around the ring snidely.

"Shouldn't you be spending your earnings on some woman?" he rebukes.

Rebby gives Westin his sunniest smile. "Don't have to." He scuffs the dirt with his sandal and rubs his chin with a thumb. "You've had some luck. Truth be told, I prefer to make my mark with the ladies, but . . . this interests me."

Westin grins at Rebby, wearing his charisma like a tightly fitted tunic. He grabs the wrist of a nearby female. Yanking her to him, he gives her a turbulent kiss and then releases her back into the crowd.

My insides explode with torridity—the tenth commandment ringing in my ears.

Thou shalt not covet.

So much for exclusivity.

"Ask the ladies what they think of me, if you must," Westin taunts. "I *make* my luck among men."

"I can see that," Rebby murmurs, his eyes flitting to Westin's knuckles. He blasts the crowd with a smile. "Enough of this." He beckons. "Let us go eat. You can elaborate on this secret endeavor of yours to bully."

An embryonic threat evolves in Westin's ice-blue gaze. I'd always found it so attractive. That rebellious, immature side of me enjoyed his devious ways. In this setting they repel me.

Rebby's usual merry expression darkens in response, his willingness to *force* Westin out of the ring morphing from playful to dangerous.

I ditch Mikyla and wiggle through the group until I reach Orren's side.

"Officer," I entreat. "You have to put an end to this."

Orren takes a moment to look down at me, as if the two competitors require all his attention and *I* am an unwanted distraction.

"Leave, stable girl," he hisses.

I realize I am covered in bits of hay and oat, and I haven't even been to the barnyard today.

"It is your duty to keep these soldiers in line," I argue. "This match is not regulated. These men will hurt each other. Does Joshua know about this?"

Orren glares at me. "As *Officer*, I see it a necessary experience for these men to fight their own battles as well as God's. If you aren't going to place bets then you have no business here. And if you touch me again, I shall see you are disavowed!"

He turns his back, officially cutting me out of the circle. Furious, I make my way back to Mikyla.

"We have to do something," I tell her.

"What are you so worried about?" she asks haughtily. "They're just having a little fun. Rebby can handle himself. Besides, you should be honored. Westin is exceedingly great out there. Untouchable. Just like Joshua."

She is lusting after him, too, and it sickens me.

A thump draws my attention back inside the ring. Westin and Rebby are on the ground wrestling. Grunts and punches ricochet out from the dusty brawl. They're matched in strength and size. It is their motives that frighten me.

I push apart the soldiers and break into the circle just as the fighters separate. Rebby scrambles to his feet and prepares to attack. His face is a cryptogram imprinted by the pebbles adhered to Westin's fingers. Rebby licks the blood from the corner of his mouth and grins cunningly. Westin reaches down and grabs a stone the size of his fist. He spins, whirling it around in his fist as he does so. The rock slams into Rebby's jaw with a crack, sending saliva and the smile sideways. Rebby falls backward onto a knee. Westin punches again, but Rebby rotates and dodges his arm. He kicks out and catches Westin's knees with his foot. Westin falls onto his back, dropping the rock.

The audience roars.

Rebby finds his footing once more, shooting a ferocious stare at his flattened rival. Orren still refuses to intervene. Kicking the stone aside, Rebby hovers over Westin. The soldiers chant and antagonize and offer to double the bets. But when encouraged by the audience to end the match with more violence, Rebby ceases.

"Mercy," Rebby broadcasts loudly, "is a gift. Reserved only for the godly."

He backs away.

Westin stands, not acknowledging defeat. Chest heaving, blood flowing, adrenaline raging. He curses, and then turns to steal an ax off a nearby soldier. Rebby swiftly withdraws a short blade from his belt. The viewers hush their wagers in a concerned awareness of peril. This has gone too far. Before the men can act, I leap out into the ring and do the only thing I can think of.

"Hooray, to my hero! Wessssssstin," I slur purposefully.

I fling my arms around his neck, pressing my body against his sweaty one. My appearance of wine-induced flippancy makes the spectators chuckle. It takes Westin a minute to drag his eyes away from Rebby. They scale down to mine, shining with rabidity. His chest inflates with each heavy breath. For a second, I look like the other woman he kissed. I *feel* like her. Like nothing but a prize. That's what I am to him. A generic, female, prize.

His eyes clear of the aggression, and he sees me, Kaya Lucan.

"I think you deserve a real reward," I state loud enough for others to hear. Besides, our audience is uncomfortably quiet. I wink at them and receive the expected response. Smiles replace the expressions of worry. "Come back to my tent, and I'll treat you to a *true* winner's trophy."

I kiss his cheek, moist from perspiration. The men hoot and

whistle. The women sigh with jealousy.

Westin finally cracks a smile, bending to sweep me off my feet with one strong arm. I link my arms around him, aware of his pulse pounding beneath his skin. He lowers his ax, cradling me closer. Ultimately, he drops the weapon and carries me through the parting crowd. Over his muscled shoulder I see Rebby, turning purple around the edges, glowering at both of us. Behind him, Travin bursts through the soldiers, barefoot, bare-chested, and wet-haired. He is followed shortly after by Gorrow and a very winded Rionn.

The crowd immediately disperses in every direction like a pack of rats, nervously concealing the funds they've gambled with. Each soldier melts away into camp, the fight abandoned, leaving only two innocuous tool sheds for testimonials. Between them stands Travin. His eyes do not leave mine until Westin carries me out of sight.

WESTIN

Men Might Have Joy

"I WANT YOU TO let loose," I tell her, leading the way deep into the barracks. "You're tense. It's time to relax."

In the back of the furthest quadrant, a structure of tents has been arranged, offering similar amenities to the taverns of Avoca. Kaya isn't convinced she will be pleased. I stop walking and turn her toward me, lifting both her hands to my lips.

"It will be fine," I assure her. "Just like home."

"I don't know," she murmurs, offering a gloomy smile.

"If you want to go to the stables after, we can do that together. Whatever you want. I just want to make you happy."

She blinks and nods. "You're right. Let's go have fun."

I kiss her cheek. "Come on."

There are two soldiers sitting outside the large, dimly lit tent. The open tarps emit visceral laughter, both male and female. I nod to the soldiers who permit our entrance. Ducking through the entrance, we emerge inside the Violet Room. Those in charge of this enterprise gave it that title, nicknamed for the female drapery hanging throughout the supporting posts of the tent. Torchlight is refracted in the multi-colored material, producing the purple hue. It is within the Violet Room that one can fulfill the meaning of the prophecy: men might have joy.

Kaya stops the moment we enter. Taking in the sights, she releases my hand.

"I don't want to be here, Westin. Can we go somewhere else?"

I slither my arm around her, reassuring her that even my own officer visits the Violet Room on occasion.

"I'm uncomfortable," she protests.

"Kaya, I guarantee you will enjoy yourself."

A harlot inches between us and the gathering soldiers.

"We have wine of Apiruh this evening, Westin," the concubine says.

I avoid eye contact with her and escort Kaya forward.

"It's just like The Cellar. Look, there's a game of Grab going on."

Kaya's eyes scan the graven images cluttering corners, falling upon an altar set upon the center fireplace. The bones of a lamb rest on top of it. Her body goes rigid.

"We are allowed to rejoice." I glance at her, reciting scriptural passages. "As the day of the harvest brings people joy, so does the day soldiers divide their plunder."

She steps backwards, exiting the tent. I stalk after her, watchful of soldiers perusing the aisles at night.

"I thought it would make you happy," I state, pacing a few lengths behind Kaya as she retreats towards the women's barracks. "Kaya? Kaya, wait."

When she doesn't reply, or even slow, I skip to catch up. I grab her hand and whirl her around.

"Is it because Miki Rox was in there?"

Her eyes look like chartreuse silk in the moonlight. But much less soft.

"Do you want me to do something to him?" I ask.

She frowns a remonstration. "Like what, hurt him?"

"Whatever you want."

"That won't be necessary," she answers, continuing her walk.

I let her go. "You know, Kaya, I would do anything for you."

"Sometimes, it's what you shouldn't do," she murmurs.

It makes little sense, but it persecutes me just the same.

I return to the Violet Room, burst through the tarps, and shove a harlot aside. Two more steps are all I take before realizing Officer Orren sits next to Miki Rox. The harlot, Iblis, lies cradled in Miki's arms. The men share a laugh comparing male soldiers to battering rams. A similar taste in politics and machinations has formed a friendship between them.

My hands, having turned white, tingle with the sensation of blood flow as I unclench my fingers. Miki's black eyes glitter at me from across the room, having observed my entrance with Kaya, our departure, and my intentions for returning. I want to hurt him, but that's not going to help my situation. What I need is for *him* to hurt *me*.

KAYA

What Now

A DEAFENING BOOM RATTLES the walls around me. I wake up with a start. The wooden planks of the shed shift and balls of stale dust cascade down around me. I've made it a habit of loitering in here lately, in an attempt to elude Mikyla and Jac. Travin and Bronwynn. Rebby and Westin. And people.

Another boom echoes. Seconds later, the door flies open and Westin stumbles in. He still has a black eye and a swollen upper lip. Relief floods his face upon finding me here.

"Get dressed!" he screams at me. "Hurry!"

Unable to ditch my morning stupor, I mumble, "What's going on?"

He jerks me to my feet without an answer.

I heard about his fight from Mikyla, as she demanded I be present at the men's judgment. Apparently her admiration of Westin transfigured into contempt after witnessing him get into a brawl with Miki. Although Miki threw the first punch, Westin threw the last. I did not participate in the hearing, mostly because I was not a key witness. Even if I had been, I don't want anything to do with Miki. He deserves every punch to the face he will ever receive.

It was after an argument between Mikyla and I, her defending Miki, and me defending Westin, that I sought refuge in the shed. I couldn't sleep. Hours of lying awake, wishing I could go down with the sun and hide on the dark side of the earth, leaves me exhausted. I'd only just given in to slumber when the noise outside woke me up. I guess it is better than the noise of my nightmares.

Miki and Westin were both disciplined for their disputation, a consequence that has left everyone involved disagreeable. Miki was put on probation by army officials for getting physical with Westin, but many of the soldiers at the Violet Room that night faced reprimanding by the judges simply for the activities of that establishment. Westin's lack of response to his punishment told me he had larger ploys in mind.

The Rox siblings murmured against me for siding with Westin—whom I have particularly distanced myself from after Joshua and thirty thousand soldiers departed for Bashan. Officers Jair, Nobah, Lachlan, and Gorrow, and their soldiers went with him, Rebby and Travin included.

Today, the remaining units will march out of Shittim. My company will march to Ashtaroth, the capitol of Og's territory.

Is that why the trump is sounding this early?

I duck as a few of the ceiling beams collapse around us. "Is this a drill?"

Westin scans the room, picking up an old sledgehammer and spear, and then beckons for me to follow. I crouch behind his shoulder, listening to the cacophony of commotion outside. We make our way out of the shed and into the campgrounds, where soldiers are in disarray. Men and women are running up and down the barracks, shouting at one another. The officers yell orders, riding horseback through the labyrinth of tents.

"Aim for the catapults!" Mert shouts.

"Westin?"

"Stay close," he demands as he leads me behind the shed—what is left of it. He hands me the spear and presses me down.

"Don't move," he commands, turning toward camp. "I'll return."

"Westin!" I call out after him, but he only glances back long enough to motion for me to stay quiet.

Israelite soldiers weave through the maze of dwellings. I glance outward to where Mert is leading a brigade of long-range-weapons infantry. Bowmen assemble in preparation for attack.

"Left is clear!" Officer Mert hollers.

"No good, no good!" Officer Carac corrects him.

From my position near the shed, I can see a good distance around the periphery. A line of shapes emerges along Shittim's outer limits. Outlining the boundary of our camp, sprinting full speed into the barracks, is an enemy force. The assailants reach the barnyard, shooting arrows, throwing javelins. A giant mechanism hurtles flaming saucers the size of sheep. The first wave hits a returning force of Israelite soldiers and combat ensues.

Injured animals wail from within the barn. Determined to rescue them, I stand up, but the barnyard has been set aflame. Charkish and Azsh race by on horseback, commanding their companies to contain the fires in each quadrant of our camp.

"Go right!" Azsh barks to a militia of short-range infantry. "Spread out. Gain some real estate."

I freeze, watching Officers Tabor, Orren, and Carac structuring formations for defense all around the stronghold.

"I'm hit! I'm hit!" a young recruit cries.

"We're all hit!" Tabor yells, grabbing the man by his weapons harness and dragging him to his appointed station. "Fight!"

Brandishing their weapons, the Israelites retaliate with extraordinary exactitude as enemies continue to fuse with our forces. Violence and bloodshed abounding, I panic.

I drop the spear Westin gave me, crouch, and run into the hills. *Flee.*

A drop of moisture hits my arm. I peer up at the blustering brumes swarming a once clear blue sky. Rain trills from the heavens, increasing into a downpour. The dirt beneath my sandals begins to soften. My robes are soaked in seconds. I try to wipe my eyes clear but the water is falling down in sheets. All I can do is keep moving. The animals are forgotten. I must find cover.

As soon as I feel safe enough to stand upright, I force myself to move hastily away from the battle. Dodging soldiers and weapons, I dash into the wilderness. The storm increases by the second. A burst of lightning cracks nearby. There's a small overhang cut into the side of a small mountain, and I hide beneath it, Avoca's politics still influencing my reaction to war.

I cover my ears as a collection of unpleasant memories flashes before my eyes. Miki Rox. The woman's face from the alley in Avoca. Me sitting and waiting in that cold pit in the wilderness where Travin rescued me. I can hear the battle at camp through the torrent, wishing I hadn't dropped the spear. Wishing I hadn't fled. Wishing I knew what to do.

The temperature declines, and I shiver, blinking against the rain. None of the Israelite soldiers were fleeing. They were defending themselves, prepared for attack, devoid of hesitation and cowardice. Pressing my fingertips against the mountainside behind me, I inch forward, eager to move. But several sets of feet trample passed me.

A dozen or so soldiers engaged in combat. The bearded Canaanites are slain by the hands of quicker Israelites. Two of them remain by the deceased, enumerating the day's plan for departure that has gone awry. They are no more than two cubits away. I cover my mouth to hide the steam released by my breath. Standing beneath the storm, they speak urgently.

"Did a Canaanite spy infiltrate our perimeter?"

"Unlikely."

"Then there must be a conspirator among us who tipped off the enemy."

"One that knew Joshua had departed for Bashan and that we would all be leaving to Ashtaroth."

"Who knew we were without our High Commander and that our posts were less guarded?"

I recognize one of their voices. He is one of the Bottker twins. From the back, it is impossible to tell which brother. The two Israelites begin to jog away. I know I should go with them. Stepping out of my disclosed location, I jump out and shout.

"Halt!"

The Bottker boy spins and hurls something at me. I do not have fast enough reflexes to move. A bladed star slices into my right shoulder. The shorter man next to him retrieves an arrow from a quiver on his back and pulls it taut in his arbalest, aiming straight for my heart.

"Wait!"

The twin thrusts himself into the man's side just as he releases the arrow. It zings past me, bouncing off a rock wall and into the ground.

Clutching my right arm, I sink to my knees. The pain is excruciating.

I gape down at my wound. The object sticking out of my shoulder is a six-inch long, handmade, metal star favored by the Bottker brothers. Two inches of that is lodged in my shoulder. Blood has stained the entire right side of my outer tunic. I feel so much pain I must be close to fainting. It makes me want to scream and cry and throw up all at the same time.

The Bottker boy runs up to me, murmuring profane things under his breath. The shorter, older soldier follows more cautiously, glancing nervously behind every few steps with his arbalest at the ready.

"We should be reuniting with our officer," he states. "They'll presume us dead and move out."

I fall onto my back and let the rain wet my face. It's then I realize I've been holding my breath since the impact. I let out an unintelligible lamentation as Gring kneels next to my head. I recognize him by his dimpled chin. He is wearing a tse'adah like Jac and Travin's, but has little on by way of armor. The surprise raid caught most soldiers off guard.

"Next time," Gring warns, "you won't do that. We communicate with sounds and signals."

I can't make words form in my mouth. The taste of salt and the smell of blood have my insides reeling.

"You're going to have to lie very still for a minute," he says.

I try to say no, but it sounds more like an inaudible squawk.

The older man is hovering over us, glowering.

"Gring, we must make haste," he says again.

In the rush of the attack, he did not put on his chain mail. With only a breastplate and his arbalest, he defends our position.

Meanwhile, Gring finds a stick and holds it up to my mouth. "Bite down. Hard."

But I can't open my mouth to accept the stick. My teeth are clenched tightly together, and all I can think about is the pain. Searing, tormenting pain!

Is my arm on fire?
I chance another glance at it. All I see is red.

"Kaya!" Gring slaps my face until I look him in the eye. "Do you want to lose your arm or not?"

I heave.

"Bite."

Gring holds the stick up to my lips. I snatch it out of his hand like unto a homeless dog stealing a piece of meat out of the garbage. He pushes up his sleeves, revealing massive muscles in his forearms. His hands are strong, unnaturally strong, as he presses one against my sternum and fastens the other around the metal star.

"On the count of three," he states. "One . . . "

He yanks.

It hurts almost more coming out than it did going in. But Gring doesn't allow me to maintain the fetal position I'm fighting for. He presses both hands against the open wound.

"Stuff this with dirt," he orders, whether to me or the older man, I'm not sure.

Gring cuts the bloody sleeve off of my simlah. "Nasr, put pressure here."

Nasr hands him a handful of dirt. Gring shoves it into my shoulder to staunch the bleeding. Nasr holds his palm against it. Gring then ties the torn piece of cloth around my shoulder. Black spots flicker before my eyes, but he slaps my face again.

"Keep your eyes open, Kaya," Gring commands.

I feel like they are, but all I see are the black splotches, and every now and then glimpses of him and Nasr.

"You have to get up," Gring demands. "We have to move."

I'm too afflicted to argue, but my limbs won't oblige. Gring and Nasr help me to my feet, avoiding my injured arm in a manner that any apathetic soldier would. They urge my feet forward.

We pass by the dead Canaanites on our backtrack to the campsite, where the men pause to overlook the scene.

"Look," Nasr says, nodding.

Israelite officers, visible from the distance by their uniquely shaped helmets, are gathering their units at the north side of Shittim.

"They're going to draw the enemy into the wilderness," Gring says.

The two males exchange a few hand signals. I've been around the soldiers long enough to understand some of them, but right now, with the weather and in my current condition, I don't comprehend much.

"We won't be able to cross this way," says Nasr. "Let's circle high and wide."

The three of us head away from camp, trying to find easy trails through the hills. We hike up, away from the battlefront and fire-enclosed site. If my senses are right, and that's debatable, we are traveling west.

"Wait," I moan. "Shouldn't we . . ."

"Fear not," Gring states. "We'll reconvene with the others before we reach Ashtaroth."

"Who are these Canaanites?" I ask.

"I'm not sure. Our spies are thorough. We did not anticipate an attack today. Someone probably leaked information."

Nasr grunts. *An approval? Disapproval?*

"They are smaller in numbers than we are," Gring adds. "They won't stand a chance once we draw them into the wooded hillside. We had detailed orders for the march to Ashtaroth, which for now are a little kinked, but it won't matter. Joshua and his men must be in Bashan. They are probably smiting down Og as we speak. The hearts of other Canaanite kings will melt when they hear of our conquest."

Gring speaks as if Joshua has already conquered Canaan on this side of the river. He does not view rebels or Canaanites as a threat and talks of Og, the giant, as a delicate butterfly. There is no fear. All trust.

I tell Gring I need to rest, that the pain in my arm is unbearable, but he protests, insisting we have to find shelter. After a half hour more of hiking, Gring spies a grotto in a nearby knoll. He tugs me up into the cavern, where I immediately crumble from shock. There is a natural cistern with gathered rainwater. The men collect it in their palms and quench their thirst. Gring offers some to me. I fade in and out of consciousness, while he rewraps my throbbing shoulder. He touches the back of his hand to my forehead and murmurs something before his face fades into darkness.

When I open my eyes again, a fire is burning next to me. An animal hide lies across my body. A few extra soldiers are gathered along the other side of the flames, but their faces are out of focus. I recognize Gring's voice when he says, "She'll be well." But my mind drifts off again into a fitful rest.

IT'S BACK.

I'm in the alleyway. Miki is on top of me. I kick at him, clawing at his face. His elbow digs painfully into my clavicle. My hips grind into the gravel beneath me.

"Kaya, wake up!"

My eyes click open. A wide, alert *click*.

It is no longer Miki, but Gring whose face I am scratching.

Four witnesses stand around him. Nasr, two other men, and an adolescent girl. Her expression is even more addled than the rest. Gring, towering above me on his knees, gives my good arm another shake. I remember to release my grip on his scalp, no longer anesthetized by my nightmare. Conscious of the thrumming pain in my right shoulder, a flow of vulgar language escapes my mouth.

"Be still," Gring murmurs.

"Sorry."

He examines my arm and then rests back onto his heels with a sigh. His teenage face looks pale and stressed, but tough. He has transitioned from youth to warrior—a warrior with scraped hands and a blackened eye. I study the strangers around me, frightened of my vulnerable state. I then observe my surroundings. We are indoors. It's a building, like my home in Avoca. The windows, though covered with boards, emit an ocher glow.

I smell Heshbon. The fetid odor of sizzled skin, hair, and life.

"Where am I?" I question.

"Bashan," Nasr replies.

His face is one large contusion, with a gash opening up part of his cheek and his left eye swollen shut. He impatiently introduces the newcomers. Haldor, a middle-aged man who is built like a bull, carries a shield and has a long sword sheathed in his ezowr. He has a dirt-stuffed wound like mine on his thigh. A younger man, named Rajmund, who has lengthy blonde hair, stands beside him. Rajmund looks regal in a colorful ketonet, a symbol of wealth and prosperity. He appears to be about my age. They are able-bodied, strong, warriors. Men. With men-like instinct.

I try to sit up, squelching my nausea. The little girl watches me diffidently.

"She's eight years old," Rajmund says. "She was salvaged from Ashtaroth. Her name is Svana."

Svana's long, dark hair is accented by bright eyes. A ragged dress covers her dusty figure. The law requires fair treatment for orphaned children.

I sit a little taller. "Bashan?"

"Rest," Gring orders.

"What happened? Where is everyone? Where are *we*?"

The men swap glances. Nasr is the one who speaks.

"You've been out for several days. We are in the capitol of Bashan now."

"*What?*"

Gring's hand covers my mouth. Rajmund flinches, moving to a window and peeking outside. Haldor picks up a blade in the shape of a crescent moon.

"Quiet now, Kaya," Gring says softly. He smiles. "The fighting continues throughout Ashtaroth. But . . . Og is no more."

"The king is dead?" I ask, aghast.

He nods. "We intercepted a Canaanite epistle. The king fell at Mount Edrei."

Haldor places the tip of his weapon in the fire until the blade glows. He then lifts it, pressing the metal to an open wound on his left tricep. The sound it makes is like an ill-tempered cat. It smells worse.

Svana is shaking. Clearly, she is frightened of these strangers, and I don't blame her. You're never too young to learn whom you can and cannot trust. And it's always better not to trust men. I decide not to ask too many questions in front of her, to respect the destruction of her home, king, and kingdom. If she lost her family, we have a lot in common.

"Joshua . . . he was right?" I inquire. "All along?"

"God is great," Haldor rasps. "Og was delivered into our hands. Joshua has already moved out. He travels across Bashan, terminating outstanding threats of Bashan's sixty other cities. After this land is secure, he will march to Giles with Officer Lachlan and Officer Gorrow. We've been charged with staying behind to ensure the obliteration of Ashtaroth. In a matter of days, this city will be burnt to ash. Every living thing must be destroyed. Every breathing creature."

Rajmund shifts to stand sentinel in front of Svana. She doesn't understand what Haldor says, but she can understand his tone of voice.

Haldor ignores them both. "We've been separated from our unit. You can hear our army near the city gates. A few enemies are holed up in a watchtower. We must starve them out or slay them. From here, we cannot see beyond the city walls, but we believe Officers Tabor, Mert and Orren are just outside. We need to reconvene with them hastily, lest they perceive us dead. We should arrive just in time for the execution of the prisoners—"

Rajmund interrupts him. "You should eat something, Kaya."

Haldor glares at him.

So the war is not over? Sixty more cities? Joshua is hungry for more death?

I can't believe I've been out for several days. I can't believe they managed to transport me here, let alone keep me alive. My wound has been tended to. I am not ill from dehydration. I glance over to Gring. He is roasting some animal over a fire. A bowl of figs sits on the ground. The men laugh and rejoice as they eat. It is a happy thing for them to devour an enemy city.

I don't participate in their discussions of position and strategy, disgusted and afraid and thirsty beyond reason. It is not water I desire. I cannot bring myself to eat, or to look outside, lest I witness this great destruction of Ashtaroth. I do not know what time of day it is. The smoke blocks the sun in the sky. My body trembles inasmuch as the crumbling buildings.

Svana follows my every move but utters little more than a sound. We cannot speak to one another well in our native dialects. Rajmund keeps his eyes on her always, his gaze bouncing between me and the girl. I take it she is one of the *every man, woman, and child* command, but the law protecting orphans has thus far protected her. She is a point of contention amongst the soldiers, as Nasr firmly believes she should be put to death, but due to more prevalent issues the men decide not to take any immediate action against our hostage.

I am in agreement with Rajmund's rescue of her. I would have done the same thing. Nonetheless, we are all wary of the repercussions. Our High Commander warned against reclaiming anything from our enemy cities, lest the wrath of God shall smite us. Yet, it is a contradiction to part of the law pertaining to orphans. We must bring Svana before the Israelite judges. They shall determine her fate.

I regard Rajmund, his breastplates and armor. An Israelite, who has seen many battlefronts. He had to have known Svana would slow him down—like Nasr had known about *me*. He also must worry concerning his salvation. If Svana is, in fact, an accursed, she may be the death of us all.

The little girl nibbles a bite off Rajmund's plate, and then brings a piece of meat to share with me. I have a hard time eating. And watching Gring drink the animal's blood turns my stomach. Reclining into the hard wall, I try to rest. It isn't easy to do, while the soldiers around me talk militia jargon. When night falls, Nasr exits our abode to scout out surrounding streets and to mark a map of our exit. He is an employed Israelite spy. These scouts evade all eyes as they move in secret, carrying messages between officers, extracting information from captives or neighboring cities, predicting the enemy's attacks. Nasr is how we know what is currently going on.

The epistle Nasr intercepted spoke of the destruction on Mount Edrei. Joshua had departed and a large part of the army began marching towards Giles. *We* are to see to the end of Ashtaroth, then fortify the city limits. A couple officers have led their units to the remaining sixty cities that—reportedly—have already surrendered.

Nasr returns at supper-time, though there is no supper. He holds a scroll in his hand. It reminds me of Avoca, the day my home was ambushed. The message I'd discovered attached to the peafowl could have been a warning. But who would've sent it? And why? Sorrow and agitation build within me. I realize I do not handle genocide well.

"It is time," Nasr explains, pointing to his handwritten map. "We move to the city gates."

His eyes travel to Svana, moving up to Rajmund, and I know he is thinking that we will *all* be punished when discovered assisting an enemy refugee. Rajmund's returning look objects to any disagreement on the matter. Svana will remain untouched until presented before the judges. It affirms my trust in him as an honorable soldier.

"Ready?" Nasr asks.

The armed men nod.

"Can you defend yourself?" Gring asks me, eyes skeptical on my wound.

"I . . ."

Haldor withdraws his giant sword, the blade as tall as Svana. Rajmund reveals a whip that breaks into five, lethal fibers each tipped with a caltrop. Svana flinches at the sight of it. Frightened, she hides behind me. Rajmund's eyes flit to mine.

Bending at the waist, he says softly to her, "Fear not, child."

She does not come out of hiding.

Gring stares at me and my quivering accomplice. He chooses to speak to Svana first.

"Be brave, little one," he states. "No harm will come to you."

When he looks up, the expression he gives the other men is doubtful. Svana stares at Nasr's arbalest, Haldor's blade, and Rajmund's whip, her little mind comprehending the terror. Gring pulls out a star from the satchel at his hip and hands it to her. Suspiciously, she accepts it. She moves the spike between her hands, running her fingers along the smooth, warped edges and pricking her finger on a tip.

"You can throw this," he says "if you are scared."

Svana nods in that way children do when opting to believe an adult. I want her to be too young for this, to remain innocent and fragile, but I want her to survive *more*. Had the women and children of Avoca been learned in the art of self-defense, many more of them would've survived. I'm appreciative of what I've been taught at Shittim, but my injury prevents me from utilizing a lot of it. Inside, I am as alarmed as Svana.

Despite communication troubles, I assure the girl with facial gestures. She warms up to Rajmund again, her rescuer, forgetting I am there. Gring shifts his assessment to me, analyzing my height, weight, and wound.

"We've got to figure something out, or she is walking dead," barrages Nasr. "Both the girls."

"Look out for Svana," Gring orders me. "That can be your duty, Kaya."

"I can do that."

"We just have to move to the city gates. The rest of Mert's unit should be congregating there. But we must make haste. We will be presumed dead if we do not hurry." Gring tells us to shout the word "bug" if we spy a rebel, assailant, or someone posing a threat. The word "tonic" if we spy another soldier or ally. For weapons, medicines, and anything else deemed usable, we will use the word "booster." This way, with one word we can deliver a quick message to one another without any unwelcome ears deciphering it. Besides that, the men use their silent signals to converse.

With our concise instruction, we depart from our dwelling and enter the vestige of Ashtaroth. The sun has set, and I'm grateful. It is worse than Avoca, with not even the plant life spared. Scorched buildings and bones are all that remain. The city is in ruins. An extreme trepidation toward Joshua rises in my chest, and I wonder how such a religious man could carry out such desecration.

Haldor follows Gring, then come Rajmund, Svana, and I. Nasr and his arbalest have the advantage of hitting a target from the farthest distance, therefore he is last.

"Checking right," Haldor whispers.

Gring replies, "Got it. Checking left."

We travel cautiously through the increasingly darkening evening, which Gring says will be to our advantage. We are less likely to be seen. Honestly, I don't want to be seen any more than I want to see what is around me. I keep my head lowered as the men lead us through the city.

"Clear," Haldor says quietly.

I hold onto Svana's hand at all times, helping her over crumpled buildings and fire-glazed glass. We pass by a well, and the soldiers stock up on water. I try to clean my arm. The swelling is exceedingly worrisome. Without medical supplies, the gaping wound is susceptible to infection, not to mention it hurts remarkably.

An hour later, with the ashen moon shining between ghost-story clouds, we come to a slot between two tall, collapsing buildings. Embers glow in the crevices like magma, an eerie diagram of our passageway. Only one of us will be able to squeeze through at a time. Gring eyes the narrow slit, holding a spiked star in one hand, making a strange signal with the other. He slips through.

A minute passes before the call of a bird tweets. Haldor returns the chirrup. Hand on the hilt, he gives a signal to Rajmund before he and his sword move out of our sight. Rajmund turns and holds up two fingers, index and middle, close together. Nasr mouths something silently and traces a line from his ear to his mouth. Rajmund's eyes flicker to mine. He pivots around and squeezes through the crack, when Gring's voice bellows through the quiet night.

"Bugs!"

TRAVIN

A Living, Breathing, Nightmare

WE ARE COMMANDED TO march to Bashan in the night. Thirty thousand men depart out of Shittim in secret, under the authority of High Commander Joshua, and his two highest-ranking lieutenant officers, Jair and Nobah. We make the journey to Bashan where rich soil yields abundant crops. Lush pasture-lands produce choice cattle. Joshua specifically called the most elite soldiers to attend these siege battles, and Rebby and I were chief among them. We have been favored amongst the new draftees. The two of us will follow Joshua and Jair toward the strange city of Edrei. The maps depict this city to be cut out of a rock in the upper Yarmuk valley. Nobah will march toward Gilead, to a territory called Kenath.

The kingdom of Og has threescore cities. The territory extends from the Jabbok River to Mount Hermon. We receive intel that Og fled his capitol of Ashtaroth and has taken residence a few miles southeast in the city within Mount Edrei. Officer Lachlan reminds us that Og has very few equals, either in the size of his body or handsomeness. Men can easily guess his magnitude and strength.

I am grateful for the officers' trust and faith in me, but I fear my lack of experience. There will be a great destruction. I plead to be favored by God this day.

The army separates into two divisions. Under Officer Lachlan, I march behind Joshua and thousands of infantry to the gates of Edrei. It is in unordinary circumstances that we find this city to be almost unassailable. The metropolis is set in a mountain-spur, built within a hollow hill that has been artificially scooped out. Ramparts of stamped earth surround the ravine-girt hilltop. Glacis, alternating layers of beaten earth and sand atop a foundation of bricks, support the fortifications. Rionn, one of Joshua's esteemed priests and skilled trenchers, leads the sappers in building a zigzag of dugouts around the perimeter. Soldiers are stationed in these canals, both to sneak up on the city, and to avoid being hit by arrows. Jair and his professional engineers construct siege ramps made of earth and wood.

We then encircle the city, transporting the ramps and battering rams towards the front-lines. Spearmen and archers prepare to cover their short-range military. Specialized swordsmen plan to storm the first breach in the wall. It is within moments of our rest that King Og marshals his men to attack. The bowmen are first to assail. Iron-tipped arrows rain down on us.

"Shields!" Lachlan yells.

Joshua commands us forward, a great sermon of God's will and justice upon his lips. *These are mine enemies.*

"Be strong and of good courage," our High Commander declares, his bravery showcased in his physical and spiritual strength. "God will fight our battles for us."

The Israelites fire back, spearmen launching javelins upon the city walls. The footmen propel the battering rams into the city gates until they crack. Once a breach has been made, the swordsmen penetrate the wall. Rebby and I follow the second wave of infantry.

"Watch your flanks!" Lachlan shouts as we infiltrate the gates. "Let's make this a quick infil."

A subsequent flock of arrows fall upon us.

"Shields!" Joshua bellows.

An arrowhead skims my calf. Another bounces of my shin greaves. My last thought before entering the city is Avoca's diplomatic policy, a credence buried in layers of ash and bone. With knowledge of the Canaanites evil trespasses, their incestuous relations, the robbers and sorcerers, the soothsayers and charmers, necromancers and wizards, I support God's command to put an end to such wickedness.

A brigade of Og's cedar-tall warriors waits directly inside the city gates, rows of soldiers, eight men deep. Enemies sprint through the geometric pattern of buildings. The city is a prosperous one, and the weapons of our enemies exceed our own. Yay, a great and marvelous and bloody battle ensues.

Joshua orders the soldiers to disperse, to the north and the south gates, to the east and the west. Jair leads a company that will fall upon the east and west gates. I remain with Rebby and Officer Lachlan, under the direction of Joshua himself. I knew not what a powerful leader Joshua really is until I see him in action. He is a man of honor and discipline and vigil, but he is also a man of immense physical strength. He does not sit on his stallion and order his men to do his bidding, but charges into battle. His soldiers do not question him. They turn their hearts to his and have faith in God.

But faith does not protect the eyes from witnessing the ending of life. It is my first time battling the enemy. Having Rebby at my side is encouraging. We engage in warfare of all manner. The Israelites have trained us in proficiency such that we do not hesitate to slaughter the people of Edrei.

The Israelites smite down a bevy of Canaanite guards. We push into the city square that is so crowded, soldiers bump shoulders. Swords clash. Shields smack. Fists wallop helmets. Rebby moves on my right flank. With him as a right-handed fighter, and me as a left-handed fighter, we press forward equally protecting one another and ourselves.

We follow Joshua to the king's temple, where Og and his personal guards stand firm. The king exceeds the height of any living man. Every footstep is like unto an earthquake. The girth of his belly like unto a whale. We climb the stairs as the king of Bashan comes down upon us. The pillars of the structure crack and crumble as the fighting permeates the vicinity. Israelite long-range soldiers fire weapons at the Canaanites on the steps. One of them falls, tumbling down towards me. I leap over him.

"Spread out!" Joshua commands, reaching the top of the stairs first.

His red cape flutters behind him, the wind lifting and tossing it as if it were under water. A spear ricochets off his helmet. He spins, expertly attacking three of Og's sentries at once.

One pillar collapses. The roof of the temple tilts, a segment of it breaking free and crushing soldiers beneath it. An enemy combatant approaches me and, stunned from the scene, I react poorly. My knife is knocked free from my hands.

"Trav!" Rebby shouts, ascending the stairs two at a time.

Without slowing his stride, he bends and retrieves something from a fallen soldier. He tosses me the small broadsword and pursues a descending contender all in one motion. I snatch the sword from the air with my left hand, whirling to brace myself against my aggressor's next move. I barely stop the Canaanite from cutting my head clean off. His sword grazes my neck, catching my breastplate. He lifts his foot and kicks at my stomach. I thrust my right arm under his elevated foot, hooking my elbow beneath his ankle, and wrench him off the ground. With my left hand, I smite him with my sword.

I do not know what happens next, but I do know one thing: God fights the battle for me.

KAYA

I Did Not Know What to Expect

Nasr shoves his way in front of Svana and I. Holding up his loaded arbalest, he guards our side of the slot while Svana buries her face in my back. Once more, I have to be the responsible adult I'm not.

The familiar sound of Gring's metal stars whizzing through the air is followed by grunts, blades crashing, and the snapping of Rajmund's whip.

"Behind you!" a man shouts.

"I see him. I see him."

It doesn't take long. A minute later, the air falls silent again.

I notice I've been running my hand gently across Svana's hair. It's a little strange, but then I guess it's what I would have done to comfort a scared animal in my shop. I stop when she pulls back to peek up at me. Her round eyes are so terrified and so full of dependence. I'm dreading the moment she realizes I'm no more of a warrior than she is.

"You and I, let's stick together," I whisper, and she hides her face again.

Gring's voice shouts for us to come through. I make it through the crevice first, snagging my tunic on the edges of the fallen building. On the other side, darkness has muted the colors of gore before me. The blood is dark like the Salt Sea at night. Three bodies lie still on the ground, cut open and mutilated.

Every man, woman, and child.

The soldiers wait, cautious and armed. A strand of Rajmund's blonde hair is hanging over his shoulder, the tip stained pink. Haldor has a small gash on his cheek, his sword gleaming with liquid in his hand. Gring begins retrieving his spikes from the surrounding areas.

I remember Svana.

She's squeezing out of the passage behind me. I scoop her up with my good arm, ignoring the angry pulse from my injury that spreads across my upper back, down into every muscle I'm using. I turn so that her back is to the bloody scene and hold her head against my good shoulder with my hand.

Nasr enters the site through the gap in the walls and scans the area, pointing his arbalest into the shadows.

"Citizens," Haldor states in a husky voice.

Svana jumps at the sound.

"It's important to keep moving," Gring says.

I'm starting to admire his capacity to lead. The men follow him down the street.

"How's your shoulder?" Rajmund asks.

He's looking at me, holding his arms out. I pass Svana to him. The pain lessens dramatically.

"Just keep her face down," I say between gritted teeth. "Don't let her see."

Rajmund nods, cradling Svana effortlessly. The shadows of the night give him a ghoulish resemblance, the way his flowing hair swathes down his shoulders and the layers of fine clothing.

"Your arm?" he questions again.

"I don't know." If any of them thinks I am a weak woman, who's to say they won't turn on me themselves? "It needs to be sterilized."

Haldor indicates the direction we must head. Gring has already begun crunching over . . . *bones.* I feel queasy, finding it difficult to persuade my feet to walk.

"I won't let anything happen to Svana. Or you," Rajmund says softly. It reminds me of a similar promise I received at the beginning of summer.

For a moment, I forget my surroundings. I forget that I'm in the middle of the enemy city, the enemy territory of Bashan, with strangers standing around me. I think of Travin. *His* promise.

The furnace that is Ashtaroth is nothing compared to the

broiling inside my heart. I clutch the lapel of my simlah with my fingers. Travin had promised to look out for me, and so did someone else. Westin.

Where are they now?

I feel faint. Very faint.

"Kaya," a vague voice calls. "Are you well?"

I shake my head a little, trying to level a steady gaze at Rajmund. "I think . . . I'll be fine. I just need water."

He gives me his ration, and we manage to reach the city wall without encountering any more adversaries. The stars up above Bashan begin to vanish, promising another sunrise. The sky is balefully orange in reflection of the dissolution of a civilization. We are almost to the city gates. Unfortunately, the swelling in my shoulder has spread down into my bicep and is red and hot to the touch. I know I need to find a remedy soon if I'm to keep my arm. Amputating limbs from animals has taught me that much.

Yawns spread contagiously through all of us as the sky begins to lighten. Svana is sleeping soundlessly in Rajmund's grasp. One of her arms dangles limply at her side, her mouth hanging open. I feel dizzy, from the pain, the thirst, and fatigue. I crave my bubble. This is probably what causes my foot to catch on the protrusion of a fallen cart. I try to recover, but instead I tumble to the ground, knocking over a blanket that had been hanging over a fallen tent post, and into a pile of soot.

Inhaling the sting of pain, I dust my hands off and peek at my wounded shoulder that's now pulsating furiously.

"Kaya?" Gring gasps.

"Cease!" Haldor shouts.

He's withdrawn his sword. Nasr has raised his arbalest straight at me. Gring stands rigid. Rajmund has retreated a few steps, still holding Svana close against him.

"Stop!" Gring hisses, moving a hand ever so slowly to his pouch. "Don't. Move."

He's looking just beyond my shoulder. They all are. Mortified that Canaanite soldiers could be lurking behind me, I turn my head as slowly as I can, until I'm faced directly with the tip of an arrow.

A woman, older but not much larger than I, has the arrow pulled taut in a bow right at my forehead. One glance at her, and I know she is no rebel. She's alone. And shaking. With a quick assessment of the situation, I surmise she was hiding behind the blanket in a makeshift asylum, until I came crashing into it. Her eyes dart to all of us, but they come to a rest upon Svana.

In the least threatening voice possible, I part my lips just enough to be heard and say, "Tonic?"

She seems to realize what I already have: we are not a threat to each other. Her eyebrows furrow as she jerks her chin toward the male soldiers.

"Can you lower your weapons?" I ask my companions out of the corner of my mouth.

They do so, and the woman takes a step back. Her gaze narrows on my bloody shoulder. She lowers the arrow, but keeps it pulled tight as a precaution. Her face is smudged with dirt, her clothes tattered. Her curly hair is tangled around her collarbone.

I struggle to my feet, clutching my wound.

"My name is Kaya," I state. She's another woman. I need her. "We are traveling to Giles."

She does not reply. She cannot understand me.

"You should come with us."

She does not look happy to see me, but neither is she afraid. The men have backed off, while Svana has drawn closer. The three of us form an unseen bond in sisterhood, in spite of our situation. I beckon to the older woman. She drops her bow and arrow completely. Her shoulders droop, and she covers her face with her hands, the extent of her loss visible in every part of her being.

I turn back to the men behind me, who are exchanging rapid sequences of hand signals. Nasr appears ferociously in disagreement with Rajmund and Gring. Haldor is trying to play the wordless mediator between them. I irritably wave at them to stop. They will do her *no* harm, or they will have to go through me first.

"You!" Nasr barks. "We shall be stoned, because of *you*, if we salvage her."

I ignore the outburst of testosterone-filled condescension.

I summon the woman, who halfheartedly picks up her bow and arrow. She doesn't say another word, and I shake my head sternly at Gring when he tries to question her. He sees her as an outlet of information regarding Bashan. The other men see her as an accursed object. I see her as no object, but as a living, breathing thing. And no matter what Joshua has commanded these soldiers, I cannot watch this woman's cold-blooded murder. Not after all she has been through.

Surely, God will show mercy upon her.

At dawn, we take a few hours to rest, invading yet another abandoned home. In the daylight, more of the city is visible. I let my eyes blur when I look around, dulling the scene of despoliation before me. There are distant echoes of ongoing battle, but no soldiers in sight. The fighting must be occurring in the distant plains. Inside our dwelling, the soldiers pore over Nasr's map. The older woman secludes herself from the others, peering out a window. She is not as hesitant as I am to view the smoking city.

Rajmund accompanies me on the floor in a corner, placing Svana between us. He has the look of a conversationalist. Rather than feel put off by his presence, I make it apparent I am ready to sleep. I stretch out my good arm, allowing Svana to lay her head on it rather than the hard floor, and close my eyes. Even after settling in, Rajmund speaks.

"Do you have a younger sister?"

I mumble, "Nay."

"Young kin?"

I shake my head.

"Hm."

I peek an eye at him. A soft smile spreads across his lips, and he touches Svana's cheek.

"Me either," he admits.

He has the face of a soldier, one that so typically deforms internal emotion and dispenses only one in particular: duty. But his features *do* have friendliness. Up close, I can see his eyes are a rich brown with gold flecks. The lines of his jaw are strong, stabilizing the structure of his long neck. His lips are full. He's not the kind of man I would normally be attracted to, but I can appreciate his attractiveness.

I stifle a yawn. "Why do you ask?"

"You just seem so maternal with her," Rajmund answers, with a glance. "It's quite selfless."

"Ha." My eyes roll closed. "Good one."

"It's the truth," he adds. "You have a way with people."

I hate people.

Have I not made that abundantly clear?

Rajmund smirks at my expression.

Svana is so young. So innocent. She shouldn't have to experience the things she's going through now. I could not hate one such as her.

"You have . . . been in many battles before?" I inquire. What I really want to know, now that Svana is asleep, is if this is normal. The way Joshua leads his army. So much destruction. I want to know what Rajmund thinks of war and God and their land of inheritance.

"Yay, I have," Rajmund responds quietly. Several minutes tick by. If he doesn't keep talking, I will be asleep in seconds. He does continue. "I met Joshua in Kadesh-Barnea, which is where I grew up. He enlisted me there. Some of the men brought their families to Gilgal, since it exists as Joshua's main logistics arena. Many of our supplies, commercial enterprises, and weapons manufacturers reside in Gilgal. I hear we will cross the River Jordan and replenish there after conquering Bashan. We must first gather the army in Giles, the fishing port thirty miles from here."

"This is quite the adventure," I mumble.

"It is, but it is God's work," he grins. "The Israelites, though they be innumerable, worship the same God. They understand Joshua is called of God. He is the greatest general the Israelite army has ever seen and a holy man. We are not a blind people. The Canaanites are a wicked populace. They partake in sin and whoredoms, and they worship false idols. They were called to repentance, but because of their iniquities, we have been commanded to destroy them.

"I can tell you doubt him." He smiles broader, and it is attractive. "Joshua. You do not show faith in him, or God. But know this. I have seen Joshua work mighty miracles. Sihon, king of Heshbon, was delivered into our hands. Og was delivered into our hands, when he might not otherwise have been. It is our rightful inheritance, these kingdoms. Bashan must be destroyed, and all of Canaan, for their abominations."

Thoughts stream through my mind. Rajmund's eyes follow mine to Svana. It is impossible to see her as a sinful creature.

"Tell me about your home," I whisper to change the subject.

Rajmund shifts slightly, the smile returning to his face. "I miss it."

"Was it hard to leave?"

"Nay. God has been good to me. You see the fire of Bashan, but *I* see the spirit of God burning. His way is the only way."

I don't recall falling asleep, but when I wake up, it is late morning. Everyone is still sleeping. Rajmund's voice repeats in my mind. *His way is the only way.*

I roll onto my side and throw up the empty contents of my stomach. My body is wet with perspiration. My fingers tremble. Brain thumps. The inflammation of my injured shoulder has reached my elbow.

"Rough start," I grumble.

Svana is no longer next to me, but standing at the window, peering through a broken board.

"Sh!" she says, pointing a finger outside.

The stink of the city makes my nausea worse. Nonetheless, I stretch and go to the window. A short distance away, near the city gates, a group of two dozen soldiers has gathered. *Others.* I say it aloud, and Rajmund snaps instantly awake. Seeing allies at Ashtaroth's front wall, I suddenly feel alight. We can leave this wretched place.

"We're going to join them, right?" I ask.

Rajmund picks Svana up, placing her on his hip like she is part of his armor. Whip and child.

"We should teach them to speak your dialect," I blurt. "The woman and her."

The men glance at me and each other. It is a feasible idea. Otherwise, the females may be executed on sight. Not to mention the five of us, for harboring them. *Just how, exactly, does Joshua punish an insubordinate soldier*, I wonder? We will have to plead to be taken before the judges if our hostages are discovered.

At our discussion, the lady with the bow and arrow mutters something. It's the first time we've heard her voice.

"What do you speak of?" Gring interrogates.

"Amaris," she responds, almost too hushed to hear. Her eyes are glazed over, as she stares out into her burnt city.

My heart mourns for her. I remember watching Avoca burn.

"Write that down!" Gring orders Nasr, who scrawls it quickly onto his map, convinced it is an important piece of information.

It is like walking through a nightmare, heading to the city gate. I am glad I was unconscious when the men brought me here, when the buildings and streets weren't all black and scorched, without evidence of life. We approach the outer wall clandestinely, the soldiers using signals to communicate, me and the older woman watching them in jealous frustration. Unsuccessfully, I try to tell her a few crucial words. *Danger. Run. Shout.* She is not interested in speaking to me, or anyone, or even looking alive. I turn my attention back to the front wall. A thin string of smoke rises above the stones. A campfire.

"Let's go!" I declare to the group, eager to meet up with our allies.

Gring gently touches my forearm, slowing my pace. His signal is easy to interpret.

Quietly. Slowly.

We inch up to the towering wall on the left side of the gate, the men conversing in hand signals. Some of the stone walls have crumbled down, forming boulders we have to climb over to reach the wall. Svana trails after Rajmund like a cub. Every few feet, he looks down at her, hand ready at his hip. His compassion for the child earns him points in my book of less-hated individuals. I make a mental note to show him gratitude and perhaps to the others for rescuing the females, myself included.

Gring reaches the open gate, the gaping mouth of Ashtaroth. Once heavily guarded, it now stands an abandoned post. Several battering rams used to destroy the entry lay discarded to the side of it. Bodies are everywhere. Optimistically, the majority of the deceased are Canaanites.

Gring peers around the corner into the valley beyond, withdrawing a metal star. Whistling the sound of a wild bird, he propels the spike across the opening of the gate, into the opposite wall. It sinks into the rock, spewing debris outwards.

A returning bird call.

A second metal star strikes the wall, directly above Gring's. It had been thrown from outside the city gates.

Tink!

The soldiers lower their weapons. Gring's double appears around the corner, an identical fusion of happiness and caution in the man's face. The two soldiers run toward one another and lock in a firm embrace, smiles of relief on their faces.

"Brother!" Grond shouts.

"I see you've been separated from your unit as well," Gring replies, pulling back.

Rajmund, Nasr, and the woman walk up to the twins. I follow Haldor, with Svana shuffling along beside me, bending down a couple of times to pick up what appears to be a playful item. I do not bother telling her they are remnants of soldiers' weapons.

"Make haste," Grond states, beckoning to us. "There is much to discuss."

KAYA

I've Made a New Friend

No MATTER HOW MUCH I argue, Rajmund demands I get my arm checked before searching for my friends. The two dozen allies have turned into several hundred, as Israelite soldiers amass outside of Ashtaroth. Mert, Dank, and Tabor organize the brigade and share intel concerning Joshua's whereabouts. An epistle arrives with instruction to march to Giles promptly. The congregation praises God mightily, giving thanks and offerings for the victory against Og.

Rajmund boils some water while another man, an Israelite medicus, unwraps my bandaged shoulder, removing soiled sections of my tunic. The bleeding secretion is revolting, swollen to my elbow and oozing. Even the medicus turns up his nose in disgust. My father would have amputated such an injury on an animal. In better news, my condition supersedes that of the other injured soldiers lying in agony throughout our encamped hosts.

The battle of Bashan was momentous.

The medicus puts herbs and myrrh into the water Rajmund is boiling. He then soaks a cloth in it. The cleaning process is horrendous. I turn away as they squeeze out the wound, removing the dirt Gring expertly stuffed in it. The medicus drenches the gouged hole with the herb water and attempts to disinfect it. I know the condition is lethal.

"Pour some wine on it," I grind out.

The medicus glances at Rajmund, and then at me.

"Do it," I state again.

Rajmund gives a pithy nod. The medicus fetches a bottle of wine. He pours it over my shoulder. I let out a cry that does not belong to me. Rajmund is dismayed. He clutches my wrists but says nothing. He expects the same from me as any injured soldier. I want to be brave, but I am frantic with suffering. After a few more ointments, stitching and bandaging, the medicus is finished with me. And I, certainly, with *him*.

"It looks better," Rajmund comments. "You know a lot about medicine?"

"I know a lot about wine," I correct him.

"Maybe you should lie down," he suggests, worry crinkling his brow. He suffered a few knife wounds himself, but nothing critical.

Svana is at his side, nibbling on manna. She hands me a morsel. I offer a grim smile to her, telling Rajmund, "I will."

What I mean is, after I comb the site in search of some very important people. It could take me a while to uncover each bloodied face in pursuit of those I seek. I may not even have time before we depart to Giles. On the plus side, no one has given much attention to our fugitives, Svana and the nameless woman. The officers are focused on making a swift exit.

Rajmund gathers some food, insisting I finish it before any further action. Then, while I'm eating a potato as fast as I can, he states, "I shall go with you."

"Where? To lie down?" I grumble. "That won't be necessary."

He smiles and blushes, putting rose petals to shame. I comprehend my stupidity too late. If there was any way to prove myself a wily temptress, I've just done so.

Before I can correct my error, he leans down and remarks, "If I thought you wanted an escort to a bed, I would have worked on my presentation."

It is funny and a little improper. I don't know how to react. I guess Rajmund speaks fluent sarcasm as well as I do. Rebby and Westin take such a blunt approach to flirting, and Travin flirts as well as a roasted chicken wing. I still consider Rajmund a stranger, one straddling the columns of people I do and do not hate, but I will admit he has a talent with flirting.

"It was a joke," Rajmund adds. "I-I-I'd actually never take you to bed. I mean, not right now. Well, I would court you first, because—"

"I understand," I reply, lamely rescuing him. "But I'm kind of . . ."

"Oh!" he replies, surprise giving way to pensiveness. "I apologize for my rudeness."

"I mean, I'm not married . . . I'm just . . .." I don't even know. "Don't apologize. I'm the one who needs to apologize. I haven't even thanked you. So, thank you for everything. Thank you for bringing me to Ashtaroth, if you had any part in it. For rescuing Svana. For not trying to kill the woman. And with this." I point at my sickly injury. "Bleh."

Rajmund looks relieved for a moment, then bewildered. He glances away at the tents and the horses and the soldiers. Two officers are huddled over a map staked to a table across from us.

"A plague has descended upon many of the uncalled cities of Bashan," one of them states. "Hornets. Many Canaanites have fled already."

"Then we may not face many more battles in this region," the replying officer agrees. "The hearts of kings have melted, as prophesied."

"There are enough soldiers here to comprise a defensive military unit, but not enough to survive an onslaught of enemy forces. How are our supplies looking?"

"We lost some of our cattle and provisions from Shittim, but Azsh and his unit have returned with many materials and equipment. We have enough necessities to make the journey to Giles. Our crops will be replanted. Gebidiah and Kinley have been sent to the river to receive a shipment of imported goods from Egypt. With the continued production and selling of olive oil, we will profit enough to purchase steel and warhorses."

Rajmund desires to join Officer Tabor and the lieutenants in their communion. With a nod, he says to me, "Take care, Kaya Lucan. I will see you soon."

An Israelite scout arrives at Ashtaroth moments later, with an epistle from Joshua. It informs the officers that Joshua has commanded his army to congregate in Giles without delay, where we will prepare to make the journey across the River Jordan. Having been victorious on the east side of the river, it is now time to cross. I listen, even though I prefer to be left out of the schematics.

"You've looked better."

My eyes flit up. The familiar voice matches the familiar face.

"Rebby!" I cry, reminiscent of the dozens of women he's spell-bound throughout his life.

His wavy brown hair is pushed out of his face, partially by dried blood and partially by a headband. Parts of his jaw are bruised and split. But he's ever the handsome chap I know him to be, decked out in battle gear and a warm smile. His presence is compelling as he widens his arms. I fling myself at him, only to wince. Wary of my bandaged arm, Rebby embraces me, lifting me off my toes. I linger a little bit longer until I remember how much he enjoys female affection.

Grinning, Rebby sets me down. "I could get used to this."

"I don't doubt that," I tease. He made it here alive, which means others could have too. "Why are you always following me?"

"A stunning girl?" he laughs. "I can't help it. And what is *this* new accessory to your beauty?"

"An *error*," I respond, prodding my injury. "I'm not sure I make a decent soldier."

"I'll kiss it better for you."

We sit down together. I can't help but note his armor and weapon, a broadsword, stale with enemy blood.

His face darkens with an unwonted guilt. "First day in battle was a little rocky for me, too."

"And the second?" I question dryly.

His hand does a weeble-wobble.

Rebby tells me he was there when Og was killed. *The giant.* The story he retells is a gruesome, magnificent tale. I've never imagined such warfare.

The Israelites came upon the city at Mount Edrei. Many enemy soldiers fled at the approach of Joshua. But Og was adamant, and he ordered his guards and soldiers to battle against Joshua. The king was executed in his own temple and hung on a tree outside the city gates. Rebby and Travin were separated during this confrontation. Many lesser battles ensued as the opposing forces fought in bewilderment, lacking their ruler. Rebby remained near Lachlan in the city. He watched it burn, later helping remove the king's body from the tree, where it was then thrust into the embers.

Rebby says he has not seen Travin since their first night in Edrei, but he knows that according to an epistle from Joshua, the Israelite army did not suffer much loss. There is a very high chance Travin survived.

High chance or not, my heart sinks. Travin is not here.

"He'll be fine," Rebby commentates. "He *is* fine. He is probably with Joshua by now."

I've never seen Rebby's confidence waver. He's fidgeting with the hilt of his sword, his expression conveying an apprehension his voice does not. The battle against Og must have been remarkable. It makes me feel less insecure that my own emotions have lost their defenses at the witness of such violence.

"What if Trav . . . " I hate to say it out loud. "What if Travin didn't make it? Joshua cannot guarantee every soldier will survive this war. What if . . .?

"I saw him fight, Kaya," Rebby tells me, and his mind drifts into those brutal memories. "Do you remember watching Travin fight Luko?"

I don't reply, traveling back in time to the awestruck moment I realized Travin was indeed a warrior.

"Travin was fighting the Canaanites, two at a time sometimes," he says. "When we stormed Og's temple, we went in different directions. But I kept an eye on him. Honestly, I thought *I* would have to come to *his* aid . . . like when we were children."

I lean my head against his arm, silent.

"Travin was in the room when King Og fell. Joshua, too. They fought side by side, and you couldn't even tell the difference. Their skill and precision was equivalent. I — I envied Travin. I was fighting on the steps, and by the time I ran to the king's chambers, Og had already fallen. His massive body was a pincushion of spears. One of Og's men almost got me. I had to use my hands to . . . " His voice fades, while he makes a strangling motion. His brief pause is accompanied by a rueful shake of his head. "I was frightened."

My eyes shift upward. "I would have been afraid, too."

"Yay, but it isn't your job to be the bravest of soldiers."

He cocks a sly grin. I mirror it.

"Unless our enemy's mortal weakness is oats and hay, I am certainly doomed. Maybe you and Rajmund can show me how to defend myself?"

Rebby raises a brow. "Rajmund?"

"Over there," I point. "Long, blonde hair. He was with us. You should see his whip. It's exceedingly deadly." This sounds funny coming from my mouth, like I'm marveling at him. Apparently, Rebby thinks I'm marveling at Rajmund, too. Rebby gives me a smile foreshadowing an embarrassing comment, so I quickly move on, "Anyway, I guess conflict on our journey to Giles should be minimal. That's what the first wave of soldiers was for. To clear the way. Great job, by the way."

Rebby playfully pushes my head away from his shoulder and stands. "If you aren't going to fawn over me anymore, I'm afraid my job here is complete."

"Rebby?"

"Hm?"

"Would you care if Svana and I sleep next to you tonight?"

"Of course," he smiles. "I'd never turn a woman away from my bed, let alone two."

His joke does not make me blush. He is just Rebby. I roll my eyes, scolding him when I reveal Svana's age.

"Come find me if you need me," Rebby adds, a bit more serious.

There are no luxurious tents like at the Israelite camp of Shittim. Our food and drink is minimal. I try to quench my thirst with water, but it does not cease the shaking of my hands or the headache in my skull. Most soldiers make do with the ground, blankets, hunted game, spare nuts and fruits. It's kind of entrancing, actually, lying beneath the stars. There are so many, a swirling stream of them traveling a current in the oceanic heavens. They are more beautiful than any nezem.

Svana curls up behind me and falls asleep quickly. Rebby, lying by my other side, snoozes on his back with his knife clutched in his hands. Trying to sleep in a state of sobriety is something I've not done in an exceedingly long time. My mind won't stop reeling. I try to calm my thoughts and let the sounds of the night lull me to sleep, but my stomach is ill. I'm thirsty and overcome with sickness. First hot, then cold. I check my arm. It is ailing me.

Several hours and a few dry heaves later, I'm drifting in and out of consciousness when a woman's voice breaks the silent night.

"Amaris!"

It's the woman with the bow and arrow and that's the only word she's spoken. She repeats the word a few times, and then falls quiet again. I can hear the yearning in her voice. The ache for something she loves. Some*one*?

KAYA

Is This Life for Me

TODAY, THE SUN IS shining tremendously. By late morning, we are moving along a stream. This land is filled with springs that flow into the River Jordan. The soldiers call this one Prawn. It drains into Jordan, an eleven-day journey from where we are now. Green palms and ferns line the banks, creating shade against the blazing sunshine. Groggily, I help Svana press on with the rest of the group. Rebby takes a liking to the little girl, promising to wait for her to grow up so he can court her. I don't think she has any idea of what he is talking about, but she smiles playfully as they promenade. I know Rebby knows of her origins, but he does not seem to mind, and I am thankful.

As I stare at them, I wonder if the woman with the bow and arrow was calling out the name of her child, Amaris. Or, maybe, a lover.

I wonder how many nights I've awakened to my own voice shouting out to my father, only to remember he was dead.

"Is he your betrothed?"

Rajmund falls into step with me, his eyes of maturity gazing down at me.

"Who? Rebby?" I ask him, bemused. "Definitely not."

"I thought—"

"He's a good friend from Avoca," I interpose. Rajmund opens his mouth, but I quickly add, "Like a brother."

"Excuse me," he smiles, tucking his pale hair behind his ears. He tosses a rock out into the water and achieves the effective expression of cordiality. "There's an admirable ease between you two. I assumed a fair maiden like you would be betrothed."

I cough stupidly. I do not qualify as a fair maiden.

"Nay," I reply awkwardly. Rajmund's not the charmer Rebby is, but his modest flirting is appealing. "I don't think anyone . . . can handle me as a wife."

"I have to disagree," he chuckles.

"I'm serious," I counter. "Complicated wrecks should never get married."

He laughs loudly enough that Svana turns to look back at us. I think she has already promised her heart to a different soldier. The blonde one. Rebby allows a casual glance at me and Rajmund, which is anything but casual. Then he bends down to splash some water at Svana, pretending not to eavesdrop.

I look up at Rajmund. He has a nice laugh. Nice like Westin's. But not as contagious as Travin's. Right now, I don't tell Rajmund about my relationships with either of them.

"Where I come from," Rajmund resumes, "when a man meets a woman he finds worthy, worthy of making a good family and good life, he proposes she be his wife. There is no prolonged courtship. A man's greatest duty is to his wife and land."

How quaint.

"There are many women to choose from," he continues, "but only one woman for each man."

I murmur, "Sounds romantic."

Rajmund gives me a knowing glance and declares, "I'll know her when I find her."

Later that day, our entourage encounters a half dozen rebels munching on gruesomely mutilated cadavers. They are contaminated by the disease, every inch of their flesh a testament of the repulsive disorder. When they move, their limbs jerk and stagger. The stench is awful. The Israelite officers jump into action, commanding several men to surround the rebels and eliminate them.

Once more, I worry concerning the safety of Svana and the woman. Their fate is unknown, left up to the Israelite judges. Surely, at the time of the next census, they will be discovered, if not before then. My hope is they will convert to the Israelite ways and make enough acquaintances that the people can vouch for them in front of the judges.

I have made progress with the little girl and, when required, she has begun to speak to others in concise sentences. The woman, with the same dark skin as Westin, and wildly curly hair like a black sheep, does not say anything at all.

By nightfall, we approach a wide marsh, the fishy ingress to the River Jordan. We've reached the outskirts of Giles. The residents have gone to rest. In place of bustling society, I hear the hum of camels, the squawk of chickens, the bawl of rams. A small fishing port, the village is prehistoric. The dwellings are chiseled into the rocky, sandy bluffs, some with log doors, some without. Silhouettes of palm trees rise against the sky, adding color to this desert land. I can hear and smell the running water.

Officer Mert orders a dozen guards to stand sentinel around the township while he and the other officers awake the slumbering villager elders. The rest of the soldiers are at ease. At this point, I don't mind where I rest. I am desperate for sleep. I yearn for my wine bubble. The nightmares keep me conscious, and my bandaged arm could use the numbness. I also wouldn't mind bathing. The skin on my exposed face and arms show the signs of excessive sun exposure, my clothing thick with grime.

Svana and I are setting up a small place to rest with Rebby, close enough to the water's edge to have disturbed the home of many insects, when the nameless woman begins wailing again. I can hear here calling out, "Amaris!"

"Not again," I mumble.

"What does she say?" Rebby asks.

"That woman," I answer. "She's said nothing but *Amaris* since we found her in Ashtaroth."

"Should I tell her I am Amaris?" he grins enigmatically.

"Do you have no respect?"

"In every form," he rejoins, outlining the shape of a female figure with his palms.

"Maybe we should ask her if she wants to sleep next to us," Svana suggests in a tiny, less understandable voice.

Rebby and I glance over at the young child. Sparing us another dry remark, Rebby sends Svana to invite her over.

"Thank you, Rebby," I tell him. "You're the best."

Removing his ezowr, he ruffles his hair and says, "Are you willing to prove it?"

I keep a straight face and reply, "Nay, kind man. I do not trust you. I simply distrust you the least."

The woman approaches gingerly, looking haggard and depressed. Even though Svana chatters in their native dialect, the older female refuses to respond. Svana takes her hand and helps her lie down next to us, but after Svana and Rebby are asleep, I find myself lying awake with her. Her eyes never stay focused on one spot for too long, like she's continually awaiting something. She bites her lip and whimpers, "Amaris."

"Hello," I whisper, careful not to wake the others.

The woman glances over for a moment. She doesn't reply as she peers back into the black sky, then at the dark shapes of trees, then to her left. I try again.

"What's your name?"

She stares at me, her weathered skin wrinkling.

"Kaya." I point to my chest and then to hers. "Name? What is your name?"

After a few seconds, she answers, "Tasia."

"I'm Kaya." I point to my chest a second time and then to Svana. "Svana." I point to Rebby. "Rebby."

Tasia eyes the girl. The two of them are still holding hands. Relative hostages. I imagine myself in their place, overcome with the weight of ignominy and sorrow for losing my home. The burden of an unknown fate. Surely Joshua would not have them executed. Even though I try to convince myself, it doesn't rest well in my mind. What would I do in Tasia's position?

I sit up, a reckless idea springing forth.

"I'll help you escape," I whisper.

Tasia watches me, befuddled.

"Get up!" I hiss. "You two," I point to her and Svana. "Get up. I'll help you escape."

I make the motions with my hands. Stand. Run. Far, far away.

Tasia swallows, moving steadily to her feet. Svana remains sleeping as the woman bends to pick her up. Tasia's wide eyes dart around the night, at sleeping soldiers, at me, to the east.

"Yay," I murmur. "You can go home. Or . . . somewhere. Wherever you'd like."

We begin to tiptoe away from Rebby, into the dark ferns. There are a couple of soldiers awake, so we won't look too out of place. The rest are sleeping, propped up by the hilt of their swords. The gravel is noisy under my toes, and I motion for Tasia to stay quiet. A hen scuttles by our feet. *Ba-cock!* We only make it twenty cubits when a hand clenches my arm. A second hand smothers my mouth. I lose my footing, fall into a man's chest. Tasia whirls around, Svana cradled to her bosom. Arms flailing wildly, I gape at the panic on Tasia's face until my body is restrained.

Twisting, I can barely see his face. His hair, his smell. Rebby's warm brown eyes blink intensely down into mine, his strong hands preventing me from moving or screaming. And then the soldier in him evanesces, and he's my friend again.

"Curse the Almighty, Kaya," he grunts. "What do you think you are doing?"

"I was helping them—"

"To their death?" he growls. Still constraining me in his arms, he jerks his chin toward Tasia. "Return," he orders. He says another word in a different dialect and then speaks in the Israelite tongue. "That way. Go. Now. Before the others see you were trying to escape."

Bowing her head, Tasia carries Svana back to our blankets. Rebby and I remain out in the brush, under a low hanging sky of darkness. Just the two of us, we stand unseen by any Israelite guards, listening to the sounds of the distant River Jordan.

"Kaya—"

And then I am gnashing my teeth in anger. An unbearable release of anti-numbness. "It isn't fair!" I curse. "To take someone against their wishes. It isn't fair."

Rebby's restrictive hold turns into an embrace. I drip like lava against him. A volcanic remittance of emotions.

"Would you rather they be killed?" Rebby asks. "Sending them out there into the unknown, they will surely die. Here, they will be protected by our army, at least until their fate can be decided by Joshua's judges."

"But Gring said all of Bashan must be destroyed. Joshua commanded his army to burn the city. Every man, woman, and child. *Every* breathing creature."

Rebby lifts my face from his collar, cupping my chin in one hand. "Yay, great and terrible things have come to pass. This was a wicked people. But, Kaya, Tasia and Svana will be saved. God has wrought many miracles. He will see to it they are forgiven if they come unto Him. Both will join Israel, as you have. Help them. Do not send them to their graves."

I nod, embarrassed . . . and cold.

"Come," Rebby says.

He turns, keeping his arms around my shoulders, and herds me back to where we lay. Flattened on my back, glancing up at the black sky, I think of smoke and death and love. The love between Tasia and her Amaris. Surely, my father taught me to love. *Do I love like Tasia? Do I love Westin? Is that why I pine for his companionship?* I pine for the wine, but I do *not* love it. *Is there a difference between enjoying being around someone and loving them?*

Are Travin and Bronwynn in love?

If so, I'd rather live alone the rest of my life than be in love like that.

"Rest, Kaya."

Rebby's voice is barely audible as I pass over into my nightmare.

TRAVIN

Making a Name for Myself

OFFICER CHARKISH HAS BEEN trying to organize his army for hours, delaying our departure for the River Jordan. We are leaving behind our station at Folomon, the nearest trading post outside of Bashan. Charkish's orders are for us to circle high and wide to the north, coming down upon Giles, while Officer Gorrow and his army loop to the south. A scout has been dispatched into the western territory, to chart out our course.

Joshua commands us to gather at Giles before crossing the river, but many of our men have been murmuring. Thus preparation and departure have been postponed. We were separated from Lachlan and his squadron shortly after the king of Bashan fell. There has been contention among us ever since.

Subsequent to success at Edrei, some of the soldiers took for themselves gold and silver, left behind by deceased Canaanites. The officers are exceedingly wroth. Joshua has warned against taking spoils of our enemy nations for ourselves. The cities are considered cursed. What precious things the soldiers do find are to be donated to subsidize the army's fund. Charkish wishes to punish the rebellious soldiers who have laid claim to the booty confiscated at Edrei, while Gorrow wants to await Joshua's orders.

In addition, contention has arisen within our ranks over the fate of the people of Folomon. No harm has come upon the residents thus far. This has divided the pleasure of the Israelites. Some soldiers are appeased, while others are bloodthirsty. With only an epistle

from Joshua to lead our actions, and those actions lead us out of
Folomon without destroying it, causes soldiers who desire its anni-
hilation to be angered.

Many different tribes inhabit this village. People from across the
land come here to exchange goods, setting up displays of their wares
in the quadrant of trading posts. With control of Folomon, and all
of the trading ports along the River Jordan and copious fjords, it will
be easy to retain control over the spine of Canaan. However, they
are not a wicked people. Joshua has commanded us to let them be,
further recommending that we make league with them.

The weather is fickle. Showers of star rock puncture the atmo-
sphere amidst the thunderous chants of the heavens. Tremendous
quakes split the earth. God is unhappy with our dissensions. I isolate
myself from the others and take up lodging in an empty trading cu-
bicle, watching the sky crackle. Thankful for the solitude, I crouch
against the back wall and sit. And pray.

A RUCKUS DRAWS ME from my sanctuary at nightfall. Charkish is
losing his ability to remain calm. He engages in an argument with
several soldiers, disputing the necessity to leave Folomon. Some of
the Israelite soldiers attempt to bribe Charkish with their stolen gold
and silver. These soldiers want to subdue Folomon. Officer Gorrow
is urging them all to do away with contention and to turn their
hearts to God. If we have not been commanded to attack by Joshua,
we will not overcome this city.

Gorrow forbids the use of the stolen property, further chastising
Charkish for his participation in bribery. A physical spat ensues,
during which I intervene. I help separate the quarrelsome men, giving my support to Gorrow. In a final act of leadership, Gorrow grabs
Charkish by the front of his tunic and dismisses him as officer, a job
technically reserved for the general of the army.

Gorrow, having trained and educated me all my days in Shittim,
then entrusts *me* with officering Charkish's unit. "Until a replacement

officer is ordained, you will lead these men. Take this tse'adah on your other wrist." He removes one of his from his right wrist and puts it on mine. "The men will heed your command."

He exerts proficient management in ordering the men to give up the precious things they stole from Ashtaroth, using the dispatch of Charkish as an example of what can happen when men use their agency to sin. The soldiers comply, bringing forth silver and gold.

After the quarrel has settled, Gorrow asks me to arrange a unit of one hundred men, with enough provisions to make the trek to Giles. Without delay, I begin ordering the men to prepare for the journey. To my surprise, they hold their murmurings and obey me. None of them mock me for being a Shemolo. Some of the men build gurneys for injured soldiers, others pack food and water and supplies.

We are ready to depart when Officer Lachlan arrives. The scout Gorrow sent out earlier gallops on horseback next to him. Examining the procrastination of soldiers keenly, Lachlan pulls his mare to a stop beside me, dragging a hand up the nose of his beast in a consoling motion.

"Is Officer Charkish unwell?" Lachlan asks me, dismounting his steed.

Lachlan is a large man with a thick beard. His hair is brown and gray, brushing his shoulders. The scout trots up after him, climbing down from his horse. Both men wear the signs of mêlée on their armor.

"Charkish was unstable," I tell Lachlan. "Gorrow asked me to step in."

"You've done well," he replies, acknowledging my efforts. "We will depart for Giles on the morrow. Joshua is ensuring the safe transportation of our provisions from Shittim. If we follow this route, through this pass, we can trail Officer Orren and his unit."

Lachlan watches me closely, hand at the hilt of his sword. Across his back is a large shield. The scout adjusts a mace and chain over his shoulder. The officers can afford great artillery. Even the lower ranking soldiers have fine, handcrafted weapons. I feel slightly inhibited, owning only the blade Father Lucan gave me. I'd retrieved it from the temple grounds after battling Og. It may appear simple, but I fight well with it.

Eager to reunite with Joshua and hand over the torch of leadership to those who are worthy of it, I beseech Lachlan for news.

"Officer . . . " I begin.

"I need to speak to Charkish," he sighs, a hint of annoyance lacing his voice. "You two get some sleep. You need your strength for tomorrow." The scout answers dutifully and departs. As I turn to walk away, Lachlan says under his breath, "You're the young man who beat Luko at Shittim, are you not?"

I hesitate. "I am."

He grins. "You helped defeat Og, I hear. And you've taken over a company of soldiers on a whim." Looking around the area, his grin expands. "You've proven to beat many giants. It looks like there is much more to be heard of you, young Shelomo."

It is the first time I like the sound of my name.

KAYA

Denial and Other Words That Start with D

THEY GET STRANGER AND stranger each time. Recent traumatic events carry disturbance into my dreams. The woman I witnessed being dragged through the alleyway in Avoca visits this time. I see her face, screaming as the rebel tortures her into defeat. And then I am she, and the rebel is Miki.

A soft, real kiss on my forehead startles me awake. The sun is blinding, leaving only a dark silhouette towering above me. A head. A face. I blink a few times, and his eyes come into view. Those striking, glacier-like eyes.

Westin dodges my skull as I bolt upright. Svana, Rebby, Tasia. They're gone. The village of Giles is awakening. Children play in the road. Camels stand tied to posts, chewing and spitting. A goat jingles the bell on its neck as it trots to its home. Rajmund is near the water well introducing some Israelite newcomers. I move my gaze back to Westin, remembering the kiss.

"Hello."

"Hello?" he asks, a bit ill-disposed. "Expecting someone else?"

"What?"

I've been eying the people in the village again. Beyond them, the River Jordan is visible, flowing rapidly in blue-gray currents. The oasis surrounding it reminds me of the Salt Sea.

"It's me," Westin says, moving his head into my line of vision. His hair is ratted and dusty. He is not wearing his armor, and he shows no signs of battle. "We just arrived."

We?

"Kaya?"

"I'm sorry," I stammer. "I'm just a little unwell." I subconsciously touch my hurt shoulder. "It's been an exhausting few days."

Westin follows my stares to the intermingling crowd of residents and soldiers. "You were having a nightmare. It's why I woke you. Otherwise, I would've let you sleep longer."

I cringe. "Do I talk in my sleep?"

"Just some muttering," he replies, looking at me. "I know it has something to do with Miki."

I sit and pull my knees up under my frayed simlah, wrapping my arms around them. I will not tell him the truth about that.

Westin nudges my shoulder with his nose. "Your arm—it looks hideous."

I flinch. "It will be fine."

It does look hideous, but at least my fever has diminished. I have not rid myself of the shakes since departing Shittim. I often lose more food than I ingest.

An inscrutable expression crosses Westin's face as he regards me. He spreads his arms, inviting me into an embrace. I lean my head on his chest, closing my eyes, and try to open that part of my soul that has been yearning for comfort. It doesn't open.

"Where is Svana?" I question suddenly.

"Who?"

"The little girl. I came here with a little girl. She was this tall—"

"The one over there?" Westin confirms, holding me close.

I crane my neck around to see where he is pointing, unwilling to reveal her as an accursed.

"Don't worry, she's safe." Westin proclaims this nonchalantly. "She's with the elder women of the village who can take care of her. I promise. An expedition is being arranged. A brigade of soldiers will lead some women, children, and injured to the Great Sea. There is an island, called Caphtor. A few of the Israelites will make their journey to it. I saw your friend, Mikyla Rox, helping organize the travels. But she's with her prodigal twin brother." He pauses, glancing around. "Miki Rox is running a census."

"Island?"

"It's out in the middle of the Great Sea. You wouldn't want to go. Travel would be unsafe on ships. What if a storm hit and you were tossed into the ocean? You could be swallowed by a whale."

"A whale wouldn't swallow a human."

"If it pleases you so much, then I will take you there someday. I promise." He helps me stand, saying nothing more of my shoulder, or the swelling of my ankles from so much walking. "Now, I've got something that will please you *today*."

I feel rotten as Westin leads me through Giles. No one even gives us a second glance, and I'm glad I don't have to fake a smile or pretend to be friendly. Behold, I am wrought with apprehension.

The homes are just what I imagined they'd be like, clay huts with dirt floors. Wood planks prop up the walls for stability. There are hammocks installed between trees, with pastures for beasts of all kinds, gardens, and a market. The people look the same, dressed earthy and unpolished, with long unruly hair and fingernails. Rajmund stands out like a sore thumb in his expensive armaments and glossy blonde tresses. I duck my head as we pass by him, unwilling to greet his friendliness with my sullenness. I'll speak to him later.

Westin and I advance toward one of the huts along the dry riverbank, enclosed on both sides by beautiful ferns. A rooster scuttles in front of us, bobbing its head and then clucking into flight as Westin ushers it roughly aside with a toe. He pulls open the wooden door of the hut, following me in.

"Be merry," Westin says. "Your friends are here."

My eyes fly up. Lock onto Travin's.

Everything goes white. I see a flash of Travin from the night of his fight against Luko. He was almost afraid of his victory but too thrilled to hide it. His skin was flushed and sweaty, and a little bloody, but he was smiling. It was the last time he smiled at me. The memory fades, and the hut comes back into view.

Travin, sitting on the edge of a bed, reading scrolls, leaps to his feet. Bronwynn is slumbering on the straw pallet. She whines something and rolls over, disturbed by his movement. There is an adjacent room where voices can be heard. Belongings and weapons are stacked in a corner, a stove is along the far wall, and a washing basin sits between them. Somewhere in the back of my mind, I register that Westin closes the door behind us. I stare, paralyzed, into Travin's mirrored expression. My heart is pounding so hard I can hear it in my ears.

I hold my breath. If I try to move, I will disassemble limb by limb.

Travin is bare-chested and barefoot. Near the stove, his armor and robes are drying from a recent wash. His hair, now below his ears, brushes his neck. At his full height, he looks taller than I remember. Taller and stronger. The soldier weight has compacted around his ribcage and done away with any remaining adolescence. Divots of might form in his firm sides. His arms, both bandaged, are full. The bones of his shoulders and wrists, once sharp and protruding, are now padded. There's a fresh, nasty gash near his bare collarbone, surrounded by the cushion of muscle.

Travin has not spoken to me since our big fight the night of the dance at Shittim, and the tension is still there. But I don't care. As long as he's safe.

I try to clear my throat quietly, but the room is so silent it sounds more like a dying goat. The discussion of those in the next room is clearly overheard. Guiltily, I tear my eyes away from Travin. Westin struts passed me to a second straw pallet. I can't look at him either.

"This is just temporary lodging for the day," he tells me. "You and Bronwynn can abide in here. The male soldiers are two doors down."

He begins shuffling through a satchel and retrieves a well-known corked bottle. Turning back to the rest of us, he pauses to send Travin a baffled expression. I can feel Travin's stare, but if I look at him now, I might just faint.

Westin motions between the two of us.

"Aren't you pleased?" he asks coolly.

I don't know who he is speaking to, Travin or me.

Travin shifts awkwardly. I use the opportunity to clear my throat again, dying-goat noise and all. I've seen him in his underclothes before, but right now it feels indecent. When I find the courage to look, I see Travin's eyes travel up and down me, coming to a rest on my bandaged shoulder.

"I wasn't sure if I'd see you again," I murmur, evading his eyes.

Travin's mouth opens. "I prayed for you."

He prayed for me? It makes me deliriously happy.

"I knew you'd be safe," Westin cuts in, promptly at my side. "What's the use of praying if you don't get an answer?" The last part he says in that quiet way you hope will be overheard. He hands the bottle, along with a wilted flower, to me. "For my trophy."

My happiness is trodden upon. The bottle feels immensely heavy in my grasp, heavy and magnetized. I feel my gaze creep back to Travin's. I recognize the frown on his face, the one I received shortly after joining the Israelite army, the one that adorned his face the first few weeks at Shittim, the one from the night of the dance. Travin frowns upon the indulgence of wine. A subtle but resolute warning shines in his eyes.

Westin tugs me close with an arm and plants a kiss on my hair.

"I missed you," he whispers in my ear. "I want to hear all about your travels, beloved. When I lost you at Shittim, I nearly burst with trepidation."

My face heats while my eyes dart between the two men. I don't like public displays of affection, and Westin has never once referred to me as his beloved. His behavior is just shy of scandalous.

I start to say something, but Travin spins away. He departs through the curtain separating this room from the adjacent one, the frown accompanying him. *Bon-won* spasms on the bed, bothered by a loud bang, but she doesn't wake. I notice she is wearing one of Travin's tunics, and it barely fits. I hand the bottle back to Westin. Crossing the room, I reach for the curtain.

"Trav?" I call.

Peeking into the room, I recognize several of the officers.

"I wouldn't bother them," Westin says from behind my shoulder.

Travin is beside Lachlan, the two speaking quietly with Rionn. The priest recommends having any prisoners of war sent to be judged and the spoils of Bashan to be blessed and distributed. Lachlan then mentions a special mission Joshua has for two spies who will be sent across the river on reconnaissance.

For a moment, I am concerned about Tasia and Svana facing judgment, but the concern is replaced by curiosity. What does all this have to do with Travin?

He glances up, and then again, spotting me in the doorway. Lachlan and Rionn do as well. I start to say something, but Lachlan speaks first.

"I apologize, but this is a private matter." He looks at Travin. "Would you like to discuss this elsewhere?"

Trav sucks in a breath to speak.

"I'll leave," I state, the look on Travin's face revealing a worry that he might disappoint the high-ranking officer. It compels me into swallowing my feelings. "I didn't mean to intrude."

I step back into the front room, gazing around the vicinity, down at my simlah, my tattered sandals, touching my loose hair. The flower in my palm crunches in my fist, and I let it drop to the floor. Gulping, I reach for the bottle in Westin's hand. I take a needy swig and pass it back. My thirst, the thirst for numbing an emotive ailment I've been suffering from, is satiated.

Eight hours and three bottles later, I'm more of a mess than I ever thought possible. At least my injured arm isn't quite as bothersome. Insobriety is a miracle in disguise. *Nothing* hurts.

"I'm going to go find more wine for our supper," Westin announces as he saunters to the door. "Will that please you, Kaya?"

Travin and Bronwynn sit opposite me. After spending the elongated day in the other room, Travin left with Lachlan. He returned only moments ago, awaking his snoring girlfriend with supper. Rebby and a couple others eat in the adjoining room.

"I'll go with you," I reply, shuffling after Westin.

"Kaya, tell Elam to give you as much to eat as you like," Travin says. "He'll oblige if you tell him I insisted."

Westin scoffs. "What about wine?"

Travin's eyes dart to his. "There is a cistern of rain water and copious streams to supply you with drink."

"I'll tell the stream you *insist*."

"Alright," I cut in, "*I* insist we go for a walk. I don't want to eat anything."

I'll most likely lose it.

"You should eat," Travin states, taking a step forward.

So does Westin.

So does Travin.

Bronwynn rolls her eyes. "Just let them go, Travin. Maybe we can finally have some privacy."

"'I apologize, but this is a private matter.'" I recite, dumbly. These two, without a chaperone? I fake a puking sound. "Bluah!"

Westin cracks a smile, one that reaches his mesmerizing eyes. I remember how handsome he is and what it feels like to have a relationship with him. We have much in common.

My joke does not delight either Travin or Bronwynn.

Sober people.

"Goodnight, boss-man," Westin says.

He captures my hand, and we promenade out into the darkening night.

Across from us, a tent set up by the Israelites is well illuminated, with officers feasting and laughing about their victories. Fat rams and bulls have been sacrificed. Grapes, fish, and bottles of wine lie scattered across the table. Westin grabs a bottle clandestinely. We pass by our dwelling. The sound of Travin and Bronwynn arguing permeates the walls.

I feel sorry for him. But I feel sorrier for me.

"There's a rabid hyena out of its natural habitat in there," I murmur. "I fear she wants to eat us."

It was mean—stooping to her level.

I've really let myself go.

"Let's go to the riverbank," Westin suggests.

Leaning on each other, we follow the fragrance and reverberation of the River Jordan to its banks. It's too dark to really appreciate the splendor, but the water awakens something inside of me. Inebriated or not, I find joy in being near the water. Water is cleansing.

Memories of the Salt Sea creep into my hazy mind. Memories of midnight swims, the hollowed out cave on its shore . . .

"This is the spot." I fall onto my rear and sit cross-legged in the grainy sand.

It's not as soft as back home. The smell is different, too. Waves hum a couple of feet away. Beachy air tickles my hair. I can faintly recognize the outlines of the port down the shore, where the officers have ordered the construction of commerce ships that will sail up and down the river frequently. Examining the transportation crafts of the Giles' fishermen, I wonder how the High Commander expects us to cross the river before anything larger is built.

I don't want to think about war anymore. For just a moment, I close my eyes. I am back in Avoca. Young and free and not facing savage battles. But the instant dizziness I feel forces me to open my eyes and try to focus my vision.

Westin takes a seat next to me. "Do you like the wine?"

I shrug, finding difficulty in liking anything these days. "It is strong."

"It's not as good as back home." He sets the bottle between his knees. "Nothing is."

"Hm. There's something dangerous about wanting more, don't you think? Is it ever possible to just be satisfied with what one has?"

"I want more with you."

The breeze blows a few loose strands of hair across my face. Reaching over, Westin tucks them behind my ear. His fingers trace my jaw, lingering below my chin. His sapphire-eyes glimmer. That face. Those lips. The laxity of my thoughts highlights a reality I haven't admitted before. My attraction to Westin's outside outweighs my attraction to his inside.

I do care about him. I care about what we share, and the times like this, when I don't have to be alone. I want more—but that more is pending.

I've got to be ready sometime. Ready for "us."

"I'm so lucky to have you," he purrs in that tone of his. "I don't know what I'd do with myself if I didn't have you. I'm so glad you made it back to me. I need you."

Need.

That's an unsafe word.

"I've been—lonely," I respond, my mind traveling to my own

needs. Speaking aloud, I voice a reflection. "Lately, I've felt like no one understands me. But *you* understand me."

Westin smiles my favorite half smile. "I do."

He'd asked me earlier to tell him about my travels. I have been itching to bare my grief about Ashtaroth.

"The destruction of Bashan was terrifying," I say.

"To be truthful," Westin replies, "I didn't see much of it. Officer Orren and our unit mainly dealt with cities that had already been evacuated. We were not present at Ashtaroth or Mount Edrei."

"Oh, it was—"

"Let's talk about something else. Something less depressing." He takes a drink. His eyes sway. "You're the greatest thing that's happened to me, Kaya. You give me hope and ideas. I would like to journey with you to the Great Sea and sail to Caphtor. I spent my entire voyage from Shittim to here thinking of our future. I confess I did not have to fight any Canaanites. Our dealings were diplomatic—political even. War isn't for us, Kaya. I wish to go back to the peaceful days of Avoca."

I hate that I can't tell if he's lying or not. No matter how hard I try, I still find it difficult to trust him. *Why is that?*

"Would you consider leaving the Israelites?" Westin inquires. "If you had the chance?"

"I'm not sure."

"Are you sure you want to fight for them?"

"I thought we were fighting for all of us, for freedom," I answer. "Someone has to fight for it. Don't they?"

He speculates a minute. "I just don't know if I support their conquest. I'd much rather run away with you." He links his fingers in mine. "We could believe whatever we want to believe. We could plow our fields with an ox and a mule at the same time."

"You know that rule is for the benefit of the animals, right?"

"That's not the point." He flicks the air with the back of his hand. "Rules, rules, rules."

The religious sermons I've so often relayed in my mind pop up. I try to dig deep and find faith, find hope, find trust in a higher being. I want to know that Joshua is truly called of God to lead us, that we are doing what is right. That Heshbon and Bashan were wicked territories.

Travin believes in God, which is almost enough for me to believe, too.

I trust Travin.

KAYA

A Turn for the Worst

ONCE AGAIN, I HAVE busied myself with duties pertaining to four-legged and winged creatures. After tending to the cattle and the horses, I gather a few eggs and return to my hut.

At the noonday meal, Bronwynn and Travin enter, awaking me from my rest. They are both carrying two servings of food. Neither speaks to me. Bronwynn sits as far away from me as possible and has finished her meal before Travin's even dented his first bowl. She is donning a new dress today, one that fits her expanding frame. I haven't cared to ask, but I wonder what her journey to Giles was like. Lo, my hate for her consumes my heart.

I do not wish to do evil today by judging her. If I can refrain from that, and from drinking wine, I will call it my own personal conquest. For motivation, I decide to head to the river and bathe. Waves and sun and sand. It shall be good.

I gather a small towel and chunk of soap from our hut's washroom when Travin asks, "Where are you going?"

I can see him through the curtain, watching me.

"To the river," I reply.

"Can Bronwynn go with you?" He shushes her when she disagrees as much as I do and enters the washroom. Speaking more quietly, he adds, "She mentioned wanting to see the river. And I need to join Rebby and Officer Lachlan for . . . I've been called on a mission. I will be gone for two weeks. Bronwynn doesn't have anyone. It would mean a lot to me if you could just be there for her."

"Where are you going?" I question.

Travin bites the corner of his lip. "I can't say."

The washroom is suddenly small for the two of us.

"Right. Your 'private' matters. In fact, that is what I would like my bath to be. A private matter."

"Please," Travin says. "Can you just befriend Bronwynn at this time? You're going to be living together for the next few weeks, and I would appreciate it if . . . "

"Trav."

"It's a public river." His tone turns testy. "Can you do me this favor?"

"You've got the authority to *insist* it. Why don't you order me to take her?"

Frustration mists his gray eyes. I've seen this look. Lost. Defeated. Usually he looks this way after a particularly hurtful discrepancy with Bronwynn. I'd seen it plenty of times growing up when he faced discrimination from Avoca bigots. I am wrought with disappointment. This is not what I want to happen between us.

I squeeze by him and reenter the front room. Shortly after, he appears. Bronwynn levels a carping scowl at him, avoiding my attention.

"Well, I'm leaving now," I mutter. "Bronwynn can do whatever she wants."

"She's ready to go," Travin states brutishly. "Aren't you, Bronwynn?"

Bronwynn shakes her head at Travin, even though he takes her by the arm and shepherds her to the front door. I don't wait to see if she follows. I pace by her and out the door in pursuit of a quick head start. Maybe I can ditch her on the trails, and she'll have to find her own place to bathe.

I'm not so lucky. She maintains a safe distance behind me, so we don't have to converse, but close enough to find her way down to the sandy shoreline. I undress, take my soap, and wade my way into the river, careful of the forceful currents. I do not go too deep, making sure my feet can reach the riverbed. A nook of shallows, surrounded by shrubs, provides the coverage I desire. Diving, I paddle over to it and blink against the sunny sky.

This is my happy place.

Letting the motion of the waves lift my toes off the riverbed and swing me side to side, I coach myself to relax, to meditate, to mend. I've felt sick lately. Without my wine bubble, I feel many unpleasant things.

In my peripheral vision, I see Bronwynn on the shore unclothing. I glance in her direction, meaning for it to be just a quick, nosy peek at her chubby weight gain so that out of all the fetid things going on in my life I might at least be assured that I am better looking than her. But I freeze with shock. Her stout figure appears. The spare wheel that had formed around her belly has projected horizontally. She warmly rubs a hand across it, patting.

Time seems to stand still.

Her second helpings. The weight.

How far along is she?

Thoughts spark like star showers in my mind.

An infant.

Condemnation.

Travin as a father.

His one *allowable child.*

I turn away from Bronwynn and look down at my trembling hands, the thought pollution crowding my mind. Exiting the waters, I grab my clothing, haphazardly draping them over me, and stomp my way back into the village. My insides are churning. I reach the hut in a state of semi-conscious stupefaction, bursting inside to find Westin bent over a scroll. He hurriedly rolls it up.

"Get your stuff!" I order. "We are leaving."

He stares at me, puzzled. "Huh? Why?"

"We're not staying *here* any longer," I shout, trying to throw what few belongings I have into his satchel. There isn't much room. My hands fumble with it until everything falls back to the floor. "We should run away, like you said."

He stares at me, unresponsive for a moment. My eyes travel to the scroll in his right hand, subtly tucked behind his back.

"You know what, I don't even care," I say. "I guess we all have our secrets."

I kneel to repack everything I've just dumped out, ignoring the look on his face that says he thinks I'm acting crazy again.

"Here, give this to me," he states softy, reaching for his satchel. It is unnecessarily heavy. When it passes from my hand to his, I hear the jingling of shekels.

"Never mind." I lift both hands to the sides of my face. "Can we just get out of this room?"

"Kaya, let's talk about this."

"What is there to talk about? You said you would do anything for me. You also expressed interest in absconding from the Israelites. It sounds like you've got enough silver in there to buy us passage to the Great Sea."

Westin straightens his shoulders, tucking the scroll from his right hand into his satchel. Slipping it over his shoulder, he walks to a cupboard and pulls a bottle off a shelf.

"The silver isn't all mine," he answers quietly. "Why don't we sit down for supper tonight, over a nice bottle of wine. We can talk about your desires."

"I desire to know what you're hiding," I reply.

"Welcome to the club."

I snatch the bottle from his hands and stalk out of the room. The strap on my sandal breaks just outside. I groan loudly, kicking it off my foot. I'll have to save up to buy a new pair, but I'd so much rather buy something else: passage to the islands. I could live barefoot the rest of my life. The wind in my hair. The sun on my face. Not a soul around. Hiking down to the river's edge, I resume the comfort of my wine bubble.

I don't need Westin right now, and I certainly don't need anyone watching my *crazy*.

It is morning, two weeks later. My least favorite time of day. Prying an eye open, I groan at the instant thumping happening within my skull. Always with the thumping. I feel around the bed for a drink, coming up empty-handed. I curse the man who has left me without it. Curse the drought my body will soon face if I don't get it.

My second eye opens. The front door to the hut hangs open, letting the lemon sunshine in. Raising my head a fraction, I see the empty straw pallet along the other wall, the blankets neatly folded. A blurry memory from last night portrays Bronwynn moving out of this room and into the next, an argument, Travin begging me to find reason. Reason has abandoned me. Like all else.

I tried to be reasonably friendly to Bronwynn while Travin was gone, I really did. And only because of the look on his face when he asked me to. I even purchased a pair of sandals for her when I bought my own, as I had noticed her feet were swollen and the straps left imprints around her ankles. I'd put in extra hours at the stables to afford them. Her response to my gift was, "They didn't have any in black?"

I compared her to a fat ram and spent the night raking hay.

Pushing the hair off my face, I roll off the bed and totter to the doorway where the sounds of a dispute increase. Horsehair and grains cover my simlah. I don a cleaner outer robe, run a hand down my long, tangled hair, and take a few steps outside. My headache accelerates. Soldiers and citizens intermingle in the busy morning. Mikyla and Miki are working as scribes. Several priests carry these documents etched in stone to their tabernacle. Haldor is carrying a stack of sharpened swords. The Bottker brothers are having a contest to see who can do the most push-ups.

Following my feet, I near the mass of bickering soldiers that has formed near the water well. Water is not as good as wine, and it offers no bubble, but I have to do something about my throat.

The well is crowded, Israelites engaging in a debate over a missing battalion. Rajmund stands next to Officers Lachlan and Carac. He is dressed fully in his regal armaments, with his whip attached to his girdle. The sunlight makes his eyes look bronze, like his breastplate. I have to squeeze by him to get a pail of water from the well. Only slightly acknowledging him, I take a drink. He does a once over on my appearance, vaguely sympathetic.

"What is going on?" I ask.

Rajmund points, and I look. Joshua is approaching Lachlan and Carac. It is *he*. He is here. Joshua appears the mythical creature everyone believes him to be. Virulent, large, magnificent. His power commands attention, his red cape flaring. When the officers notice him, their contention immediately ceases. Carac snatches the detailed provisions assignment and holds it up, declaring his insistence that the other soldiers listen. Joshua waves him to a hush, his calm manner tailored for leadership.

"Officer Azsh and an army of one thousand are missing," he states. "They must be recovered before we can depart from Giles."

The soldiers discuss this in several opinions.

"Shouldn't we presume them dead?" Officer Carac questions.

"Nay," Joshua answers. "I will ride with a small unit of soldiers to locate Azsh. The officer's last known location was somewhere in the mountains north of Edrei. After accounting for the soldiers, I will traverse back to Giles. Immediately upon returning, we will make the voyage across the River Jordan to Gilgal. Jair will be in charge in my absence."

Joshua asks for volunteers, a strange request seeing as he could simply order anyone to do anything and they would.

"The mountains are a known rebel territory," he confirms. "It will be a perilous mission."

That is why he'd prefer volunteers. And it amazes me that Joshua wants to take on this mission himself, when he has many important things he could be doing.

Tasia is standing alone, just beyond the soldiers. Her curly hair is wild and frizzed. She's been watching Joshua, although I don't know how much of his language she understands. It seems she comprehends what the soldiers have been talking about. Her limbs are rigid with anticipation. Her lips move.

Amaris.

"Fear not, my valiant soldiers," Joshua proclaims. "God is with us."

I can't believe I'm standing this close to him. He has yet to realize I, a humble stable maid, am lingering in the shadow of Rajmund, quenching my thirst. I am entranced listening to Joshua's voice, witnessing the absolute faith in his eyes, the calmness about him, the affability. He is fearless. A model of discernment. A holy man. A good friend. Despite knowing the mountains he must enter are filled with enemies, he is going to rescue his unaccounted-for soldiers.

A parable concerning the shepherd in search of his lost sheep comes to mind. And then another idea joins it.

I want to go with him.

Rajmund raises his hand, among many volunteers. I raise my fist into his, locking our fingers. He glances down at me, tightening his grip on my hand.

"For Israel," he states.

I nod. "For Israel."

"We journey toward Narr, the city to the northeast," Joshua dictates. "It is part of the Bashan kingdom. It has been vacated, but rebel inhabitants have increased. They're plagued by the disease. The land will be treacherous. Hittite migrants have taken up residence in a few resigned cities. My scouts have revealed there may be a dictator over the vagabond settlers. The Hittite movements have been deliberate and prudent, unlike rogue rebels. We will encounter trials and tribulations, but be strong and have courage."

A group of forty soldiers has gathered around the High Commander. He holds out a small drawing of the mountainous region.

"We will search here, here, and here. Pack light. We leave in an hour."

I follow Rajmund out of the circle, excitement walloping my chest.

"I'm not a warrior," I whisper.

Rajmund grins and says out of the side of his mouth, "You trust in God. It is the same."

Do I?

Westin suddenly materializes, yanking me away from Rajmund. "Kaya, are you insane?" he gasps.

And where has he been?

"I'm not staying here," I return. Rajmund, startled by Westin's conduct, takes action. But I shake my head to advise against it, knowing an unnecessary dispute between them will come about.

In a second's time, Rajmund absorbs my relationship with Westin Fahim. A slight scowl dims Rajmund's expression. I lift a palm to him, but say to Westin, "I can get out of this . . . place." Place being a state of the mind, rather than a physical location. "Joshua says we need not fear. We will find Officer Azsh and return in no time."

I start down the road. Rajmund follows, a countenance of caution and opposition stiffening his movements. Right now, I'd rather be with him than Westin.

"*Joshua says,*" Westin spits, keeping stride. "Joshua speaks for his army, for his Israelites, the men he must encourage to do all the dirty work. *Of course* he says what they want to hear. They would not follow him otherwise."

"You accuse him of bearing false witness?" I demand.

"An exceedingly dangerous thing to do."

That would be Travin's voice. He is standing outside of the munitions tent, where Rajmund, Westin, and I advance. Travin's chagowr is wrapped around his torso, his tse'adah on his wrists. Tassels hang from the bottom of his tunic, similar to the "tsit tsit" seen on the robes of Joshua, Jair, and Nobah. They're a reminder for the righteous of their covenants with God.

Travin's arms are folded across his chest. The bandages have been removed, revealing strings of fresh scars. His hair flops over his ears, and he has an errant smirk on his face. But his eyes shimmer darkly at Westin.

I want to smile at Trav, but I don't, because I don't think we are friends right now. Westin glowers at him in defense, inveigling zero response from my childhood friend. I do smile then. Trav misses it because his eyes are still on Westin.

Bending to retrieve a lightweight sword from the stockpile, Rajmund nods a greeting to Travin, the latter responding in like manner. Rajmund hands the weapon to me. I'm vaguely aware of Travin's eyes examining the transfer. It is the only part of his body moving.

The sword is no heavier than a horseshoe. I feel cool.

Travin's gaze glues to mine. I wiggle the sword and my eyebrows. Without looking away, he offers a rapid hand signal that Rajmund reciprocates.

"Where is Rebby?" I ask.

Travin finally moves, shifting his weight. "He's staying here with Jair. Joshua's order."

"We must make haste," Rajmund reminds.

I hustle back to my hut, sword and cool-factor in tow. My adrenaline is piquing. Grabbing my small satchel of supplies, bread and cheese, water, and herbs, I can't contain a grin of excitement. In the intervening moments, Westin persistently tells me I'm unwise and tries to convince me this is just a suicidal mistake.

"You don't even know what you're doing!" he huffs, trailing me through the hut like a querulous child determined to out-stubborn his mother. "This is madness. You're going to get yourself killed."

He's probably right.

"I've never been all that attracted to life," I mutter dryly.

Travin and Rajmund stand in my doorway. They split apart when Bronwynn approaches, stepping between them. Her thin hair has finally grown below her chin, a more flattering look for her fuller cheeks. A basket of olives sits on her hip.

"You're not leaving again?" she asks Travin. Before he can respond, she says, "You were just gone for two weeks."

For the first time in history, Travin ignores her. But she doesn't stop.

"Travin, I need you right now. You cannot abandon me on some rescue mission. Joshua has plenty of volunteers. Don't be selfish about this!"

I exit my premise, stepping over olives that tumble from Bronwynn's basket. Rajmund smiles at my expression, but his eyes flash with exasperation when Westin follows hot on my heels.

"Kaya," Westin pleads. "You don't know what you're doing. You've hardly had any combat practice. We can stay here and be safe. You love the river. It will be just like home. We can even leave if you want."

"I *am* leaving."

"Then let's leave together. We'll leave these violent people. You and I—Kaya!" He grabs my right bicep, jerking me to a halt. My right shoulder smarts. His icy eyes peer into mine as he bends forward. "Kaya, wait. I — I love you."

Aghast, I quickly gather Travin and Rajmund's reactions. Both of them appear on the verge of aggression, their eyes fastened to Westin. I physically shake Westin's hand off of me, but an impression of his fingers lingers on my upper arm. I psychologically shake off the mortification. I can handle myself. Besides, if he hadn't grabbed me, the other two men might have heard what Westin said—which was worse.

Ingesting my anger, I start across the road. Travin's gaze follows me. Rajmund's remains on Westin. He hasn't given up.

"And this?" Westin snorts, snatching the thin sword from my hands. "What makes you think you have what it takes?"

Rajmund captures the sword in one fluid movement and hands it back to me. "If you have a problem," he comments tigerishly, "take it up with Joshua."

He springs to the top of my list of "liked people," but I'm a little surprised it wasn't Travin coming to my rescue. My lifelong protagonist stands casually to the side, concealing the torridity in his eyes well. He whistles one descending note. Ignoring Westin and Bronwynn, Rajmund points to the edge of the village.

"Joshua is waiting."

Several dozen armed soldiers have amalgamated around him. With delight, I see that a couple of them are female. I twirl the sword in my grasp once, and then charge after Rajmund, aware of Travin's footsteps behind me. *Let's do this.*

Halfway there, Tasia steps out in front of us. Her leathery face is stern, no longer the face of a torn woman. She holds her bow in her hands and has a quiver of arrows slung over her shoulder.

"Amaris," she exclaims.

I give her the universal signal for approval.

"Say your goodbyes," Rajmund says nonchalantly. "Do not keep Joshua waiting."

He paces ahead of us a bit. Behind me, Travin is reassuring Bronwynn.

"You will remain here," he asserts. "I have to do this. Joshua needs me. We won't be gone long. You will be safe here in Giles with the other Israelites to strengthen you."

Bronwynn's reply is cacophonous like unto an anthropoid giving birth.

My patience has run short, so I turn to Westin, hoping to give him as succinct a goodbye. But he's not there. Reappearing a second later, he exits the munitions tent with his satchel slung on his back and a war hammer in his weapon's harness.

Returning to me, he announces angrily, "Fine. I'm coming with you."

WESTIN

Vitalities and Virtue

THE SOLDIERS SPREAD OUT in a field, slumbering after a day of hiking. Several guards circle the area where we have camped. They will switch shifts in another hour. I lie awake studying the coals of our fire. Tasia is awake also, or she sleeps with her eyes open. I'm not sure how to tell the difference, but she does not blink. Next to her, Kaya has found sleep, but it is fitful.

Forty men and women have volunteered for this mission, those I know include Officer Lachlan, Officer Carac, Haldor, the twin Bottker boys, Rajmund, and Travin. Travin is currently on night guard with Joshua and Officer Lachlan. He thinks he is one of *them* now.

I don't need to be Joshua's puppet. As soon as we cross the River Jordan, I plan on renouncing the Israelites. Kaya and I can find somewhere to make our home. We don't need an inheritance to do so. The islands are welcoming migrants. Caphtor and the surrounding oceans are not confined by rules.

Morning arrives in a hurry. We are awakened by horses galloping through our caravansary. One of the steeds is dragging something—*someone*—tied to a rope. The body, a captured rebel, bounces in a flatus of dirt as the horse is brought to a halt before Joshua. The captive, not yet dead, has maggots burrowing into sores on his flesh.

Bits of his skin are worn off, chunks dangling from his elbows. The odor is rank. Even from several cubits away I have to cover my nose.

Lachlan dismounts his horse to which the enemy is tied. "He tried to infiltrate our perimeter. Should we question him?"

Joshua surveys the culprit and replies, "Nay. He is contaminated. Let us make an example of him."

Our High Commander commands the man to be hanged. Joshua mounts his mare, overlooking the scene as the officers drag the diseased body to the limb of a tree where he will remain for the last few minutes of his life. Grond assembles the rope around the captive's neck. Travin and Rajmund hoist the other end, lifting the man's feet from the ground.

Kaya is confounded by the brutality, her green eyes glued to the soldiers carrying out their duties. I fear she has surrendered to the Israelite authoritarianism. When it is finished, she moves to the horses, brushing their tails as if nothing had happened at all.

Picking up my satchel, I start toward her when I notice Travin. He is *also* watching her. On the other side of the swinging corpse, he stands hesitant. He flattens a wayward hair atop his head and paces in Kaya's direction. The two of us, striding toward the same destination, cease when Rajmund beats us to her.

I envision their hands, held together, as Rajmund and Kaya both agreed to volunteer with Joshua.

They converse a moment before Rajmund turns to walk away. Kaya stuns both Travin and I as she smiles wryly at him. Though the transaction is negligible, it is a precursor for worse things to come. Travin's face agrees, revealing what I feel inside. The very thought of her gaining rapport with the other male soldiers fills me with contention. A new distaste rises in my throat, pondering the way she looked at Rajmund, the way he looked at her, and the way Travin looked at *them*.

KAYA

Narr and Far

THE FIRST DAY WE move vertically, climbing out of Giles to the northeast. Narr is not too distant, but the journey will take longer than anticipated considering the steep mountainside. We should reach the perimeter by tomorrow. At least the weather is mild. There is little discussion amongst us. I focus on our trajectory instead of our company. Besides, the soldiers communicate in that silent way. I've been watching their hands, their fingers, the signals. And I watch Joshua. He makes me feel invincible.

Behold, I have a sword. And it has propelled me into an interest of weaponry.

Today, as we hike through the slot canyons, Tasia and Travin talk bows and arrows. Surprising me and Rajmund, she speaks the Israelite dialect effortlessly. I am glad, for she has not been judged. Joshua has not shown any sign of condemning her, and she has not shown any sign that she is a Canaanite. Travin teaches her hand signals, she performs the proper way to lace a feather delicately between one's fingers. As a kid, Trav made a lot of bows and arrows, but they were flimsy and paled in comparison to Tasia's.

Their discussion breaks up the silence the rest of us employ. As I listen, I can recognize vexation in Travin's voice. He is grievous today. His frown portrays less of the chronic irritation I've familiarized it with and more of a peculiar nervousness. I get the feeling it does not have to do with war. Perhaps he's anxious because Rebby stayed behind in Giles. They don't operate quite the same without each other. Maybe he misses *Bon-won.*

Our unit approaches a narrow slit of mountainside that drops off about fifteen feet, then forks. There is no other passage. Joshua orders the Bottker twins, Haldor, and nineteen others to venture right with him. The rest of us will venture left with Lachlan. If we do not reconnect within the hour, we will return and find an alternate route through which to pass.

Descending the rock face is a balancing act of placing both hands and both feet onto the sides of the mountainside and inching down cautiously. Once at the bottom, our unit splits. Lachlan leads eighteen of us through the slim passage to the left, as Joshua's group disappears to the right.

Broken chariots and empty baskets line the trail, but the passage is otherwise vacant. At least, it would seem the entire mountain range is deserted. Twenty minutes later, the reverberation of rocks tumbling stops us. Lachlan raises a flat palm. Rajmund repeats the motion. All of the men do.

We instinctively crouch beneath a shady outcropping of rock. Hand signals are exchanged. I observe. *Alert. Unknown. At least ten.*

Rajmund's whip dances in his fingers. Travin and Westin are armed at the ready, Travin with his knife in his left hand, Westin with his war hammer. Tasia's bow is loaded, pulled taut at her side.

Swallowing, I lift my sword.

"Guard your flanks," Lachlan states calmly.

Rajmund turns to Westin and grins crookedly at him. "Hope you like bugs."

KAYA

This Really Bugs

THE SOUND OF HORSES approaching resonates throughout the canyon, growing louder. My grip on my sword slips. Westin says something to me, but I'm not listening. I can only think of the nearing footsteps, the sound of tired horses whinnying, the creak of Tasia's bow stretching.

"Bugs?" Travin whispers.

More hand signals.

An impact near the side of my head stuns me. I flinch, but my hair is pinned between the mountain and a blade that made the sound. Suddenly, six, seven men clothed in dark fabric, faces concealed, leap out at us. Their skin has been covered in whitish mud to camouflage their flesh. They blend into the mountains around us. Each of them carries an oddly shaped weapon, the sharp edges coated in dried blood. Short-range infantry.

Lachlan hollers an order. The Israelites react in unison, ready and willing for the enemy confrontation. Rajmund is on two of them, maneuvering his whip melodically to attack. Tasia plucks one of the assailants with her arrows. But more are swarming into the slot canyon. They materialize out of cracks like unto a spider's egg sac hatching. Many of them are long-range soldiers. We are outnumbered, and the enemy has high ground.

A huge, beastly man attacks, throwing a pinwheel made of steel blades. It misses Rajmund's head, sinking into the rock behind him.

"Kaya!"

A sharp, prickling on my scalp causes me to respond to the voice. On the other side of the large, metal ax stuck pinioning me to the mountainside, Travin is hacking away at my hair with his knife. Westin tugs on my sleeves. When a rival soldier rebounds off an adjacent rock, vaulting toward us, Travin pauses his barbering to kick the man mid-flight to the ground. Tasia ends him with an arrow.

At last my hair is cut free. I fall to my knees and cover the sides of my head with my hands, my sword rendered useless.

"Get up!" Westin screams, grabbing hold of my arms. "Get up, we have to run."

Travin twirls his knife, absorbing the scene in less than a second. Lachlan is still shooting off commands. Rajmund and Tasia continue to battle the enemies alongside the other Israelites.

Gring and Grond appear, running into the ravine toward us, from the opposite entrance. They had originally followed Joshua. From the liquid on their arms, it's clear they, too, have seen an ambush. The twins move in incredible acrobatic motion. Their awareness and sense of each other is magnificently innate. One of them lets out a rabbit's scream. It travels up my spine and rattles my bones.

Entering the commotion, the brothers arm themselves with their metal stars, gaining speed. Gring stoops to his hands and knees in a slide, while Grond steps onto his shoulders and leaps into the air. Grond soars toward an attacker, tackling him and striking him in the throat with a metal star.

Haldor advances behind them, clamoring raucously as he charges into the skirmish. His massive blade sways as he moves toward a bald man in black. The rebel meets Haldor in the narrowest sector of the gorge, engaging him in a cramped spar. Other Israelites integrate themselves into the battle, smiting down our enemies as they come to our assistance. *And Joshua.* Joshua is like an angel, hair blowing behind him.

At this point, I am dragged away. Westin hauls me into a retreat, Travin defending it.

"Run!" Travin shouts urgently.

The three of us move clumsily. Every few feet, Travin contests a rebel opponent. Sometimes two or three. Ignoring the adversary,

Westin concentrates on our exit strategy. We wind through the narrows, sprinting as fast as we can. The grunt of a fallen foe echoes behind me as Travin catches up. We must have taken a different route than before, for we approach a large obstructing wall of rock that wasn't there before.

Westin helps Travin up the boulder and then lifts me into Travin's grasp. It happens haphazardly with our weapons getting in the way, and I realize my mediocre training has not prepared me for this. My inabilities will encumber Travin and Westin. I fear that all the faith in the world cannot save us.

My right shoulder hasn't completely healed and, despite every effort, I whimper at the blood-curdling pain as Westin hands me off. Travin assists me to a stable position atop the rock face. Looking first at my injured arm, he turns troubled gray eyes on my face. I spin from him to help Westin, unaccustomed to showing weakness, least of all to Trav. My longtime friend clasps one of Westin's wrists, and I clasp the other.

Below us, a bloodied Rajmund, the twins, Haldor, and Tasia pursue our trail. The high mountain walls echo with horse hooves, indicating the enemy behind them. Tasia is running low on arrows, limiting her shots to those she trusts will leave a deadly impression. The metal stars thrown by the Bottker twins resound off the mountainside like musical chimes. Haldor is taking an inclined route, combating multiple assailants. Soldiers are yelling orders, but we've become separated from our High Commander.

When the last enemy pursuant is killed, Rajmund climbs up the rock wall to where I stand, the others close behind. Two arrows obtrude from his scale armor. He jerks them out. Grond Bottker picks up the sharpened tip of one, snapping it free from the wooden shaft by cracking the arrow against his knee. He tucks the arrowhead into his chagowr. Tasia picks up the other arrow, adding it to her diminished reserves. Haldor smears the blood across his face in an effort to clear his vision. He spits into the dirt. A tooth joins his saliva. Travin points to Haldor's head.

"You're hit."

Haldor pats the back of his head with his fingertips. A spear grazed his scalp.

"Let's move," Gring barks. His lips are split, and there is a knife wound on his chin. He shoves dirt in it. "Get to high ground. That's where Joshua will be."

Up the slanted landslide, out into an open gorge, past a half dozen sun dried corpses, we veer off the pathway and search for cover. Westin pushes me to move. Travin pulls me. The lapse in battle allows us the opportunity to slow to a jog. We travel a few more minutes, until we hit a dead end.

"Where is everyone else?" I gasp.

"I told you this was suicide!" Westin snaps at me. "There's no way out."

"*Cease*, Westin!" Travin snaps.

"*You cease!*" he growls back, thrusting a finger at me. "This is all *your* fault!"

I don't acknowledge Westin's behavior. My heart feels like it is going to explode in my chest. Water. I need it, from my satchel. But when I try to retrieve it, my hands shake so badly I drop everything. Travin sends me a look of alarm, which disintegrates into indisputable hatred the second Westin speaks again.

"We are all going to die. If we'd just stayed back at Giles, none of this would be happening!"

Travin steps up to Westin, the heat from his glare flagrant.

"Shut your mouth," Travin grinds out, his chest an inch from Westin's, "before I shut it for you. It is men like *you* who are going to die! Soldiers rely on one another for protection. They are not cowardly. We do not run. We fight for the man on our right! We fight for the man on our left! It is our *unity* that gives us strength!"

Travin's hell-hot vehemence simmers around the two of them, burgeoning outwards in a quality of leadership I'd never imagined. I can't believe my own ears. My own eyes. I've never seen someone look more powerful. More powerful than Joshua.

"There is no room among us for inessential personnel," Travin snarls in conclusion.

Westin lands a gruff push in Travin's chest, shouting, "And where's your badge?"

Shoving him right back, Travin replies furiously, "We *all* carry a symbol of our allegiance, Westin. Mine is a badge of scars. What is yours?"

We don't have time for this.

I grab them individually by their wrists and say so. Westin huffs, refusing to surrender the argument. Travin's eyes drop to mine. The ferocity softens. Kindness and loyalty replace it, his two most endearing attributes. I release his wrist, offering a gentle, swift smile. This moment passes between us, but we are still under attack. Squatting down, I collect my satchel and sword.

"We'll have to head back the way we came," Rajmund states. Tasia and the twins nod in agreement.

Before we have a moment to retrace our steps in search of an alternate exit and the rest of our convoy, the echo of trampling hooves crescendos. Several of the rebel mercenaries materialize on the rocky ledge above us, their blood-stained weapons shimmering under the sun. They are all around us. Defense is futile.

Travin's back hits mine, Westin on one side me, Rajmund on the other. Tasia and the twins close in, with Haldor completing our circle. More of them pop up from the ground amidst us, like gerbils. *Pop. Pop, pop, pop. Pop, pop.* The black-clothed enemies have the upper hand.

We are surrounded.

A hiss draws my attention down to the rattlesnake several inches from my sandals. I disregard it, glancing up at the Canaanites. One of the men, face hidden in black drapery, descends from his stallion. He gradually approaches us, climbing dexterously over rocks and sagebrush. All of his rebel comrades pause, monitoring his actions with regard. He is built like an experienced soldier, the size and shape of Luko. His scalp has been shaved, and the only part of his face that is visible are his eyes, the white in them covered by tiny red vessels. He is diseased.

"Israelites?" he inquires.

His accent his thick. To our silence, he flicks his hand out to his side. Seven other men also dismount and join him, revolving around us like unto vultures to prey. They force us into a line, two of them invoking a short physical skirmish with the twins. They then stand sentinel before the trail, blocking us into the dead end. We are stripped of our belongings and weapons, the man who'd addressed us combining several dialects to direct his minions. My satchel and sword are taken. I feel the rebel behind me snake his icy fingers around my neck. It sends a familiar shiver down my spine, and I blanch.

"Leave her!" spits the enormous man in front of us, causing the drapery across his face to flutter. The rebel behind me releases my throat as his leader continues, "She may be of value."

"Yay, Sable," a voice at my ear hisses crossly.

My mind and stomach begin to gyrate.

Value?

They're going to sell us.

At least Tasia and I.

I glance right. Tasia has sunk to a kneel. Her eyes portray extreme horror as she stares at the man, Sable. He snatches her bow and sheath of arrows. On the other side of her, the twins are being restrained and disarmed separately. Near them, Travin wrestles against his contender. The bald Canaanite thumps Travin on the head with the hilt of his weapon, knocking Travin unconscious.

"Trav!" I shout.

He gives no sign of response. An open slash from the blow begins to ooze down his temple.

I glance to my left. Haldor also struggles against his captor. He has been forced to his knees with his arms bound behind his back. His face shows the utmost disdain. Rajmund is being constrained beside Westin, who gazes back at me. The Canaanite holding Westin has a knife between Westin's teeth, prohibiting him from speaking. Westin's eyebrows move up and down while the fingers of his right hand take a shape. I've seen it before. I should know what it means.

"Are you an Israelite?"

Sable is in front of me. He removes the drapery from his face, letting it fall around his neck. His features are strong, his nose flat. His expression is composed. I'm too frightened to respond, let alone look into his blood-shot stare. It is likely he is contagious.

He calls me the worst name I've ever heard and bellows, "Answer me!"

The back of his hand slams across the side of my face. I've felt worse pain, but the impact causes my vision to momentarily waver.

"Leave her alone," Tasia sputters.

Sable struts over and squats to Tasia's eye level. She meets his glare. Sable's fingers glide through her tangled hair. Fusty, infected fingers. Lingering, he laughs and looks at all of us one by one. Then he saunters further down toward the twins.

"These aren't officers," he scoffs, and he motions for the two Canaanites confining the young boys to bring the twins to him. The sentries obey, jolting the brothers forward until they are standing directly in front of us. Haldor shifts uncomfortably, fighting against the ties on his arms while Sable declares, "They're not even spies. You'll reap little at an auction."

A rumble of chuckling erupts. Travin stirs at the noise. The largest of Sable's men takes Gring and Grond, strips them of their clothing, and pushes them apart. Meanwhile, Sable removes a thick rope whip from his horse's saddle.

The enemies smile at one another. They are all sickly, with purple rings around their eyes. It could be the plague. Their muscled arms and legs are strung with contagions, hearts full of wickedness.

"Sable," Travin's guard exclaims, maintaining the weight of my unconscious friend. "This is meaningless! Vaclav said bring *all* captives to him alive. We cannot sell spoiled goods."

Suddenly Sable looks even more noxious. The fire burns in his reddened eyes as he glowers at his subordinate.

"These *boys* are useless, Falgan!" Sable spits, insulting the ripe age of the Bottker brothers. "They'll make pathetic slaves."

Slaves?

Spoiled goods?

These words bounce around in my head. And then nothing is in my head at all, as Sable contracts his arm, throws it forward, and lashes Gring across his back with the whip. Gring slumps to all fours, followed shortly after by Grond. Sable continues lashing them until their backs are tiger-striped and bleeding.

Taking a breath, Sable hands the whip to one of his men and reaches into a sheath at his hip, pulling out a jagged scimitar. He runs the blade across his palm before impelling it into the ground between his feet. I eye it, feeling like the handle is stuck in my throat.

A crafty grin splits Sable's face. Observing the twins and my allies, he states, "We'll let one of you free. The one that lives."

In the silence that follows, I can hear the beating of my pulse in my ears. I no longer feel the residual ache from my slapped face, for a new kind of stupefaction supersedes it.

Sable walks casually to the sidelines while calling, "Release them!"

Both boys are unleashed with a final thrust. Their captors move out of the way, leaving the scimitar twinkling as an omen between them. The brothers don't move. They gape confusedly between each other and us and the weapon. Grond is ashamed of his nakedness. I look to Travin for, I don't know, help. But he is still cataleptic, his eyes rolling beneath his half-shuttered lids. Tasia begins weeping. Westin grunts against the steel in his teeth. And Haldor is moving.

He attempts to break free from his captor's grasp, lunging for the scimitar. His effort is fruitless. A bladed pinwheel hits him in the back of the head, sinking into his skull bone. His body slumps to the ground in twitches.

Gring and Grond grimace, their expressions fading into something I've been dreading. An instinct to survive.

A second time, cold, smelly fingers curl around my neck.

"Nay!" I lament in an outburst of legitimate panic. The hand on my neck covers my mouth, cutting off any further bewailing. The rebel then smashes me into the soil and pins me there, stomach to dirt.

Sable only enjoys this. "Handle her, Thur," he muses. "Our entertainment has just commenced."

Another physical bout sparks. This time, it is between Westin and his adversary. Westin kicks himself free from the degenerate detaining him, and the two commence a fistfight.

"Hiin!" Sable snaps, looking mildly perturbed. "End that boy."

Hiin, the man who'd killed Haldor, *not* the one challenging

Westin, paces to the side of his horse and pulls out a long, wooden slugger. Carrying it at the base, he walks serenely back to where Westin still struggles with his rival. A cyclone of turmoil churns inside of me in the form of bile, attempting to surface from the ever tightening of my throat. I scream. Thur compresses himself against me to stop the noise. He is exceedingly heavy.

My vision focuses in time to see an unprepared Westin peering up at the wooden shaft as it descends, smacking into the side of his head. His eyes roll to a close. He falls to the earth, senseless.

"Remove him," Sable demands with a flick of his wrist.

A female cry pierces the air, either mine or Tasia's.

Hiin drags Westin to a cart hitched to the back of his horse, throwing Westin's flaccid body into it. Mounting the beast, Hiin kicks his heels into the horse's belly, and they disappear into the mountains. I gasp for air, straining my ears, but I only hear the clicking of the horse's hooves against gravel. It slowly fades away to nothing. Silence.

And then Gring takes a step forward. It's subtle, but we see it. The brothers stand motionless a few more seconds, and then Gring bolts. He races forward, slides onto the side of his leg, and jerks the scimitar out of the ground. Hovering on his feet with his knees bent, he scrutinizes the soldiers, the rebels. Grond remains rooted in the same position, the look in his eyes showing the defeat he feels.

"Brother, *please*," he pleads.

"I knew you wouldn't be able to do it," Gring replies.

"Do not become one of them," Grond implores. "We are not savages."

Gring scans the area, thoughtfully eying Sable, Travin and his captor, Thur and I, Tasia, Rajmund, and the rest of the rebels. He rises and deftly twirls the scimitar in his hand. One quick flick, and he could easily lodge it into his brother's body. We all know he has the skill. Then he'd be free to run to safety.

Grond's voice shakes. "I won't fight you."

I don't doubt him. It will be a fast and boring "entertainment" for these sinful rebels.

Gring turns to his brother, still twirling the weapon. He reaches down and probes the deceased Haldor's laceration with the tip of the blade.

"Either way," he says to Grond quietly, "they're going to kill us."

"I won't fight you!" Grond screams back. "I'm *not* going to do it!"

"I know," Gring answers with a sad smile. "I know you won't. Goodbye, brother."

With lightening speed and perfect aim, Gring spins and propels the jagged scimitar, sinking it straight between Sable's eyes.

A few people shout, and then an arrow is shot. Gring slumps to his knees with the feathered tip sticking out of his chest. Streams of deep crimson flow down his bare rib cage, blending into the markings from being whipped. Grond dashes to his brother's side while mayhem ensues. The rebels clump around their leader's corpse, leaving Rajmund, Tasia and I temporarily free. Neglected, Travin flops to the earth. I turn and sprint frantically toward him.

"Run!" Tasia yells at Grond.

He is stroking his brother's cheek, sobbing.

"Run, you fool," she repeats. "He died for you! Run! Find Joshua!"

This seems to motivate Grond. With a kiss to his brother's hand, he stands and limps away into the canyons, the rebels unresponsive.

Travin is still lying lifeless in the commotion. I'm almost to him when I'm clotheslined by Hiin. Rajmund calls my name. Thur grabs my arm while Rajmund tries to wrestle me free. I'm knocked in the face, the sky twisting wildly above me. Tasia enters the grapple, using her fingernails on the enemy until the rest of the rebels intervene. They have twice the forces we do. We are incarcerated again, doubly injured.

"We're taking them to auction," Thur growls. "Load them into the carts."

Two men pick Travin up by his ankles and wrists. The other rebels lead us to the carts hitched behind two horses. Arms bound behind our backs, Tasia, Travin, and I are thrown into one cart. Our weapons are thrown into the other. Rajmund is noosed and tied up behind a single horse, forced to walk. His hair, the shade of morning glory, cascades unkempt over beaten shoulders, but he holds his chin high, keeping his eyes straight ahead—on mine—as we exit the canyon. An image that will forever haunt my crowded nightmares.

TRAVIN

A Soldier Am I

Consciousness comes intermittently.

The throbbing in my head increases. Every jolt sends a sweltering twinge through my skull, down my spine, along with a hot drizzling fluid. My brain registers my body. I'm being carried . . . transported . . . jostling over the ground. The swish of a horsetail. The *click-clack* of hooves. Then darkness.

I wheedle my eyes open, catching a glimpse of Kaya Lucan. She is sitting next to me in a wooden cart. Her arms are bound behind her back. Streaks of red cover her clothing, and her lips are cracked. Enemy rebels are on all sides of us, on foot, on horseback, riding camels. Behind one horse, Rajmund is being dragged. He barely stays on his blistered feet. His lips are dry, eyes swollen, his whole body covered in dust.

Tasia is dead, or asleep, beside Kaya. Westin, Haldor, the Bottker twins . . . they're missing. And I . . .

I was told once by our High Commander that to demonstrate inferiority could amplify the enemy's arrogance and thus cause uncertainty in who had the upper hand. I am inferiority at its finest. We do *not* have the upper hand.

My mind drifts back into unconsciousness. Into a dream. A wonderful place without pain.

Avoca.

Home.

We were in the cave.

We were best friends.
We did something preposterous.
Kaya and I shared all our firsts.

I'M STARTLED AWAKE AS my body is dropped to the dirt. The happiness from those pastimes is minced in an instant. My tied elbows and knees collide with the earth first, the contact echoing painfully throughout my limbs. My lungs lose air momentarily. I gulp a few times before it comes back, tasting the tang of my own blood.

Slowly I regain coherence. Tasia, Rajmund, and Kaya are all tied up next to me. Heads bowed. Slave merchants swarm around us, bartering rabidly with our captors. On the cusp of delirium, I finger the belt at my hip. My knife is gone. The knife Father Lucan gave me. It was he who inseminated my enthusiasm to become a man, a *good* one, and an even better soldier. It was the only reason I was accepted among the secret combinations of Avoca, where I was introduced to the topics of warfare and liberty. My whole life's ambition was to succeed and please him, and to keep his cherished daughter safe.

If I fail now, I've failed him.

KAYA

Is This Real Life or Reality

We are sold. To a wealthy tradesman named Vaclav. His faithful servants Eamon, Bence, and Nicol collect and guide us like animals headed for slaughter. They will deliver us to Vaclav, to the palace of Zaheth. I have no idea where we are. Which means neither do the Israelites. I pray we are not far off course, and that we will not be pronounced dead. If we are close enough to Narr, Joshua may be able to find us.

Since the spine of Canaan has undergone destruction, leaving whole cities abdicated and in ruins, nomadic rebels from throughout the mountains have come to dwell in them. Those residing in the relics of this city appear in no better condition than the fallen structures around us. They are most certainly Hittites, enemy migrants. They push us through the streets, feeding us only a single spoonful of syrup and a single ladle of water, for nourishment.

This area of Canaan is unlike anything I've ever seen. Being dehumanized is unlike anything I've ever experienced.

Tasia and Rajmund are both virtually catatonic. Travin is breathing irregularly behind me. His head wound has not been tended to. Traveling by camel, our entourage is ushered into the city's temple grounds. Pillars lie in pieces, ash replacing the floor of the incinerated buildings. None of us speaks until night, when we are led into a prison cell below ground. The rebel guards establish a makeshift door of wood spears, locking us in, before departing.

"They can't," Tasia whispers into the night. "They *can't* find him."

I keep my face from hers and the men. I frown at the stars seen through the bars of our cell. A pit, more or less. Similar to the one I fell into when fleeing Avoca. Memories and emotions drivel away any and all of my hope for salvation.

"If they find him," Tasia continues, "I'll never see him again. They will manipulate him, enslave him, torture him for his gift."

I don't know what you're talking about. But stop.

"Do you understand?" Tasia says quietly.

I have no energy for this, no energy to focus on anything but survival. I pull at the chains on my arms, uselessly.

"If they find him," Tasia persists, though I pretend I'm not listening, "they will destroy him. Whosoever gains control of Amaris can possess him and his gift. His gift is special, sacred. He is an hourglass. *I'll never see him again!"*

I groan, longing to massage the cramping in my forehead and bones and organs. Rajmund is silent beside Tasia, sleeping. It is nothing short of a miracle he is still alive, though it can't be for long in his state of exhaustion. Shifting, I listen for the sound of Travin's lungs. I cannot bear to see him wounded. I sigh. My chains rattle.

Tasia wiggles against her own restraints and murmurs, "Vaclav . . . he is an aberrant. A sorcerer of evil. Amaris has told me about him."

I finally give in to response. "You know this man we've been sold to?"

"I've heard of him. Amaris has warned of him. An evil dictator from far north, determined to besiege all nations and kindred."

"Then Amaris will know not to go near him," I reply under my breath.

"But I am here," Tasia weeps. "He always comes back to me."

He always comes back.

I give up on the conversation, uninterested in Tasia's murmurings, and crane my neck around to glance at Travin's shadow. He is lying on his back a few feet from me, gray eyes closed. His clothing is in rags, hair disheveled, belongings stolen. A favorite memory of him comes into my mind, so clearly it could be a dream. We had just finished swimming in the Salt Sea and were sunbathing in the sand. Travin's hair was still damp, pasted to his ears and neck in unruly curls. Divots formed in his adolescent arm muscles as he leaned back onto his elbows.

"It's so amazing out here," I'd said. "I can't get enough of it."

I'd looked at Travin. The side of his mouth twisted up in agreement as he stared at me. In his eyes, I could see that he was thinking the same thing.

Pointing a slim finger at my nose, he'd said, "Wear your hair down more often."

WE ARE ROUSED IN the middle of the night. Several repugnant men remove our ankle bindings and hoist us to our feet.

"Move!"

Falgan has returned to deliver us to the palace, to our master, ruler of these monstrous rovers. Gusts of wind slap at our chapped skin as we are marched through the quiet city, up stone steps, through shattered pillars and wide, enormous doors. The dwelling is ominous, with only remnants of walls and rooftops. The moon shines in a ghostly manner through the gaping chasms. Some of it has been haphazardly reconstructed, and plant life has begun to grow again in the fertile soil. Ferns and vines curl around the buildings. An irrigation system consisting of a pulley, a bucket, and a lever-arm provides access to water from a small spring.

"Zaheth," Falgan declares at the entrance.

Armed guards receive our group, the stench of them, and Zaheth, repulsive. The fog of dawn thickens around the palace so that the tall pillars look like they're levitating. Torches are lit along the walls, sending streaks of firelight across engravings. Falgan carries one in front of him, casting a russet glow into the humid mist. The hairs on my arms begin to stand up. Travin is semi-conscious. I whisper his name, but he doesn't respond. Tasia is nearly blind with fatigue. Rajmund's clothing is in tatters, his feet swollen and bubbling with blisters.

We climb the ascending staircase and enter the main hall. Two magicians in jeweled robes stroll by. A female carrying a bowl of liquid ventures toward us. A low snarl rumbles from the shadows, the figure responsible drawing near. The creature appears to be floating. Cutting through the mist, a lion prowls forward slowly, zigzagging across the ashen floor. Behind it, six . . . eight . . . twelve men dressed all in black, with shiny bald heads, emerge.

A sharp pain stretches up my back, causing me to hunch over. This is not physical infliction caused by Falgan or one of our captors. It comes from inside, smiting my cognizance, making the tendons in my arms and hands constrict. My muscles begin to spasm uncontrollably. I moan, crouching, my blood boiling, the torture forcing me to my kneecaps. Then, all at once, the agony stops. I try to catch my breath, blinking back the teeming solution of pain in my eyes.

I peer up in desperation. The Hittites stare down amusedly. Rajmund is restrained by Falgan, but his eyes convey a message to me. *Get up.* To his side, Travin is propped up against a pillar, the loss of blood rendering my friend disabled. Between them, Tasia gapes down at me, abhorred.

I get up.

But my chest heaves. Once more, I fling myself forward just in time for the mad rush of vomiting that follows. There is no bile. Instead, a thick, black, gas-like substance spews from my mouth. I choke on it, the taste of Heshbon and Bashan vile on my tongue. Coughing and spitting, I gulp for oxygen until the last fumes escape my lungs. My allies observe in disbelief, having remained unaffected.

Sputtering, I watch as the airy matter floats upward and begins forming itself into a long, oblong shape. The substance forms itself into the silhouette of a human. A man. Like unto an Egyptian hieroglyphic that progressively becomes real.

Sorcery.

The apparition stands with his back to me, facing the grand hall. The rebels around us bow their heads in submission. I seize the front of my collar miserably, as tiny hissing sounds drag my focus to his shoulders. Small drops of dew vaporize as they fall upon him, the steam orbiting around him devotedly. Blue veins elongated through his arms begin to clot and expand with the flow of blood. He is dressed in the same manner as our captors, with black robes and a bald head. Extraordinarily tall in stature, he is fortified to maximization. Every curve of his muscles is visible beneath his clothing. The width of his arms is such that they hang abnormally out from his sides.

An internal alarm ignites within me.

Sorcery is of the devil.

The lion, which I'd momentarily disregarded, now paces gracefully at the man's feet, its tail slithering up the back of his knees. His belt is adorned in gold, reflecting the torchlight.

"Vaclav."

It is Falgan who speaks first.

Our master whips his head around to face us, black matter floating up from beneath his robes and disintegrating into the fog. The man's face is square with broad cheekbones framing a complexion of healthy pallor. His oval eyes are a brindle of hazel, not suffering from the widespread disease. A gleaming grin transforms his face. It is handsome, though it harbors no warmth. No feeling. No essence of humanity.

The kind of smile that sends daggers.

"Eamon. Bence. Nicol."

Vaclav's voice is deep and hypnotic. It has a harrowing effect on me, like the sensation of a drunken stupor. My head swivels at the sound.

The three men he'd called immediately converge, stepping up to the right of their master.

"Take our guests to their quarters. And this one," Vaclav pauses, "take this one to my personal chamber."

When his eyes meet mine, a chill of inhuman quality raises the goose bumps on the back of my neck. It's almost as if I can sense him inside of me. Inside my mind. *An aberrant.* Is that what Tasia called him? He is surely of the devil.

I quickly break eye contact, remembering the sense of choking on the black smoke that became him. In all my life, I have not been blessed with the gift of discernment, but at this moment, having spent a goodly number of months alongside the Israelites,

I can discern between right and wrong. This is wrong. This man, this place. I desire to rid myself of the feeling of Zaheth or meet the same fate as Gring.

Bence escorts Rajmund and Tasia away. Nicol hauls an unresponsive Travin over his shoulder, following them. Eamon then takes me by the arm. Vaclav lifts a hand to stop him. Eamon maneuvers me in front of Vaclav, presenting me, and then lowers his head. His master stares fixedly down at me from a height taller than my father stood, his supremacy equivalent to that of Joshua. How he became a monarch over this rebel society, I know not, but it is clear he was born of omnipotent people.

Vaclav beckons to the shadows and a harem appears, lifting trays of pomegranates, grapes, and fresh meat from bulls. He plucks a few grapes from a tray, popping them into his mouth one at a time. Slowly, he lifts a grape towards my mouth.

"Eat," he commands quietly.

My mouth opens. The grape bursts under my teeth, the juice delicious. That strange, febrile daze enters my mind once more. A devil's handiwork. Vaclav leans, closer and closer, until the reflection of his multi-hued eyes amalgamates with mine.

He appraises me deliberately. Like I am a stolen prize, an easy victory.

The way Miki sees me.

I shake the hypnosis from my head, feeling as if I'm lost in some out-of-body experience. I relive that moment in that alley, the abolition of my virtue. The infiltration. The despoiling. I understand now what soldiers mean when they say there are worse things than death.

I try to look away, but Vaclav extends one finger beneath my chin. He pulls my face toward his, Eamon pressing behind me to hold me still. I can feel the heat of Vaclav's living, breathing body. He has purchased me for a marionette. A slave. He examines me, inside and out, and suddenly—I don't know why—I get the odd sensation he recognizes me.

His eyes shrink to pinholes, the only movement of his face. He lifts up a hand to stroke my hair, his brindle gaze scrutinizing.

Grabbing a few strands, he holds them to his face and breathes in. His eyelids flutter and then snap open to reveal the lusty dilation of his pupils. I can see his hunger.

A hunger for something . . . neither food nor water.

TRAVIN

I Do Not Fear for My Own Fate

ALL I CAN SEE are chains.

All I can feel is the cold.

All I can smell is decay.

I allow my swollen eyes to remain shut rather than fight to open them. On the back of my eyelids, I watch memories play. Memories of my lifetime. It's what happens when death is upon one, I guess. One thinks of the things he loves, and the times he would change. Mostly, I think about Maleah. I think of her little hands, grabbing my blanket in the night. I hear her tiny cries as she tried to sleep on the floor, while father yelled down the hall. And then she grows up and her face becomes Kaya Lucan's.

I remember envying the life of a soldier as a teenager. A man with such valor, honor, and bravery. A man worthy of respect. I had assumed Avoca's secret combinations were full of robbers and criminals, but in fact they were formed by the most honorable men I knew—those desirous of eradicating evil and obeying the law of God. It is hard to resent the ambush of my home now, when it led me to my greatest ambition, discovering freedom, God, adventure, and excelling as a warrior in the Israelite militia. I couldn't wait to join Joshua.

I remember what it was like, seeing him for the first time. Witnessing his army. Being called one of them, instead of just a Shelomo. It meant I was becoming something more. I would be the first of my bloodline to prove I was a good, honest man.

Somewhere in the room, the cry of a man in pain slices into my head. Rajmund is being tortured again. This means I am next.

Although sermons of faith and fortitude trigger my stamina, they are oppressed by an influence beyond my control. Fear.

What good is an honest man if he is dead?

KAYA

He is One of Them

I'M NOT VISITED AGAIN by the dream of Miki Rox. Instead, I endure a nightmare. A new, endless nightmare. I remember pain and murder and captivity. I remember a night, quiet and eerie, only the sounds of insects chirping in the evening air. The prison cell. The palace. *Vaclav.*

A noise startles me awake. My eyes open. The cobwebs of sleep and withdrawal cling to my consciousness like unto a sodden robe. I blink repeatedly against a pale shaft of light. I'm lying on a giant, cushiony bed covered in white and gold pillows with no recollection of how I got here. The sheer fabric draping down on all sides of the cushion is fastened to an ornate chandelier on the ceiling directly above me. Beyond the sheer cloth is a large room with ornate walls and furniture. There is a vase of lilies, a gold mirror, and a chaise. Animal furs cover the floor. An open furnace is burning hot logs. A door is closed, the only access point.

My exit.

I throw myself off the cushion, pausing to examine my attire. My frayed simlah has been replaced by a new, linen one. My hair is washed clean and braided intricately. Several nezem embellish my fingers. I probe my weakened body, finding several bruises, along with the soreness from my shoulder injury. But I am not sick. I am not beaten. I am nourished and well.

A slave.

I know what it is Vaclav wants me for, and it is not household chores. My tongue tingles in remembrance of the sticky syrup I was fed before arriving in Zaheth. I shall never desire to eat it again in all my days.

Stepping toward the door, I hesitate as my head swivels, the *pyretic* swivel that I endured upon meeting Vaclav for the first time. It is accompanied by the discernment of evil. I try to ignore the compelling impression in my mind, advancing toward the door in pursuit of escape. Reaching for the handle, I waver. A soldier would have a plan. *What is my plan?*

Before I can come up with one, the lock on the door clicks, and it swings outward.

No plan.

Under the door frame, in full restoration, stands a man I recognize.

"Westin?" I gasp.

I throw my arms around his neck, the originations of hope birthed inside of me. After a few seconds, I pull back enough to inspect him. It's really him. An ally, a soldier. I am saved!

Wearing fitted black robes, Westin is alive, healthy, and mildly smiling. His eyes, the piercing blue I remember, now look white against his tan, hairless scalp. It makes his features even more exotic. His arms and chest are full with muscle, his skin unblemished. He is well.

"May I come in?" he asks.

He enters the room carrying a black, corked bottle and shuts the door behind him.

"You're alive!" I stutter. "What has happened? Where have you been?"

I reach out to touch him, retracting my hand at a blip of fear. The last time I saw him . . .

Westin pulls the cork from the bottle and offers it to me. Dumbfounded, I can only stare.

"I've just been with Daedrina."

"Daedrina?" I question. "Who is Daedrina?"

"You will meet her soon." His eyes narrow as he sets the bottle down on a table.

I glimpse the door behind him, the latticed designs and illegible inscriptions. We could escape, the two of us. We mustn't delay.

"Is it night?" I whisper.

Westin shakes his head contemplatively. "Nay, it is just after sunrise."

How did you—I mean, how long have you been here? How many days has it been? And why do you look like *this*?"

"Kaya. Everything is going according to His plans." Westin steps toward me, and I gape into those beautiful eyes. Squinting, I spot a minuscule red line that has begun to creep into the corner of his left eye. It wasn't there before.

"Who is Daedrina?" I ask determinedly.

"She lives here in Zaheth," Westin answers calmly.

"Let us depart!" I urge. "*Now*. If you know the palace, you can lead us out of it. We can escape into the mountains and return to Giles. We have to find Joshua. We must rid ourselves of this place and . . ."

I whirl toward the door, grabbing the handle. But Westin smoothly catches my wrist and guides me back to his side.

"She has revealed the prophecy," he tells me. "Daedrina. She is an oracle, Vaclav says. She has seen Him, a ruler over all the land from the borders near the seashore until the ends of the earth. You and I, Kaya, are on His right hand."

"Oracle?" I scoff, comprehension dawning. "It is sorcery, Westin. The work of the devil!"

For the first time since entering my room, Westin's eyes stray from my face. They rake over the vicinity, lingering on the bed, and then return to gaze upon me.

"Westin, you cannot believe what she says," I plead. "You speak of Vaclav like he is a god. There is only one God. It is the first commandment. Joshua says—"

"Joshua is mistaken, Kaya," he replies pensively. "He has been corrupted by greed and false visions."

"Nay. Vaclav is a false prophet," I object, surprised by my declaration of conviction. "Where are the others?"

"Others?"

"Travin!" I hiss. "Tasia. Rajmund."

I pull Westin toward the door. He resists. "Vaclav's forces have gathered in preparation for our departure. We are going to battle against Joshua's army. We can stop him!" His voice darkens with exigency. He caresses the side of my hair, his palm skimming down my linen simlah to my thigh. "Vaclav will put an end to Joshua's crusade. The Israelites will become our slaves. You and I—"

"You are confused," I interpose nervously. A pressure has built up in my head. I feel extremely dizzy, like I've been hanging upside down for way too long, or drinking way too much wine. My knees start to wobble. A tingling unease siphons through my stomach and into my veins. I want to vomit. Grabbing his wrist for support, I stammer, "We need to . . . this isn't . . ."

Out in the hallway another door opens and closes. Westin jumps and then presses a finger gently to my lips.

"Shush, now," he murmurs.

"But—"

"I will be back."

"Wait—"

He kisses me hard. It is odd, our lips touching in this circumstance. I miss him, but I do not wish to be kissed.

When he draws away, he smiles. "We have forever," he says, and then he slips out the door as if he'd never been there.

TRAVIN

Failure is a Killer

HISTORY HAS TAUGHT US that there have been men so vile they could perform every atrocious and debasing act of abomination without an ounce of penitence. In the dungeons of Zaheth, I witness these atrocities. We are stripped of the virtues we hold dear and fed only upon the flesh of dead prisoners. Except we do not eat. Fearful of consuming infected flesh, we resist the victuals they provide.

When Tasia becomes desperate for food, she almost consumes the diseased meat of deceased rebels. But Rajmund grabs her chains and wrestles her back. We are so hungry, rationality has deserted us. I sit motionless, contemplating eating my own flesh instead.

It gets me to thinking about who holds the power in the situation. A real man of real worth would not cause such depravity to another human being. Weak men, insecure, doubtful, frightened, and motivated by the powers of evil, attack those they fear are stronger. And the three of us, chained to separate corners but sharing a cell, have not yet turned on one another when we easily could have. We have remained true. We have prayed. And we have been sustained by God's power.

All my life I have wanted to be a soldier. I spent years unlawfully participating in Avoca's secret combinations with Rebby and other locals who support the right to defend our lives, our homes, our families. I hid my desires from my own mother, from Kaya Lucan and her father. I had not yet separated my identity from hers. How close we had grown throughout our childhoods. Hoping and fearing her father viewed me as a son, I did not want to disappoint him. It wasn't until he gave me my first knife that his true belief and support of the right to bear arms was revealed. Still, I did not share my involvement in those activities with Kaya, having heard *her* opinions of violence.

I will never forget when Father Lucan asked me one day, *Do you know when you become a man?* I didn't know then, but over the years, I thought I'd figured it out. Maybe after my first drink, I'd be a man. But after my first drink, which was with Kaya, nothing changed. I still didn't feel like a man. The older I got, I thought, maybe when I have my first kiss. But my first kiss was with Kaya. It wasn't at all what Rebby said it would be like, and I still didn't feel like a man. Maybe, I considered in young adulthood, if I work harder, I would be a man. But no one would hire a Shelomo, except for Father Lucan. I did what I could to get by, and I still didn't feel like a man.

I worked diligently during the day to provide for my family and steadfastly through the night to be able to protect them when the dawn of war came. I couldn't figure out what I was doing wrong. *What had he wanted me to do?*

Joining the Israelite multitude at Taavetti felt like the right thing to do, deep down to the marrow in my bones. Yet, as I sit in this prison, with a few of those bones broken, I can't help but think.

I don't feel much like a man.

KAYA

A Leader from the Underworld

I AWAKE WITH A scream, hauling myself off the bed and into a mess of sheer fabric. The more I try to break free, the more entwined I become. I'm being asphyxiated. Ravaged. Miki, Canaanites, rebels. Dark pits of despair. Ever since I fell into that hole in the wilderness, claustrophobia has been an issue of mine. My body trembles in panic, wriggling against the cloth encompassing me. And it only gets tighter and tighter.

The door opens and heavy footsteps tread toward me. Strong, manly hands grope at my legs. I kick out at them.

"Stop it!" I yell. "Stop, Miki! *Stop!*"

One hand grabs my shoulder, the wounded one, sending a crippling pain down my arm and back.

"Hold still!" a voice barks.

It is Eamon. I recognize his face. He drags me to my feet, freeing me from the fabric.

"I said, hold still!" he grunts again, but I can't shake the feeling I'm being strangled to death.

I brush my arms like they're covered in flesh-eating beetles, loathing the ornamentation decorating my body. I hate that I am so well kept, but so unbearably used according to Vaclav's desires. I would rather spend a night alone with Miki Rox than one more night in Zaheth.

Eamon releases my arm. "You're wanted in Vaclav's chamber."

I freeze, not wanting to go anywhere near Vaclav. I've been

locked in this room a whole day and night, my only company the tray of food I haven't touched. Although desperate to get out, I do not want to see the master of Zaheth.

"Come with me," Eamon demands.

Sputtered protests spew from my mouth, none of which are heard. He drags me toward the door, past the mirror that I quickly glance at. The woman staring back at me is hardly recognizable. Like a stranger. I feel ill.

Overwhelmed by my loss of self, I give in to despair. In the absence of identity, humans are defined by their circumstances. My circumstance is bondage. I belong to Vaclav.

The hallways of Zaheth are long with wide corridors, all lined with grand pillars and engraved walls. Pots of plants and channels of flowing water decorate the floors. Despite being previously unoccupied, the city is grand. It is daytime, therefore the torches are not lit. Sun shines through the cracks in the edifice forming rectangles of light. Spiraling staircases lead to different parts of the palace, fallen beams and piles of rubble supporting what is left of them.

Eamon escorts me up a flight of stairs and to the right. The vaulted ceilings echo our footsteps, which are loud against the stone floors. Down another hallway, a handful of females skitter past us. Their bellies are bare, their robes slit to reveal their legs. Bells jingle on their wrists and ankles. I cringe against such usage of whoredoms. For that is what is to become of me in Zaheth.

At the end of the final hallway, we reach a set of large, double doors. Eamon squishes me toward them, as they unlock and swing inward. He stops at the entrance, ushering me forward. I enter the room by myself, and the doors close behind me with an ominous *click*.

Three stairs ascend to the main floor of the room. It has been cleansed of ash, the marble and stone polished. A Canaanite shrine of basalt statues takes up most of the far wall. There are two erect fireplaces on either side of it, which emit a smoky, hypnotizing fragrance. It reminds me of the black gas I coughed up the night I met *him*. That bizarre febrile daze envelops me once again. It mutes the fear just enough to prick curiosity in me. I want to know where my friends are. If he called them here, too.

I climb the three steps onto the landing and see Vaclav waiting for me. He sits provocatively in an elaborate chair, a platter of fruits beside him. Two maidservants dressed like the females in the hall fan him with gigantic ferns. He's donning the same black robes. His bald scalp reflects the flickering flames. I dare to make eye contact. He is smiling, an attractive smile that hides his teeth.

He speaks in his harsh accent, "Sit, my treasure."

I notice a woman, about the age of Yespin Roteruth, sitting in the chair beside Vaclav. She's a beautiful woman with straight, purple hair that cascades to her knees. She wears a gown like mine, with a high collar that follows her neck and scoops outward just below her jawline. A large, white fur shawl drapes loosely over her shoulders. Her eyes and lips are painted. Many nezem shine on her wrists and fingers. She stares blankly ahead.

Something about the word *treasure* makes my skin crawl. With no choice left, I follow the motion of Vaclav's hand, taking the empty seat across from the woman.

"There's someone I'd like you to meet," Vaclav says. "Kaya, this is Daedrina."

Daedrina.

The oracle? I shift to the edge of my seat.

"I've asked her to do me a favor," Vaclav remarks in a threateningly calm manner. "You see, Daedrina is a special person with a remarkable gift. This gift slowly kills her. Therefore, I rarely request it. Unless, of course, there's something I need desperately. Right now, Kaya Lucan, I need something desperately."

I stare in bemusement, between Vaclav and Daedrina. Did Westin tell them my tribal name? The woman seems comatose, glaring unresponsive at me. I can't help but think of her as a witch in league with the devil. Vaclav leans over and places his elbows on his knees, steepling his fingers beneath his chin. In a hushed voice, he says something to her in a language I've never heard before. She answers him with one word.

"You've been treated very well here in Zaheth." Vaclav's eyes are back on me, dark eyes that do not showcase the terrorizing threat of evil I witnessed the night I met him. "And you will cooperate."

I want to flee.

My life has not been modeled after righteousness, and I fear the repercussion is eternal enslavement to this man.

The two of them stare at me with such an intensity I cannot look away. I lose my gumption, still concerned with my friends' whereabouts, but too afraid to inquire of them. Vaclav remains immobile. But Daedrina's dull eyes burn vibrantly black, full of new energy. No color, no white. An eccentric expression crosses her face. The pulse in her temple begins to twitch. She begins chanting.

"The Lucan tribe," Daedrina murmurs.

In my peripheral vision, I see Vaclav sneer.

"I knew it," he hisses.

Just then, a pain shoots through my neck and into my brain. Daedrina starts to mumble in that foreign language. Slumping to my knees, I squeeze my ears with my palms. I start to hear voices. Angry, whispering, voices I can't understand. The pain turns to a prickling, like someone is digging around in my skull. Daedrina's incantation grows in volume. From inside the trance, I see a monster. No other words can describe it. He is ruler of the underworld, a tyrant of all manner of evil, with horns of wickedness and a trident of immorality. His smile is murder and his power enmity.

Daedrina withdraws from my head, and I collapse to my elbows, seeing spots.

The monster is gone.

Vaclav is towering over me, the evils of his enterprise shining in his eyes. There was purpose, after all, in Joshua's orders to destroy every living inhabitant of Canaan. Look what's become of whose left.

Daedrina's fingers turn white as she grips her armchair, leaning forward an inch. My head splits with a second unsurpassable pain. Her invasive picking resumes. *Chanting. Chanting. Chanting.* This goes on for several long minutes, until Daedrina's incantation ceases. I blink up from the ground. Vaclav materializes at my side with a cloth. He pats my perspiring forehead and helps me to my feet.

"Drink," he states, offering a chalice of pure water.

My lips are trembling. Most of the water spills down the front of me. Just then, the door to the room opens. A man enters. Daedrina shifts her black gaze to the intruder.

"They've escaped!" Bence shouts to his leader, paying no attention to me on the floor. "We've searched the grounds and found nothing. There is no evidence of struggle. Chas and the prison sentries sent men into the valley to find them but—"

Vaclav's demeanor changes slightly.

"Take her back to her room," he orders Bence, "and bring Chas to me. He will pay for his mistake."

"She doesn't know anything."

Vaclav ceases mid-stride. Languidly, he turns to Daedrina, his black robes flowing. I peer up at the woman who'd spoken from my position on the marble flooring. Her eyes have fallen back into their misty state, no longer black and lively. She looks even more drained and old than before.

"What?" Vaclav snarls through gritted teeth.

"It's not there," Daedrina continues, her voice gritty with age. "The information you're looking for. Kaya doesn't have it."

Vaclav's hands ball into fists, the blue veins visible beneath his skin swell. "You said she was of Lucan descent."

Daedrina does not answer him.

His seething eyes fall on me, bestowing a lethal fervor comparable to *the monster*. He loses the control he'd fought for and storms over, yanking me to my feet by my hair. There is nothing handsome left in his face. He is the color only seen by the eye in perfect darkness. His murderous bearing proves I'm not currently a *treasure* to him. He grabs my throat, constricting my pathway for air, and tilts my head back.

He shakes me back and forth violently. "What are you hiding, Israelite?"

I can't breathe or speak against his firm hold on my throat.

Bence reenters the room, dragging another man who's been severely flogged. Vaclav throws me aside as the two men approach. I gasp for air, the spasm in my airway lingering. Daedrina is staring wraith-like ahead, as if turned to stone. I would beg her for help, but she does not appear coherent. Although she is not ailing from the disease, she is nearing her end.

Chas, the beaten man, begins to speak. "Vaclav, I don't know how—"

Vaclav holds up a hand, silencing him immediately.

With his palm toward Chas, Vaclav slowly lifts his hand to eye level. Chas rises into the air, a few inches above the ground. He begs for Vaclav to spare his life, but it's a useless plea. Vaclav curls one of his fingers down, and I hear a snapping sound as Chas screams in pain. Vaclav curls another two of his fingers down, and two more cracking sounds are followed by Chas's cries. The man's right hand is dangling at his side, and three of his fingers are twisted and contorted. Bone is exposed and blood is dripping onto the floor.

With a final movement of Vaclav's hand, Chas's head twists sideways and his neck breaks. I look away. Vaclav lowers his arms to his sides, and Chas flops limply to the floor. Insatiable with greed, Vaclav shouts several commands. In a flurry of mania, Bence whirls me back to my room. At the door, he thrusts me inside. I knock over the tray of food. Grapes bounce across the floor.

Reeling around, I attempt to ask Bence, "Is Vaclav going to let me go? Since I don't have what he's looking for?"

My voice sounds ridiculous. I've never heard such dread come from my throat, not even with Miki.

Bence leaves me without a reply.

I sit back on my bed, isolated in this horrendous room. All I can think about is Chas. I can hear the popping of his bones over and over again. My thoughts are overrun by a myriad of depressing fates. When will my end come, and will it be as afflictive? I cannot carry on this way.

I run across the room to bang at the door with all my strength. I scream, curse, cry out. When I've achieved no response at the door, I begin throwing furniture at it. After breaking a few objects, I spot a black bottle sitting on top of the table. The bottle Westin brought me.

Westin. He was one of them.

I yank the bottle off the table and take a sniff at the opened top. *Wine.* Is it poisoned? *I pray so.* I take a long sip and sink to the floor. The monster. I can feel it within me. I am consumed with anger.

"Get out of my head!" I shriek, chugging more of the drink. "Leave me be!"

I slam the bottle on the ground. It's more than half gone.

My stomach protests. My head swims. But I need this to poison me, before Vaclav can break my bones and torture me slowly to death. I will not stay here. *Not like this.*

The bile fights its way into my throat again, but I force it back down. I finish the wine, coughing and gagging. Rolling onto my back, I stare at the rotary above me. The lights, the gold embellishments on the ceiling, the slices of sky visible in cracks in the building, everything turns before my eyes, blending together. My stomach heaves again, but now I don't have the ability to stop it. The burning liquid spews out of my nose and mouth.

Even as I try to spit the vomit out, it rests in my airway, blocking the flow of oxygen.

This is it. The end. It frightens me. How I welcome it.

A dark shape moves into my twirling perspective. Is this my salutation? My entrance to the underworld? I should've known I would not be greeted by angels.

The shape hovers in the swirls above my face. I tell myself to reach up and touch it, but my limbs don't move. I can't breathe.

A force shoves me onto my side. I flop over and vomit again, wasting so much of the precious poison. Arms, long and strong, wrap around my waist, hoisting me to my feet. Eamon is back, to take me to Vaclav and Daedrina for more suffering. I must die before then.

"No," I slur. "Let . . . me . . . be."

My legs can't support my body, and I fall. The arms enclose around me, tightly, while a voice whispers in my ear.

"Be at ease."

I gasp for air. "Who. Are. You?"

The voice responds curtly.

"Amaris."

WESTIN

Still a Slave

"I ᴋɴᴏᴡ ʜᴏᴡ ʏᴏᴜ feel about her."

Vaclav towers over me, his eyes hostile. His ever-deepening apathy bristles around him. His Israelite slaves have escaped. Rajmund, Tasia, Travin, and Kaya. All of them.

Dragged to the dungeons, my body has been crammed into a small barrel. I am squashed into the small wood cavity, except for my head. A spiked metal collar is fastened around my neck, restraining me from much movement. The barrel requires me to kneel, and I've been confined in my own filth for two days now. My hollow stomach aches, my eyes burn from exhaustion.

Vaclav continues his ordeal, bending at the waist to enforce his anger. "The maggots won't stay in your feces for long. They'll find the source from which your foulness comes. They'll enter your body from your lower passageways . . . "

"I don't know where they are," I moan, spewing saliva.

Vaclav grins, his lips pulling back tightly as they reveal his teeth.

"I swear!" I plead. "I don't know how they escaped. I don't know where they are. I've done everything you've asked of me."

"I recognized you from a portrait my insider drew. He suggested we recruit you to help him extract information in exchange for shekels of gold and silver. You do realize the position I am in, don't you? One of your own has been willing to sell Israelite intelligence. The army is weak, led by disillusioned elders. I have power and riches to rule over this kingdom. Joshua and his soldiers will fall. You can swear allegiance to me or fall with them."

I grimace, his words tumbling around in my head.

"Eamon," Vaclav calls, and the bald man appears. "Are my men ready?"

Eamon answers, "They await your command."

"Young slave," Vaclav directs toward me. I twist my head to try and get a better view of him. The spikes dig into my neck, and the pain of it piercing my skin causes me to wince. "You are going to accompany me and my soldiers. They are waiting on my word. You know where the Israelites are camped?"

"Joshua . . . has stationed the army at Giles," I hiss. "But it is fortified. They plan to move across the River Jordan. They may have already."

"Westin." He leans farther over so that his eyes, shining with covetousness, are at my level. "Daedrina's prophecy will not be fulfilled if you do not find the Lucan girl. And you will suffer exceedingly if you do not lead me to them. The Israelites must bow to us. We can overcome them. They shall be *our* slaves. I will reward you greatly for your efforts."

The prophecy.

My and Kaya's future. Together. Ruling over all the land.

Vaclav withdraws a pouch of silver from his robes and tosses it onto the floor.

"Release him," Vaclav demands. "And bring him to Daedrina."

Eamon unlatches the collar around my neck first, and then opens the barrel, shrinking in disgust from the smell of waste. He winches me out and pulls me to my feet. My legs are weak. Standing entails all of my strength, and I still require assistance. Vaclav exits the dungeons, and Eamon drags me after him. They don't bother cleansing me. I leave a stinking trail along the floor until we reach Vaclav's chambers.

Bursting through the doors, Vaclav orders Eamon to present me to Daedrina. The oracle is sitting in her chair, slumbering. All around her, idols of gold and silver shine from the flames of a burning offering. The skeletal remains of a child lay atop the altar. Several armed servants kneel before it, chanting in worship.

A harlot, holding a palm fern, bows as her master approaches.

"Daedrina!" Vaclav's voice bellows.

The woman's glassy eyes open and meet his.

"Tell me what you see."

On command, Daedrina directs her blank stare toward me. Asserting her magic rites, energy fills her ailing frame. Her eyes light up. An ebony film swirls over them until they are completely black. She begins chanting, her sorcery crackling around the room. The stabbing pain perforates my brain, increasing into my neck until my knees crumple. Eamon grabs hold of me, keeping me upright.

Several minutes later, the pain ceases. I collapse into Eamon's grasp, and he groans at having to touch my soiled body.

"He will find her," Daedrina says, deadpan. "He knows the way to the Israelite commander. We will defeat his army and reign across these nations."

The intensity in her eyes fades along with her consciousness.

Vaclav roars in triumph. He turns toward me once again with confidence.

His voice booms throughout the palace walls, "You will take me to them!" He spins toward Eamon. "Behold," he demands, "take him to be cleansed. We depart at nightfall."

KAYA

I Can't Trust Anyone

THE NEXT SET OF events is only connected by my various moments of consciousness. I feel as if I'm trapped inside a vortex. I'm flipped and turned and tugged about. My main focus is to continue breathing. This has become exceedingly difficult, since I seem to be vomiting every waking moment. My throat and nose chafe due to the unwelcome stomach acid.

"She needs water."

"It will flush her insides out."

"Do something! Now! We can't lose her!"

Several people speak far too loudly, intimidating the throbbing inside my skull. I think my clothes have been removed. I get the sensation I'm being dipped into water. A cool cloth on my face, my neck. Cool water on my tongue.

"Back up, son."

"Give her to me!"

"It's not going to be enough! Too much is in her blood."

"It's all we have!"

The hands of a stranger fall upon my head, his voice uttering words too sacred to repeat. Then I am dried, clothed, wrapped snuggly in a warm blanket, laid next to a crackling fire and regurgitating into a small hole in the dirt beside my head.

"She's getting better."

"*Stay strong.*"

My father's voice?

I try to locate him, to urge my eyes open so I might scan my surroundings, to find his face and see him for myself. But they roll involuntarily closed.

"Your work is not finished."

And another quiet voice whispers, "Stay with me, Kaya."

I PEEL MY EYES open. My first cognitive thought is there is a person sleeping in front of me. Eventually, the figure forms with clarity. A collection of beaten extremities curled into themselves. I blink away the bleariness and inspect him. His knees are in his chest, his hands tucked underneath his neck. Deep shadows hover beneath his closed eyes, accentuating his sallow complexion. His cheekbones are noticeably sharp under his sunken face. It only takes a moment to estimate how much weight he's lost. And the injuries—bones have been broken and healed without being set. He is a dead body breathing.

I try to say his name, but the sickness overcomes me, and I end up vomiting instead. Nothing comes out but bile. My coughing wakes him. He quickly sits ups, rubbing beneath one eye with his thumb. Crawling to my side, he assists me onto my back and pushes my hair off of my face. His winnowed form moves like a spider.

"Sorry," I cough, wiping my mouth against the blanket around me. "I didn't mean to disturb you."

"How do you feel?" Travin asks somberly.

"Deceased," I croak. "How long have I been here?"

"A few days." Even though his appearance has changed dramatically, his voice still sounds the same. Warm and husky.

The last thing I remember was my prison in Zaheth. The palace. The room. Daedrina. Sorcery. The wine bottle.

"Azsh was recovered," he continues. "Joshua and Lachlan march with him across the plain as we speak. Joshua . . . he sent Amaris after us. He rescued us, Kaya. God told him where to look and we have been saved."

His voice is shaky, overcome with gratitude. I take a second to survey our environment. I'm not sure I'm seeing things correctly. It looks as though we are sitting alone in the sand, in that old cave from my memories. Beyond the stench of vomit, a slightly coastal breeze whiffs around us, and I can faintly hear the sounds of the crashing waves of the Salt Sea.

I am back in Avoca.

"Is this a dream?" I murmur, not particularly to anyone.

It's odd, but I start to cry. Not a blubbering cry, but an uncontrollable flow of silent tears that stream down my cheeks. And right now, I have no motivation to hide them.

Travin reacts unexpectedly, offering comforting words while awkwardly trying to clean my face of the tears. His fingers are rough and knobby, like tree bark, and the sight of them only worsens my current state. I start to heave again.

Leaving my side momentarily, Travin retrieves a bottle of water. I force some into my arguing belly. After one last gulp, the bottle of water is empty.

I can't believe I am crying in front of him. I haven't cried in front of Travin since my favorite chicken died. Thaddeus. I was ten years old.

"Be at peace," Travin whispers softly. "Avoca is deserted. Everything has been—never mind. I knew this is where you'd want to be when you . . . um . . . when we . . ."

Before I really lose it, he scoots beside me, turning me so we are facing the Salt Sea. It's nighttime, for all I know the middle of it. The full moon is reflected perfectly in the dark water. The grayish waves roll up onto the shore one after another. It's my absolute favorite place in the world. He knows that. It's his as well.

Travin maneuvers his arm around me, but I recoil instinctively. I didn't mean to. I just did. Turning away, Travin glares down at his knuckles. For the better part of a minute, I let him. Then, slowly, I take his arm and lift it around my shoulders, leaning into him. He releases a sigh. With his other hand, he brushes the tip of his pinky across my brow.

"Be not afraid, Kaya. We're in our cave."

That's what I'm afraid of.

"What has become of us, Trav?" The stinging in my eyes is unbearable. I try my best to keep it subdued. "What are we doing?"

Resting his cheek against my temple, he replies, "Have you ever felt something, and you just *knew* it was right?"

I have felt something and knew it was *wrong*, certainly.

"Kaya, I have felt it." Travin stares out at the water. I stare up at him. "Whenever I am near Joshua, I feel lifted up with strength. I hear his words as if they are spoken from the mouth of angels. The spirit of God is like a fire, *burning*. I can tell you there were numbers amongst us in the battle of Bashan, numbers not of this world. It wasn't me who was fighting. It was . . . *Him*. And when I pray, God answers my prayers. Not always in the way I anticipate, but . . . have you ever noticed *your* prayers being answered? In strange ways?"

My mind is jarred to the handful of times I've been reduced to the desperation of praying.

I am astonished by what I find.

"We have been exceedingly blessed," Travin murmurs amidst my discovery. "Though we face obstacles, we overcome them."

I regard him wearily, his optimism endearing. He deserves to have been much more blessed than this.

"I was going to give it to you, you know," I confess.

His throat rumbles, "Hm?"

"Lucan Care. I wanted it to be yours. I wanted to give it to you. I always thought—it should have been handed down to someone my father respected and knew would look after it."

He doesn't respond for awhile. I can tell by his mannerisms that emotion is warring within him. Travin would have been the first Shelomo to own a business at the venue. It would have done wonders for his reputation. I don't know what inspires me to speak of such personal affairs, but I continue to do so.

"It would have made everything better, wouldn't it?" I ask. "What if—what if I'd signed over tenure sooner? Maybe you'd have earned more for your family. The people wouldn't have treated you so poorly. And Maleah—"

"Sh," Travin hushes me. He squeezes me tightly. "Sh."

Minutes pass. Until his voice penetrates the dark.

"Do you know where we're sitting?"

I nod.

"We promised never to talk about it—"

My body tenses. Travin pulls back enough to look me in the eye.

"Kaya," he states, still holding one thin arm around my waist, "it's just me and you here. It will keep our minds off . . . other things."

I take a moment, decide I don't care to put up a fight, and shrug in response. We had sworn each other to secrecy. *But who cares?* We were much younger then, much less accountable. And it was such an embarrassment for both of us, I never once actually *wanted* to bring it up.

"What?" Travin questions. He tips my chin up with a finger. "It can be one of those stories we fall back on when we need a boost of cheer. One that gets better and better with repetition. Like the day I taught you to swim."

I glare dryly at him. "You mean the day you tested the fruition of human gills?"

His eyes see something I do not. He smiles benevolently.

"Fine," I burble, feeling close to throwing up again. "Let's tell the story."

He nudges my shoulder in agreement, stating affectionately, "There she is." He rearranges himself onto his stomach and elbows, with his legs stretched out behind him. The muscle atrophy has left them bony. "Where do we start?"

"I think that's *exactly* what you said," I mumble.

"Yay, I think you're right."

He bites his lip and cocks his head to the side, looking frighteningly similar to his childhood self. Goofy. Knobby. So exceedingly lovable.

So. We are finally going to talk about the cave.

The memory surfaces, this time out of a once happy place.

"It was a night like this," I reminisce, recalling the slightly nippy breeze.

Trav grins. The smile looks more boyish with the lack of muscle and substance in his neck and face.

I mirror it.

"I have to be honest," he comments, "I'm glad it was with you. I mean, it was going to be uncomfortable no matter what. But at least it was with my best friend, you know? We're in the middle of a war, and, in case I never get a chance to say it, I just want you to know that . . . I'm glad I shared it. With *you*."

Despite our circumstances and the grueling headache wreaking havoc on my brain, I attempt to feel happiness. I don't need to hate this cave, and I don't need to hate the memory of it. *If I'm not going to be around much longer, what's the point in letting old stories embarrass me?*

"*Me, too, Travin*," he says in a girly voice, poking a finger tenderly against my thigh.

"Me, too, Travin," I respond quietly and glance away.

Extending a hand, he scoops up some sand and lets it slide through his fingers. The firelight flits about the cave, and his face shines in intervals. "Do you think kissing is supposed to be like that?"

I roll my eyes.

But Travin presses forward. "You do know, if my marriage suffers because of a deficiency in kissing skills, I am coming after *you*."

Travin . . . married? My thoughts turn far away from kissing, to grown up endeavors and forever-afters. Suddenly, I want to be away from him. I *do* hate this cave. I want to be away from the memories of it, away from the story of how we stupidly, immaturely, decided to be each other's "first." We were dumb. And sloppy. Having kissed others since then, I know my childhood kiss with Travin lacked artistic facility. We couldn't concentrate and kept giggling.

We were young and not yet religious enough to know better. It's a good thing, too, because such conduct among the Israelites is considered indecent outside of wedlock. We'd be stoned in the streets.

"What's wrong?" Travin's voice pulls me out of my thoughts.

I notice the tears have commenced once again, and this time they're accompanied by torrential sobs. This is blubbering. I've never felt it before. Such a throttling failure. I hurt in places I didn't know could hurt. Bewildered, I stare at the palms of my hands, unable to grasp this concept of crying beyond my control.

Travin is equally confused.

"Sh," he coos, attempting to embrace me with both arms. "Shush, now."

But I refuse his touch. "Let me go!"

"Kaya, it's alright," he insists, reaching for me again. "Was it something I said?"

My sobs transform into hysterics. I pound my fists into his chest.

"I'm disgusting!" I wail, pushing him away. "I am filled with wickedness and abominations!"

"I'm sorry, I didn't—"

"Let me go!"

Travin's arms continue to dismiss my thrashing. I try to withstand his hold. But he doesn't let me win. I feel like a comet on a crash course. My lungs inflate in short, concise gasps, exhaling the air in disjointed breaths. Words tumble out of my mouth.

"I am not pure or virtuous. I just didn't want to feel it anymore, this emptiness. I don't want to feel anything. Because when I do, it means I can remember. And when I remember, it is my living nightmare. I know I have been compromised, but sometimes I like to pretend that I haven't."

Travin struggles to follow. I struggle to breath against my sobs.

"I'm—a wicked—person!"

"Kaya, your sins can be washed away as mine have."

"Nay!" I gasp. "I am . . . r-ruined."

"How?" He tries to cajole me into his lap, but I withdraw firmly.

"I know I messed up after I lost my father, alright? But then . . . after Miki Rox . . . I just gave up on it all. I have been unchaste ever since." I sniff. "Even if it wasn't my desire."

"Slow down," Travin murmurs, not allowing me to entirely slither away. "What is this about Miki?"

"Don't you understand?" I choke.

Travin clumsily wipes a few of my tears away with his thumbs. I can see the memory turning in his mind. Back at camp, when he discovered Miki punched in the face by Westin, and I standing nearby—I never told Travin the truth. Now, I very briefly explain why that occurred, the night in the alleyway a year ago, and then the nights in Zaheth, keeping as many gruesome details as possible to myself. By the end of the grisly tale, Travin is clutching both my wrists.

"I've never told anyone," I conclude, "because nobody needs to know what a whore I am."

"Enough of that language!" Travin barks. He shakes me, an intensity appearing behind his eyes. "You are not! Never say that again! *Ever!*" He looks as wild and vicious as Westin did while beating up Miki. "I don't care what has happened in the past. You can be clean again. Though your sins be as scarlet, your soul can be made whole. Do you hear me?"

"I hate myself," I grumble.

"Look at my face," Travin orders calmly until I do so. "You're my best friend, and I'll never let Miki, or anyone, molest you ever again. We look out for each other, remember? I know I haven't been there for you recently, but all of that has changed now. Everything has changed. I'm sorry they took Westin. We're . . . we'll get him back."

His tone is underlined with the nonverbal statement, "It will mollify your reputation."

Furious, I stare fixedly back at this person I've known my whole life.

"Things will all work out," he murmurs. "It just takes time."

"We look out for each other?" I repeat, my voice shaking. "You haven't been there for me *recently*? Things have changed *now*? Everything will all work out? You couldn't be more wrong!"

"I am *not* wrong!" Travin argues. He's still clinging to me, and I'm still trying to wiggle free. "You will be well, Kaya. Everything will be well. Joshua has promised us freedoms, inheritances, and health. God will protect us. You just have to come unto Him. Have faith to see it come true. See it in your head first, and you can make it happen."

"See it in my head first. Is that right?" Refusing to make eye contact, I let my hands fall into my lap and stare at my palms. "You don't want to know what I see in my head."

When I stand, Travin doesn't stop me. His arms slip down to his sides, and he gazes up at me from the ground, helplessly. I rock, my balance infantile.

"What false world are you living in?" I demand, motioning around us. "Where is our freedom? Where is our protection? *We* don't take care of each other. I hardly know you at all. You've been in support of this war all along! Since when, Trav? How old were you when you first learned to fight? To hurt others?"

"I would *never* intentionally hurt another unless—"

"And you and Bronwynn . . . I mean, I knew she was your prospect for marriage, but I just thought . . . with all your talk about resisting temptation and fearing God . . ." I shake my head while Travin's eyebrows draw together. "At least *you* have each other. I'll never see Westin again. He is one of them now, one of Vaclav's servants. He has given his loyalty to our enemies. I know it. I saw it. Believe in *that*!"

I shuffle a few steps away from the burning cinders, my body sore and stiff.

"I can't even trust you," I say with resignation. "The one person I want to trust most."

Travin makes no response, his expression unmoved. I leave him in *that cave* with his own thoughts. With my bare feet in the sand, I gaze out at the Salt Sea. This may be my last chance to swim in it. So I traipse down to the water's edge. My robes of Zaheth have been replaced. I prefer this economical wool. Removing the simlah, I enter the waves. I sink to my knees, let the water tickle my collarbone, and think about this crazy war that is tearing my life apart.

Your soul will be made whole. I heard that message at an Israelite sermon once.

A crack of lightning startles me as it strikes off in the rolling hills. Thunder follows shortly after, and I retreat to my clothes. The storm proceeds rapidly, releasing a downpour of rain. I walk back to the cave beneath it, wishing it would purify more than just earth. Fighting my dread, I take a seat across the fire, away from Travin.

Have you ever felt it? he'd asked.

I wish I hadn't let him see me cry.

Prayer.

Have I truly prayed?

Were my prayers answered, even if they were answered in a way I didn't expect them to be?

I startle to an intense strike of lightening. Travin sits close to the flames, staring at the coals and at nothing at all. The soldier in him has become accustomed to reigning in emotion. Lightning strikes again, only this time two figures appear in the cave's entrance. They're dripping wet, gripping each other's hands. I jump back as they step into the light of the blaze.

Tasia?

She is much thinner than when I last saw her, with her curly hair untamed all around her. Next to her stands a man of equal height, shaggy brown hair, wearing long robes and animal skins. He's her age and devastatingly handsome. With a grandiose flap of his robes, he charges into the cave.

"You are well?" Tasia asks, following quickly after him and squatting at my side.

"I . . . I suppose." I want to ask her so many things—about being in Zaheth, our escape—but her eyes tell me it's not the time. I opt for one crucial detail. "Where is Rajmund?"

Travin's eyes dart to my face.

"I took him to Officer Carac's unit," the man with Tasia announces.

I faintly recognize his voice. He reaches for something inside of his robe. I see a flash of gadgets and gizmos as he withdraws a short, thick sword. Where or how he stashed it, I have no idea. Shaking out his hair, he glances beyond me to Travin, handing him the weapon.

"We bring good tidings," Amaris begins. "And bad tidings."

Tasia smiles at me as she helps me to my feet. I can see a new brilliance in her face. A glow of happiness. I peek back to the handsome stranger. This is he? The *one and only.* Amaris rescued me from Zaheth. I owe him my life. But I do not want to bring up those moments of our imprisonment now, not with the way Tasia is looking at him. Their adoration for one another is frighteningly tangible, especially in the close confines of the cave. Even with the tiniest glances, a flare of sensuality crackles between them.

"We need to travel north immediately," Amaris declares. "Over this pass, the enemy forces march toward Giles. We can intercept them, but we must hurry. Joshua and several units can march against them. You must return to Giles and warn the soldiers there."

Tasia confirms with a nod.

"An enemy force approaches," I repeat. "Vaclav's soldiers?"

Amaris nods.

"How did they find us?" I question.

"One of Joshua's spies intercepted a Canaanite epistle. Vaclav has intel concerning Joshua's plans. They intend to attack Joshua's stronghold at Giles and restrict the Israelites from crossing the River Jordan with—"

"What?" Travin interjects. "Vaclav is coming after Joshua?"

"Not just Joshua."

"We need to get to Giles," Tasia states, assisting Amaris in the sense of urgency. "Joshua, Officers Gorrow, Lachlan, and their soldiers will hold off Vaclav's men, but we have to return to the stronghold and report of their intentions. In case any enemies break into the village. There are—" her eyes flit to Amaris, "—artifacts and provisions Joshua's army must transport across the river. This cannot be impeded by anyone. It is understood that Vaclav is after these artifacts. If we get there in time, the Israelites in Giles can begin the exportation before the Canaanites arrive. Travin, you may rejoin Amaris at the front-lines of battle after you've helped Kaya return safely and delivered the warning."

"We have to leave Avoca?" I ask.

"I cannot join the battle now?" Travin says at the same time.

"We need armed guidance," Tasia answers. "This is your direct mission. Vaclav may know more than we wish. If we don't hurry, the village and these artifacts will be in grave danger."

Amaris, appearing every bit the enigmatic spy I believe him to be, leads Travin out of the cave. The man is unusually mysterious, but full of wonder. I worry he is an aberrant, but I do not feel he is wicked. When Tasia takes off after him, I capture her elbow.

"Is Amaris . . . immortal?" I mumble quietly.

Her eyes don't leave her beloved. She grins covertly and answers simply, "He is God's servant."

I vow to myself to find out more. Tasia trusts him. It is expedient that I do, too.

Down on the shoreline, Amaris is explaining something to Travin. They exchange hand signals. Standing next to them, I start to feel something.

It.

Even though part of me has died, I am alive. Awakened. The sublimity of Amaris, the doubtlessness of Tasia, the faith of Travin. I am starting to see what *is* right, and how these souls have been blessed because of their obedience.

Amaris touches Tasia's face, kisses her forehead, and then her lips. Their embrace is so passionate, I blush and turn away. I have not thought to ask if they were wed.

"Don't stop. Don't turn back," Amaris orders her. Still clinging tightly to Tasia, he turns his attention to Travin. "If you follow my instruction, you will reach Giles swiftly and safely. It is a two-day journey. I vow you will make it in less than one. Have faith."

He turns to me and shock, mixed with an impression of truth, rushes through me.

"Kaya, give this epistle to one of the officers. Tell them what you have seen and warn them of Vaclav's Canaanite army. Travin, return to Joshua's convoy as soon as your mission is complete. Here is a map of the Israelite locations. If Vaclav pushes Gorrow and his men from here into Giles, we will have to cross the river sooner than planned. Joshua will impede any attackers who threaten to stop him. He will need your assistance."

With a final, but sound, kiss to Tasia, Amaris turns and sprints toward the Salt Sea. Before he reaches the water, another crack of lightning strikes, and his figure is gone. I stare at his departure in wonderment.

"Come," Tasia beckons, moving forward through the rain without further explanation.

Travin follows Tasia, gently ushering me along. It pains me to leave Avoca again. He sheaths the sword Amaris gave him. I notice his tse'adah are missing. The chagowr Joshua awarded him is also gone. The taupe ketonet he wears is clean, however, and he has a small pouch attached to his belt. From it, he removes water and a slice of manna, offering them to me. Then he tucks the maps inside.

I trip in the sand trying to keep up with them, my body having exceeded much of its physical limits. The manna tastes like mud, but nourishment placates my roiling stomach. Nothing can be done for my headache.

Behind us, Avoca looks like a ghost town in the dim light. Desolate. Forsaken. I miss it, but I understand now why and how it met extinction. The three of us must make haste, lest Giles and the inhabitants thereof meet a similar fate.

We travel north as the sun starts to rise against the horizon, casting a hint of luminosity across the rolling hills. Although wooded-plains and mountainous ravines separate us from Giles, a passage always appears. Our travels are made easy. The miracle Amaris foretold unfolds. It takes all night, but we reach the edge of the wilderness in fewer than ten hours. Pausing, we take a moment to gaze across the vast, green valley below us. A snare of creeks winds through lawns and meadows. They feed into the River Jordan.

Morning touches the land, but the sun withholds its yellow fingers. Swarthy clouds roll against the firmament, swarming over dawn like an oil spill. Another crack of thunder perforates the air, leaving a consistent, low thrum. The storm conceals every inch of the sky, leaving only dark shadows over the valley. A blinding white shaft blasts a tree next to us, and we huddle closer.

I'm squeezing a hand I don't remember grabbing. It's willowy and coarse, and I know it belongs to Travin, who hovers behind me, peeking over my shoulder. Part of me wants to let go. I can't allow him back in. Not now. He's right, everything has changed.

Suddenly, the earth begins to tremble. That constant thrum grows louder. Branches break off trees and tumble to the ground. Leaves flutter loose and spill down. The waters of the streams start to tremor and swirl. Then, from over the furthermost hill, hundreds of little black dots appear. Like termites, they crawl over the distant mounds, pile into the dell, infesting the whole valley. Vaclav's army.

Thunder booms loudly from the opposite end of the vale. The three of us turn. Surmounting the neighboring tor, a multitude of Israelite soldiers marches forth. Officer Gorrow is at their lead. Rumbling sounds of horses and chariots and oxen hooves pound the earth, challenging the growling heavens.

Tasia climbs a large stump, perching herself on it. Travin and I stand beneath her.

"Even the elements have chosen a side," she whispers.

I follow her gaze heavenward.

The clouds follow in sync with the soldiers' promenade, whirling closely overhead like they have elected to participate. The black nimbus crosses the valley, breaking sporadically so that gaps of the sky blast through with starry elucidations. The ground beneath us begins to quake. The armies charge one another.

It has begun.

TRAVIN

Courage Is the Fiercest Weapon

I GAPE AT THE commencement of another battle, wishing I could bring back last night. Pacing the cave, visiting the Salt Sea, allowing solitude *and* the company of Kaya to remind me who I am. I am a warrior. I must be strong.

I'd fallen asleep by the blazing embers, only to drift into a nightmare. I was in the dungeons of Zaheth with Rajmund and Tasia. We were tied up by our wrists, suspended from wooden beams. Hanging from our ankles were heavy weights, which pulled on our bodies until our shoulders dislocated. I'd shouted from the pain, awakening myself. Kaya was still asleep, her breathing entering and exiting her mouth in short gasps. She was having a nightmare, too.

I had not understood the complexity of her pain. I had not known it existed until she told me the truth about Miki Rox. When she was robbed of that precious piece of her soul, she no longer felt virtue was valuable enough to keep sacred. Love and intimacy did not coexist anymore. She let Westin have what she thought he needed in hopes that he would reciprocate with what *she* desired. If only she knew what she *really* wanted, and that lust has very little to do with love.

It's complicated, but it all makes sense. Kaya did not have a mother to teach her how to be a lady, and her untoward encounters with physical intimacy have taught her to be someone she is not. It is not my burden to bear, but I feel trodden by her sufferings just the same.

I truly miss her father. The knife he gave me was taken in Zaheth, and I feel like it means Father Lucan is forever gone, too. I do not wish to let his memory die. Perhaps it doesn't need to. Maybe it just means I need to gain strength and go forth as my own man, and be there for Kaya the way he would want me to. I must take these things and learn of them, and be the person *I* know I should be.

I let my gaze travel over the mass of two armies, over one land, under one God, and I pray with all my might. *Withersoever thou sendest me, I will go.*

I can feel His divination buoying me up. No matter the toll captivity had on my body, my faculties are magnified. Instead of hate, I feel love. I feel His grace.

Failure is a closing door.

I don't live there anymore.

KAYA

Blessings and Battlefronts

As THE TWO RIVALS blitz across the hills, Tasia, Travin, and I watch from a secluded hillock near the wilderness, a family of trees providing cover. Vaclav's Canaanite militia, the Israelite soldiers, the "elements" as Tasia calls them, are all so mesmerizing.

War.

Horse-drawn chariots race toward one another. Single stallions and soldiers on foot rout betwixt them. Other beasts of the field are present. Wolves. Lions. Fowls in the air soar and dip above the warriors. Shouts emerge from the trees behind us. I whip around, clutching Travin's shoulder. Climbing down through the wilderness and into the valley, more Israelites come forth only a few cubits from where we huddle, concealed by our slight elevation. Officer Carac and his horse hurtle through trees, Grond Bottker right behind him.

Grond's eyes are cold and angry, his fists clenched around two scimitars. Closely following Grond is Rajmund, whip in hand. His blonde tresses sweep elegantly above over his shoulders. His arms have diminished in muscular strength after being held in captivity in Zaheth, but a different power of reckoning arms his body.

Nasr, among the many others, is wearing next to nothing. Brute force and a couple patches of fur are his only armaments. He speeds valiantly toward the clashing front-lines, smiting down anything in his path with a hefty blade. Then I see Rebby. He sprints beautifully alongside these crusaders, a vision of purebred vanquisher. His father would be proud. He vanishes into the mix of soldiers dumping like buckets into the gorge.

I understand what the Israelites intend to do. Surround the Canaanites from all angles.

Trav desires to join them. He flinches, hesitates. His hand is still linked in mine. I try to extract my fingers, wanting him to fulfill this lifelong dream of his, wanting to slip away from the comfort of his fingers, wanting to stay and watch, but also wanting to run. But he clasps my hand more firmly, following the soldiers with his eyes.

Tasia's gaze slides over to us, a small nod emphasizing our orders from Amaris. Return to Giles. Warn the soldiers at the stronghold. Make preparations for crossing the River Jordan.

We devise a plan, descending from our lookout. All the elements are livid. Molecules sparkle in disorder. Sunbursts scorch into a wintry spray of sleet. The sparks fizzle from flame into evaporations upon contact. The moisture that hangs in the air begins to freeze as the temperature declines. Thick, jagged icicles form on stiffened tree limbs and rocky overhangs.

Grond leaps from the ground toward a tree, propelling himself inches underneath a branch. He breaks off a big icicle in a twist of motion and pitches it into the crazed battle. The knife of ice pierces a lion in the chest. The beast tumbles to a halt, twitches, and then it is dead. A thin layer of frost coats the dead lion's fur. Several feet away, a tall Canaanite stands motionless. Vaclav.

He is staring down at the lion. His dead pet. From the distance, I cannot discern his expression, but he begins moving frighteningly slowly amidst the multitude of soldiers, as if he is a spirit skating over the earth. Bald and built large with stature, his muscles protrude from his skin, clothed in black armor. He is not afflicted by disease, like unto his rebel servants. Ignoring the contenders drawing near, he reaches a hand out toward the lion's carcass. As his hand clenches into a tight fist, the animal's body begins to hover and shake.

I quiver, remembering his torturous sorcery. I feel *it*, the opposite of what Travin defines as God's spirit. I sense the adversary. Vaclav is employed by the devil.

The warlord yanks his fist back into his chest, and the lion's hide is stripped with a ripping sound. It reminds me of Chas's breaking bones. The hide floats above the heads of the fighting men, levitating over Vaclav's body, until it lowers on him like a cape. The mane droops over his head like a hood, while the remainder hangs down his back. A pool of blood forms beneath the tail, streaks of red sliding down Vaclav's arms and hands. In a final elegant motion, he launches into the fight, scooping up a fallen shield and ax along the way.

Javelins fly through the air. Bowmen shoot arrows. Chains with huge spiked balls swing into skulls. The beasts charge savagely down the hill. Spears sink into trees, wobbling from the mighty tempest. The grassland below becomes smeared red, covered with lifeless bodies. Various weapons stick out of their corpses.

The conflict is spreading, despite the number of dead lying on the ground. Soldiers from either side pour endlessly into the valley, closing in on our refuge near the wilderness with each passing minute. Tearing our eyes from the spectacle, Tasia, Travin and I stand, and begin to retreat farther into the forest.

"Go, go, go!" Travin yells, the clashing of metal echoing around us.

"This way!" Tasia cries, turning toward a skinny trail.

Giles is only a short distance away. Our mission needs to be completed. We flee across the rough terrain, ignoring our bodily stress, dodging weapons as the battle corrupts the peaceful woodlands. But we've waited a moment too long. The soldiers are gaining on us.

Out of nowhere, Amaris appears beside Tasia. In a single movement, he grabs hold of her hand and disappears as if running directly into the mountainside, becoming one with the rock. My feet stop. I gape at the place where she once stood, alarm transfusing through me.

"What happened?" I shout. "Behold, it is evil!"

"I can explain," Travin answers breathily. "Later. Follow me to the Praun River. It will lead us to Jordan faster."

"I d-don't understand," I stutter, fear gripping me.

Travin backtracks to grab my wrist. "Trust in the Lord with all thine heart. And watch the miracle of His hand at work."

We run down the trail, Travin in the lead.

"Look out!" he yells, shoving me into the trunk of a tree.

An ax flies past our heads. He flattens me into the bark, while arrows zoom by. His shoulder blades protrude pointedly into my sternum. His ribs are defined and skeletal beneath his thin shirt. *What did Vaclav do to him?*

"We're not going to make it!" I whimper, my faith slipping.

"We'll make it!" Travin urges, reaching behind himself to grab my hand.

We wait for a recess in the weapons scrimmage and hurry on. Following a discreet pathway to the River Jordan, which Amaris commanded us to take, we manage to outrun the battle. There is only one last mountain to cross, and then we will enter Giles.

The blood-hungry convoy of soldiers takes respite for the night. Sounds of battle diminish. Wheezing, I tell Travin I have to catch my breath. We stop in an arid tract, Travin circling the area to make sure it is clear. I lean over, pressing my hands into my exhausted legs. From my lungs into my throat, my body stings.

"I can't breathe," I exhale.

Nothing comes out of my stomach, but the taste of fatality is there. I cough and gasp. Travin is two shades better, but he conceals it well, examining our surroundings with a soldier's aptitude.

"Did you see Rajmund back there?" I ask. "He was with us in Zaheth, right? Did Amaris save him too?"

"Yay," Travin replies. "Let us move."

"Amaris came back for Tasia." I spit the foul taste from my mouth, drawing in another deep breath. It hurts, all over. "He always comes back for her. She said that."

Travin takes a few steps away, reviewing a window in the gully. He says nothing.

"Trav?"

"Hm?"

"I thought he was God's servant . . . I thought . . . I mean, I felt his goodness when I was around him. But this—how did he—why would he—it is like he is a phantom. How was he lifted up into nothingness? How did he speak truth and allow us to travel this distance in a remarkable time?"

Travin is still inspecting the landscape. "Kaya, there are soldiers who are called by Joshua to fulfill God's work. Then there are men called by God. I do not have the scientific explanation you desire, but I do know God can move mountains. He distributes that authority to men who are special and gifted, like Amaris. He can perform miracles, but they are conditioned upon faith."

Travin peers back at me from a cleft he's beginning to hike and beckons.

I still yearn for answers. "Why did you want to be a soldier? This destruction has brought you great sadness."

"That is not true. It is what I was born to do."

"But what about Bronwynn? Didn't it concern you to leave her in Giles? Do you think—?"

"It is God's will that we fulfill His work. I can hear Him speak to my heart, Kaya. I heed Joshua's command. When I do what I'm supposed to things just . . . work out. Are you coming or not?"

I skip to catch up, following him up the steep ledge. That explanation, *things just work out*, is really starting to plague me.

"Why did *you*?" he asks suddenly. "Why did you join the Israelites? You don't even believe in God."

I position my feet against the stone, wondering if it is a good time to tell Trav I have started to feel *it*. Mostly just around him, and those who are exceedingly righteous, like Amaris, but I know there is something in the heavens the same way I know it is daytime even when I am inside a tent.

"I had nothing left to believe in at home, Trav," I reply. "Is it not better to wish for something without knowing it is there, than to pretend like it is not when it really exists?"

"Do you know you speak of faith?" he questions. "Watch this crack. Put your foot there."

"Isn't faith and doubt the same thing?"

"Nay, faith is choosing to believe, even when you do not see. That is part of the religious freedom."

"You know, you don't have to be religious to want freedom."

Travin helps haul me up over the ridge to a slim path. "Here, take my other hand."

I obey, admiring his willingness to defend his beliefs. His faith is contagious. And I want it to be.

At the top of a ridge, we face a massive chasm that separates us from a southern shoreline of the Praun River. It will lead us directly to the River Jordan. Nevertheless, the only thing connecting our side of the gorge to the other is a feeble, deteriorated, not at all trustworthy, rope bridge. I approximate it to be nearly one hundred cubits in length. I send Travin a look to fend off any fostering ideas, but he disregards it.

Stepping up to the first wooden plank, he tests the stability of it with a toe. The timber immediately splinters and breaks free, free-falling down to the culvert, hundreds of feet below. He stops to evaluate the situation, as I glance around the area for enemies. A dimming sunset shines a light the color of nectarines across the dry land. It would be beautiful if it weren't for the distant detonations shaking the mountain range. One peak begins to split, a landslide of rock and earth crumbling to sea level. The skies above are a clashing eddy.

I turn back to Travin and realize he is praying. It is such a humble, unassuming moment, I can't help but glance away. A minute later, he starts toward me. His eyes penetrate mine while he lifts a hand in my direction.

"Come with me."

It is like he fears nothing. Like Joshua.

I've never had a reason *not* to trust Travin, which is the only reason I allow the idea of God to resonate. Maybe this will qualify as one of the *things* that will *just work out.*

With my back to Travin's front, we begin inching backward down the rope bridge, he watchful of potential assailants ahead of us. I am watchful of anything in pursuit. Every time Travin takes a step back, I imitate his actions. Step by step, we make it halfway across before a decayed board beneath my foot shatters. My leg plunges through the gap, and I tumble. For a split second, I know Travin's prayer will not be answered. We will fail. The bridge will not hold. We will not travel through time to Giles in a manner that should take several days.

But Travin lunges forward, seizing me around the shoulders with a nimble arm. He muscles me toward his chest, holding us still, with the strength of four men.

My stomach churns sickly inside of me, replicating the vertigo in my head. Neither of us says a word as we stare downward. The trees look like specks of ash at the bottom of the ravine. Slowly, I retract my leg from the empty air and maneuver myself into a standing position. The rope bridge settles underneath us, but Travin does not relinquish his hold on me. His heart is lambasting into my spine.

I stutter a tuckered, "Th-thank y-you."

His forehead falls onto my back. I hear him swallow.

And then, somehow, it is over.

Our feet are on solid ground. We gape out at the rope bridge. There are only a dozen or so wooden steps spanning the entire length of it.

Navigating the trail along the Praun, we then encounter a high wall of sandstone twinkling against the sunset. We'll have to find another route. Travin suggests we take a moment to eat, plucking olives off one of the abundant olive trees. I chew on a handful at a time. Cows are grazing at a nearby patch of clover, displaying a counterfeit portrait of calm. They are not at risk, but *we* are, if we are caught out here after dark.

When it is time to begin moving again, we use the small fissures and attempt to climb the sandstone. I lack the expertise of the Bottker twins, the best-known climbers in the Israelite army. Travin gives me a few tips. Digging the toe of my sandal into the deepest crack, I manage to make it a few feet up, when I hear something unpleasant behind me. It was the sound I imagine a huge, hungry belly might make.

A gurgle.

A rumble.

I glance down at Travin and follow the focus of his attention in the direction we've just come from. I never totally believed Joshua when he spoke of Og as a giant. I never believed in giants at all. Nonetheless, approaching us now is a creature over eight cubits in height. I can tell it's human and male. The ill-boding sounds only assent to its genetic composition. *A giant.*

"I thought you killed Og," I voice.

"We did," is Trav's reply.

The giant's huge ears stick straight out from his head, thick and ogre-like. A few long, greasy hairs dangle forward down his face. His stinking body is covered in animal furs, except for his arms and legs. From his armpits, sprouts dark, curly hair matching that of his legs. The fat nose scrunches up, and his mouth curves into a gaping smile, revealing several rotten, square teeth.

With each step the giant takes toward us, the ground trembles. He's viewing us as his next meal. From the belt at his hip, the giant withdraws a sickle so grand it could harvest an entire cornfield in one swoop. Travin crouches slightly, rocking back and forth between his feet, his hands hovering out to his sides. The sword Amaris gave him is at the ready in one. He is prepared for attack.

"Trav!" I hiss.

He doesn't look up.

"Trav!" I try again.

"Kaya," he murmurs without meeting my eyes. "Whatever happens. Don't. Move."

"What?"

"If I can distract him, try getting to the top of that point. You'll be safe up there."

"Nay." I can't quit saying it. "Nay. Nay. Nay."

"I want you to run. Don't look back."

"Nay!"

As the giant approaches, I see thick saliva oozing out the side of his mouth. His sickle is rusted, or covered in dried blood, and no doubt contaminated with the disease.

My fingers begin to ache. I cannot hold myself to the mountainside much longer.

A few things happen all at once. The giant pitches toward Travin, swinging his large sickle. Travin hunches and rolls between the giant's legs, but his sword is knocked from his grasp. The sickle sinks into the stone beside me, and I shriek. The giant swivels around in search of Travin, who is dodging the giant's deathly swings. My fingers finally give out. I fall to the dirt and land flat on my back.

Laboring for air, I fumble to my feet. This time the sickle sinks into the stone and sticks. The giant yanks at it repeatedly in frustration. Travin's sword is nowhere to be seen. He sneaks behind the creature. In one quick motion, he leaps onto the giant's back. The giant spins around in loops, trying to shake Travin off of him. It raises a chubby hand and clubs Travin in the side of the head. Again and again.

Travin shouts back to me, "Get the sickle! Get the weapon! Get it out!"

I scuttle past them, avoiding getting trampled. Grabbing the handle, I pull on the sickle. Nothing. I kick at it. Nothing. I kick again, and again, and again, until it wiggles. Ever so slowly, I notice the blade shifting. Positioning myself so I can stand on the handle, I press all my weight down on it. Finally, the weapon breaks free.

"Now what?" I wail, watching the giant's arms reach around crazily, trying to remove Travin's body from his back.

"Stab him!" Travin hollers back. "Stab him, quick!"

I gulp, staring at the bloody weapon. It's too heavy for me to raise. I am unable to summon the strength. But Travin is still shouting encouragement.

"Now! Kaya, get him! Now!"

The giant is reeling toward me. His big, round belly nears my face. I can't see Travin hiding on his back, but I hear his coaching.

Lift. Point. Stab.

I close my eyes.

Help.

My eyes spring open with sensation. Two arms clothed in white encircle mine, lift the sickle, and point the tip at the enclosing flesh. Not a second too late, the giant staggers into me. I feel the blade sink into his gooey flesh, swallowing my hand. Hot blood spatters across my cheeks and neck. With a final gurgle, the giant falls forward and crushes my legs to the earth beneath him.

Travin dismounts from the giant's back, but the giant is not dead. It pushes onto all fours. Swiftly, I tuck my limbs into a ball. Travin tears the bloody sickle from the giant's belly and picks it up.

Without hesitation, he steps beside the creature's cranium, skillfully raises the blade, and slams it down across the giant's neck.

Sticky fluid covers my body. My arms, my hands, my legs. I'm drenched, shaking. Blood. Diseased blood. I crawl backward until my back hits the boulder behind me, the jolt resonating in each part of me like a giant bruise. My eyes trace the crimson rivulet leading back to the headless corpse. And Travin. He drops the sickle, breathing heavily.

"Are you okay?" he calls. "Are you hurt?"

And God will deliver them into our hands.

The spirit of God is like a fire, burning.

I feel like I *am* burning. The things which I feel cannot be written, but I bear record of the miracle I have seen.

Travin is standing over me, his figure no less frail than he had seemed in the cave but completely transformed. Fortitude defines him. He reaches out to me. His hand, though covered in slime, appears to be glowing.

"Kaya," he says shakily. "Are you alright? Are you injured?"

He studies his hands, rubbing them on his clothing, but it does not remove the gore. Anxiously, he rips off the hem of his tunic to scrub at his knuckles before throwing the fabric as far as he can. Breathless, he falls to his side next to me. He rests his forehead on my knee, letting out a gust of air.

"You are well," he whispers. "*We* are well."

We both fall into a deep sleep, the otherworldly energy leaving our bodies in a state of total exhaustion, not waking until morning. The mordant odor of the giant's blood grows gamier as the heat of day arises. It smells like poison. Distant rumbling attests to the commencement of battle. Travin pushes himself up, examining his arms and legs. He retrieves his sword, but I do not heed his suggestion to carry the sickle. I can't. I don't even think I can move. But the soldier in him takes precedence over the friend.

"Come," he demands. "We need to keep moving."

The air has dried the blood on our skin, and there isn't time to clean it off. Henceforth, the two of us look unrecognizable in our new disguise. I haven't shaken the worry of that giant's contagious blood somehow infecting mine. When I look down at my flesh and over at Travin's, my internals plait with worry. *The disease.* Travin reminds me in a still, small manner: Joshua promised health to the righteous.

It doesn't entirely convince me. Travin perceives my doubtfulness. He strides over and places his hands on my shoulders.

"Let me see your eyes," he declares.

I hold perfectly still, staring back as he scans me for any indication of infection. His gaze withdraws from my eyes, seeing my whole face. The corner of his mouth turns up.

"They're exceptionally green," he confirms.

We reach the mouth of the River Jordan, glancing behind us in awe at how far we have traveled, in such a short amount of time. The clairvoyant, Amaris, was correct. The tips of the rocky summits are irradiated by the progressive blaze of war. The land surrounding us is on fire. Ahead of us, the fjord expands into the marshes of Giles. It is a miracle.

I know I should tell Travin about the other miracle I experienced against the giant, but the more time passes, the more I question if it even happened. *Was I hallucinating?*

When we come upon the village gates, I momentarily forget. There are two pikes with scalped heads atop them. Huts have been turned inside out. Plumes of smoke rise into the air above them. There are no busy soldiers, no bustling activities. Blood covers the earth. Several bodies lie dead in the walkway, burnt animal carcasses and humans. Dead sheep and cattle are scattered over trampled crop. The whole scene is in complete disarray. Giles has been ruinously looted.

My soul stings as I realize another horror. We are too late. The artifacts have been stolen. *And what has become of Svana? And all of the citizens?*

"Let me see the epistle," Travin states.

We open it and read.

"Consecrate yourselves, for tomorrow the Lord will do wonders among you."

"Vaclav sent spies to Giles," Travin murmurs.

"What does the rest say?"

"Vaclav purposefully drew out a large part of our army by waging war against us. With Giles momentarily lacking strong defenses, his spies slipped inside, in search of the artifacts."

"Vaclav tricked our forces?"

"It appears so."

"What do we do?"

He points towards the Tent of Meetings, the structure near collapse. We creep past the debris, staring at the lynched corpses.

"Careful," Travin whispers, lifting his sword.

The whole village is derelict, with only the sounds of the river eerily serenading the flurry of ash. Travin signals he is going left to investigate. I nod, inching carefully toward a dead body. Still clasped in the lifeless hand is a weapon I could probably carry. I glance around, leery of villains that may be lurking. My eyes come to rest on a heap of unresponsive bodies in a pile of mulch. Covering my mouth, I hold back a retch. There has been a battle here, but there are not enough deceased persons to account for all of the villagers and Israelites. Even the ships of fishermen at the port of the river sit unattended.

Where has everyone gone?

A noise in the distance catches my attention. I peer backward from whence we came, listening to the increasing din of battle. Amaris wanted us to warn the officers on location of Vaclav's crusade and urge the Israelites to cross the River Jordan as soon as possible. But Giles is deserted.

Stooping, I grab the weapon by my feet and continue cautiously around a bend where I spy a cluster of people, all of them women, tied up near the central fire pit. Their arms are restrained behind their backs. Cloths cover their mouths and noses. Many of them are stripped of their clothing. But they are alive, wide-eyed, staring at me.

"Trav—"

I'm snatched by the elbow before I can scream for help. A disgusting, diseased face smiles down at me, his hand smothering my mouth. I drop my weapon. A second rebel grabs my arms. He binds them tightly behind my back and ties my feet with cords. They stuff a sordid piece of rag into my mouth, jerking me back and forth. The particularly ugly one, with warts polluting his face, drags me to the pile of remaining survivors, kicking the backs of my knees so I fall beside them.

Panicked, I try and count the captives around me. I think there are fifteen. No Svana. No Mikyla. A face I do know is behind the woman closest to me. Bronwynn's dress is torn and soused in blood, but she appears unharmed.

Guarding us are six, maybe seven infected rebels. One man's skin has even begun to peel back on his forearms. Another's eyes are so bloodshot that red veins string down into his cheeks. They must be Vaclav's men. The spies he sent in. I don't understand how they have overtaken Giles. *Wouldn't a pair of Israelite soldiers easily have slain half a dozen enemies? Why would the officers have abandoned their post?*

After ensuring their female captives are confined, Vaclav's spies begin to chop up a cadaver, dispersing the human mutton and eating it.

My mind spins, trying to pinpoint the actions of a soldier, particularly one intent on escaping. I glance into the shadows of misshapen buildings in search of Travin. Perhaps Amaris returned to rescue him a second time, stealing him straight from the air and returning him to the front-lines to help Joshua. The voice of my childhood friend cancels that theory.

"Kaya?"

Travin reappears, ceasing his casual stride as he emerges from down the road. At the same time, he becomes aware of the captive females, the Canaanite spies become aware of him. Deficient in hunting tactics, two of the rebels hightail after Travin, who bolts down the winding streets of Giles, disappearing from sight. The other mercenaries lurch toward us, one wrenching Bronwynn to her feet. I fight against my bindings, desperate to evade the rebel swiftly approaching me, when the echo of clashing metal reverberates.

The battle between the Israelites and the Canaanites detonates the perimeter of Giles. The sounds of war rebound off the rocks as contending soldiers approach, entering the city gates, descending nearby hills. They rush in from every direction, opponents engaged in combat. The port of Giles explodes into flame as Canaanites throw burning torches into ships and barrels. Joshua, galloping on horseback, is carrying a large flag as he moves toward the river. Twelve soldiers flank him—his loyal priests. Rionn rides a traveling chariot filled with weapons, a large chest, and multiple barrels.

Canaanites are in swift pursuit. Israelite officers are commanding the soldiers to head toward the riverbank. Our army pushes toward the water's edge, not in a sense of fleeing, but with a sense of purpose. This is not a surrender. My first thought is they have gone mad, for they intend on running straight into the river. But Joshua raises his flag and points the staff toward the water.

Rionn enters first, followed by the eleven other priests. The moment their feet meet the riverbed, billows of clouds from the heavens whorl down toward the earth, crashing into the fuming currents. Out of the river, a spiral of water slowly rises into the air. Like an upside-down tornado, the water is channeled up toward the sky, leaving a tunnel of moist earth. The cylinder continues sky high, with white caps crashing at the top, effectively splitting the river in two. A pathway through the heart of the River Jordan remains clear, as if obstructed by an unseen dam on both sides.

Astonished at the scene, Vaclav's spies stagger a moment. The ugly one then calls his associates to action.

"Pnun, Yishnah, Leq!" He points to an enemy force with Vaclav at the lead. "Our master!"

Vaclav commands his soldiers to pursue Joshua. Veering around contenders, our rebel captors begin to shepherd us out of the village, toward the banks of the River Jordan. Our feet shuffle along, still bound, as we are pushed and shoved down to the water's edge. The muddy earth continually slurps at and swallows my sandals. One of the female captives falls behind, abandoned by the spies in their attempt to abscond from the skirmish.

We reach the riverbank, ducking as weapons fly. Horses gallop across the wet surface, flicking chunks of mud. Soldiers use slings to hurtle massive stones at one another. Javelins whiz into buildings and bodies. It is too noisy to discern between the voices shouting, but officers from either army point toward the Israelite High Commander. To my amazement, Joshua proceeds into the riverbed, following the earthy path newly formed from the parting of the river. In a matter of seconds, the earth on which he travels becomes dry.

His soldiers diligently follow, the water ascending all around them. Officers Lachlan, Gorrow, and Orren lead their units into the tunnel of water. Time seems to stand still as this procession moves toward the western banks. Joshua and the Israelites. Vaclav and his army of intermixed Canaanites. The enemy forces retaliate thoroughly, desirous to bar many of the Israelites from crossing the river. Engulfed in the pandemonium, I hardly notice the bearded Canaanite lunging straight for me.

"Kaya?"

Twisting, I recognize Nasr, the Israelite spy. He smites down the bearded enemy whose goal was my blood. Without pause, Nasr lifts his right hand and signals men to follow him. Two soldiers do so. Nasr aims his arbalest. He plucks out one of the rebels beside me expertly before reloading. On his right flank, Rebby runs, wielding his hefty blade with aptitude. The third soldier, Travin, materializes from behind Rebby, cutting down his competitors alongside his childhood companion until the two of them are moving as one. Artful and perfect, predicting each other's moves before they are complete.

"Watch your right side!" Rebby calls.

With his weapon in his left-hand, Travin's right side is exposed to the enemy. When a Canaanite approaches it, Travin tosses his sword to his right fist, smiting his opponent down with ambidextrous beauty.

Rebby gives Travin a gaping smile. "Stop showing off!"

Weaving in and around airborne weapons, they steadily draw nearer and nearer to where we inch along through the exodus, but their route is continually stymied. With little direction available during this massive migration, the rebel captors herd us, the female prisoners, into the river tunnel. The supernatural force defies gravity. Mountains of water on either side of us swish and suck and push in torrents of air. The noise is deafening.

The wise soldiers postpone their fighting with the knowledge they are pressed for time. Foolish mercenaries continue slaying one another or being slain. Every soldier moves with haste and little consideration for each other. My arms are tied behind my back, my ankles strung together. It is difficult to stay on my feet. My claustrophobia is exaggerated by the incredulity of this miracle *and* the danger of it. We are doomed.

The moment the High Commander reaches the banks on the other side, the land starts to shake. The elements clamor virulently. A flash of nebulosity clobbers the sky. River floods curl overhead, threatening to immerse us at any moment. Water sprays down in a mist, then progresses into a cloudburst that pelts our bodies like pebbles in a slingshot. Through the tempest, I can see Canaanite soldiers giving up on their destination. Many of the enemies turn and retreat toward Giles. My gaze shifts to follow their retraction, once again locating my friends, hell bent on rescuing us.

Rebby gives Travin a hand signal, simultaneously engaging an incoming reprobate. A stream of red blood rockets out of the enemy as Rebby's blade chops through him. A fallen shield slides through the earth at his feet. He jumps onto it, surfing a moment before jumping off. He lands on one of Vaclav's men caught in the chaos. Driving him down, Rebby fends off any pursuing offenders as Travin and Nasr continue forward.

One of the spies, Pnun, shoves me into motion, eager to reach the western riverbank. We are more than halfway across. His other rebel friends have given up. They and many Canaanites have fled back to Giles on the east shore.

For a moment, the deafening thunder of swishing waves subsides to a quiet grouse. Insidious brumes lower, generating a fast absorption of precipitation. Rain and fog and wind encompass us. There are no words to describe the bedlam.

Then, a shrill light inseminates in the sky. It gets larger, nearing, crashing into the center of Giles behind us. The star rock lacerates a hill in two, causing the quake to shake the ground beneath us. Scintillations shoot up and outwards in all directions, illuminating the charging soldiers in a white flash, before extinguishing into the walls of water.

I catch glimpses of Travin in motion during these bursts of light. He slices his blade toward one attacker. The enemy dodges the swipe, returning with a swing of his own. Travin drops to his knees as the Canaanite machete barely misses the top of his head. Travin stabs the contender through the stomach.

Nasr is keeping stride. He plucks two men out with his arrows, leaving only a handful impeding their pathway. Travin charges the one nearest him. This enemy soldier is carrying a whip similar to Rajmund's. Each of the three tips has a spiked shard of metal attached to it. The Canaanite is taller than Travin. Much taller. And much stronger. He slashes his whip toward Travin. One barb catches Travin's wrist as he raises his arm to shield his face. The adversary recoils, tearing Travin's skin off his arm, then circling him in a spherical dance. Travin moves like a warrior five times his capability. *The way he did against Luko. The way he did on the bridge.* The way *I* did, when divine assistance aided me in raising the sickle to kill the giant.

Skidding across the ground, Travin slides onto his hind and strikes his foe's right leg, severing a vital artery. The rival attempts to whip Travin again, but Travin flips to his knees, spins, and narrowly escapes. The rapid loss of blood disorients his opponent, and the man begins to stagger. Disarming the enemy fiercely, Travin decapitates him without hesitation.

Wiping the blood splattered across his face, Travin looks up. His eyes lock onto mine. The front of his tunic is soaked through from a combination of bodily fluids. Slabs of thin muscle contract in his forearms as he lifts his glistening sword, his only armament. Nasr runs up to his side, grabbing Travin's shoulder. Four arrows stick out of Nasr's right arm as he raises it and points. Joshua, having reached his destination, sits astride his horse on the western shore opposite the port of Giles. He once again raises his flag.

The ground quakes in affray. Above us, the river starts to descend to its original formation. Water pours down onto the footpath Joshua had paved, beginning closest to Giles, immersing retreating Canaanites as the currents careen in our direction. I scream into the cloth in my mouth, forcing it out. Looking around frantically for a way to cut my ankles free, I spy a fallen sword. I jump over to it, position my feet, and slice through the bindings.

I push to a kneel, stand, and sprint toward dry land.

With only thirty feet separating me from safety, I hop across twelve stones marking a path through the wet ground, climbing a slippery ledge, gaining optimism and elevation as I near the riverbank where the multitude of Israelites has gathered. Rebby and Travin are seconds behind me, Nasr shouting intelligibly as the river surges toward us.

Just a little bit further.

Dying men wail, sucked into a watery abyss.

Twenty feet.

A tidal wave curls overhead.

Ten.

Hands bound, limbs aching, I leap.

I land on my chest, my breastbone colliding painfully with rock, just in time. The water consumes land and soldiers beneath it as the River Jordan resumes its previous arrangement. It swishes and swirls, but doesn't come near the ridge on which I lie. I'm at least several horse-lengths above it. The elevation of my position alone saves me from joining those lost.

Protected atop the cliff side, I gape at the swishing river, floating heads and weapons traveling through the whitecaps. The water is red, like unto pure wine of the fruit. My gaze passes over the mass of soldiers who have congregated on the western shore, from Nasr to Travin to Rebby, all of them panting heavily at the water's edge. A rocky incline separates them from me and multiple soldiers who also landed on the higher rim.

As my adrenaline abates, the pain in my right shoulder increases. I wriggle to my feet, peeking over the small but steep bluff, and exhale. The others beside me also stand, many of them limping, some of them missing fingers or earlobes. They express gratitude and sincere thanks to one another, the heavens, Joshua. The sky opens up, and, for a blip of a second, a ray of sunshine brightens the stream of anarchists.

A woman, Bronwynn, lets out a yelp. She is half-sitting, half-crawling on the precipice on which I stand. Her simlah is sopping and splattered with blood, clinging to her pudgy frame. Her ankles are swollen twice their normal size. A crazed rebel that escaped the lethal river crawls over to her, releasing a gargled laugh as he yanks her to her feet.

"Look out!" Nasr shouts from the shoreline below.

Lifting a knife to Bronwynn's throat, the rebel licks her cheek with a brown tongue. She pushes against him with a cry, and they trip backward into the man beside me. He loses his footing on the slick surface, grabs hold of my sleeve.

Travin screams.

Then, I am falling.

I swear I never see, nor feel, the impact of the river. Submerged, the oxygen is swept from my lungs. My bound arms make it impossible to swim. The undertow sucks me deeper, and deeper, and deeper. The pressure increases as I sink, the flood thrusting me into bodies, planks of wood, sharp weapons. My right shoulder throbs, the pain escalating to my ribs. I inhale water, chest burning, ears popping. The nautical black creates an absolute feeling of departure.

From life.

WESTIN

I Will Do as You Command

I LED THEM RIGHT to Giles. We encountered several Israelite bat-
talions, drawing them out of the village and into battle. Vaclav's
spies infiltrated the vicinity as his armies distracted the Israelites.
The Canaanites underestimated Joshua's forces, *and* his brilliance.
Where they thought they had the upper hand, and a village vacated
to be looted, they had been led right into a trap.

Joshua's military cleverness was inveigled further as Vaclav ordered his men to pursue the Israelite soldiers through the River Jordan. Vaclav had seen the Israelite's backward trek as a retreat, but
Joshua had planned to draw his opponents to the water all along.
A miracle in and of itself, Joshua split the river in two, allowing
passage. It proved to be the winning factor for today's battle. The
water destroyed most of Vaclav's forces. I narrowly escaped death by
retracing my steps, fleeing the riverbed to the harbor of Giles just
before the water lowered.

From my position on the shoreline, I can see Joshua and his
army, a smear of shapes spanning the length of the western banks.
Vaclav ordered me to fight against them, the men who'd trained
me, welcomed me. But then again, Vaclav has told me many things
about Joshua and the false preaching of the Israelites. I do not know
whom to call an ally anymore.

I know the men of these nations delight in the shedding of
blood. Growing up in a non-violent community, I find it frightening and detestable. Regardless, I do not have much of a choice.

There is nothing great or rewarding about the destruction of people, but I have been offered a vast reward for my knowledge concerning Israelite intelligence. If I use my resources, I will be employed as one of Vaclav's spies. In exchange for money, Vaclav's Israelite insider will deliver me detailed epistles concerning Joshua's army. I know their structure, their campsites. I know where the Tent of Meetings is held and the tabernacle of valuables.

As reward for my help, Vaclav will pay me with shekels of gold and silver. He has promised to compensate me with leadership over the spies and an entire palace, with servants and bountiful necessities, should I prove myself worthy. I will not be mired by the Canaanites the way Orren hindered my advancement.

Not wanting to delay, Vaclav demands the construction of ships that we may cross the river and stop Joshua before he triumphs over the western spine of Canaan. Joshua may have more soldiers, but Vaclav has more riches. With gold and silver, Vaclav will bribe neighboring kingdoms and roaming migrants into supporting his cause using flattery, force, and fear.

This dictatorship is reminiscent of a sermon the Israelite priest, Rionn, once shared. A long time ago, a single man wanted to rule the world. He wanted to revoke free will and ensure the compliance of every living thing using the same deportment as Vaclav.

He and a third of the hosts of heaven were banished to outer darkness.

KAYA

My Soul to Rest

I MUST BE DYING.

Shaking, convulsing, writhing. Everything is muffled by the water, arctic from the fit of weather. My thoughts are sporadic in the miasma of death. Nothing congeals. There is no light, only pain, and it is worse than I ever thought imaginable.

I don't know if I've broken the surface of the river, or passed on into another life, but I gulp reflexively at the awareness of oxygen. The sharp intake of breath awakens the chance at a revivification. I am drifting towards land. Not drifting. I am being carried.

There is a blur of war wreckage around me. Soldiers. Smoke. Weapons. My body is being cradled by strong, scarred arms. Carried to the top of the hill where a base camp, larger than Shittim, is established. We approach the infirmary, filled with other injured soldiers. I'm taken inside one of the dwellings. The stonewalls perfectly resemble how my bones feel. Cold, emotionless, dead. The arms transport me to the back room where a wide cistern sits filled with water.

Half a dozen female Israelites enter, bustling quickly. I am given over to them. My simlah is torn away from my body, large splinters of wood removed from my skin. They lower me into the water, which is warm from the earthen container. The temperature change in my body is excruciating. *Too* excruciating. As the sound of a man in distress pierces my alertness, I try to force my eyes into focus. I look down at my bluish-gray form. My flesh looks like wax. My limbs feel broken and beyond my control. My body trembles, each muscle constricting in spasm. Wheedling a small breath here or there, I toil fervently to keep my lungs functioning.

Keep your eyes open, Gring once said.

Memories of the last year sputter. Swimming in the Salt Sea. Westin. Travin. Zaheth. Throats slashed. Giants. Travin. Bodies decapitated. Travin.

The door explodes opens. I hear a hoard of demanding voices.

"She may be dying!"

"We'll see to her needs—"

"Let me through!"

"Get him out of here. It isn't proper."

"Rebby, go get a medicus!"

"Her injuries are extensive. You shouldn't be here just in case."

"Let me through, I command you, as your superior!"

All followed by a very unseemly slew of profanities. The women scatter. A face appears, forcing its way through the Israelite women.

"Kaya?"

His voice is faint.

"Kaya?"

I hear him, calling me back from the end.

Travin.

He's standing by the side of the cistern. I can see him, this boy I once called my best friend. Now I'm not sure I know him at all. He is a man, a warrior who fought the king of Bashan, who killed a giant, who killed hundreds of enemy soldiers. He's a hero.

Travin's sodden hair frisks the tips of his ears and brows in disorderly configurations, dripping down his swollen nose and the layer of scruff on his cheeks. Bloody scratches cover his hands, which are also slightly inflamed and unnaturally bluish. A cut on his wrist intermittently squirts blood over the cicatrix covering his arms. And his eyes. His eyes are the color of the river and harbor the same loud hysteria.

Shaking, Travin removes his sopping tunic, leaving only his under garments. He looks fourteen again, all knees and ribs and shoulders. I gasp at the sight of his lanky body and the contusions garnishing it. What has happened to him? And *how* did he fight with such strength?

"Kaya," Travin says gingerly, leaning over the tub.

I shift my head slightly so I can look at him. It hurts, insufferably. *Stay alive*, I tell myself with each heartbeat.

Travin proceeds to step delicately into the cistern, sitting opposite me. He positions himself across from me, extending an arm out to find my hand. His fingers rest tentatively on top of mine. They are ruefully skeletal.

"You're wounded," he voices. "Badly."

All soldier. No emotion.

Until I look into his eyes.

He doesn't *look* like a soldier of no emotion.

His face breaks into an expression of sadness so raw I look away. I long to tell him how strong he is, how brave, and that if I go I will always remember him. I will *always* be with him. But I simply cannot speak. My teeth clamor from the shivers, and every part of me sears with pain. If I am dying, I don't want him to know what my last feelings are. How much of them are shadowed by shame. What I would've done differently. That I regret so much of it.

"Trav," I whisper. "Y-you're my best f-friend."

The water ripples against his clavicle, wetting his first battle scar. He tilts his head to one side, wistfulness in the margins of his eyes.

"Do you remember that necklace I made you?" he asks softly. "The one out of seashells?"

I remember.

I was only twelve or thirteen years old. Travin strung a bunch of my favorite seashells onto a piece of twine and gave it to me for my birthday. He has celebrated every one of my birthdays. And he was so proud of that necklace. I remember how his eyes lit up when he presented it, like the richest man in all the land.

"You've never worn it once," Travin whispers with a quiet laugh. "I suppose it wasn't very fashionable."

I force my eyes back up.

"Stay away from here!" he exclaims with quiet force. "No more of this soldier life for you. Let those who know how to fight do the fighting. You need to go somewhere safe, where . . . people . . . can watch out for you. I'll find . . . someone to help you get into an established community. The place where the Israelite families are living. You don't know how to survive—" He chokes on the words, swallowing with difficulty.

An impression covers me. Something beyond the deep ache in my bones and bruised muscles. It kills my hatred for people.

"Did you save me?" I croak.

Travin's answer is immediate. "Of course!"

His eyes then shift from the water, to mine, and back down again. He shakes his head frowning.

"Who would I have if you were gone?" he murmurs, dragging a hand down his face. In a voice no bigger than a rain drop, he repeats, *"Who would I have?"*

Suddenly, my body is moving.

"Wo," he cautions, but I ignore him and the grueling pain.

I force myself to cross the small space between us, where I find a place between his legs and curl up. Nuzzling my face into his chest, I tuck my knees up into my stomach. Travin rescued me. He came for me. *He* saved *me.* I shut my eyes. Only a moment later, Travin's arms fold around me. He rests his cheek on top of my head.

I don't want to die. Not yet.

This is my happy place.

"Th-thank y-you."

Silent tears sluice my cheeks. They come, endlessly, and I let them. There's no room for shame. My body wants to cry, so I allow it to cry. What little willpower I have left I target toward breathing and bearing the suffering.

If Travin notices, he says nothing. He only cleaves to me like no one ever has before. As a parent might hold on to a lost child. As if it really is the end, and we have only moments to say goodbye. Unconcerned with propriety, we return to our childlike state of friendship until my tears eventually stop.

Neither of us says anything. My eyes sag heavily, but I continually drag them open for fear of falling into a sleep I won't wake from. I stare at the water droplets dotting the hair on Travin's arm. His one palm is directly below my chin, and I'm not at all embarrassed at where the other is. We sit like this, quietly, until the water turns cold.

I never want to leave this place in time, but medicinal purposes take priority over emotional needs. Travin must leave so I may be examined. His exit is as boisterous as his entrance, with a plump and confident older woman returning to stipulate propriety.

A medicus comes in, helps me from the cistern, and determines I have broken several ribs. He wraps my torso tightly with white straps, indicating bruises around my lower abdomen that suggest I may have internal bleeding. I have a deep slash in the back of my calf that is sewn together. I'm nursed for two days before I make the mental judgment that I am not, in fact, dying. Even though I feel like it, I know I'm getting better. My physical injuries, at least, are healing.

But I haven't seen Travin since the day he rescued me from the river, and something about this stirs my insides. At *least* I would like to know he is alright. I *need* to know it.

Rajmund has been my only regular visitor over the past two days. When I asked him if he'd seen Travin, Rajmund said Joshua had called Travin into his tent with the officers, and Rajmund hadn't seen Travin since. I notice a twinge of jealousy on Rajmund's face at my mention of Travin, but I can't help it. As soon as I can walk, I have to talk to Travin.

I can't complain about Rajmund's kindness, though. He brings a chaperone to wait outside the door of my room, sits at my bedside, and informs me of the war updates. We are camped on the borders of the city of Gilgal, a main logistics point for Joshua on the western side of the River Jordan. The Israelite army has enforced a stronghold around the vicinity with mighty fortifications. Their numbers are ever increasing, such that Joshua has appointed *several* High Commanders. Joshua is preparing the army to invade Jericho. More battles. More death.

I tell Rajmund about my nightmares, not for sympathy but to purge the images from my mind. In alliance, he tells me about his own, where he sees the faces of all the people he has killed. I describe the river, with wave after wave crashing down upon me, the water sucking me toward the muddy floor. I could sense the others drowning around me. One even grabbed hold of my arm, momentarily pulling me further under as he tried to resurface.

"I don't feel like I deserve to be alive," I murmur.

Rajmund answers simply, "You're not the only one."

KAYA

He Wants More

TODAY IS DAY FIVE at Gilgal.

Still no Travin.

Rajmund arrives in my tent to join me for breakfast, as usual. He brings good tidings. Sitting up in bed, I gaze at him wryly, awaiting whatever information has him so excited. I see it glimmering within his golden-brown eyes.

"I have received permission from the High Commanders," Rajmund starts, eventually perching himself on the foot of my bed. I gaze at him in anticipation. He smiles. "I've finally found the woman I desire to marry."

A tension unrelated to my injuries arises.

"I'll have to approve," I smirk, hoping to conceal my worry.

"I'm sure you will," Rajmund replies confidently. His face changes color until he looks like a blonde apple. "We have two more weeks before we march to Jericho." He inches closer. "I have spoken with my officer, Gorrow. He has approved of it and allotted a time." He pauses for effect. "Kaya, I'd very much like to depart in matrimony."

"You're not . . . saying what I think you are, are you?"

"Kaya Lucan?" Rajmund takes my hand while reaching into his pocket. Pulling out a ring, he displays the slender nezem layered in jewels. "Before I leave to Jericho," he asks, "will you be my wife?"

"Rajmund."

"This one isn't permanent," he comments nervously, "but it's of the finest silver. It belonged to my tribe and was bestowed upon me before I departed Kadesh. I've worn it on my tse'adah, but I would like to give it to you. I have much wealth, Kaya. When we settle into our home, you can pick out any ring. Any color, any size—"

"I told you already," I exhale, gaping at the bejeweled nezem. It's got to be the most expensive thing I've ever seen. "I'm not meant for any of that."

But Rajmund's expression doesn't wane. "I know. But I think your fear of companionship will pass, and you will understand what I can provide for you."

Fear of companionship?

"When we inherit these lands, we will fortify our cities and begin a new life. You won't suffer attacks from rebels or enemies, like in Avoca. I will protect you, and we will prosper."

I could buy all of Avoca with that ring.

"I will provide for you. You will never worry about being poor or hungry. And I will be gentle with you."

Gentle.

It's an unfair argument. Naturally, I hesitate.

"What if you don't return from Jericho for months?" I counter lamely. This isn't the biggest issue. "I will have to convert to the Israelites? Officially?"

"Yay," Rajmund replies. Boldly, he reaches out to take my hand in his. His palm dwarfs my own as he sets the nezem in my fingers. "I'm not asking you to make a decision today. All I ask is for you to think about it. It may be a decade before Avoca is reconstructed enough to be habitable. Where will you go? Where will you live?"

The ring weighs a thousand pounds.

"Give me a chance?" he asks.

I want to say no, to let Rajmund down now and be upfront about how I feel.

But . . . how *do* I feel?

He's a confidant, an *attractive* friend, a soldier. He can promise me a safe, and wealthy, future. My home would be lavished with all the opulence of God's chosen people. Sounds like a better marriage than most I've known. Is that wrong? Am I insane if I decline?

Maybe he is right.

Rajmund's large brown eyes search mine expectantly. There's a kindness in them, a real fondness.

Someone once said affection is a shy flower that takes time to blossom. I think it was my father. I think he was speaking to Travin.

Perhaps over time I will feel more than friendship for *this* man? I can't make a decision today, so I promise Rajmund I'll think about it, and he leaves me with the heirloom.

I twist the nezem around my finger. I don't want to lose him, but I don't think I'd make a good wife. It is true, what he said. I have a fear of companionship. I yearn for that bond, the closeness of intimacy I imagine people in love feel, people like Tasia and Amaris, but I push people away. Maybe even my parents felt it, before my mother left. But that's the problem. She left. Anyone can leave—or die—at any given time, no matter how much love you *think* you share.

I'd desired intimacy with Westin. He had something I could rely on regularly. Contact and convenience. I probably didn't love him. But I cared. *Still*, I care. But he is gone, lost to Vaclav.

If I pass up on Rajmund's offer, will anyone else come along to care about me the way Westin did?

Travin's voice surfaces in my mind.

You don't know how to survive.

If I marry a soldier, I can survive. I'll live through their victories and defeats as a warrior's wife, but I will face no more battlefronts and wars. While my husband is off conquering Canaan, I will be at home, alone, sewing, cooking, and tending the livestock. How different is *that* way of life to the life I've always lived?

Outside, the stormy weather has subsided, returning the full sun to the skies and heat to the air. It is beautiful.

I sit by the window and watch with a heavy heart.

KAYA

God, if You're There

IT HAS BEEN THREE weeks since we passed through the River Jordan. They've moved me from the sanatorium to a residential dwelling. The homes are larger than those in both Avoca and Taavetti, with two or three bedrooms each. Most of them are made from stone, with thick wooden doors and wool drapery over the windows.

My body's recuperation has been incremental. Physically, my injuries have healed enough that I can walk with ease, but my organs have not been well. The medicus has banned the intake of fermented wine, as it slows the recovery process. Withdrawal has been ugly.

The only consistent thing in my life is Rajmund and the tremors.

Gilgal is prosperous, the inhabitants welcoming. The soldiers mingle with the long-term populace as the army makes preparations for the march to Jericho. There is a rumor that many women and children will travel by camel and boat to the Great Sea to seek life on the islands. I've never seen the Great Sea, but the tradesmen of Gilgal speak of Caphtor and the endless ocean. Waterfalls, tributaries, and ponds embellish the coastline. And fish. All the fish you could dream of.

I don't dream.

But I *can* walk. I'm preparing to head out when I hear Travin and Rebby outside my front door. I peek through a side window. Behind them, a clump of young women walks by in the street. The females smile girlishly while staring at Rebby, who, of course, guiltlessly waves back. But then, I realize, they are not staring at Rebby at all. The girls point at Travin, whose face takes on a ruddy shade.

For a moment, I am stunned by the confusing heat coming over me. I want to slap the lustful smiles from their faces.

My eyes travel slowly back to the two men standing by the front door of my dwelling. Travin has put on some weight. His muscles have sustenance again. The color has returned to his skin. He's even washed and trimmed his hair. It's better to see him like this. It is better to see him, than to not see him at all.

One of them knocks.

"Let's make this a quick infil," Rebby says.

I open the door. "Welcome."

Travin moves past me without a word. Rebby follows, a strapping smile gilding his face. I shut the door, half expecting to see *Bon-won* lurking behind them.

"You look much better," Travin declares. Reaching out, he touches the side of my face and gradually turns my head from side to side. "You almost look like my friend Kaya."

"But prettier?" I quip.

His smile doesn't reach his eyes.

"Walking helps a lot," I state. "I've never realized how much I enjoy it. And the mountains, actually. I mean, nothing compares to Avoca. The Salt Sea. Home."

"Miki Rox is holding a funeral service today," Travin shares.

He must know that would make me feel better. But he must know I will not be attending. I've paid my condolences to Mikyla Rox, and all of the Avoca natives that passed away during the crossing of the River Jordan. I will not go anywhere near Miki Rox.

"I'll visit the grave site tonight," I sigh.

"What is this?" Rebby asks, lifting my hand and his eyebrows simultaneously.

Uh-oh.

"About that," I chuckle timidly.

I retract my hand quickly with a frown as large as Rebby's grin.

"I guess Rajmund has plans for me in his future," I mutter. "Um, *us*. He sort of proposed."

Rebby bursts into laughter.

Travin's upper lip curls in repugnance.

I immediately regret telling them.

"Men from Kadesh are absurd," Travin scoffs. "You don't even know each other!"

"False," I laugh nervously. "Rajmund and I know plenty about each other. He's . . . my friend. He's doing what he thinks is traditional. And he can offer security, wealth, safety." I shrug, vocalizing the internal debate I've been having for many days. "It's worth pondering."

"Are you listening to yourself?" Travin gapes.

"I'm sure plenty of people find customs in Avoca bizarre," I argue.

Rebby gives one solid, supportive nod.

"So, you accepted?" Travin exclaims.

"Of course, not!" I shout at the same time Rebby says, "*I* would." He is admiring the costly ring. I glare at him.

I don't want to admit the fact that I actually might be considering Rajmund's proposal. How different my life could be. How less lonely.

I look down at the jewels and say with a subservient tone, "I promised him I'd think about it."

Travin waves a hand. "But you're wearing the nezem?"

Rebby leans in to my ear, whispering far too loudly for confidentiality, "I think I've had enough of Travin's gaiety for the day." He canters to the door and hollers mid-flee, "You two are on your own for this one. Glad you're doing better, Kaya."

The door shuts behind him.

"Trav?" I exhale heavily. I've wanted to talk to him for so long. Not about this. "I'm just being realistic. Probably for the first time in my life. I told Rajmund I'm most likely not meant for marriage."

Travin huffs crossly. "Well, he's never going to believe you if you keep leading him on the way you do. Trust me. A man doesn't just hang around to get to know a woman for no reason. A man *always* has an agenda—"

He stops short, moving his gaze from my face, to the ring on my hand, to the window.

"Well," I refute, "talking with him helps me feel better. Besides, everyone *else* is preoccupied."

I don't have to explain anything more. Travin gets my point, looking up slightly annoyed.

"Did *I* help?" he asks spitefully.

Behind the peevish tone, I see the exhaustion in his eyes. There's such an obvious need for approval.

"You did," is all I can manage to utter.

His hands fidget.

Directing my attention to my injuries, I try desperately to think of something—*anything* else—to talk about. Unfortunately, all that comes to mind is Bronwynn.

"She's . . . recovering just fine?" I ask, trying to sound hopeful.

"Yay, Bronwynn is at ease," Travin replies tensely. "I suppose."

"That is good. Good, Trav."

A small muscle ticks in his clamped jaw. Neither of us wants to say out loud what we both know is coming.

I feel guilty over wishing he spent less time with Bronwynn. I wish to express that I know he should be doting on her at this time, and planning to wed her, and comforting her from the trauma I know she has endured. I wish to free him from the guilt that he chose to save me. Instead of her.

Bronwynn was pulled into the river by the crazed rebel that had attacked her. When Travin jumped into the oncoming river tide, he dove straight for me. He'd risked his life to rescue me from the whirlpool of death. *Me.* It was by chance that Nasr saved Bronwynn.

Yesterday, when I visited the medicus to have my stitches removed, the man expressed his concern for Bronwynn's baby. According to the medicus's calculations, Bronwynn is five months with child. That would mean she conceived sometime at Shittim. She made the medicus swear not to tell anyone, which is probably the nicest thing she's ever done. Israelite commandments have been broken. God's laws have been disobeyed. And Travin's salvaged reputation, and rapport, will be bankrupt if they don't make this right.

"All that matters is we are all alive." I declare, eager to deter the topic. I want to talk to him, but I don't want to discuss wedding details. "I mean, Bronwynn and I—we're both alive and well.

Everything *worked out.*" I drive a fist down and up in a mock gesture of conquest. It doesn't make him laugh. "Trav, I'm glad you came by to visit me. I've wanted to thank you. I've wanted you to know that your choice actually . . . meant . . . I survived . . ."

I'm rambling, voice and mind alike. *Am* I surviving? Or am I just alive?

Travin paces the length of my bed a few times. He pauses in front of me, as if to say something, only to continue pacing some more. He heads to the door. Standing in front of it, his fingers tap the wood, he shakes his head. *Shame.* I feel it, too. I'm going to have to live with this remorse the rest of my life, knowing Travin saved me over his beloved and her unborn. Every time he sees me, he will be reminded that she could have died, the baby could have died, because he came after *me.*

While he's looking away, I analyze him. The growing hair and returning muscles. The scars left on his arms. The blade attached to his belt. He's matured into such a man, a fierce soldier. He will make a fine father.

Travin glances up. Pushes back his floppy hair.

I murmur, "Just tell me what you came here to say."

They are to be married, of course. Before anyone finds out about the conception. Is that why he came here? For my blessing?

"You said it yourself," Travin answers. "It meant *you* survived."

Then, he is gone, and I'm on my own. As always.

KAYA

Ask and Ye Shall Receive

ANOTHER DAY PASSES. NEITHER Travin nor Rajmund comes to visit me. They are preoccupied with Joshua's comprehensive preparation. I'm fine. I definitely need some space from both the predicaments I've found myself in because of the two of them. Instead, I want female companionship. Tasia and Svana are going to relocate to Caphtor. Amaris, who had kept the two females from the wretchedness of the war front, will help them travel in safety. I invite them over one last time before their relocation.

I haven't had an opportunity to speak to Tasia since before crossing the river. She seems glad to see me, too.

"I want to thank you," she says the moment she enters my dwelling. She embraces me, stunning me. "If it weren't for you, I may not be alive."

When she draws back, I smile. "You're very welcome."

She touches my cheek. "The judgment went well. I've been acquitted of criminal charges. Thanks to the law, I will live as a free woman."

"That is such a relief."

Taking my hand, she pulls me to the floor. We sprawl out like children. It is reminiscent of my adolescence, with Mikyla Rox. Although I feel oddly closer to Tasia.

"Tell me about Amaris," I probe.

"What do you want to know?" she asks bashfully.

She's glowing and looks nothing like the woman I first met,

when she pointed an arrow directly into my face. We can communicate. Her skin, her eyes, her smile, everything has a new radiance. Ever since they arrived in the city, she and Amaris have been inseparable. They tour around in unison, like they've become one being altogether. It's so adorable it's revolting.

I say, "Everything. How did you meet Amaris? How did you know he was the one?"

He's an odd fellow, Amaris. Always skulking around as if everything needs investigation, wearing that long coat and touching things. Once, I saw a small chalice roll out of his sleeve. He hurriedly scooped it up and returned it to a hidden compartment within the folds of his robes, glancing around suspiciously. When I refer to him as an aberrant, Tasia corrects me by calling him God's emissary. When I hint at some ability to time-travel, she clandestinely averts the topic. I'm still trying to absorb it all.

"Wasn't it scandalous? You're from Ashtaroth, a city God commanded Joshua to destroy for its wickedness."

She grins coyly. "Just because I was living there, doesn't mean that's where I'm from."

I ponder this, quietly. It's none of my business, but there is much I wish to know. Tasia reveals a small piece of information that satisfies me for now.

"I'm an immigrant from Egypt," she states. "I bought passage to Ashtaroth on my journey south. Amaris was visiting the palace I worked at in Egypt when I was in my youth. He—he always came back to me. When Egypt became a plagued city, he urged me to leave. As the presiding hourglass, he assisted me in crossing the Transjordan. But then he was called on a mission. I lived in Ashtaroth many years awaiting his return."

"Wow."

Narrowing her eyes, Tasia questions, "Have you never heard of an hourglass?"

I shake my head.

"Not many have been known to roam the earth," she reveals, playing with a strand of her hair. "They are servants of The Most High. Ordained seers and revelators. Kaya, they are like unto angels living among mortals."

"I knew he was immortal!" I gasp.

Tasia laughs. "Nay, he can be killed. But he has the sight of our father in heaven. He was one of the original twelve spies of Israel. Joshua was, too."

This notion has begun to grow on me. A father in heaven. His servants. His will. Faith does odd things to a believer's cognitive mind. And it seems, the more one tries, the more one's heart is touched.

"Don't you miss him?" I ask. "He must travel a lot."

"You'd be surprised what you will do for love," Tasia responds. "Every time Amaris is called on a mission, I worry I'll never see him again. And when I see the burden he carries on his shoulders, I just wish I could take it away from him. I never know what our future holds . . . but I love him." She gives me a teary smile. "I wouldn't have it any other way."

"Even in a marriage?"

She winks, "It's worth it."

I disagree too fast. "I don't ever want to get married."

"You'll change your mind," she giggles, looking down at my bare finger. "Just wait for the right man."

"I've been proposed to already," I admit. "Rajmund. He wants to 'leave in matrimony' when he marches to Jericho," I relay in a manly voice. "He's a good man, a good soldier."

"But?"

"Being a wife doesn't sound very interesting, except for maybe the promise of a safe, secure life for the rest of my days."

"Do you really want a safe, secure life the rest of your days?" Tasia quirks an eyebrow at me, but continues before I can answer. "Let me know how you feel about it in a few years."

Even though I desire to know all she knows about Amaris, and why she was in Ashtaroth, I decide only one more question is important today.

"Tasia?"

"Hm?"

"What do you mean 'you'd be surprised what you will do for love'?"

A wide smile grows across her face. "That is the existential question." I open my mouth to respond, but she cuts me off. "I think you already know the answer to that. Trust me, everything happens for a reason. And at the precise moment it's supposed to. If you are righteous, your calling and election will be made sure. Just believe."

A million different things spin through my mind. Avoca. Zaheth. Giants. Rebels. Conversions. Pregnancies. Letting go.

I bite my tongue to refrain from a cynical riposte and, instead, confess, "I fear I dwindle in unbelief."

She gives my hand a squeeze. "Then surround yourself with those who don't."

I spend the afternoon cheerfully with Tasia. Later, Amaris drops by with Svana. The three of them have grown close, a little family. The little girl has been kept safe all this time by Amaris. It amazes me the way Amaris looks at her, like a daughter. But it is even more amazing the way Tasia sees Svana as *her* daughter. Tasia does not say it aloud, but I see the hurt of a barren woman in her eyes.

It also amazes me how I look at Amaris, like he's a secret I'm not supposed to know about. When he catches me staring, he glances at Tasia, a playful glower on his handsome face questioning whether she has exposed his identity. Tasia simply distracts him with physical condolences of love and affection.

Though I still have a soft spot in my heart for the little girl, I'm glad Svana has them to look out for her. They can provide her with excellent sources of love she needs to develop appropriately. A mother *and* a father. In return, Svana provides Tasia with a feeling of unexplainable completeness, transferable to Amaris within their marriage. The idea that he would love Tasia, and want to be with her under such circumstances, heals the part of my heart that never believed a man could be so good.

You'd be surprised what you will do for love.

I imagine Bronwynn delivering an innocent baby into this world. What kind of mother will she be? What kind of mother would *I* be?

I sleep restlessly that night, tossing and turning as the nightmares force their way into my mind. I see Westin's eyes, covered in more red blood vessels. The disease is taking him. Then, I am drowning in the river as bald soldiers from Zaheth swarm around me, groping my arms and legs, pulling me to the depths of the sea.

I wake up screaming, only to find myself alone.

Always alone.

I cross the space in my room, dragging my blanket behind me and curl up on the floor in the corner. I want more than anything to be back in my home in Avoca, to talk to my father. He would console me after my nightmares. He would reassure me everything was fine until I fell back asleep. But I am alone.

Always alone.

KAYA

I Miss My Friend

IT'S TOMORROW.

The dreaded day that never fails to remind me: I'm still lost.

Today, I wake up in the worst mood of my life, and I've known some bad moods.

If I wanted to die of organ failure, I'd stay inside all afternoon and consume toxic amounts of wine. I have not seen my friend, the wine bubble, in a remarkably long time. It is what I desire today.

In a lame attempt to imitate Travin's obedience, I try talking to God. I don't understand. The peace I'd felt when listening to Travin talk about faith, and after I received divine assistance in killing the giant, has ceased to abide in me.

Joshua ordered a census last night. Miki Rox is the scribe, sent to each dwelling to record every Israelite denizen that survived the crossing of the river. He came to my abode to document the names of all living Lucan tribe members—which is a whopping *one*. It was after dark. There was supposed to be a chaperone.

"Aren't you going to invite me in?" Miki asked. "I thought we could share a final farewell to Mikyla and those who lost their lives protecting our freedoms."

I have to admit, there was sadness around his eyes. It didn't change my hate for him. I put on the ring from Rajmund and speciously told Miki I'm going to be married.

"To a prosperous, strong, righteous soldier."

Miki gave me a heartless smirk. "Does Rajmund enjoy harlotry?"

"You tell me. You spend enough time in their dens."

His smile was endowed with a politicians smile.

"I guess the Lucan Tribe is dead," Miki retorted before he left.

Now I feel melancholy. There are worse things than death. Lies and scars and hellfire. Word of my betrothal will spread like all three.

I decide to go on another walk today. It's warm and sunny and looks like Avoca. The sun has a whole new splendor to me after witnessing darkness, and not just the kind that appears at night. Hiking around the mountains, I contemplate the course my life has taken. The course it could take. The course I *ought* to take. I need closure before I choose.

Sunshine prickles my skin. Exercising brings strength to my limbs. I see a herd of bighorn sheep tackling the intricate terrain. It brings a smile to my face. I have sorely missed the contact with animals and the ability to sit with them for hours to avoid the less tolerable species of humans. If I maintain my station in Gilgal, I can resume my occupation with the Israelite beasts. I long to break the new mare. She is a gorgeous bay horse, standing fifteen hands tall. Her nose is long, her chest narrow, and her feet good and sound.

I decide to head to the stables now, when I hear them arguing. Always arguing.

Bronwynn is waddling down the street after Travin. Lucky for her, her stomach has not been the only part of her body to acquire roundness, thus she has avoided scorn by keeping the baby a secret. I am surprised they have not yet wed. I am *not* surprised they are contending with one another.

I unexpectedly feel sorry for Bronwynn and Travin. They spend their lives so miserably together. At least I make myself miserable on my own. And that's when it hits me. I do not have the right to make *other* people miserable. I cannot burden someone else with my problems. There is a reason I block people out. It's what I'm good at.

If I am going to be a good friend to Travin, I need to forgive him of his transgression and at least give him my blessing. I owe him. If I'm going to be honest with Rajmund, I need to tell him how I really feel, that I'm not ready. He deserves the kind of woman that will appreciate what he has to offer.

If this is my destiny, to be on my own, then that's what I'll be. At least I won't be hurting anyone anymore.

Knowing the course I will take, I venture into the marketplace. Gilgal is a boisterous province. It won't be hard to find fermented wine. There are some indulgers who have been filled with pride for the victories. Their hearts are hardened, and when wine is produced in bulk, it flies off the shelf. Joshua observed the increasing wrongdoing among his people, and he instructed them to use caution and moderation. The obedient obliged. For the prideful, or exceedingly miserable, consumption has continued on.

People like me drink wine to feel normal, not high. We don't consume of the strong drink because we feel great, we do so to forget how we feel. It is a temptation of mine to forget the bad choices I've made, the ones I've been tallying up since daybreak.

It becomes a greater temptation when I pass by a brewery. The aroma surrounding the shop is strong with fermentation. I breathe it in, removing two jugs from the storage and bartering with a worker there for free care of his cattle in exchange for them. I return home with the intentions of simply storing the jugs, just in case, when I find someone standing in my room.

At first, I'm startled by the intruder. But then I realize who the person is. He faces the little shelving unit against the wall, hands intertwined in the small of his back, below a new chagowr. There are tse'adah on each of his wrists, but no weapon or harness. His posture is valorous, demeanor gallant. But his hair is waving in delinquent directions over shoulders, round beneath his tunic. I see in him the strength of a grown man, a warrior, the way his muscles sustain his arms and back, the way his faith sustains everything else.

I clear my throat.

"Ah-hem."

Travin whirls around. The color of his eyes is soft, dove-gray, not hardened like they are when he is in battle. A sandy curl dangles over his forehead and he moves it aside tentatively. There he is, the quintessential boy I know.

His eyes fall upon the jugs in my hands and then rake back up to mine. He tips his head and frowns a scolding tantamount to the judgment of God.

I clutch them to my breast. "I haven't had wine in a very long time. I'm fine." I leave out the parts about throwing up and shaking and the nightmares. "Joshua said use caution and moderation. I need this. I deserve—"

"Sh."

Lifting a hand, Travin moves toward me. He gently reaches for the jugs. I snatch them back. It is actually wise, my consumption of wine, to dull my mania instead of inflicting others with it.

I'll make whatever excuses necessary. I yearn for the numbness. *My wine bubble.* It will make everything go away. No more shakes and ill-tempered fevers. No more heartache. If I'm lucky, there won't be any more nightmares either. I will *finally* feel free.

"Can we talk?" Travin asks in a calm voice.

"Uh. I need to . . . I don't have . . ." I clench my jaw, embarrassed at being caught with the wine. Embarrassed by the moment we shared in the cistern, when I thought I was dying. *Because* I thought I was dying, I didn't care.

Travin is studying the back of my head.

My mouth salivates as I taste the scent of the wine.

Just a little.

Just enough.

My fingers move of their own accord, removing the cork to one of the jugs.

"Wait!" Travin brushes up against my shoulder.

I don't meet his patronizing look. I can only imagine what he's thinking.

"I hate when you do this," he murmurs.

He would.

"You don't have to," he reiterates, this time reaching out toward my wrist.

I pull back, eying him sideways with a glare.

"Kaya," he pleads.

It's not fair. That face. His dreamy eyes.

"I can't, Travin. I can't."

His gaze drops below my eyes. "You didn't call me Trav."

"Because!" I groan in frustration. "Trav, it's not me and you anymore, running through the chicken coop, scrambling to catch the chickens. It's you and her." I'm shaking. "You are . . . remarkable. She is *not* a decent woman."

"You are right."

I turn away, my emotions uncontrollable. My fingers outline the rim of one jug.

"I need you right now," Travin is saying. "I need you *here*."

He points to his temple.

My voice quivers. "What do you need *me* for?"

I've shamed him enough already. That must be why Bronwynn hasn't married him. She is going to expose him, and their infidelity, out of revenge. She will tarnish his reputation, *then* trap him into matrimony. I don't care how evil it sounds. I think she jumped into the River Jordan on purpose.

A minute passes. I take a drink.

"Don't," Travin states, but it doesn't come across as a request.

I didn't even realize it. My hands just performed the motions. I lifted the bottle and swallowed. The release is instantly gratifying. Like a leech sucking the lifeblood from me, I am in bondage from the wine once more.

I take another sip, and suddenly Travin has me by the upper arm. He smacks the jug from my hand. It bangs loudly on the ground, rolling against the wall and spilling the remainder of its contents.

"Enough!" he growls, slit-eyed.

"You," I hiss, "are not my father."

"At least you had one that loved you!" he bites back.

My temper thuds against my ribs. I wrench my arm away, but Travin holds tight, scowling at me with a challenge that shimmers darkly in his gaze.

"I care for you, Kaya. I cared for him. I promised him I'd see you were taken care of."

I can't help it. I scoff.

"I heard you will soon be taken care of by someone else."

His voice is monotone. I close my eyes and shake my head, trying to force all the hideous visuals from my thoughts. If he could see this, what goes on in my head, he would want to numb it for me.

"I am happy for you," he states.

"Rajmund—"

"Is a good man."

The walls of my small room seem to shrink, closing in all around me. Travin's grip on my bicep remains, but his fingers loosen. The air is dry and suffocating.

"Kaya?"

Miki Rox thieves what is left of my goodness.

I'm in a cold pit.

Vaclav is garroting me.

Daedrina is hypnotizing me.

"Kaya!"

Water is consuming me.

Westin is gone.

Travin is not mine.

My lungs labor to draw breath.

"He's gone," I bemoan. "My father is gone! Westin is gone. *You* will be gone, as soon as Joshua marches to Jericho. The people that matter to me leave."

Travin stares back at me stonily. His hand strays a bit from my elbow.

"I'm sorry you chose me, okay?" I stammer. "I didn't ask for that. You shouldn't have. You've worked so hard to get where you are, a-and I d-don't want to encumber you. Oh, Trav. You shouldn't have come after me instead of Bronwynn. I don't—have a reason to—"

"Kaya."

"Why couldn't you just *let me go?*"

His voice quavers. "Cease!"

"You think I'm not ashamed of this? You think I'm happy about it? I am not. I *wanted* to die!"

Recognizing my confession as a lot of dumb things I've never admitted before, but deem true, I try to push Travin away from me. I am making him miserable—I can see it in his enormous eyes that sear into mine, indignation accentuating his cheekbones.

"Please." I beseech. "Just let me go."

Because I will never *be able to let you go.*

His fingers on my arm clench with bruising force that matches his voice. "Cease."

The one word echoes throughout my tent, the message powerful beyond recognition, inasmuch as the prayer Amaris performed for me in the cave of Avoca. A sensation like wind flows forward and fills me. The hardness of my heart softens. I feel *it*, the right side of things, when Travin is near.

Near he is.

His hands are cupping my wrists. My elbows. My shoulders. I feel one palm slither behind me, pulling me tighter against him. His face is so close I can see the growth of his sideburns. He seems to have grown even larger in strength than when he was training with the Israelites. Possibly larger with intolerance, too, for the grumpy divot in his forehead emerges.

I give up. I give in.

Resting my forehead on his sternum, I blow out a puff of air. My hair falls across my face. Resignation. I tender my resignation for life.

At one point, we were the closest of friends. I'm not sure what we are now—what *this* is—and how to deal with it. This is persecution. He is persecuting me. Life has taken us down separate roads, and I cannot see us arriving at the same destination.

It would be better if he left. It would be best if I never had to see him and Bronwynn again. The torture of having to live by or see them together in the future brings affliction to front-lines of my emotional battle. The battle I am quickly losing. Travin has so much going for him. So much potential in the army, as a person, as a servant of God. *How can he jeopardize that?*

I don't have the courage to look up into his face, but I reach up to push my hair aside. Travin releases one hand from behind my back. His fingers miss mine by a millisecond, and the back of his knuckles graze my cheek delicately. Mortified, I feel hot instantly. My face flushes scarlet. The anger building beneath my chest torpedoes through.

"Get out!" I shout into his face. "Get out! Get out! Get out!"

I'm not sure if I'm shouting to him or the demon inside.

The effect of my words is illustrated in perfect detail in Travin's dazed eyes. His hands drop to his sides. Somewhere, beyond my control, a tear or two leaks from my eyelid. The instant they are free, I want to dry them up and put them back where they came from. I hate that this keeps happening. I abhor tears. I despise crying. I detest being weak. I want to erase every moment of this feeling I have, that isn't numb *at all.*

"You did the right thing staying away from me." I fight the susceptibility lodged in my throat. "It w-will help us all forget. That's all w-we need to do. Forget. Move on. We're better off apart now. Things are just too different. You have Bronwynn, and I understand that you need to wed soon. You should've saved *her*, Travin. You should've saved your baby."

Travin's face goes white at once, so white it would make snow appear gray.

"That's right," I announce, my eyes sliding over his face, down his throat to the tanned flesh at his collar, and back up. His gray eyes are blank, his mouth agape. He stares right through me while I repeat, "I know of your transgression."

"Baby?" Travin whispers.

"Mmhm."

"How do you know?"

"Well," I sniffle, "at first, I thought Bronwynn was just putting on a few comfort pounds. No one would notice, unless you knew what to look for. And I've been around enough pregnant sows to see the resemblance." I smile sinfully at the comparison. "And to confirm my suspicions, I overheard the medicus say it. She didn't lose the baby."

He takes a step backward. "This can't be."

"It is what it is. Now I know, and you don't have to hide it anymore. Don't worry, I won't tell anyone else. You can go forward with your wedding. Congratulations."

"No, you don't understand!" he barks, something beastly coming alive within him.

I raise my eyebrows in response, shrugging my shoulders.

"*Pregnant?*" he questions a third time, teeming with disbelief. He stumbles a few steps away. His eyebrows dip lower and lower each second.

"Well, when one man and one woman get together . . ." I link my two pointer fingers together. "What did you think would happen if you two kept fornicating?"

Travin glares up at me. After a moment of immobility, he stomps back over. He places his hands on both of my shoulders, tilts his face toward mine, and looks at me, eyes to eyes, nose to nose.

"She didn't lose . . . the baby?" he demands, his voice strung with emotion.

"Travin, I'm one hundred percent positive."

Was she manipulating him with *that* as well? Did she lie to him about losing the baby? I laugh, even though there is nothing funny to laugh about.

"She is having your baby, Travin. Do not fret."

Then, as if channeling all this built up rage, Travin yells at me, "I'VE NEVER LAIN WITH HER!"

His hands fall off my shoulders, and he turns to pace the room from side to side. He rakes his fingers through his hair, then places his palms together over his mouth.

"What . . . wh-what did you say?" I stutter.

Travin wheels around on me, eyes wild.

"You mean to tell me . . ." I begin, but I can't finish.

"I've been chaste!" he grunts, thrusting his hands out to his sides.

"Then, how—"

"Exactly!" he spits, stopping his pacing to lean against my bed. Neither of us says anything for a length of a time.

Could this be true?

Travin drops onto the edge of my bed. "It makes sense."

"Nothing makes sense."

I silently drop onto the bed, taking a seat next to him.

"I told you we've been apart lately," he continues. "I've had too many other things going on to worry concerning her increase in size, and the last few weeks Joshua has taken those of us he recruited into the Israelites for a second medical evaluation. You're right.

Bronwynn *is* an indecent woman. I have desired to end our courtship . . ."

"Everything happens for a reason."

I don't know why I said it. It just came out.

Travin doesn't reply right away. We sit in silence as the seconds tick by. I feel too alert right now. Every nerve exposed. Travin strikes the one most precious.

"You are the only person I've ever . . . been with."

The air catches in my throat. I choke.

"What?" I squawk.

He shifts nervously beside me, his hand absently fussing with his hair.

"You are the only person I've ever, you know . . . kissed. That way. There, I said it," he declares, falling onto his back next to me so that his legs drape off the edge of the bed.

All this time, I thought Travin was so in love. Miserable, but in love. I didn't know there was a difference. I love wine. It makes me miserable.

So much of his relationship is becoming clear. While I take a moment to explore the things I've learned about Travin Samuli Shelomo, I come to the conclusion that he is somewhat dysfunctional.

Like me.

Our childhoods have been the most important thing in our adult trajectories. It's one of the many things we have in common.

Staring at the opposite wall, I search for a proper response. This is strange.

I say the only thing I can think of. "I'm really, really sorry."

"Don't be," Travin replies, caressing his lips with his left thumb. "You are right. Everything happens for a reason."

"If that's true," I counter, "then why is there all this tragedy? Why do I hurt myself? Why did you let Bronwynn hurt you? Why must we be at war?"

I fall back onto the bed, landing on Travin's arm that has been extended out to his side. He adjusts it, so that the inside of his elbow lies behind my neck. We inhale in unison, turning to look at each other.

"How are you feeling right about now?" he asks.

Since I'm on an honest kick. "Not *numb* . . . like I was hoping."

"Lush," he quips. But then his eyes crinkle with a silent smile.

"I'm sorry." And I mean it this time. "I'm sorry I have a tendency to be self-absorbed. I'm sorry for acting this way in front of you. I know it's not good for me. It's just so hard not to. This is what I do. I don't know how else to cope, to forget."

Once I've said it out loud, a colossal weight has been lifted off of me.

He nods. "You and I both."

"And I'm sorry about *Bon-won*. Really."

Travin's lips curve in a grin. "I'm not. I'm relieved. It's over for me. Finally."

Finally?

I shake my head. "I wish my problem was over for me."

He angles his body toward me a bit, staring at my profile. "I think I know of a solution."

Closing my eyes, I mumble, "What do you mean?"

"Be converted."

"And it will all just go away, like that," I mutter.

"Not *all* the way," Travin consents. "But you will find your weaknesses can be made into strengths. Repentance will wash away your sins. Converting your life to God will make you whole again."

I chew on a cynical rebuttal.

"Are you going to help me?" I ask, squinting at him.

"I'll do what I can, if you'll listen and not swat me away!" He mimics my hand motions from earlier animatedly.

"If you'll come around and not abandon me!" I snap playfully, but also stern.

"Alright, but it's going to require some personality adjustment."

"Adjustment?"

"On your part."

"Says the man with no flaws."

Travin beams wolfishly. "To the woman who won't court the nice guy, and instead goes for the shiny one, tries to change him, lets him break her heart, and then complains that all men are the same."

I smile toward the ceiling. "That would be me."

I'm such a mess.

"You can do it," Travin affirms.

"And if I can't?"

"Don't be such a pessimist." He smacks my leg hard, his tongue sticking out of his smile.

"I'm not—ouch!—a pessimist," I jest. "I'm a realist."

"God is a realist," he muses. "Kaya, I say unto you, all things are possible through God. You *must* believe."

"Sure, Trav." I pat the top of his head, briefly combing my fingers through his hair. "Sure."

His eyelids close. For a moment, we just sit in silence and savor the pleasant feeling of talking again. After keeping so much inside, it's remedial. This is us, the way we should be. He was right, at the Roteruth's in Taavetti. I've blocked him out. I've been so unbelievably, foolishly, selfish.

"Do you want to know why I avoided you?" Travin asks quietly. "Why I didn't come around the last few weeks? The honest truth?"

I don't think I want to know. At the same time, I don't think I've ever wanted anything more.

Travin's eyes open. Staring at his hand, he spreads his fingers out along the mattress, inching them closer to mine.

"I'll know if you're lying," I reply, and his grin brightens.

"When I lost my sister—"

The door of my tent opens just then. Rebby and a newly promoted High Commander Gorrow march in without preempt. They both look ready to go into battle, outfitted with breastplates, swords, and helmets. That is, until the mischief in Rebby's eye catches my attention. Travin and I sit up. Gorrow surveys the room with soldier instinct. I forgot we don't have a chaperone.

"Travin," Gorrow states beneath his growing beard. Travin straightens off the bed hastily. "Our scouts have just returned. We have new intel concerning the fortifications of Jericho. Joshua wants to meet with you immediately."

There is no admonishment in Gorrow's voice. In fact, there is a discernible trust and friendship between him and my best friend. As for what's going on between Rebby and Travin, I notice a wordless message pass between them. Rebby's eyes swing a teasing accusation at me, heightening my feelings of being caught—at what, I'm uncertain.

Something fuzzy involuntarily inhabits my cheeks. I mouth a curse at Rebby, but it is ineffective.

"Right away," Travin replies.

"Joshua is calling all of his officers together for a conference. Jericho will be exceedingly more difficult to destroy than Bashan. A unit of soldiers will also be overseeing the safe travel of the women and children of Gilgal to their destination. We will establish a permanent post here for transporters, but the remaining inhabitants shall relocate to the western seashores. Orren has been charged with the acquittal of the prisoners of war." The High Commander's eyes dart to mine. "Come, we'll talk more."

Travin steals a glimpse at me, but with the presence of Rebby and Gorrow, his exit consists of a quick, "I'll see you later."

I know he means it.

They disappear out the door with Rebby giving Travin a rough shove.

I stare at the back of the door.

When I lost my sister . . .

It dawns on me. I am Maleah to Travin. His lost sister. He feels accountable for me because I'm younger and helpless, and he thinks saving me will bring her back. This isn't comforting. It's . . . it's . . . disappointing.

Being by myself, I realize I could easily drink the rest of my night away. Forget what needs to be forgotten. But then, I'd also forget about the conversation Travin and I just had, which seems to be important to me. We were getting somewhere. Sharing things. Being *us* again. There will be no baby for him. He is not going to marry that wanton woman.

My eyes flit toward the spilled jug on the floor. The scent of the wine floods the room, tempting me.

Nay, I tell myself.

I don't want to let Travin down. He said I could do this, that I was strong enough.

I peek over at the other jug, the one still full. Approaching it, I slide my hand across its surface, resting my fingers on the lid.

Just a little more. A little more and I will feel numb, for sure. Not haunted by the nightmares awaiting me in my dreams.

I start to back away, down the hall. Travin has learned to be strong. So can I.

Maybe.

I can't tear my gaze off my toxic old friend until I reach the washroom. Once there, I leap inside and shut the door behind me.

"I can do this," I whisper out loud.

I take a deep breath in, and exhale slowly as I pace the tiny space of the washroom. Knowing there's wine just beyond this door traps me within. It reminds me of being trapped in the pit in the ground in the wilderness. Striding to the tiny window, I gulp the fresh evening breeze. I'll have to face the dreadfulness of my dreams tonight. I'll have to see the blood and broken bodies, over and over. I'll have to feel those rebel hands on me. I'll have to *feel*.

Or, I could just go retrieve the jug. I'm alone, anyway. Always alone.

What harm could it do?

"Nay!" I reprimand myself, sitting with my spine against the door, reminding it to stay shut.

I say a most desperate prayer, fighting back tears and the sting they mete out in my throat. As if I have something to prove, I spend the night on the floor in the washroom. Either my body is trembling like unto an earthquake, or the walls are trembling. I feel the darkness looming around me, the anger of it losing the battle. Tucking my knees up to my chin, I pretend there are two strong arms wrapped around me, keeping me safe. The closed door muffles my screams when I awake throughout the night to some awful part of the nightmare. I don't hear the person come into my room during the pre-dawn hours, sit with their ear against the washroom door, and then leave just before sunrise.

TRAVIN

A Villain within a Villain

HIGH COMMANDER GORROW LINES up the prisoners outside of the village, down in a dusty ravine. Only a handful of Canaanites survived the crossing of the River Jordan. Seized upon by guards, the enemies have been imprisoned since reaching the western shore. Today, they are to be judged for their crimes. Rionn is present to preside as priest as the judges call out the final verdict. Each criminal shall lose his fighting hand and be banished from the holy land.

Officer Orren is charged with this assignment, and Gorrow departs with instruction for Orren to return to Joshua's tent immediately after the sentence has been carried out and report of the captives' departure. Forty Israelite soldiers stand at attention, awaiting orders. The one to my right starts whispering.

"So," Rebby says out of the side of his mouth. "You and Kaya . . ."

I roll my eyes over to his. "Not now."

He shrugs and purses his lips, nodding to himself. "Kaya and Westin . . ."

My left hand raises a fraction, forming a signal. Rebby snorts a laugh, hastily swallowing it. Orren's eye flicks in our direction. When he returns to his duty of scribing the names of the prisoners and their tribal ancestry, Rebby's teeth begin to move.

"Kaya and Rajmund?"

That stings.

"It's up to her," I state.

"You and . . . Bronwynn?"

My head twists the needed degree to give Rebby a thorough chastisement. "This isn't a therapy session," I grunt.

A few of the nearby soldiers subtly glance our way.

Rebby jerks his chin forward, his eyebrows dipping. "Tell that to Orren."

Officer Orren paces the length of the captives, commanding each of us to regard our enemies and heed carefully. These are the men that have killed our families, defiled our women, and stolen our freedoms. Orren has a look of greed in his eye, his desire to inflict merciless torment on them evident. Without Joshua present, it is certain to happen.

To my left, the young soldier Rionn anxiously fidgets. His features are slightly crooked. He is missing several fingers and teeth, but he has a pleasant appeal about him. I am glad he has survived thus far. He lost every one of his combat simulations during training at Shittim, and his speech impediment has made it difficult for him to gather friends. But he has the testimony of a prophet and can recite each one of Joshua's sermons by heart.

The prisoners are commanded to their knees, arms restrained behind their backs. I count thirty of them. Orren paces over to the first of these, slipping his sword from the sheath on his belt. Rebby and I exchange questioning glances. Orren raises his weapon, a double-bladed scimitar and executes the first prisoner. Twenty-nine.

Rionn flinches.

"This can't be good," Rebby mumbles.

"We rid this, God's chosen land, of our enemies," Orren dictates.

He strides to the second prisoner, stomping on the enemy's chest, pinning him to the earth. His blade drags across the Canaanite's throat languidly.

I flinch forward.

The back of Rebby's hand brushes my forearm, communicating the need to hold still.

"We end this wickedness, this plague," Orren continues, "so that Israel may possess this promised land. Do not fear the wrath of God, my soldiers. For we are protected from evil." *Another execution.* "All of Canaan will hear of our victories. They will know we are upon them, and they will fear us. The righteous will come off conqueror!"

The third prisoner is killed in the same slow manner with Orren delighting in the man's dying gargles. A pool of blood forms below him. Orren dips his toe in it, dreamily dragging the fluid through the dirt. This scene continues until only one captive remains alive. The last man does well hiding his fright from my officer. It is how I would hope to look on my dying day. Ready. Willing. A triumvirate of pride. Orren pauses in front of the enemy Canaanite, scanning the Israelite soldiers at his leisure. He aims his scimitar at Rionn.

"You," he declares. "Finish this."

My body turns cold, a wave of dread and injustice coursing through me. Orren stomps closer, raising the scimitar in our direction. Rionn begins to stutter quietly. His fear transfers through his body to me. I try to think of something to say to persuade Orren that Rionn is not suited for such a trial, that *this* assassination has not been part of righteous judgment. My fears double when I realize Orren is not pointing his weapon at Rionn. Orren is pointing the blade at me.

"Finish this," he says, now face to face with me.

The other soldiers are deadly silent. I can feel their eyes on me. I can smell the blood on Orren's weapon.

The officer's eyes and voice turn cruel. "Finish. This."

The temptation to shake my head overwhelms me, and I know in an instant I am going to be dismissed from my position as one of Joshua's soldiers. I will fail. At the one thing I've wanted to succeed at most in this life. Joshua's sermons and prophecies echo in my mind. The dominions and promises and protection and freedom. God's will. God's army. The psychological message we are sending our wicked enemies. Destroy every living creature. Obey your superiors.

Cowardice betrays me.

"This man has murdered the young and innocent," Orren states, eying me distrustfully. "Joshua has commanded us to bring an end to the wickedness of these people. Every man, woman, and child."

Over Orren's shoulder, I scrutinize the man I'm supposed to kill, the bloody head of an enemy combatant who is vicariously responsible for the death of my mother and Maleah. Responsible for my captivity in Zaheth. And so much more. An anger builds within me. I wonder if I will do it. But the anger is overpowered by a heavy sorrow. I feel sorry for him.

"Mercy is for the weak!" Orren shouts brazenly. I blanch, as do the rest of the men. "End him!"

"I'll do it," Rebby declares. He edges carefully in front of me and reaches for Orren's weapon.

Orren jerks back, his teeth gnashing. He lands a palm roughly in Rebby's chest. Rebby resists the shove but does not retaliate.

"You will fall into line and obey your commanding superior!" Orren roars.

Rebby does no such thing.

"I'll do it," he repeats evenly. And before Orren can disagree, Rebby snatches the scimitar from his hands, marches over to the captive prisoner and slits his throat. Rebby watches the dying man, dropping the weapon into the blood-softened dirt. Sixty agonizing seconds later, the prisoner has bled out. Rebby rotates toward the rest of the Israelites. "Mercy is a gift," he says. His eyes meet mine. "Reserved for the godly."

Fuming, Orren stabs a finger at Rebby. "He's to be suspended from the army for three days for direct disobedience of an officer's order! Remove his armor. He will bury each one of these prisoners by hand, digging their graves with his sword. Do not assist him. Noncompliance is reserved for weaklings." Quieter, he says to Rebby, "You will *never* be promoted in this army. I will see to that. And may God be a witness to this rebellion against His work. He will judge you for your sins."

A soldier guides Rebby from the scene while I gape at the dead men. A cloud of emasculation envelops me. What have I done?

Beside me, Rionn is praying. His demure voice thanks the Almighty for sparing him such trial and asks a blessing on the souls of those who have died.

Orren orders the soldiers back to their posts, pausing as he passes Rionn and I. His mouth gnarls, his voice frothy. "As for you—"

But High Commander Azsh rides into the ravine on horseback, saving me further tribulation.

"Joshua will hear of this," is Orren's parting *gift* to me.

KAYA

Let's Face It, I Don't Know What I'm Doing

THE LONELINESS I EXPERIENCE when I wake is strangling.

Feeling like I'm murdering an innocent animal, I take my full jug of wine to the spigot out back and dump it out. Westin's face still lingers on the back of my eyelids from my nightmares. It's likely I'll never see him again and, although I'm not completely heartbroken, it does leave me with a void. An empty feeling in my soul that wants to be filled so longingly with companionship. And wine. Lots of wine.

I skip breakfast and opt for five glasses of water, throwing up the first three.

I need a new vice if I'm to stay sober.

Which gets me thinking. Which makes me move. Which is how I end up in front of Rajmund.

Joshua is departing tomorrow with an army of men to conquer Jericho and many of the inhabitants of Gilgal are traveling to distant cities to start their life. I want to say goodbye to Rajmund. I want to see him when he returns from battle. After only two knocks, he opens his door. His long, blonde hair has been cut a few inches, hanging down his shoulders sleek and shiny. He looks every bit a soldier, armored, dignified.

I don't have to long for companionship anymore. It's right in front of me.

I smile. "May I come in?"

"Certainly," Rajmund replies cordially. His brindle eyes gleam.

He scans the village over my shoulder in true soldier fashion and beckons me in, leaving the door open since we don't have a chaperone. "You look astonishing. How are you feeling?"

"Much better, thank you." Biting the corner of my lip, I summon the stupid reckless part of me and reach beyond him to close the door. "And . . . I've been thinking about your offer."

I press myself into him. Rajmund's back hits the door. His eyes widen, his jaw drops open for two full seconds of pure surprise. He lifts one hand to my waist, but I can't tell if he's pulling me closer or pushing me away. I splay my hands at his collar, inviting myself closer.

"Uh, are you well?" Rajmund questions.

"Absolutely," I respond. *Not even close.* "I just thought, what better way to get to know each other before you leave, than, you know . . ."

"I wanted a betrothal, Kaya," he tells me. "Not your virtue."

I dismiss a flash of embarrassment. "Think about it," I argue. "We've spent so much time talking, and I really feel like I know you, but I'm ready to know you . . . more. I've thought I've known men before, but it turns out I didn't know anything about them. I don't really know how you are supposed to get to know someone, but I imagine it has something to do with knowing them better. You know? Especially since you're asking me to think about spending the rest of my life with you."

At least that's the truth.

Rajmund doesn't see it that way. He is looking at me like I've just flung a piece of conversational phlegm at him.

"It's not fair," he forces through the conundrum, "of me to ask something of you without even acknowledging your feelings." He blinks once and then sinks into the door an inch. "But this is not wise."

He's taller than Travin. I have to tilt my head all the way back to look into his face.

"I'm considering it, your proposal, I truly am," I breathe heavily. "I thought you would want this too, after all our time together."

"There are rules," he murmurs.

"There are *precautions*," I counter.

I run a hand up his shoulder, prodding the hardened muscle beneath it. It is shaped different than Westin's, but every bit as strong.

Rajmund lowers an eyebrow, unconvinced. Westin would have been enchanted. I don't understand.

Placing a hand on either side of Rajmund's face, I kiss him. A mouth-to-mouth kiss. It is not my first, but it is every bit as uncomfortable. His full lips cover mine as a low, mannish groan rumbles in the back of his throat.

Affection is a shy flower.
I can make it bloom.

His mouth opens softly against mine, when a knock at the door startles us. We break apart shyly, unsure of what to do. Rajmund desires the knock go ignored, while I see it as an opportunity to stop the kiss.

The knock comes again.

"Just . . . stay put," I whisper nervously. "I'll see who it is."

Rajmund's eyes are locked onto me as I slide away. I don't care that it isn't my home. Scooting aside, I reach for the door and open it.

"Oh!"

"Good, I thought I saw you come over here," Travin gasps, out of breath. He observes my simlah, my loose hair. "Are you unwell?"

I stare, stupefied.

"I am fine," I lie.

Travin's enormous raincloud-colored eyes expand even more. "We need to talk."

"Now's not . . . a good time, Trav." I contemplate making an escape by shutting the door in his face and parting Rajmund's home in two with my mortification, the way Joshua parted the River Jordan.

"Nay, nay." Travin summons fervently. Curiosity keeps me at the door long enough for him to say, "This time it's about *me*. And I feel like you can . . . he . . . lp . . ."

Travin's voice trails off as Rajmund appears behind me in the doorway. Rajmund's face is flushed, his lips moistened from our kiss. Travin knew I was lying about being fine, but now he knows *why.*

"I'm sorry," Travin snaps. "Didn't mean to intrude."

He rotates around on his heel and departs.

"Wait!" I call after him, leaving Rajmund behind.

Travin doesn't listen. He just keeps walking faster down the road.

"Wait, we can talk," I stammer.

Travin pivots promptly, and I bump into him. His familiar face warps in unfamiliar outrage.

"*You know what?*" he growls. "It . . . doesn't matter. You would *never* understand. *Ever!*"

"Excuse me?"

Baring his teeth, he fumes, "All you understand is wine and . . . the desires of men!"

"Cheap shot, genius," I snort. "You're just figuring that out?"

"Yay, I tried to ignore it. You don't waste any time, do you?" He takes a long inhale through his nose, his nostrils flaring. "I get it, Kaya. You think Rajmund is your one shot at a respectable marriage, the way you thought Westin was your one shot at love. But *this*— this thing you do—the immoral way you live, it is no way to live. I gave you time to grieve, took time to heal from my own surgical procedure."

Surgical procedure?

Oh!

"I tried to pretend there was some decency in you, Kaya Lucan. You're from the Lucan tribe. Your father was an exceedingly wonderful man. I thought you would be like him." He provokes the prohibited part within me speaking of my father. "Even when I didn't, I tried to help you. I did everything I could to convince you that what you are doing to yourself is slowly deteriorating what I—"

"So, *I'm* deteriorating?" I interrupt. Two can play this game. "*I'm* miserable, and deteriorating, and *you're* the walking picture of happiness. That's right, Trav. I've been totally blind all this time. Please, please teach me how to be happy like you!"

"Agh!" He throws his hands up into the air.

I take this brief pause to glare at our spectators. Nasr, Tasia, and Amaris are among the multitude. Oh, and Rajmund. He's standing in puzzlement behind Amaris, who scratches his chin and exchanges a parental nod with Tasia.

Travin begins to march away, but I swiftly move in front of him.

He doesn't get to point out all of my flaws without acknowledging his own. And he does not get to treat me like a helpless little girl. He's lost loved ones. I've lost loved ones.

My emotions are beyond my control. Thanks to my ever-breeding feelings. These feelings that make me go berserk. Feelings I'm choosing not to numb.

"You want to know why I never wore that necklace you gave me?" I exclaim.

Travin gives me a heartless smile and backs away, turning in a circle with his hands out to his sides.

"Ha," he huffs, shaking a finger at me. He then reaches into his robes, and magically withdraws the tiny shell necklace I'd left back in my jewelry box, in my home in Avoca, where it was obliterated. "You mean this one?" He holds it up for me to see and my mouth falls open. "Let's hear it! I've actually been trying to figure this out. For years!" He lets out a nutty laugh. "What's the big reason?"

Travin's sarcasm only infuriates me more. I know some of the villagers, including our acquaintances, are watching our argument. It makes me feel vulnerable, the feeling I hate most.

When I don't answer immediately, Travin thrusts the fist clenching my shell necklace forward. I know he must be aware of our audience, but he doesn't seem to mind. He's never been quite as introverted as I have. He's also never been quite this irrational. Right now, he is furious. His pupils are completely dilated, making his whole expression batty. An angry pulse pumps at his temple where his unkempt hair frisks his ears.

I chance a glance sideways. Two individuals quickly turn and scuttle away. Morning is a busy time of day for Gilgal. Lucky me.

"Why don't you just spit it out already!" Travin barks scathingly, and I jerk my head back to him.

I feel my cheeks redden as ripened fruit. God, help us all if I'm about to open up. I cannot be held accountable for what comes out.

Travin drops his arms to his sides and rotates away from me. He covers his nose and mouth with a hand and takes a step. If I'm going to say it, it's now or never.

I hurriedly reach out to grab his arm before he can leave. Only his eyes move, staring down at me with reluctance. It's that look I've seen him get over and over, as he reaches the point of exhaustion. Defeat. Authentic hurt. It hurts. *He* hurts. This argument is hurting him just as much as it is me.

Here it comes.

"I never wore it—" my voice cracks. Travin's expression becomes more pained. I quickly clear my throat. "I never wore the necklace, because I never wanted to lose it."

I pause. Wait for a reaction.

Travin doesn't even blink. He glares back at me like he's frozen in time

"I just thought—if I kept it in a special place—I could keep it safe. I would never break it or lose it." I choke and struggle to finish. "Nobody—nobody except my father has ever given me such a gift. In a way, the necklace represented you. And I never want to l-lose you. Like I lost him."

I thought by now I'd have erupted into violent tears. I've never admitted such a revelation. It blisters every inch of me.

A part of me hopes Travin will smile in understanding, maybe offer comforting words, the way he always skillfully can. We will call a truce. Then our argument will end, all feelings having been liberated, and we'll go back to being the way we were, before leaving Avoca.

Travin chooses to do none of this.

He moves from out of my reach and turns his back to me, surveying our surroundings, audience and all. High above, the morning sun beats down on us. I feel it, roasting me, segregating me as I atone for the mistakes I've made. My necklace is in his fist. I remember the exact moment he gave it to me. Pinching my eyes shut, I see my father's face. I see the faces of the dead. Travin. Westin. Rajmund. All of my grand errors.

I hear Tasia's voice resonate in my memory. *Don't take them for granted.*

Now would be a great time to disappear.

When I reopen my eyes, Travin is twisting back to face me. Like I've said before, I'm a bad liar. Travin knows this. Surely, that means he knows I'm telling the truth. And, if that's the case, he must also know how unwell I feel over this whole mess. That I just want it to end, so I can retreat to solitude and drown out my worries. To hell with defeating demons.

To my surprise, Travin closes the gap between us once more. A single tear leaks from his left eye.

"I was up all night." His voice is low, and I know his words are meant only for my ears. "I ended it with her. Forever."

My pride relents due to the heartache engraved *so* unbridled in his soldier face. My initial response is regret. And then, relief. Like I'd been carrying around a three hundred pound pack and just set it down.

Travin continues, quickly wiping away the drop on his cheek like an itch.

"I don't know what my future holds, Kaya. But I'll tell you what I do know: I knew the moment—when it was you or Bronwynn in the river—I just knew. I feel terrible if that hurt her. Terrible that if Nasr hadn't been there, she may not have made it. But when I saw you drowning, I can't explain what went through my mind. It all happened so fast. I just knew. I thought about Westin, and how he always saved his wine in times of escape. He asked me what I would take, if I knew I only had a moment to save something, before getting out alive. I never answered him . . ."

Travin examines the necklace in his hands, running his fingers across the tiny shells. Then, he closes his fist tightly around it and looks up at me in earnest. There are tears in his eyes. There are tears in his voice, too.

"I went back for you."

Whether in my mind or in reality, I hear him say this several more times.

"I went back for you."

Travin inches closer toward me, and his smoky eyes ignite a fire deep inside me, unlike the one born of rage. I freeze like a deer in awe.

"When Avoca was attacked that day, I went looking for you," he says. "You weren't home. Kaya, I've never felt so crazy. After losing my mother and Maleah, not knowing if you were still alive . . . when I found you in the pit in the wilderness, there are no words to express how I felt, pulling you free.

"When you demanded to be taken to the Israelite camp to join the army, I was *so* angry with you. At first, I wanted you to remain in a non-violent community, but I realized I needed you in Shittim. *With me*. I might have lost the people I love, but . . . I – I – I will follow you everywhere, Kaya, because the truth is—I can't bear to think about never seeing *you* again."

As Travin ceases to take a short breath, I distantly remember the look of menace he'd kept giving me. The frown that couldn't quite mask his kind nature.

"When we were taken captive in Zaheth," he continues, "I cannot describe the torment I felt each minute of every day there. Not knowing where you were, what they were doing to you. When Amaris rescued us and took us to the cave at the Salt Sea, we had time before the soldiers commenced their battle. There was much I wanted to say, but I don't know how to say these kinds of things."

His teeth work over his bottom lip. He lifts his fingertips to the bridge of his nose.

"After I saw how much you were suffering, and – and – and how distant you were . . . toward me . . . I didn't know how you'd react. I thought . . . I thought you deserved better."

"Better?"

"Every time since then, when I've touched you, Kaya, I've—wanted—to do—more." As if expecting me to object, he rushes to finish. "I've never wanted to let you go. The instant you and Bronwynn disappeared beneath the river, I had only a single heartbeat to decide. There wasn't a doubt in my mind. I can't explain it, I just knew. You are the one and only I can't live without."

My heart stops.

And then, it beats again. Once. Twice.

Breathe, I tell myself.

That fire in me kindles a warm current, vitalizing my limbs. Everything fades away except for Travin. His face is a towering silhouette against the sun, windswept hair in golden waves, eyes stark and penetrating. For so long I saw a boy. I didn't want to see a man, someone who had grown up, because I didn't know how or when he did, and I didn't want to be left behind.

I repeat his words over and over in my head. *I just knew. You are the one and only I can't live without.* How many times did he say that? *I just knew.*

"Kaya?"

Travin's voice jars me back to the present. I close my eyes, but terrible things live behind my eyelids. Things I can never burden him with. He is too precious. *I* don't deserve better, *he* does.

Panic is encroaching. My neck prickles. My head is pitching. So, I run.

Run as fast as I can, out of the village, putting as much distance between the conflict and myself as I can. It's what I do best.

Wobbly in the knees, I trip down the rocky pathways. But I don't stop. I'm so used to numbing my feelings, that I don't know how to handle them radically concentrated and crashing down on me at once. I don't even notice I'm at an enormous drop off until the rolling sound of water snaps my focus to reality. A waterfall.

I'm standing on the rocky ledge, peering down at the bottom of the falls, where the cascade collides with the pool. White caps crash up and over the rocks emerging from the large pond. Ferns decorate the lush surroundings. The soil is fertile, with blossoms and jeweled stones. It is magnificent, a hidden oasis.

I close my eyes and listen to the sounds of the falls. My favorite sound in the world. I inhale deeply, catching my breath by filling my lungs with the smell of moist air. This, I tell myself, is where I belong.

It's been a long time since I've let these deep emotions out, and it's going to take a long process of meditating to put them back where they belong. Hidden and unaffected. I open my eyes and know how I'm going to start this therapeutic process.

It's a promising fact that large boulders capable of incapacitating a human lie in the pool below, but that doesn't stop me from tiptoeing through the tiny, pressing stream, until I'm peeking over the edge. Adrenaline courses through my veins, desiring the thrill of leaping into the water below. I scope out a general landing point. It can't be more than a thirty-foot drop. From what I've already survived, this should be a piece of cake. It might hurt my joints, but it would be exceedingly awesome.

Bending my knees slightly, I prepare for the jump. Except, it's much scarier than I'd anticipated. Kind of silly, almost, that I'm afraid of a little jump, when I've already faced human beings trying to kill me. I count to three numerous times in my head, without making the choice to actually move. I shake my arms out at my sides and try again.

One, two—

"Hold on!"

I whip my head around. Travin is running toward me. Frustration impedes his movements, but a strong sense of determination propels him forward.

"Wait!" he bellows a second time.

He sloshes up to my side, spraying water all over the place. His breath comes in short gasps. Beneath exasperated eyebrows is an obscured smile. The kind his pewter eyes expose. He takes a peek over the edge of the falls and leans back, exhaling a whistle through his teeth.

"I have to hand it to you," he declares, "you always were the one to keep me on my toes." After a second of catching his breath, he points a thumb over his shoulder and says, "I knew saying all of that would make you run. Kaya, sometimes you're just predictable." Closing his lips, he nods to himself. The corner of his mouth lifts sardonically. "Took me a moment to decide whether or not to come after you."

"And?"

"I always have. Why stop now?"

I flush, my eyes dropping to follow the movements of his hands. He removes his chagowr and tunic, folds them, and tosses them onto the water's edge. I gape at his bare abdomen as his lungs expand and retract heavily, his stomach contracting into sculpted lines. Every lean inch is toned perfection. The few hairs on his chest are coated in perspiration. Most of his deeper wounds have healed. The once dark purple bruises have faded, leaving a delineation of surface scars.

When I glance up, I notice Travin watching me observe his undressing. His confidence does not waver.

"Did you mean what you said back there?" he asks.

I suck in my bottom lip, shifting to gaze out into the setting sun. With the tip of a finger, Travin pulls my chin around to face him. He moves a tiny bit closer to me. I can feel his breath on my face. I look everywhere besides his eyes. I've always had a weak spot for those eyes.

"Kaya?"

I melt when he says my name.

I quickly make eye contact, determined to look away again, but my gaze fastens on his. With my back to the waterfall, I can see a complete reflection of the sunset in his eyes. The gray color in them matches that of the water. Rays of summer yellow and fall amber slash through his irises as the sun dips below the horizon. I'm completely lost in his eyes.

Travin's hands reach behind my neck. For a crazy moment, I envision him kissing me. In a crazier moment, I want him to.

His fingers fumble. About the time my ribcage blasts open, they clasp the seashell necklace into place. His fingertips graze back across my collarbone. Slowly. Agonizingly. Beautifully. Before falling back to his sides. A huge pain I had not known I'd been feeling begins to ebb. Years of grief fritter away.

An expression of satisfaction crosses Travin's face. Followed by even more discernible emotions like humor, peace, and then . . . his eyes take on that round softness of a man experiencing a miracle. I feel the smile stretching on my lips before I can stop it. Trav catches it and gives a delectably clever one back. A sensation I'm not familiar with fills my stomach. It's not an ache or nausea. It's similar to the feeling of falling, where your insides flutter into your windpipe.

Still grinning sideways, Travin brushes his cheek against mine and says close by my ear, "Do it."

I swallow. "Do what?"

"Jump," he states nonchalantly. He rocks back on his heels and cocks his head to one side. "I dare you."

The provocation wangles a smile out of me.

We've spent so much time exerting energy into other relationships. Both of us are guilty of that. And I realize now our relationship was riven *before* Avoca was attacked. I wish we could go back to the days of our youth, when our laughter would fill the stalls of Lucan Care. Age has taken us in different directions. Maybe that's how it's supposed to be. Maybe two children can't stay best friends forever. Or maybe, just maybe, they can develop into something more.

My earlier thoughts come back to me.

Maybe I've taken everything in life for granted. Maybe everything does happen for a reason.

"Trav, I've . . . I've forgotten how to live."

I don't realize I've said it out loud until I glance up at Travin's reaction. Compassion. Understanding. Forgiveness. He cradles my face in his hands and the effervescing spreads. It starts at my chin, shooting down my spine, all the way to the tips of my toes beneath the trickling water. All within a moment, the world seems right.

And then he smiles. The sweetest smile I've ever seen. It broadens across his face like unto a rainbow arching across the sky, administering an everlasting covenant that the storm has passed.

"It's not too late to remember," he rasps.

And with that, Travin turns and leaps off the edge of the waterfall.

ACKNOWLEDGMENTS

I'M SO GRATEFUL FOR my husband for letting me be annoyingly extroverted. Plugging my earphones in, diving into the "zone", and plopping my feet on his lap while he watched sports is how these novels came about. My children, who are the reason my heart beats, thank you for grounding me and reminding me—daily—what life is all about. I'm grateful for my family who moves me, rarely out of the way, and is always a source of motivation. Karen, Dayna, and Fran = mic drop, my editors, all the BookWise fingers that fondled this manuscript, so fabulous. Lastly, my God and Savior, Jesus Christ, thank you for everything.

ABOUT THE AUTHOR

As a FOURTH GRADE student, Brittany Shannon told her friends and family, "I want to be an author when I grow up." She won Author of the Month at her school and never looked back . . . but she did look up, down, and sideways, dabbling in the performance arts, and then pursuing a career as a professional cosmetologist, which allows her to paint, cut, and splash her creative talents to her heart's content. Music has a special place in her heart and, if her dreams come true, she plans on composing an entire film score. After working for a marketing agency as a creative content writer, she was summoned to her divine calling of motherhood. She now evaluates manuscripts for a local publishing company and volunteers as a facilitator for the Addiction Recovery Program.

Learn more about Brittany at www.brittanyshannon.com.

www.ingramcontent.com/pod-product-compliance
Lightning Source LLC
Chambersburg PA
CBHW020927260626
47169CB00006B/1609